THE NIGHT WE MET

HEALING IN CINCY
BOOK 1

ELLEESE BLACK

Copyright © 2024 by Elleese Black

All rights reserved.

No part of this book may be reproduced in any form or by any electronic or mechanical means, including information storage and retrieval systems, without written permission from the author, except for the use of brief quotations in a book review.

While this book takes place in real settings, the events that happen are fictionalized. Any resemblance to any person, living or dead, is purely coincidental.

Cover Artist: Kimberly Sable | KBG Designs

Proofreader: Stephanie Wheatley

Formatting: Kalie Gerwig | Good Girl Author Services

For permission to reproduce anything of this novel, please contact Elleese Black at elleeseblack.author@gmail.com

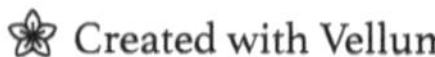 Created with Vellum

CONTENTS

THE NIGHT WE MET

Healing in Cincy Book 1
A friends to lovers, second chance, and sports romance

CONTENT WARNINGS

Homophobia, death of a main character, and mental health representation.

Book intended for mature audiences.

Disclaimer:

While this book takes place in real settings, the events that happen are fictionalized. Any resemblance to real people or places is purely coincidental.

PLAYLIST

- Bad Romance by Lady Gaga
- Rude Boy by Rihanna
- Best I Ever Had by Drake
- Pieces of Me by Ashlee Simpson
- Mine by Taylor Swift
- Use Somebody by Kings of Leon
- Give In to Me by Garrett Hedlund and Leighton Meester
- DONTTRUSTME by 3OH!3
- Fireflies by Owl City
- Pretty Wings by Maxwell
- Never Say Never by The Fray
- American Honey by Lady A
- (You Make Me Feel Like) A Natural Woman by Aretha Franklin
- All I Ask by Adele
- Make You Feel My Love by Adele
- The Night We Met by Lord Huron
- Ride by Chase Rice and Macy Maloy
- With Love by Christina Grimmie

- This Feeling by The Chainsmokers and Kelsea Ballerini
- All The Stars (with SZA) by Kendrick Lamar and SZA
- God's Plan by Drake
- Light On by Maggie Rogers
- Circles by Post Malone
- Truth Hurts by Lizzo
- Good as You by Kane Brown
- The Git Up by Blanco Brown
- Good Days by SZA
- Praying by Kesha
- Lust For Life (with The Weeknd) by Lana Del Rey and The Weeknd
- I Fall Apart by Post Malone
- Touch (feat. Kid Ink) by Little Mix and Kid Ink
- Feels (feat. Pharrell Willians, Katy Perry, & Big Sean) by Calvin Harris, Pharrell Williams, Katy Perry, and Big Sean

the night WE MET

HEALING IN CINCY

ELLEESE BLACK

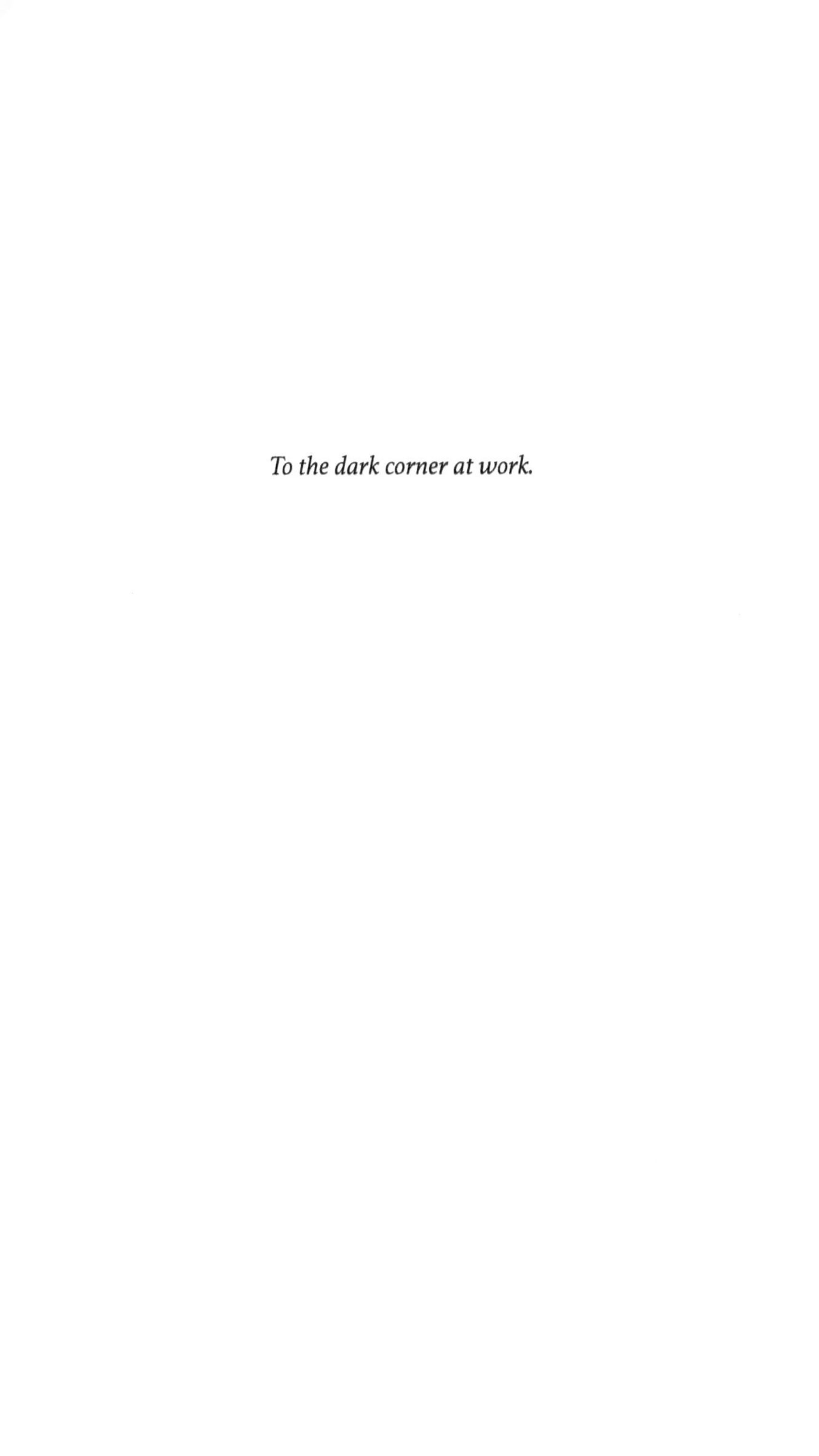

To the dark corner at work.

PART I

1

KAMRYN

AUGUST 2010

One Week Ago

The snickering sound of my closet door closing gives this move-in a bit of a series finale feeling.

"Promise to call every night?" My mom asks as she gives me a bone-crushing hug that only moms seem to possess the strength to do.

My dad and sister snort because they know that's unrealistic. As the eldest daughter, I'm moving away from the nest for college. My mom is still coming to terms that her baby isn't going to be in her room when she gets home from work.

"Yes Mom, I promise," I say because I know it's what she needs to hear.

My mom fusses with my hair as she continues to hug me as if she'll never see me again. Her fresh laundry and lavender scent invade my senses, making me miss home already. I sink into her embrace a little bit more, knowing it'll be a couple of more months before I have another hug like this.

When her hold on me gets tighter, I try with all my might to wiggle out of her embrace. The taps on her shoulder are going unnoticed so I do the one thing that'll get her in gear...time. "You guys really should get back on the road. It's a long drive back to Pennsylvania."

"Mom, let Kamryn breathe." My sister, Jax, says to coax her off of me after another thirty seconds pass without her making a move.

"Okay, okay." My mom finally says as she releases me.

When I'm out of her embrace, I look around my dorm room with a happy smile and misty eyes. I could pinch myself that I'm now in college.

I'm finally a freshman at Carolina Southern University. My decision was based on the academic programs. PhilU had a good psychology program, but CSU had a stellar psychology program. But what also drew me to the university was the city of Columbia. It's a quaint college town and the campus is beautiful. Not to mention the city is a history book in itself. It also doesn't hurt that they have my mom's sorority here as well, so I should be a shoo-in as a legacy.

Not that it was the reason that I chose this school. I'm to the point where I'm not even sure I want to join a sorority.

As a family of four, we wander out of my dorm room and back down to the parking lot. It's a little bittersweet for me as I've never been so far away from my family. But I'm determined to quite literally spread my wings.

My roommate and I, fortunately, have already become incredibly close. When I got my match, I instantly looked her up on socials and it turns out we have a few things in common. We've been in contact since becoming Facebook friends and she's set to move in tomorrow. With her liking sports and having an eclectic taste in music, my hope is that our friendship can thrive. It's what I worried about when having a roommate chosen for me as I don't make friends that are girls easily.

Once in the parking lot, my dad pulls me into a brief but tight hug. "Have fun kiddo. Just not too much fun. I'd rather not become a grandpa just yet."

Oh lord. "I promise to stay in-tact." I say with a wink. I'm far from in-tact, but I refuse to talk about that with my dad.

We're an open family, but some things have to remain private.

My mom comes to hug me again. "My sweet baby girl. I miss you already. Let me know when rush week starts."

"Mom, I'm not sure when rush week is. But I will keep you updated."

Next is my sister, best friend, and my partner in crime when it comes to keeping our parents on their toes.

"What am I gonna do for the next two years?" My sister asks as she hugs me.

"I'm sure you'll manage. It's your turn to rule the school and to live it up! Go to all of the football and basketball games, take a ton of pictures, and maybe even sneak into a college party. Just do all the fun things that I did in high school. I have officially passed the torch to you." I tell my sister this with the utmost love.

Despite the two-year age difference between my sister and me, we grew up close. We did a lot of stuff together: art, sports, music, and photography. It helped solidify our bond. But we still had our own lives despite the commonality. I know my sister felt a bit in my shadows by always being compared to me. So my hope with her still in high school, she'll be able to leave her mark as Jax and not Kamryn's little sister.

With a final hug and a kiss on the cheek from my family, I watch them pile in the car and slowly drive off.

I tell myself I will not cry. But before one tear can slip down my face, I'm startled as I'm crushed by some strong arms. "Parents are gone!"

My heart rate spikes before I realize it's Liam.

"You asshole!" I exclaim and shrug his arms off of me before turning around to face him.

"I'm just trying to comfort you, Kam. Don't be such a sad sap."

I give him a wary look. "Might I remind you how to comfort someone properly?"

"Hmm," he starts. "Maybe you should show me how to properly comfort someone." He says with a suggestive wagging of his eyebrows.

One good thing that makes this high school to college transition so easy, is that I'm also here with my best friend. Liam and I have been friends since we were seven. When he moved into town, he was placed in my class in the middle of the school year. I made him sit next to me and we've been inseparable ever since.

Turned out that Liam's dad's work transferred him to the company my dad works for. And when they found out we were in the same class they were overjoyed. It also helped that Liam and his family moved in across the street. Our families did everything together. So finding out we were thinking of applying to the majority of the same colleges, and subsequently getting into some of the same colleges, it made the separation from our parents easier.

Liam is here on a baseball scholarship. He was one of the best pitchers our high school had ever had. When he wasn't pitching he was crushing it as an all-star center fielder with a wicked batting average to show for it. And since CSU has such a winning baseball program, we found it to be a win-win when we both got accepted.

I ignore his quip about proper comfort and turn to face him, placing my hands on my hips. "So Mr. Baseball star. Wanna come help me unpack the rest of my things?"

Liam ponders my question a little too long and then answers with a shrug. "Yeah, why not. I need to help out my fans."

My jaw drops and now I really punch him in the arm. "Your fans? Is that what I am? I could've sworn I was the girl who encouraged you to start baseball. So really...I should become your agent when you make it to the pros."

Now it's Liam's turn for his jaw to go slack. "Let's not get too ahead of ourselves, Ms. Always-loses-her-phone-and-mind."

I scowl at him as I feign offense, but I know he's right. I always lose my mind...and my phone.

"THAT SHOULD DO IT." I say as I put my last empty suitcase in the closet.

Liam and I finished setting up the rest of my room. At a young age, Liam became very tech-savvy, so he made sure my internet was set up properly. Anytime the internet went out at either of our homes, our parents never bothered calling for the internet company and instead had Liam fix the outages. He also did most of the heavy lifting which wasn't too much, pushed mine and my roommates' dressers together to form a large TV stand, and helped raise my bed so I could fit more storage underneath.

"It looks good Kam." Liam says as he throws his arm around my shoulder.

"Yeah, it does. Thanks for helping me, Liam." I say and wrap my arm around his waist, leaning into him.

"Anytime shorty. Wanna get a layout of the campus and get some food?" He asks as his stomach rumbles. His 6'2" rivals my 5'5" but our appetites match in size.

I swear he is always hungry. He would eat at his house and then come over to mine and eat again. My Mom made sure to have a section in our pantry just for Liam's appetite.

"Sure. I could use that. Plus I'm really hungry anyway."

Food clearly is the way to both of our hearts.

"So how long have you two known each other?"

I'm sitting at a table across from Liam along with some of his teammates. When they say boys in the South are grown differently, they weren't joking. The guys down here are, for a lack of better words, corn-fed. I'm not saying Liam is unattractive. He could give anyone a run for his money off his looks. But his teammates...just wow!

Some of the guys' girlfriends are here early too. I'm hoping that with our mutual love for the guys that we're friends with, a mutual friendship can form too. As I said, I'm not that great at making friends that are girls so I'm hoping baseball can be a bridge for us.

"Since we were seven. And it's been all sunshine and rainbows since then. Hasn't it Liam?" I give him my most sugary smile.

"Oh yeah. You're a real peach to hang out with." He says with so much sarcasm dripping from what he said that I could scoop it up in a bowl and save it for later.

His teammates snicker at our little exchange.

For the past year my family, along with Liam, have been front and center to my always changing moods. Call them hormonal changes or planets aligning, but those in my life never knew the Kamryn they were going to get on any given day. I owe my best friend more than just my friendship.

"So Kamryn," Chance's girlfriend Allie starts. "Are you planning to join any sororities?"

That can't be the only reason she came to college. But then again some girls only go to college to get not just a Bachelor's degree, but an MRS. degree. With her bleach blonde hair, flower headband, and conservative yet, at the same time, revealing wardrobe she fits the stereotypical label.

"Yeah. Um, I think I'm a shoo-in for Kappa Beta. But I wouldn't mind another sorority. If that doesn't go the way I hope for it, maybe a club."

Allie looks at me with narrowed eyes but recovers quickly. "How's that? You have to go through the bids and rush week and all the other fun stuff."

I give her my best smile. "I'm a legacy, actually."

Her face drops when she hears that. "Oh really. What's your mom's name?"

Not even a minute into this tense conversation and I'm already over her. I cheat a glance over at Liam to see he's very invested in this exchange. His family wasn't into Greek life so for him, this is all foreign. "Elizabeth Rawlins. Thomas is her maiden name."

One of the reasons I decided to go far away from home was that everyone knows of my family. And when I say everyone, I-Mean-Everyone. My family is kind of a sorority and fraternity legend.

Both my mom and dad had family members who were

part of the founding chapters that they were in. When my mom and dad met in college, it was like Greek royalty. Apparently, PhilU has a wall dedicated just to them for helping start the chapters. They didn't go to PhilU, but once they found out that my family lived so close, those in Greek Life found it a no-brainer to dedicate a little piece of the wall to them. Weird I know, but I guess they wanted them memorialized.

And that's a big reason why I didn't go there. The comparisons and unrealistic expectations would be endless because apparently no matter what university you go to, in Greek life, the Thomas and Rawlins names carry a lot of weight. I try not to make too much of a big deal about it. I can't help who my parents are. I love them both to death.

Okay, okay. I'm not exactly a shoo-in for Kappa Beta. Just because my mom and her mom, along with the majority of the women in my family, rushed Kappa Beta, doesn't mean that I have to. But KB is a really good organization to be a part of. What they stand for, how they get involved in the community, and also the opportunities that open up for you. PhilU didn't have KB and some of the other universities that I looked at had KB but didn't have the major that I wanted. CSU had both of them. And I also had a couple of backup options if the organization turned out not to be a good fit for me.

"Then I have no doubt you'll fit right in with everyone." Allie says with undisguised venom in her voice.

I turn back to face Liam who's looking at our exchange with wide eyes. He's as shocked as I am. "We're definitely not in Philly anymore, Kam."

"No kidding. So much for Southern hospitality," I say loud enough that hopefully Allie can hear. The rest of the table snickers when I say that.

After we all finish eating, we're just hanging out when my phone beeps with a text from my sister about this boxing class that she's interested in. I encourage her to go for it.

"What are you smiling about?" Liam asks me.

"Jax. She's thinking about signing up for a boxing class." I say with a proud smile on my face.

"Taking after her big sis, huh?"

"You could say that." My sister may not like living in my shadow, but she was always interested in the hobbies I managed to pick up.

"You box, Kamryn?" One of Liam's teammates, Brandon, asks me.

I lift my shoulder in a shrug. "Kind of. Not competitively though. Liam and I would play around and we found it a good way for me to let off steam. It's also a really good workout"

"Like your life is so hard," Allie piques up.

"Allie," Chance hisses. I'm not sure how serious their relationship is but I can tell he has his hands full.

"I could use you as a punching bag if you don't think I have enough pent-up anger. I could really use a release right about now." I say as I fantasize punching her in the face over and over again. So much for making any new girl-friends.

"I don't hang out with your type."

"And what type would that be? A guy's girl? A tomboy? Please, spell it out for me." My lack of patience is threatening to boil over.

"I don't hang out with lesbians." She says matter-of-factly.

A collection of shocked gasps erupts from the table.

"What the fuck Allie?" Is what I think I hear her boyfriend say. I feel like I'm underwater. I can't hear anything. But I can see her sitting at the end of the table with a smile fit for a villain.

I always find it easy to separate the bigots. My love for the LGBTQ+ community is immense. So anyone assuming that I can't be friends with a guy and automatically be part of that community had to have been raised that way.

"What did you just say?" I spit out as a red haze covers my body.

"You heard me. Because there's no way a girl like you can be friends with a guy like Liam and not do anything about it."

"So because I haven't pounced on my best friend that makes me a lesbian?"

She shrugs her shoulders as if this doesn't set women back. "I dare you to kiss, Liam." Allie challenges.

Shaking my head, I reply to her retort. "I don't have to prove anything to anyone. Least of all you."

Allie leans forward on the table and crosses her hands in front of her. "Color me curious. Besides, if you two are just friends then this should be no problem."

I have nothing to prove to her. So why am I considering kissing my best friend? Is it because I'm genuinely curious? Or is it because I've always had a teensy crush on my best friend for years?

Again, I have nothing to prove, but I get up anyway and walk around the table to Liam. My heart is pounding so hard it's threatening to jump out of my chest. Liam slides his chair back and the noise from the legs screeching on the floor, dulls the roar of my heart beating in my ears as he eyes me warily. I swing my leg over his lap to straddle him and place my hands on his shoulders for balance. Not quite chest to chest. But close enough that I can see his pulse fluttering in his neck. I trace an invisible pattern around his face and when I reach his eyes they're as big as the moon. His hands move automatically to my hips, keeping me in place, and my thumbs rub light circles into the curve where his shoulder meets his neck.

Why does this feel so natural?

Nope! Stop that Kamryn!

Not letting myself indulge in this for too long. Despite my skin feeling warm as a swarm of butterflies threaten to take flight.

Nope! Not going there.

My hand travels to trace his jawline, to his lower lip; noting the way his breath hitches with these light touches. My other hand travels around and tangles in the hair at the nape of his neck. I slowly move in and pepper light kisses against everywhere I traced before: his jawline, his nose... the corner of his mouth.

When I pull back, our eyes connect and something changes. His breathing has deepened. His eyes have turned from sky blue to an ocean blue so dark I feel as if I'll get lost in them. They're hypnotizing and it's at this moment, that the curiosity I felt before, is thrown out with the need to kiss my best friend. And from the look in his eyes and the heavy weight of his hands on my waist with his now-growing cock that's nudging my pussy, he wants to kiss me too. Just one kiss.

What harm can it really do?

As his eyes travel down and linger on my mouth again, I lower my lips to his. And with a gentle touch of our lips, we kiss. It starts off soft as we feel each other out. This is our first kiss and when Liam's tongue traces the seam of my lips, I let him in. Blood rushes through my ears as our tongues tangle and I kiss him back with more intensity than I have ever kissed anyone. Liam uses his hands on my hips to bring me closer and settle me firmly against his erection. I roll my hips eliciting a groan from him.

His hand tangles in the curls at the nape of my neck. And angles me the way he wants.

My heart has never beat this fast before.

A kiss has never felt this good before.

My thoughts are a jumbled mess. From the feel of our lips gliding against the other to the feel of his erection underneath me. I roll my hips attempting to gain the friction I so desperately need and suck on his bottom lip before releasing it and diving in for more. Liam puts his hands on my lower back to keep rhythm and to hold me to him before he rolls his hips up into me. The friction from my jeans rubbing my clit has me moaning into his mouth.

Eleven years of friendship poured into this very first kiss. We might be two seconds from ripping each other's clothes off. Who knew that kissing your best friend could be like this? Thankfully, Liam has the foresight to slow the kiss down and pull away.

Stunned silence is the reaction of those at the table. Including us. What the hell was that? This kiss, Liam being the one that I kissed; it's the only thing that's running through my head. Hello, new spank bank material.

"Definitely not gay," Brandon says.

Liam and I stare into each other's eyes with so many questions. I don't have an answer to what just happened. I barely remember my first name.

I just kissed–scratch that–I just made out and dry-humped my best friend. All to prove to some mean bigoted girl that I can be friends with a guy and not want to hook up with him.

Joke's on me, right?

"Boxing?" I ask Liam while trying to calm my erratic

breathing and wildly beating heart. My voice? I don't recognize it.

"Yeah. Meet me in the gym in an hour," Liam says distractedly.

With an unpracticed move, I slide off Liam's lap, my face flaming hot as I walk out of the cafe and back towards my dorm.

2

KAMRYN

I quicken my pace, tripping over my feet doing so. Embarrassment coats me, that I just made out with my best friend. My body is also a live wire as I need to get back to my dorm to take care of the situation that is the need to orgasm.

I'd have to be an idiot to not notice how attractive my best friend is. We grew up together, so I've seen firsthand how he transformed from a lanky kid to a hunky young man. He sprang up in height over the summer between our junior and senior years of high school. So he now towers over me at 6'2". His dark brown hair sometimes flops over his forehead when he needs a haircut and his beautiful blue eyes have the ability to stop me in my tracks.

But I never got the urge to act on any attraction towards him. I couldn't do it.

Has the thought of being with my best friend ever crossed my mind? Of course, it has.

Have our parents ever hinted that they'd want us together? Of course, they have.

But Liam has always made his taste in girls apparent. Tall. Blonde. Supermodel skinny. The total opposite of me.

I'm not short by any means. At 5'5" I'm average height. My dark brown chocolate, almost black hair, curls if any water touches it. My light brown skin turns a golden caramel when I'm out in the sun for an extended length of time. I work out to stay in shape and to keep the curves I work hard for. I'm so far from Liam's type that it's laughable that he could want more.

For the longest time, I accepted my role in his life as his best friend. Nothing more. I accepted it and it worked for both of us.

Could this possibly be the year that changes everything? I mean we're not living with our parents and I've heard about what goes on in college dorm rooms. Do I risk this decade-long friendship over a simple kiss? Do we try for more without the pressure from our parents? Maybe.

"Kamryn, wait up!" Liam shouts behind me.

I turn to look over my shoulder as Liam jogs to catch up with me. My wayward curls have moved in front of my face, so when I feel him close enough to me, I turn back around and tuck my hair behind my ears.

We walk in a heated and awkward silence back to my dorm. I planned to use the hour until I had to meet back up with Liam to take myself over the cliff that I was on the edge of. Being friends for as long as we have, Liam is everything, including very in-tune to my moods.

Opening the door to my dorm room we both head in.

What exactly does someone say after a kiss like that loosens something inside of you? I toss my keys on my desk as Liam closes and locks the door. I can feel him watching me. But again, what do you say? I stare at a clean spot on my desk refusing to turn around.

Thoughts of what to do continue to swarm through me when I feel Liam's body heat behind me. He moves my hair to one side to expose my neck. The open mouth kisses he lays there have my chest heaving. His arm snakes around to the front of me as he pulls me against him. His erection sitting hard at my lower back pulls a whimper from my throat.

At that moment, everything moves fast. I turn around and our mouths meet. Our tongues tangle as he moves his hands to the back of my thighs picking me up and moves us to my bed. I land on my back as Liam's weight presses into me and he hooks my leg over his hip, rolling his hardness into me. My hands explore the hard planes of his biceps and the muscles flex as I rake my nails down his back. Liam flexes his hips into me again.

"Holy shit." I moan out as I break the kiss. My hands go to the bottom of his shirt and pull it up. His body heat briefly leaves mine as he breaks to pull off his shirt.

I'm momentarily speechless with how ripped his body is. I knew Liam worked out, but up close and personal is intimidating. But now that we're demolishing that friendship line, where we couldn't look too long without the other catching on, I can look as much as I want. His abs are carved to perfection, biceps perfectly sculpted with forearms that have me drooling. Liam breaks my stare by leaning in and pressing kisses to my neck.

"I have a...proposition." I pant out.

It's definitely not thought out. But one can only hope it helps both of us.

Liam continues kissing my neck as his hands move up under my shirt and teases my nipple. "What's that?" He asks as his thumb continues teasing me. His head dips to suck my nipple through my bra and all thoughts fly out of my head.

"Oh god…" I groan out. My hands tangle in his hair, pulling and pushing as the pleasure gets to be too much. My nipples are a sensitive spot and it seems he's got that figured out from the noises I'm making. "Friends with benefits. Casual. Just sex. You and me." I finally manage to get out.

"Just sex, huh?" Liam smirks at me.

I roll my eyes at him. Pushing him back, I run my hand down his chest and rest them at the waistband of his shorts to make my point. "I'm not saying I want to jump into a relationship with anyone. But I have needs and so do you." I palm his erection threatening to poke through his shorts. Rubbing my hand up and down. Teasing him the way he teased me. I watch with amusement as he swallows down a moan.

"So just sex. And if and when either of us meets someone, we stop automatically."

The last thing I want is to ruin our friendship. Adding sex to the mix isn't the smartest decision. But if the only way I know I can have Liam is like this, I won't waste a second of time.

"Deal." He says before swatting my hand away, pulling my shirt off and unhooking my bra before tossing it away. "Christ almighty, Kam." Liam groans out before grabbing a handful of my breast and sucking a nipple into his mouth. His hand moves down my body to flick the button on my jeans and pull my zipper down.

Lifting off my body, Liam pulls my jeans all the way off and tosses them over his shoulder. Naked under his gaze I bring my hands to my breasts and play with my nipples as his hand goes to the front of his shorts cupping himself.

"Shit. Keep playing with yourself." Liam says as he slides

down my body. Pulling me to the edge of the bed and throwing my legs over his shoulders, my breath hitches as he blows cool air on my clit. With a stiff swipe of his tongue and an answering groan from me, Liam dives in. Sucking my clit into his mouth with the right pressure has my hips coming off the bed. He locks his arm around my hips and pushes two fingers into me at the same time.

"Oh fuck." I say as I grab onto his hair and grind myself into his mouth. His fingers twist and hook inside me over and over until I feel myself tensing. Fighting the sensation with the need to pee as he curls his fingers inside of me. "Liam. I'm gonna come." I choke out embarrassed that he's able to make me come so fast.

He stiffens his tongue on my clit as he flutters his fingers against my walls. And that does it. My orgasm has me pulling him closer to me. Chasing a high that I've never experienced before.

"Fuck yes." Liam says as he continues to work me through my orgasm.

When I come down from my high he continues sucking my clit into his mouth and moves his hands up my body to play with my nipples.

"Let's see if you can come like this." His fingers twist and pinch until the bud is a pointy tip. Switching between stiff licks and tongue fluttering against my clit.

All of that has my second orgasm slamming into me. Moaning out his name I ride the second wave.

When the last of my climax fades, Liam moves up my body, placing kisses on my mound, my lower stomach, and sucking each sensitive nipple in his mouth, before meeting me in a bruising kiss. Tasting myself on him sends another jolt of desire running through my body. Our kiss is sloppy and has me hooking my feet into the band of his shorts, pushing them down his hips.

His erection springs free and I flip our positions. Sliding down his body I come eye level with his cock. I lick the pre-cum before taking him in my hand and pumping him slowly.

"Are you gonna put it in your mouth or just play with it?" Liam challenges.

I cut my eyes at him. Holding eye contact I lean forward and swallow him to the root. Liam is bigger than other guys I've been with, so he takes some adjusting. When I pull off of him, my saliva mixes with his cum and I use my hand to lube him up.

My hand continues to pump him as I lean forward and suck on his tip. Using my tongue to flick the head, I take my other hand and cup his balls. Gently tugging and massaging I swallow him to the back of my throat, gagging a little. I continue teasing him before he pulls me up his body in another bruising kiss.

"Condom?" Liam asks, breaking the kiss and moving to my neck.

A rush of nerves zooms through me. There's no way to prepare yourself for crossing the line than actually crossing that final line. We can chalk it up to the dare and something that pushed us to what we've never tried before.

"Nightstand," I tell him.

With a kiss to my neck, Liam leans over and stretches his body to open my nightstand and grab a condom.

Logic finally takes over. I push up on his chest and sit back on his thighs Liam follows

"Are you sure you want to do this?" I ask and do my best to cover up the shaking in my hands from the nerves that threaten to take over. My fingers play with his hair at the nape of his neck while the other traces over his jawline. "Because this is going to change, a lot."

I watch his eyes roam over my face. Liam has always been an observer so I know that's what his intention is and I know when he finds it. Yet I have no clue what he's thinking or feeling. He's as much of a blank sheet as I am.

"It's already changed. Plus, I think this will be good for us. I trust you and you trust me."

When he says it like that, maybe that's why this arrangement is so easy. He's my best friend before anything. If I needed an alibi he was it for me. And same for if he needed one. It comes down to the trust I have for Liam that this feels right.

I hear the tear of the wrapper and then Liam finally breaks the kiss, sitting back on his heels to roll the condom on. I'm still sensitive from the first two orgasms so when he rubs his cock against my clit, my body shudders. He continues to tease me, coating himself in my arousal before slowly sliding inside of me. My leg is hiked up over his shoulder, opening me up to him, before sliding in deeper.

"Shit," Liam's groan vibrates my body. "You feel so good."

I'm thankful he stays still so I can adjust to his size. But as he swivels and pumps his hips a little at a time, I can feel the tingle of another orgasm building and I'm ready for him to move.

"Move Liam," I encourage and clench around him.

And he does, boy does he. He finds his rhythm as he pistons his hips in and out of me. Slowing down the movement of his hips as his groin rubs against my clit. He repeats that until he tosses my other leg over his shoulder allowing him to slide deeper than I thought possible.

"Oh...right there," I whine as he hits that spot that has me grabbing my breasts and pinching my nipples to the point of pain. The noises that come out of me are not quiet by any means.

"Fuck, baby. That's hot. Look down Kam. Look at how well your pussy takes my cock."

My gaze moves down to where his cock slides in and out of me. "Holy shit."

The pounding of his cock takes my breath away. Tears leak out of my eyes at the intense pleasure, and I whimper at the pain I'm inflicting on my nipples as I feel my orgasm rushing at me.

Liam moves his hand so his thumb is flickering over my clit. "I can feel your pussy sucking me in. Come for me, Kamryn."

And I do. My walls spasm and my climax allows him to slide in more. He pumps in and out and continues to circle my clit with his thumb until his rhythm gets messy and he finds his own release. Swearing as he continues to pump in and out of me and work us both through our release.

When the last of Liam's orgasm fades, he pulls out and collapses on his back beside me. Our chests heaving with exertion. Our bodies hot and sticky with sweat. He reaches back over to my nightstand to grab a tissue to wrap the used condom in.

"So this arrangement seems like it will work." I finally pant out.

Liam holds up his fist for me to bump. "Absolutely."

With a chuckle I ponder what to say. The sex was good. Hot even. But I need more. It's been so long since I've had sex that these three orgasms can't satiate the sexual hunger inside of me.

"Stop thinking Kam," Liam says.

I glance over and his eyes are closed. "How do you know I'm thinking anything?"

"We've been friends for a decade. I know your tells. Your noticeable ones and your silent ones." He turns his head to face me, his blue eyes seem to see right into me making my heart stutter. The quirk of his eyebrows challenge me to challenge him.

"I was just thinking that it's totally unfair that I've already had three orgasms while you've only had one." Deflecting with a joke to turn this now serious moment back into a fun moment. The silence lasts for all of two seconds before Liam busts out laughing. My face flames as I look over at him. "Stop laughing!"

Hearing him laugh is a good sign. I didn't want one round of sex to change anything between us. So laughter is good.

"You're adorable when you get embarrassed. But for this to work you're going to have to say what's on your mind. No getting shy on me Kamryn."

I turn on my side to face him. My leg slides between his as I trace a finger through the divots in his abs. "Well there are a few positions I've always wanted to try. And you seem like the perfect body to try them out with."

My fingers trail dangerously low to his semi-hard erection. I trail kisses up his chest, my tongue flicking against his nipple before moving up to his neck.

"What did you have in mind?" His voice is huskier as I tease him.

"Me on top. Against the wall. You behind me while laying down. But if you're too tired...we can wait." I start to pull away when his arm clamps down on my thigh.

"You want to be on top?" Liam's surprised tone kicks my heart rate up.

I nod my head. Because yes, being on top gives me more control. And I orgasm faster and harder that way.

"We do it my way too." His eyes are wild and his tongue peaks out from the corner of his mouth. I've seen that look before as batters enter the batter's box, right before he throws a wicked curveball.

"Are you topping from the bottom?" I ask, my hand drops to his chest.

"No. I just see what's hiding under the surface with you. Now get up here and turn around."

Confusion takes over. But not enough to snuff the need to come again. Liam takes hold of my body and straddles me over his lap facing backward. His cock twitches against his leg. I look over my shoulder and sit up a little so he has room to slide down.

He pushes my back down so I'm eye level with his erection. I flutter my tongue over the tip of him at the same time his tongue laps at my clit.

A yelp escapes me. The sensation is overwhelming. His tongue is voracious in its assault against my pussy. My hips move on their own as I pump him up and down. Flicking my tongue and sucking the head into my mouth. His fingers replace his tongue. He falls out of my mouth when his thumb plays with my clit.

A moan breaks free when he adds his mouth back to the mix.

"Oh shit, Liam."

I pump his cock with alternating speeds, gauging his reaction to the fast and slow pumps, hard pressure and light pressure. The slow pumps and hard pressure makes his toes curl so I add my mouth back. Teasing the head of his cock with fast licks of my tongue, I hear him groan his pleasure.

My experiences with giving head are very limited. Guys that I've been with never pressured me to go down on them. They either wanted it or didn't. They were more of the gifter-types. But in the small amount of times that I did go down on them, I made sure it was good for them and for me.

I'm no saint, so I may have picked up a thing or two from reading and porn. I've gotta say...those pointers are really good.

"If you don't want a mouth full of cum, I'd stop right now," Liam warns.

I pump him faster and he swells in my mouth. A garbled curse comes right before he shoots down my throat. I work him through his orgasm making sure to not spill a drop. When I feel him start to soften in my mouth, I release him with a pop.

I turn around and kiss my way up his body. Our tongues tangle as I let him taste himself. The kiss turns heated and just as Liam reaches over to grab another condom, his phone chimes with an incoming text.

With a reminder that the outside world does indeed exist, we both deflate.

Liam swears when he looks at his phone. "It's Brandon. He said he's going to the gym to make sure we have a spot."

Rolling out from under me, Liam finds and pulls on his clothes. Watching him tuck in his semi sends a rush of heat flooding through me. I will myself to snap out of it. It's just a dick. My eyes travel back up his body and see him smirking at me. I realize I've been caught.

"See you at the gym?" I deflect as smoothly as possible.

Will he kiss me on the cheek? A high five? An awkward wave? It's not like we're now dating after being friends for years. We're just testing the waters. Seeing how this arrangement plays out.

With a nod of his head and a quick, "Yep," Liam heads to the door.

And with one hesitant awkward head nod and a half

wave, he leaves my room. I flop back on my pillows with a huff. This is what I didn't want to happen. It shouldn't be awkward with Liam. This should be easy. Just sex.

The problem with just sex is that as women, we're ashamed when we enjoy it and a liar if we say we don't. Is it bad if I enjoy sex with my best friend? I mean, I don't think we would be the first friends to cross that line.

3

KAMRYN

I've had a full twenty-four hours to come to terms with the fact that I had sex with my best friend. And I liked it a lot. I'm sure his teammates could read it all over my face when we met up at the gym to spar. Thankfully they didn't call us out. But I needed to spend the rest of the night alone to get acclimated to my door. And wash my sheets before my roommate arrived.

I've just finished getting dressed when the door opens. The butterflies swarming in my stomach as I realize it's Sarah has taken flight.

Do I sit on my bed? Stand and greet her like a hostess?

A tumble of red hair flows in the room and a girl with a cute button nose with dark blue eyes surveys the room before landing on my awkward form.

Walking over to the empty bed and plopping a suitcase on her bed, she turns around to face me once again. "Kamryn?"

"That's me. And from the key you used to come in, you're Sarah?" *God, could I be any more awkward?*

We've chatted so much online and now that we're face

to face, I'm stumped on what to say. Thankfully two people, who I'm guessing are her parents, follow in behind her.

"This place is cute. A few pictures, an area rug, and some curtains will make this place homier for you two." A woman I'm assuming is her mom chimes. "You must be Kamryn. I'm Erica and this is my husband, David. Sarah has been gushing about you and we just knew you two would have the best year."

"Mom," Sarah scolds as her ears go red from embarrassment.

It's nice to know all mom's follow the same handbook.

"Do you guys need help?" I ask. I feel awkward just standing around while they're about to bust their butts bringing Sarah's things up here.

"Oh, no sweetheart. Sarah has a few more things to bring up and then her dad and I will help get her stuff set up."

Before I can respond, Sarah and her family are out the door. With nothing to do, as the welcome orientation isn't until tomorrow, I decide to take a walk through the city. Grabbing the essentials: dorm key, phone, and wallet; I leave the door to our room open and start my journey.

I'm sweaty by the time I get to the campus entrance. The summer humidity is no joke in the south. But luckily the city is still relatively quiet. I pop into some small business and a record store. My dad loves looking at records. He's not one to collect them, but seeing albums you grew up listening to in vinyl form is magic. I get lost in the rows of music with the radio from the speakers proving the perfect background noise.

I text a few pictures to my dad. Letting him know the next time they're down here he'll have to check this store out. Before I know it, hours have passed with me wandering around the area the city calls Five Points.

~

"You ready to go?" I ask Sarah as I tie off the last of my braid.

She spritzes her body with body spray and shakes out her hair. "Yep!"

We walk arm-in-arm down the hall of our dormitory, before pushing out into the early morning muggy sunshine.

"Is it always like this?"

Sarah nods. "Every summer like clockwork."

My roommate was raised in Charleston and her parents are old money rich, which I couldn't tell from their well-worn clothes. I guess I assumed a family like the van der Woodsen's and I'm glad that's the opposite. But Sarah's style is the complete opposite of mine. While I dress for comfort and still manage to highlight the assets I do have, Sarah likes to show off her assets whichever way she can. I don't fault her for it.

Not only are we opposites in the way we dress, but also the way we look. Where I can tan, she can burn. Where my hair is a dark brown, hers is a beautiful auburn shade and depending on the light can look darker or lighter. She's two inches taller and where I have curves where it counts, Sarah's hourglass waist turns heads while we walk towards the basketball arena.

"Rawlins!" My name being shouted halts our steps. I turn and see Liam with his baseball buddies that are also freshmen.

"Who is that?" Sarah dreamily asks as Liam jogs over to us.

A pang of jealousy hits before I throw it away. Liam and I have only had sex one time. But it would be weird if my roommate and best friend ever hooked up. Right?

The smile that's present on his face sends chills down my spine. We're just friends hooking up. No need for me to go all googly-eyed for him.

"Hey," I greet him when he's a foot in front of us. "Sarah, this is Liam, my best friend. Liam, this is my roommate Sarah."

"Nice to meet you." Liam says with a nod as he throws an arm over my shoulder.

"Likewise. So how long have you two been together?"

My body tenses and I know Liam feels it if his chuckle is anything to go by. "Oh um, we're just friends."

Sarah eyes me like she knows I'm not telling her the full truth. *I'll tell you later,* is what I mouth to her. She relinks her arm with me and we resume the walk inside with Liam still hanging on my shoulder and chatting with Brandon to his other side.

"Fingers crossed this doesn't last long so we can get on with the rest of our weekend." Brandon groans as a group of us take our seats in the arena.

Liam leans in. "Party tonight? It's just some of us from the team?"

"Are any of them single?" Sarah asks and I hold in a laugh as the speaker drones on about how these are the best four years of our young adulthood.

"Hell yeah some of them are," I hear from Brandon. His excitement for tonight is like an overeager puppy just willing to be out of his crate from the night.

Someone from the row in front of us shushes us.

"Sorry," our group whispers as we focus on what's happening up front.

When the speech ends, we branch off from each other as we peruse the selection of clubs and organizations the school has to offer.

"Any sorority?" Sarah asks genuinely curious.

"Maybe. You?"

She flips through a pamphlet for the school's newspaper. "I was thinking about it. It would look good on my resume. But being around a big group of girls all the time...I don't know if I could do it."

In the twenty-four hours Sarah and I have occupied the same space, I've come to notice that while she's outgoing, she's also a solitary person. While we were with Liam and Brandon I saw a mask slip into place. And until we were around them for longer than five minutes did I see her true self show up.

"My mom was in a sorority. One of the reasons I came here was because of it. Now I'm of the idea that I don't care if I rush. So how about we scope out a few and see what happens." Is what I barter with.

"Deal."

We make our way to where some of the Greek organizations are located. There's a bunch of them.

"This is so overwhelming. Like what are we supposed to look for?" Sarah's deer-in-the-headlights look is so me.

"I have no clue. Let's just find some good ones and then get out of here."

I get lost in a sea of options. Club sports, book club, art club, culinary art club; the options are endless and my head is swimming by the time we leave.

"So what's with you and Liam?" Sarah mumbles as she puts on mascara.

I could play dumb, but after only a day of living with each other she knows me well enough. "We're best friends. Who now have sex."

"I knew it!" She fist pumps the air. "God the way he was looking at you on Sunday was so hot!"

"What? How was he looking at me?" My cheeks flame. Not from her knowing about us hooking up. But at the realization that Liam could have been looking at me the way I've always looked at him.

Sarah snorts very unlady-like. "Like he wanted to take you into the nearest bathroom and do very rude things to your body."

My mind wanders as I picture him doing just that.

A pillow hitting my head pulls me out of my hot fantasy. "Earth to Kamryn! You were totally picturing him defiling you."

I give her an *and* look before I finish getting ready for the party.

"Well I for one am Team Kamryn and whatever you choose to do. Or should I say whoever you choose to do. Just be careful."

I look into her eyes and see nothing but sister love. "I will. Thanks, Sarah."

4

KAMRYN

PRESENT DAY

Wednesday

My phone vibrates as I'm in the middle of a chapter for history class, with an incoming text. I look down and a soft smile creeps on my face.

> Liam: Food?

> Me: Yes. I'm starving. Finishing up at the library. Meet you at the cafe?

Classes started this week and I've made it my priority to get ahead. Even though they're all intro classes I know it can change quicker than I can blink. I'm to a good part of the section when my vision goes dark.

"Guess who?" Liam asks.

I choose this moment to mess with him. What harm could it do? "Am I being kidnapped by the hot Mafia boss?"

My vision is restored as Liam takes a seat next to me with a huff. "Very funny, Kam."

The study room I'm in is in the very back of the library.

When I came to the library the first time, the majority of the study rooms were empty as some students don't feel the need to be an overachiever like I do.

"What are you doing here? I said I'd meet you at the cafe," I state not breaking my focus from doing my outline.

He texted last week that he's been busy with fall practice and conditioning, so we've only seen each other for a handful of minutes in passing. And I miss him. I shouldn't admit that even to myself, but I do. It's not even the sex I miss. But him in general. Even when we were at home, we always checked in with one another.

I glance at Liam in the corner of my eye as he thumbs through my science textbook before shuddering and putting it back on the table. "I figure we'd go get a pizza and watch a movie."

"Oh, did you now?" I ask as I swivel in my chair placing my legs between his.

"Mm hmm. And then try those positions you were talking about."

My heart rate is picks up as his hands fall to my legs and massage them in a way that has me wishing for them to do more, to go higher. His hands travel back up my legs, his thumbs rub into the apex of my thighs. Moving in til his thumbs hit the seam on my jeans, and rubs my clit. Liam moves in to kiss my neck, gentle nibbles blend with licks. All the while his thumbs continue the maddening pressure on my clit.

My breathing is audible, and embarrassingly loud, as his thumbs create more friction on the seam of my jeans. "Liam..." I moan out. When I can't take it anymore, I grab his wrists and push his hands away. "Let's go grab a pizza and head to my dorm."

I do my best to get my body back under control from the

fast approaching orgasm that was building way faster than it should have been.

"Where's Sarah?" Liam asks as I put all my books back in my bag.

"She's with her newest hookup for the night. She won't be around until her class tomorrow morning."

When Sarah moved in she claimed that the school was like her buffet. I don't shame the girl for having a healthy sexual appetite as long as she stays safe. On nights she plans to spend with her hookups, she dutifully texts me and grants me free rein of our dorm.

Once my books and supplies are put away, Liam takes my bag from me and slings it over his shoulder. With a hand on my lower back, we walk out of the library and towards the pizza place.

We talk about the random things that have made our friendship the way it is. Laughing at his bout with hormonal acne and me getting my first period at school. We talk about the fictitious future where we're both sitting on hypothetical millions. Knowing that some dreams have the fortitude to succeed and some dreams fail, make the future we're both working towards somewhat daunting.

Although I have no clue what I want to do when I get older, Liam knows he wants to play in the Major's. Something that does terrify me is the after school part. School is where I'm supposed to know what and who I want to be when I graduate. But what happens after those four years when I still have no clue?

"So how has conditioning been? We've barely seen each other these last few days." I say as we walk towards my dorm room with pizza in hand.

"Did you miss me?" Liam asks cockily.

Nudging him in the ribs with my elbow. "Shut up."

Throwing an arm over my shoulder and pulling me to him, Liam calms whatever anxiety I had about the reality of me missing him a little too real.

"I missed you too." He tells me with a kiss on my temple.

I preen as if I have a right to. Him telling me he missed me. It's silly, really. We're just friends who have sex.

If I keep repeating the word *friend* in my head over and over, maybe it'll stick.

We pass by several co-eds on the sidewalk on the way to my dorm and I don't miss the appreciative looks Liam gets. Because I get how hot my best friend is.

"I felt like I never worked out a day in my life." Exhaustion is present in his response to my question.

"Really?" I ask him, surprised.

The hallway in my dorm is relatively quiet. I still haven't gotten to know a lot of the girls on my floor. It's not that I'm not a girl's girl, but it's just a lot harder for me to make female friendships. Playing sports growing up, there was this competitive streak that was hardwired into me and the girls I played with. It didn't make for a longstanding friendship when we all left the sport. Apart from my sister, Sarah, and my best friend Emily from back home, they're the only three I've trusted enough.

We make it to my room without too much more gawking that occurs when Liam is at my dorm. Once in my room, he places my bag on my desk and moves to grab plastic plates and napkins from the little kitchenette before moving to sit on my bed.

"You know those videos my dad would show me? As a preview to how hard collegiate athletes worked out."

I get us both water bottles from the mini fridge and have a mental flashback to watching those and shudder. "Oh yeah. I remember walking in on one of those videos. And I think that's when I decided I would never become a Division i athlete. I don't think I'd ever heard your dad laugh so loud."

"We really need to work on your poker face, Kam. But even I'll admit that those videos looked easy compared to what I endured. I think it was the strength and conditioning coach's way of preparing us for the actual baseball season training." He explains to me as he divides up two slices on each of our plates.

I pop in a DVD from Netflix before picking up my plate and taking a bite. "No regrets though, right?"

His response is muffled from the food in his mouth. "None. This was always my plan since I started playing baseball."

The fictitious future comes up again when I ask Liam if he could play for any MLB team, what team would it be for? The look in his eyes as he dreamed of playing for Atlanta, it gives me chills. At eighteen, it's easy to see how passionate he is about going all the way. At eighteen, it's also easy to dream bigger than your talent. Liam has the drive and the talent to go far. So I know when he makes it, it'll be the happiest day of his life. And I can't wait to be there when it happens.

Our conversation comfortably lulls as we finish off the box of pizza. Liam places the empty box on the floor before settling back on my bed and pulling me against his chest. My back to his front. My head resting against his shoulder. Is this position too intimate for our new arrangement? Maybe. But we make do with college twin size beds.

As the movie drones on, Liam's fingers trail paths up and down my arms. Whether intentional or not his fingers hit the sides of my breasts. I anticipate it happening again, when one hand continues up and wraps around my neck.

The other hand trails down my abdomen, landing on the button of my jeans.

My breath stalls and with the flick of his fingers, the button on my jeans pops open followed by the lowering of my zipper. His hand slides down inside my jeans and settles over my underwear.

I haven't taken a breath in what feels like a minute when Liam says, "Pay attention to the movie Kam."

"I can't." Sighing out, my eyes flutter closed at the sensation.

I'm vaguely aware of the high-speed car chase happening on screen when Liam's finger starts rubbing me from entrance to clit. Gathering moisture and applying just enough pressure that has me pushing into him. The friction of my underwear rubbing my clit is enough to get my heart rate up. My arms have snaked over his thighs and curled under to keep from moving too much.

Liam slips my underwear to the slide before applying dizzying pressure to my clit with his thumb while he plunges two fingers into me.

"Oh god." I throw my head back and Liam licks a trail up my neck before sucking on my earlobe.

My hips move on their own. Getting myself off with his help. His hand that's holding my neck tilts my chin up to meet his lips in a sensual kiss. I whimper into his mouth as our tongues meet and duel. Breaking the kiss I sit up and turn to slide his pants down, taking them off and throwing them over my shoulder.

I glance up at Liam before lowering my head to his cock and licking up the pre-cum that's made its way there. My hair creates a curtain over me as I take Liam all the way to the back of my throat. Gagging lightly before pulling up. I do it again and add my hand to the upward movement.

Pumping him in my hand a few times before swallowing him down again. My other hand moves to cup his balls. Massaging and gently pulling them as I continue to lick and swallow him from the tip to the base.

Liam gathers my hair in his hand and I look up to see his eyes are completely glazed over. I spit on his tip and lick it up while keeping eye contact.

"Dirty girl. You have 5 seconds to stop or I'm gonna come down your throat," he promises.

I lift my eyebrows at his "threat". Leaning down I suck and twirl my tongue over the tip as I pump him in my hand. I feel him tense before he lets out a groan and shoots himself down my throat. Not letting any drop go to waste, I swallow and lick him clean. Placing a kiss on his tip, I move off the bed to shimmy my pants down and throw my shirt behind me. Crawling back up the bed I suck him into my mouth again and hear him swear. With an audible pop as he slips from my mouth, I crawl the rest of the way up my bed and settle astride on his lap.

Liam's hands go to my hips while I run my fingers through his hair. His lips meet mine in a feverish kiss. My hips begin rocking over his still semi-hard erection. But he stops my movements by sliding down the bed and hooking his arms over my legs to keep me from moving.

"What are you doing?" I ask him, confused, nervous, and so horny.

His hands push on my butt cheeks to move me up and stop me when he's pleased. "Getting comfortable. Now sit."

My stomach dips. "What? But...you–I, huh?"

"Kamryn, I've decided that this is how you're coming. I'm gonna eat your pussy until you're begging me to stop, only after you make a mess all over my face. And then I'm gonna fuck you until you can't feel your legs. Now grab onto the headboard and sit on my face." His tone holds no room for negotiation.

With my nerves at an all-time high, I grab onto the headboard and sit on his face.

Liam's tongue plunges into me at first contact and my hips move on their own. He sucks my clit into his mouth and slides two fingers into my pussy. My moan is almost embarrassing as I gingerly continue to rock my hips. Taking my own pleasure from him. His fingers hook into that spot that has me feeling as if I need to pee. And I know he feels me tensing.

I whine at the loss of his mouth and look down into furrowed brows.

"Relax for me Kam." He says as he holds eye contact and sucks my clit back into his mouth and continues to curl his fingers in me. My thighs relax and it puts my pussy closer to his face. "That's it baby."

Liam's movements get more determined. I look down and see his eyes on mine. Salaciously kissing my pussy the way he kisses me. Holding my gaze his tongue licks at my clit over and over until he sucks my clit into his mouth, then moves back to kissing my pussy. He wraps his arms around my hips, locking me in place as he devours me.

The contact and the feel of his tongue entering me has my orgasm barreling into me as I ride his face.

"Liam," I choke his name out. "Oh god. Fuck! Fuck! Fuck!"

With a harder suck on my clit, the curling of his fingers to my g spot, and his finger pushing through my hole I shoot off like a rocket.

My release shakes through me at the same time as I hear Liam slurping me up like he's afraid he'll never get a taste of me again. He works me through my orgasm and carefully flips our position. Our lips meet and I taste myself on his tongue.

We make out like two love-struck teenagers. Gyrating on each other. Feeling each other up.

I take more control of the kiss and flip our positions again. Our tongues tangle as Liam sits up and his hands move down my body. His hands knead my ass and moves me up and down his cock.

I fling my hand out to my nightstand and feel around for a condom in the drawer. I break our kiss as Liam leans back on his hands and I roll the condom on.

Sitting up on my knees, I tease my entrance with his cock lubricating him in my arousal.

"Put it in Kam," Liam says with restraint.

Lining him up at my entrance, I slowly sink down. Giving my body time to adjust before I lift myself higher and then lower down on him.

Liam's hands go to my hips to steady me and help set a rhythm. Bouncing me on his cock while I have no choice but to hold on for the ride. My hands go to his shoulders for support. I swivel my hips in a way that has him hitting that spot that has my toes curling. I do the movement again. And again until Liam lets go.

Arching my back when the pleasure gets to be too much. A moan slips free as Liam takes a nipple in his mouth and teases the taught bud. "Hold yourself up. Good girl."

Liam pistons his hips up into me. The new movement has him hitting my g-spot better than before.

"Harder." I tell him. Needing the release more than ever.

One hand grabs mine and travels down my body to my clit. "Play with yourself." Liam tells me.

His hips piston in and out but it's still not enough. I clench my walls and feel my orgasm coming faster.

"Shit Kamryn," Liam says. His hips stutter while sweat drips down his forehead. "Are you there?"

"Yes. Harder." I say as my other hand twists and pinches with my nipple.

Sweat is dripping down his forehead. "I can feel your pussy strangling my dick. Let go Kam."

Liam angles his hips just at the right angle that has my orgasm releasing. I come with a scream that has Liam's hand covering my mouth.

"We're not done yet."

Confusion plagues me as Liam stands up with my legs wrapped around his waist. My back hits the wall and he slips further inside me with the new angle.

"You wanna be fucked against a wall? Take what you want Kam." Liam grounds out.

I grab on to Liam's shoulders and tighten my legs around his waist before using him as leverage. The pressure begins building again. Slowly bouncing on Liam's cock. His gaze where we meet has me tucking my legs up and bouncing harder.

"Fuck!" I moan out.

Liam pushes my hips against the wall and pounds into me. His hips angle at just the right spot to make my legs shake.

"Oh right there." I manage to pant out.

He sneaks a hand to rub my clit. "Come for me Kamryn. Come all over my cock like the dirty girl you are."

Liam leans forward and takes a nipple in his mouth. Rolling it with his tongue as his finger continues rubbing my clit. With a hard tug on my nipple I come with a silent scream. Liam's hips become punishing as they work me through another orgasm. He pulls out and tosses the used condom while we stand at the door. My pussy still flutters with the aftereffects.

I feel weightless as Liam walks us back to my bed. Laying us down, he takes my mouth in a lazy kiss. Our tongues tangle and that spark that I thought was little ramps up again.

His semi-hard erection grows with each roll of my hips. Rolling off me he reaches back into my bedside drawer for a new condom. I watch him roll it on and then rove my eyes up to his.

"Turn on your side." He tells me.

Turning so my back is to his front, his hand reaches for mine. Our hands move down my body to my still soaked entrance. Rubbing my clit with him feels more intimate than it should.

"Keep rubbing your clit." Liam orders as he lifts my leg over his hip and slides in effortlessly.

His tongue and lips create a trail up to my earlobe. Liam's lazy thrusts now combined with his fingers rolling and pinching my nipple.

"Are you gonna come for me like this, Kam?" *Thrust.* "Squeezing every last drop from my cock?" *Thrust.* "Moaning out my name as you come for the last time." His thrusts get harder and faster. He moves my hand from where I'm rubbing with my clit. "Let go for me."

My orgasm doesn't slam into me. It's a slow fall over the edge. Starting at my toes all the way to the top of my head. Liam's name falls from my lips in a breathless scream. His muffled curse as I feel him swell even bigger before his orgasm takes over. Our heartbeats fall in sync while he slowly pumps his hips, bringing us down from the high.

With a kiss to the side of my neck, Liam pulls out and

disposes of the condom. He gets a washcloth to clean us up, tosses it, and climbs back in bed with me.

No words are spoken. Just the hum of the air conditioner and the beat of Liam's heart under my ear.

Thursday

I wake up in a daze the next morning under the sheets alone and a text from Liam.

> Liam: You snore. I had to get to conditioning. Wear dresses for the rest of the week.

What is he up to? I continue to mull over his request as I get ready for class. Picking out a flirty dress and pairing it with some cute sandals, I throw my hair in a messy side braid. Keeping my makeup to just a couple swipes of mascara. This southern humidity is something harsh. So the less is more when it comes to stepping outside is the smartest decision one can make.

Sarah walks in our room as I finish putting my books I'll need for my classes in my bag.

"Well, well, well. Someone had an eventful night."

I look over my shoulder at her to see her looking at my bed. The sheets and comforter haphazardly on the bed and floor.

Ripping what's left of them off my bed, I toss them in the hamper with a mental promise to wash them after my final class. I walk over to the small vanity and pull out my mascara.

"I could say the same about you." Mascara is caked under her eyes and her shirt is inside out.

She smirks at me before plopping down on her bed. "Let's just say that walls and desks will never be the same for me."

My hand holding my mascara wand pauses. "Sarah!"

"Who knew a volleyball player had such upper body strength?" Her maniacal laughter pops free as she gathers her things.

I can't stop the laugh from escaping me as she walks out of our room to the showers. Her walls and desks comment hit me a little harder than it should have. Remembering where Liam had me last night sends a tingle down my spine.

Checking the time, I book it out of my dorm and to class. My phone buzzes with a text and I smile as I see my sister's name.

> Jax: Hey, sissy.

> Me: Hey dork. How's life? Miss me yet?

> Jax: Volleyball is starting so I've barely had time to miss you

> Me: 😒 Whatever

I've been here for almost two weeks. To be honest, I haven't been as homesick as I thought I would be. Sure I miss plopping on the couch with my family and getting sucked into whatever TV show my dad deems his favorite at the moment. But other than that, this newfound "adult" life has worked for me.

The blast of cool air as I open the door to the liberal arts building brings me back to my studious persona. I was a smart kid in high school. Honors and AP classes. But history was my only tough class.

I manage to make it through the rest of the day relatively unscathed. With thoughts of what happened with Liam running through my mind. Did we cross the line? Does he have another hookup? Does he want more than a hookup? God I want more than anything for it to happen again. He scratched an itch I didn't know I had.

Thinking back to the "revenge" kiss to our agreement, I find nothing amiss. I take a seat at the fountain in the quad and decide to fire off a text to him.

Me: Hey, I hope everything is okay today.

Liam: It is. Meet me in the empty classroom across from the athletic hallway.

My senses heighten. Curiosity wins as I make my way over to the athletics wing. My not being an athlete has kept me from this part of campus. As I walk the building, my senses are on overload. The athletes here are treated like royalty. As they should. The teams bring in thousands, sometimes millions, of dollars from each sport alone. I pass a trophy case of the winnings from the women's and men's sports.

Me: What room?

Liam: Do you see my flashlight?

I see a light moving around in circles and speed walk towards the dimly lit room and I look around to make sure no one sees me. He's up to something, I just hope it's what I think it is.

A startled yelp leaves me as a hand grabs me and pulls me inside. Liam's hand covers my mouth and laughter in his eyes.

"You know I don't do well being scared." I scold him.

From the time we no longer needed our parents to accompany us for trick-or-treating, Liam and I got in all kinds of mischief on Halloween. But his favorite has always been scaring me. He would even hide in plain sight and he would still manage to get a little scream out of me.

"That's what makes this so much fun," Liam responds. "Speaking of fun and scaring, how about we have a little fun ourselves?"

He turns and closes the door with a quiet snick, then turns around to face me.

My cheeks burn. With either desire or shock. I truly can't decide. "Are you talking about sex in a classroom?" My voice comes out in a panicked whisper. The terrifying notion that we could be caught isn't lost on me.

"Why not? No one is in here but us. And I've missed your pussy squeezing the life out of my cock." He says it so nonchalantly like he's talking about the weather and not sex.

"Does the door even lock?" I squeak.

"I guess we'll just have to make this quick," he says, still on the prowl.

"Well, when you put it so sweetly."

Liam crowds my space causing me to back up and rest against a desk. His arms cage me in and his lips trail a path over my exposed collarbones. His tongue peeks out and flutters up and towards my pulse point. My breathing stutters and my head falls back, exposing my neck to him.

"I can be sweet." Liam starts by kissing up my neck and to my jaw. "But we both know that's not what you need."

"Are you gonna be all talk? Or are you gonna make me come?"

My hands go for the waistband of his shorts, the mesh doing nothing to conceal his growing erection and I push them down just enough to free his cock.

Flipping our positions. I wait for him to sit on the desk. Running my hands up and down his thighs.

"See, while you're a talker, I'm a do-er."

Taking his mouth in a bruising kiss that leaves him speechless, I trail down his body. I pump him a few times and swirl my thumb over the tip, smearing the bead of pre-cum. Bending down, I kiss his tip before sucking him into my mouth.

"Jesus, Kam," Liam exclaims. He grabs my hair into one fist and I look up to see his gaze half-mast with his bottom lip between his teeth.

I take him to the back of my throat and contract around his cock. Liam's muffled curse spurs me on and I pull up to where his mushroom tip is all that's in my mouth. One thing I've quickly learned about Liam is that he loves suction on the tip of his cock.

I continue to lick and pump his cock in my fist. Watching as a bead of cum falls from the tip. I continue to pump his cock as I lean forward again and take him in my mouth. I pump him faster as I suck him harder. He tenses for a second before he spills down my throat with a groan.

I work with him through his release. Not letting a drop spill from my lips. Releasing him with a pop, I stand up and slip my underwear off under my dress.

"Condom. Backpack. Wallet." Liam says.

I arch an eyebrow at his lack of a complete sentence. Kneeling, I pick up his backpack and pull a condom from his wallet, slide it on and straddle him on the desk. Liam's hand goes to the nap of my neck and pulls me in for a bruising kiss. Our tongues dance together as I roll my hips over his erection.

Liam breaks the kiss and I see him holding onto his last shred of control. Sitting up, I tease his semi-hard cock through my pussy. Teasing my clit that has my breath stuttering.

Lining him up at my entrance, I slowly sink down. Letting his cock fill me to the brim.

"Your cock feels incredible." My hands go to his chest as I use him to bounce up and down, setting a rhythm that has my toes curling.

"Fuck," Liam says. And then he grabs my hips and takes over. Bouncing me on his dick with more force. His hips lifting off the desk and hitting that spot that makes my toes curl. The sound of our skin slapping against each other echoes off the blank walls. "Reach down and touch your clit for me, baby. I need you to come."

I reach down between us. Rubbing my clit with my two middle fingers. Before I know it everything tightens and I moan Liam's name. He moves his lips to mine and groans out as I feel him come.

My hips slow down their movement. But our lips don't stop. I like kissing Liam a lot.

Eventually he breaks the kiss and pushes a loose piece of hair that fell from my bun behind my ear. "This was a nice break. Wasn't it?"

"I will never complain about an afternoon delight again."

That gets a chuckle out of him. He moves to sit up, letting his cock slip free. I'm not sure why this weirdness around Liam sprung. Is it because we had sex in a classroom where anyone, including his teammates, could have caught us? Or is it that the physical connection is blurring with my emotional feelings for Liam.

I glance at him out of the corner of my eyes. He's picked his shirt up off the floor and flips it right-side-out.

He looks unaffected. Like this is just sex to him.

Do I keep this arrangement going? Or do I stop this for fear of becoming more attached than I should?

Friday

Liam's hand covers my mouth as he pounds into me from behind. He surprised me in the library again and said it was always a fantasy of his to have sex there. Who am I to say no? It's been a dream of mine too.

We're hidden in the science fiction section that's in the dark part of the library. For all of the time I've been coming here to study, this space has been unoccupied. We're just hidden away, but not too hidden that anyone who happens to come back here won't know what we're doing.

His hand sneaks to the front of my body. I think he's about to play with my nipples but he veers south and plays with my clit. My head falls back on his shoulder as my knees buckle.

"That's it Kam. Milk my cock."

His dirty talking does the trick. My body tightens before it lets go. My moans turn breathier as my orgasm slams into me. Liam's thrusts get sloppier as he chases his own release. His mouth latches onto my neck and with a groan he lets go.

We stand there with our hearts trying to slow down. My head resting against his shoulder. His forehead on the top of my head. A sound jolts us out of our post-coital bliss. We separate and make our way back to the study room we were in before Liam dragged me out.

It takes herculean effort to focus back on my previous task at hand. But I manage to get in an hour's worth of studying before we're packing up for the night.

5

LIAM

I'm an idiot. A coward. I took this chance to be with my best friend because I felt it was the only way to be with her. But what I felt was just a way to scratch the itch has turned into a full-blown need for me.

Yes we'd only been at this for a couple of weeks, but I'd become a lovesick fool. From wanting to spend every moment that I'm not busy with baseball or classes with her. From wanting to take this arrangement to the next level with her.

I looked at Kamryn's texts. I know she knows I looked at them. So I needed to pull away.

A baseball hitting me in the chest pulls me out of my friends with benefits fog.

"Hey!" I scold at Chance.

He holds his hands out in a WTF gesture. Something I've noticed he does a lot. It works. It says exactly what the words would.

Picking the baseball up, I throw it back to him and then rub at the sore spot on my chest.

We may be teammates, but I'm not sure I want to divulge what went down between me and Kamryn. Do I really not have anyone to talk about this with? Her roommate comes to mind but at the end of the day, Sarah is Kamryn's roommate first and my acquaintance second.

I continue running through drills with Chance in hopes that it pulls my focus back to why I'm at the university in the first place. Which is for baseball. Kamryn wasn't exaggerating when she encouraged me to keep up with this sport. I was aimless as a kid. Video games were what I did after school while I was "watching" my little sister, and on the weekends. Until one day after school, nine-year-old Kamryn knocked on my parent's front door and exclaimed "Liam come outside and play catch!"

I'll admit that I was terrible at first. Having a girl out throw me was embarrassing. But what I liked about Kamryn was her patience when she taught me. That patience moved on to competitiveness and eventually support as she cheered me on at every game she could attend.

Getting scouted in high school didn't cross my mind. I didn't even think I was good enough. Despite the honesty that bled into every statement, Kamryn told me I was good enough. I needed that more than she knew.

Chance and I wrap up our drills and shoot the shit before leaving the field house. He does his best to pull me with him, but my mind is too flooded with thoughts. Thoughts of Kamryn. Thoughts of what we've done this past week.

I've been in love with my best friend since I was twelve years old.

It sounds crazy even when I say it to myself. I hid behind different girls that didn't look like Kamryn in hopes that what I felt for her wasn't love, but a deep-seated crush.

But when she proposed a friends with benefits arrangement, I couldn't say no. If that was the only way I could have her, I took it. My not good enough bled into every aspect and thinking I can have more with Kamryn is the tip of the iceberg.

Yet here I am. Avoiding her texts because my feelings crossed over that line. Every touch, every kiss, every whispered breath against her skin had me weeping. I drank those moments up like a man without water for a month.

I'll admit that the kiss we shared in front of everyone, rewired something in my brain. I thought that was it. That we would finally be a couple. If only I had spoken up. Maybe one day. But if I have to continue loving my best friend in secret, then that's what I'll do.

It's taken everything in me as I continue to be around her, sleep with her–that I'm terrified that I'm going to blurt out that I love her. I don't even know if she'd feel the same way. I know she loves me as a friend. She's said it to me several times. And every time she said it, I'd carry those words around as if they could anchor her to me.

Pulling away, no matter how painful for both of us, is the only way our friendship can work. It's the only way that I can survive. Until I can pick up the courage to tell her the feelings I have for her are more than just friendship, I have stop this. I have to quit her.

If that requires me ghosting her then so be it. I can only hope that she comes to me first.

6

KAMRYN

NEXT SATURDAY

"Sarah! I really don't feel like going to a party tonight!" I protest and go back to the history homework spread out on my bed. This class is kicking my butt despite me having learned it in high school and lived some of it.

My outgoing roommate has been pestering me all week about the back-to-school party. Apparently, it's a can't miss and all the who's-who is going to be there.

I may be outgoing, but I've never been a big partier. That and crowds just don't mix well for me.

"Kamryn! I am begging you! This could be our in. Find some really cute guys and keep them on our regular rotation." Sarah looks close to dropping on her knees and begging for me to go to this party with her.

It's been a few weeks since classes started and we've bonded better than I could have hoped for. Which is still odd for me. But Sarah wormed her way into my life and wouldn't give up. When I haven't been with Liam or in class, Sarah and I have taken to roommate bonding. Movie nights with manicures and pedicures to screaming at the top of our lungs to Ashlee Simpson's *Pieces of Me*. With our fun, we also have our serious; with mandatory studying for one-hour every night. Apparently studying excludes the weekends.

I weigh my pros and cons, because what eighteen year old doesn't? *Can you sense my sarcasm?*

I could go and be social or I could be a hermit for the rest of the year. As well as continue my arrangement with Liam. Who I haven't heard from in over a week. Am I a little hurt that he's completely ignored me? Of course I am. This was the main reason why I never wanted him and I to hookup or date. The possibility that our friendship could end was too great of a risk to take.

I relent with a sigh. "What are we wearing?"

She shrieks so loud I fear my eardrums are going to burst. She immediately heads to my closet and picks out my favorite pair of jeans with holes strategically placed, a flowy white off-the-shoulder shirt all paired with gold earrings and brown sandals.

"Remind me again, why you're not at Parsons or any other fancy fashion school."

Sarah groans extra loud. "My parents want me to choose a *reasonable* career. They don't think that fashion or design is it. I even reminded them that they came to me all the time for opinions on what they wore to work."

"So what is your major? I don't think I've asked you that yet."

"Sports management. Well, business but my main concentration would be sports management. If I can't be a designer, I'd rather be a kick ass sports agent."

"How does you wanting to be a designer veer to sports management?"

"Long story short, my parents are both entertainment lawyers. They never tell me the nitty gritty of what their actual job is because of the confidentiality of it all. But I know they work in the entertainment side: celebrities, athletes, and some politicians. I do commend them for being as present as they could be. They were around when I needed them. We spent holidays and birthdays together. But being an only child to two lawyers whose careers were important to them, made my childhood lonely. I think they took note of that. Which, again, is why they did their best to be present parents. They had a family friend take me on their work day and he's in the sports management business. I don't know. Something about that day just clicked."

I watch her face as she talks about the clients he introduced her to. How when he was talking to his athletes he wasn't belittling them. He cared about their future.

"You and Liam should talk. I know he'd love to go to the MLB," I say to her. "It's his dream and if he already has an agent, it'd be much easier for him."

"Let's wait a few years for that Kam." A blush takes over her whole body.

"Alright, alright. I guess I'll shower and get to work."

"Yay!! We're gonna have so much fun Kamryn," Sarah cheers.

I laugh all the way to the showers. It's never a dull moment around her. As boisterous as she is around me I've noticed how shy she is around others. But the mask she throws on fools even me sometimes.

Getting ready for my first college party should have me elated. But something nags at me. Nothing goes right. From finding an outfit, to my hair...to Liam.

Sarah helps me out with an outfit of ripped jeans, a slouchy shirt, and some boots, but tells me my hair is my own problem. I don't blame her. Despite being in the south for almost a month, I still haven't gotten used to the humidity trying to revive my curly hair. From the time I could learn, I had been straightening my hair so I wouldn't have to deal with it.

Taming my curls to a beautiful blowout helped take the hassle off of getting ready. But when I decided to come to school here, I told my mom I'm going to attempt to get my natural hair back. And while it's not at it's full curl strength, it has waves and falls just to the middle of my back. So I work with that and finish the process of getting ready.

Me: Hey, I know you're probably busy, but Sarah and I are going to that big back-to-school party.

Liam: Some of the guys and I are going.

His first response in a week is that? Looking back on the unresponded-to messages makes me feel like a fool.

Is this how it's going to be? Maybe it's a good thing we haven't seen each other. I shake off Liam's sour response and fluff my hair a few more times before checking over my makeup.

Our one-hour time limit to get ready turned into two-hours before Sarah and I are walking arm-in-arm down the street towards the party. In college they never say when exactly the party starts. People just start showing up with beer, liquor, and a kick-ass soundtrack.

By the time we're half a block away, we already pass some sorority girl who's crying with the support from her "sisters" and I have a momentary freak out that that's how my life is going to turn out.

"Promise that won't be us," Sarah says when we're past them.

"Thank god you thought the same thing. I promise. 100%." I say linking our pinkies in a promise.

We continue walking and pass guys that I'm assuming are on the basketball team. It's not so much of an assumption as it is them standing next to the basketball hoop at the end of the driveway and they're taller than your average college guy that doesn't play a sport.

I turn to look at Sarah and see that she's got her jaw unhinged. I politely push it back up.

"I can give you a moment. I'm sure Liam is around here somewhere." I say taking some humor in the fact that she's going goo-goo over basketball players.

"I'll text you when I'm inside." Sarah says as she sashays towards the group.

I watch her walk away and pull out my phone to text Liam.

Me: I'm at the party.

Liam: Come out back and I'll get you a drink.

With a look back at Sarah and seeing that she's happily occupied, I take a cleansing breath and walk through the house towards the backyard. My first thought is WOW! My second is why couldn't this house have a side entryway leading to the backyard? The scent of sweat, Axe body spray, and Chanel No. 5 permeates the air. Not the best combination for a group of young adults, but it somehow works.

I finally find Liam after being knocked around by all of the grinding and writhing of bodies in the house.

"Kamryn!" Liam says when he spots me.

I walk over to him and his team and am greeted with hugs all around.

The weirdness is present as I settle next to Liam with my arm around his waist and his arm around my shoulders. He places a kiss on the top of my head before going back to his conversation.

I've been trying to wrap my mind around the shift in our relationship...no friendship. Was I ever asked why he and I never took that next step? All of the time. I'm not sure if it was because our parents were friends, or some cosmic occurrence that kept us from crossing that line back then. But now, I'm still not quite sure either of us is ready to wipe away that line in the sand and crossover into something more. Was the sex with him good? It was the best I ever had. But being with Liam would require more than just mind-blowing sex. With his lack of communication this past week it's not off to a great start.

Maybe Sarah is right and that I do need to meet someone else. I've given her a rundown on our friendship and all that's happened since we came to college. All I've truly known is Liam's friendship and if this last week with him brushing me off is any indication, then my feelings need to be squashed.

They say the best way to get over a possible situation-ship is to get under someone else. I'm not holding out hope that he and I could ever be more. Okay, maybe it sparked to life a little during our arrangement. Call it an orgasm high. As I give it more thought, maybe it's possible that Liam and I only have physical chemistry. Not relationship chemistry.

My phone buzzing in my back pocket pulls me from my warring thoughts.

> Sarah: Meet me in the garage. I want you to meet someone.

Talk about a sign.

> Me: Give me 5 minutes.

I tap Liam on the hip to give him a heads-up.

He lowers his head down to my ear. "What's up?"

"I'm gonna go meet up with Sarah." I pull back a little to see his brows furrowed.

"You want me to go with you?"

More distance will do us both some good. "No. You stay. I'll see you later."

"Are you sure?" Liam pulls back to look at me.

I nod. "Positive." Leaning up on my toes, I kiss him on the cheek. "Have fun." I tell him and walk away. I feel his gaze burning into my back as I make my way to the garage. Is that a metaphor for how this will go?

UGH! Be still my anxious heart. Maybe I'm naive, but I hoped with everything in me that this thing between us would be without the awkwardness and the feelings that come with it. If last week is any indication then I need to move on from what Liam and I almost had.

I finally make it to the garage and after squeezing through the many sweaty bodies again, when Sarah calls my name.

"Hey! Where'd you go?"

I point over my shoulder towards the general vicinity of the backyard. "I was out back with Liam and his friends. How was the basketball team?"

Sarah makes a gagging face. "Ugh. I like sports. But I can only talk about basketball so much and that's *all* they wanted to talk about. " Her nose scrunches up in the corner.

If it's one thing I'm learning about Sarah is that she's not one to mince her words once she warms up to you.

"You're insane." I tell her as I take the drink she made for me. I look around the room and it looks like a different house. "Where did you bring me?"

"Nice huh?"

I nod my head as words fail to form.

"This is unofficially the football lounge. The players apparently don't like getting too rowdy with everyone else, so they kind of claim this spot as there's. You either have to be invited in, be friends with them, related to someone on the team, or dating one of the players." Sarah takes my silence for what it is and explains this space.

I take a look around and see that she's right. It's definitely not as rowdy here. I can hear myself think and I'm not assaulted by gnarly scents.

I've noticed the hierarchy that is D-1 sports. And some of the divide between the mens and women's teams. The football, baseball, and basketball teams are the top three breadwinners amongst the men. Especially the baseball team having won four national championships in the last ten years. But the football team is in another class. While they haven't won as many championships in the last ten years, they have had the most players to be drafted to the NFL. While I'm not too sure about the basketball team, I do know they have a successful program.

With the women's teams: soccer, basketball, and volleyball are the moneymakers here. I make a mental note to support the women this year. Sarah and I have bonded with some of the girls in our dorm that play a sport. They've been slow growing friendships with their busy schedules, but we hope by the end of the year something comes out of it.

"I like it," I say as my mind snaps back to where we're at as I scan the room. "How did you get an invite?"

"I went to high school with the quarterback. Helped tutor him in AP English and we've stayed in touch ever since. I almost forgot he went here until he messaged me. He said I always had an open invitation to hang out in the football area. Figured it might be good for you too."

I look at Sarah in horror. "Is that the reason you brought me here?"

She averts her gaze to something behind me before quickly looking back at me. "Uh...not exactly. Mason, hi!"

"Sarah, how are you?"

Holy smooth-like-butter-talk-me-to-sleep voice. I turn and look at the guy that Sarah's talking to.

You know that cliché moment in movies or romance books where the whole world fades away. And it's just you two seemingly coexisting in the same space? That's this moment. The moment where I feel things may change.

Because Liam, who? I ask myself. This boy...no scratch that...this MAN is just that. He's a man. That Sarah so easily can talk to. Meanwhile, I'm next to her getting tongue-tied in my own thoughts.

He's beautiful. Like, he could be Idris Elba's twin brother. Or at the very least his cousin.

"Hi! It's so good to see you. I'm doing well, how are you?" They embrace as if it's been a while since they've seen one another. And maybe it has been a while.

I watch their interaction with fascination. It's obvious they have an easy-going friendship. But that little green-eyed devil props itself on my shoulders begging to make something out of nothing.

Sarah turns her attention to me and I note the mischief in her eyes. "Kamryn, I'd like to introduce you to Mason. Mason, this is my roommate Kamryn."

He steps up to me with a wide smile on his too beautiful face and sticks out his hand.

"It's nice to meet you."

Wordlessly, I place my hand in his and shake.

"It's nice to meet you too." I respond once I finally find my voice.

Sarah excuses herself not so discreetly, leaving Mason and I just looking at each other.

"So...where are you from?" Mason starts.

I look at him incredulously, which gives me time to gather myself. "Is that really the question that you're going to start out with?"

He looks taken aback. "Um...no?"

"Perfect! Let's start again." I'm not usually this bam in your face! But with him, I might have to be.

"Okay." He starts and looks to the ceiling for help. "If you identified with any animal, which would you say you identify with?"

"You're not opposed to marriage after only knowing someone for thirty seconds, right?" I ask jokingly, although maybe a hint of seriousness laced in my teasing question.

"You know, Khloe and Lamar seem to be going strong, so why not?" Mason jokes back.

I may have met my match. "Touché. Identify with an animal...it's a toss-up between an elephant or a horse."

"Okay. If you chose an elephant, why?" He asks as he leads us, with a hand on my lower back, to a little bench in the garage. The butterflies take flight. We're still in view of the football team, but this way we're not screaming our answers over the sound of the music.

"Elephants are kind, nurturing, loyal, and gentle. That's just one side of them. On the other, they're protective in a way that just brings goosebumps to my arms. With their young, they place them in the middle as a protective barrier from predators and sometimes those in the herd. But they'll also defend their whole entire herd from predators. Plus, they're a few of the only animals to have an impressive memory. Yeah. I think having the memory of an elephant would be better than having the memory of a goldfish. Plus elephants are my grandma's favorite animal."

Mason looks at me with a smile on his face. "And if you chose a horse instead?"

"Oh goodness. Horses come in all different shapes, sizes, and colors. They can be trained and used for very different things. But if I had to choose, it'd be the wild horses, or the ponies. Watching them adapt to an environment and then having to defend themselves against man and the earth's natural changes takes a lot of fortitude. I've seen pictures and videos of wild horses on the Eastern Shore in Virginia. It was breathtaking. But when it comes to horses they're also like elephants. They're gentle, loving, nurturing, and protective. And when it comes down to it, they'll protect those that need it."

"What's your major?" He asks, looking at me in wonderment.

"Psychology. Why?"

He shakes his head in bewilderment. "With those answers, you could have easily gone the philosopher route."

"Eh. No way to make a living off of that."

"Sure there is. Motivational speaking is one way. Conferences on how to dig deeper on things that might not make much sense to others. Think of all the book deals you could have."

He's smart and I hate that I judge athletes. My best friend is an athlete and he finished in the top ten percent of our class along with me.

"Maybe one day. Okay your turn. What would your spirit animal be?"

"Hmm. A lion."

"Why?" I ask curiously.

"Lions operate in packs. Granted they're mostly female,

I operate in a male pack so that's one major difference. But the lions work as a team with the other lions and lionesses. The lion is the leader of the pack, but also the loner."

I see where he's getting. "So even though you're probably surrounded by droves of coeds on campus, you're still a loner. How is that possible?"

"I never liked the attention." He starts and scrunches his eyebrows in concentration. "Football came easy to me. Obviously, I mean I wouldn't be on the team if I didn't like the sport or have the talent or drive. But I help the team get the wins and I've kept myself in that spot. The fanfare that comes with being the starting QB becomes a distraction more often than not. So I do my best to keep my head down and focus on football. As much as this school loves believing that us athletes juggle the girls at this school, I've always been a one-on-one type of guy."

"Interesting. No pressure though," I say while my heart is threatening to burst from my chest.

"No–shit. I mean. I didn't mean that you'd be the girl that I go after. I'd never do that to any female. My momma taught me better than that."

I breathe a sigh of relief. "Well, if I was looking for someone, you might be my top pick."

He turns his smile up a notch. "Do you wanna take a shot with me Kamryn?"

"Just one?"

"Okay. Two if we're feeling real daring. We'll do that."

"Deal."

One Week Later

"OKAY!" My professor starts to say as we start packing up to leave class. "I want you all to write a paper on what it means to be a Psychology major, what you expect to learn from studying this subject, and why you chose psychology to begin with. I want that on my desk in a week. Have a good weekend."

School's been in for a couple of weeks and I've never been so busy. I'm not complaining because I love the work, but I'd love for just a moment to breathe.

Jax: Hey sissy! How's college life treating you?

Me: It's insane. But in a good way

Jax: Meet any cute boys yet?

One boy comes to mind. But I haven't run into him since the party. I try to tell myself that it's a big campus. That he's an upperclassman. The feeling of being forgotten so easily and so quickly stings a little too much to admit to anyone.

Me: Jax! No. I'm too focused on school right now to even think about that

I also refuse to mention my kiss or any of my arrangements with Liam to any of my family. If they knew they'd throw a party and start planning our wedding. I'm not ready for that. Least of all with Liam. Don't get me wrong, he's a great guy. But he got weird after that night. And I refuse to hold out hope for someone that won't reach out to me. Sure feelings may have stirred up for me, but I'm definitely not ready to pursue a relationship with him or any man for that matter. Well maybe one man. But, again, I haven't seen him since the party.

Jax: Fair enough. So what are your plans for
the weekend?

Me: Me and Sarah are going to a football
game Saturday and maybe a frat party. And
then Sunday I'm working on homework.

Jax: Boring!

Me: This is pre-adulting my dear sister. A
delicate and equal mix of work and play.

My sister chooses to tell me how school for her is going. She's indecisive about running for Student Body President. So as her older sister, it's my job to hype her up and tell her that she'd be a great voice to have at the school.

I'm so preoccupied with texting my sister that I run… literally run (well walk) straight into someone and drop my phone.

"Ohmygod I'm so sorry!" I exclaim.

Hands land on my biceps to steady me. "It's alright sweetheart. I think I'll live." The voice says. And holy crap! If this isn't the voice that has haunted my dreams for a week. The voice I've touched myself to.

I trail my eyes up Nike-covered feet, black workout shorts that are hanging just right on his hips, over a CSU football shirt, and into the eyes of a delighted Mason.

"Wow." I mentally smack myself. "I mean, hi. I almost didn't recognize you in workout clothes."

He chuckles a little. "Yeah, I like to keep people guessing."

"I'll bet. I really am sorry. My mom always warned me about walking and texting."

"As long as you don't text and drive, I think your mom would be proud."

"Yeah." I say and get a little lost in his eyes but shake myself out of it. "Uh...well...I should get going. Don't wanna be late for class."

"Sure." He says and steps aside to let me pass.

I'm about five steps away from him when he calls out my name and I turn around to acknowledge him. "Yeah?"

"I think you'll need this." He holds out my phone to me that I somehow forgot that I dropped.

My eyes widen at my dumbness. "Oh, right! Thank you."

"Since I have you here again, do you mind if I get your number?" He asks me very nervously.

A snort escapes before I can stop it. "Sure. But does that line ever work for you?"

"It has until now."

This gets a laugh out of me. "Give me your phone." Once he unlocks it and I type in my number, send myself a text, and then I hand it back to him. "Only use it if you really need to."

"I intend to. I'll see you around Kamryn."

"Bye, Mason." A blush and smile covers my cheeks as I walk away from him.

I close the door to my dorm with a huff. Tossing my bag onto the floor and flopping onto my bed.

"What's up with you?" Sarah asks from her spot at her desk.

"I literally crashed into someone today. And not just any old someone. A hot, tall, and athletic Mason. I dissolved into a puddle of mush when I looked into his eyes."

Sarah's chuckling at my rant. "Okay. Slow it down now. Now tell me what happened?"

So I go into how I was texting Jax when I walked out of class and wasn't paying attention to where I was actually walking when I ran into someone. I omit the fumbling and gawking I did. She'd tease me for eternity.

"Wait, you ran into Mason? How did you not recognize it was him?" Sarah asks, barely containing her laugh. "This is too priceless."

My eyes widened in response. "Sarah, it's not funny! Plus I told him he looked different in workout clothes. Why was it so much easier to talk to him at a party than it was in a hallway?"

"Maybe it's because you didn't have the alcohol cloud surrounding you? I tend to lose the beer goggles once the lights turn on too," she says with a finishing smirk.

"Oh hush!" I say and dissolve into a fit of giggles.

The party where I met Mason was a dream. How I forgot what he looked like I have no idea. His voice has been the star of my most recent fantasies since we met.

In our hysteria my phone pings with an incoming text from an unknown, but South Carolina, number.

"It's him!"

"What does he want?" She asks as she looks at me expectantly.

"To know if I want to go to dinner with him on Tuesday."

"If you don't say yes, I will." Sarah says with a wink.

Me: What did you have in mind?

Mason: Pizza?

Me: Sounds good to me.

7

KAMRYN

After watching him at the game on Saturday and then being near each other at another party afterward but never engaging in conversation with one another, I realized just how out of my league I was. That night we were very coy with one another. He was getting praise the whole night for helping the team to another win for the season. The small glances we shared were enough to have me wanting to shout from the rooftop that we're going on a date.

Before I know it, it's Tuesday. And the butterflies are taking flight the only way a first date can do.

I've gone through almost my entire closet and Sarah's trying to help me figure out what to wear.

"Kam relax! It's just a casual date." She says attempting to calm me down.

"Yeah. With a hunky quarterback. Why am I so nervous?"

From her spot on her bed, she looks at me with empathy. "Maybe because you're scared that you might actually like him after tonight? Since I've known Mason, he's been nothing but a gentleman. I don't think you have anything to worry about."

I groan out my frustration. Look into my average looking closet and back at Sarah with puppy dog eyes. "Will you help me please? Your fashion taste is much better than mine."

With a laugh, Sarah hefts herself off her bed and joins me at my closet. Swiftly putting two pieces together, I never would have thought to put together. "Here...wear this maxi dress and these boots. Now go put those on." Sarah says as she pushes me into our little bathroom.

Deep breaths Kamryn. It's not like you haven't gone out on dates with insanely attractive guys before. Yeah, but not star athletes. When I go out with Liam he gathers plenty of female's eyes. The looks I get are born out of jealousy. I give myself a pep talk like that will hopefully calm me down.

With the dress and the boots on it still doesn't look right. Doubt coats my voice as I call out, "Okay. I'm coming out of the bathroom. But I don't think this looks good."

"Kamryn, stop whining and let me see."

I open the door and do a little twirl. "See. Something's off."

Sarah puts her finger to her lips to see what can be done. "Let me try something." She walks over to me and crouches down to mess with the dress. When she's done she pulls me in front of the mirror. "Done!"

I never would have thought of that. She's tied the bottom of my dress into a knot so that it kind of cascades down and is still showing off my boots. It's very bohemian chic. But something is still off.

"You don't think the boots throw it off?" They look a little clunky.

Sarah eyes my outfit again. She walks back to my closet and riffles through what I have before coming out with another dress and shoes. "Here, try this dress instead. You have really nice legs. Show them off!"

I swiftly take off the maxi dress and replace it with the shift-style mini dress. Then swap the boots for cute sandals. It is still summer in the South after all. I've never been one to wear a dress on a date because some guys take wearing a dress to mean "easy access" when it really means "less effort".

"I like this a lot better! Thanks, Sarah."

"Anytime," she tells me with a small smile.

My phone chimes with a message from Mason.

Mason: I'm out front.

"He's here." I look at Sarah. My nerves have skyrocketed to an all-time high.

"Don't keep the man waiting. Chop chop!" Sarah demands.

I gather up my little black wristlet and throw my ID, chapstick, lip gloss, debit card, some cash, my dorm key, and a couple sticks of gum in it before I leave. I also make sure I have my Blackberry, because...why wouldn't I? I say bye to Sarah and tell her not to wait up with a wink.

Walking to the front of my dorm telling myself to calm down. He's just a guy. A really hunky, athletic, and handsome guy. I push through the door and he turns around at the noise.

"Hey, you," He greets.

"Hey, yourself," I falter in my steps a little. Did I really just greet him like that?

He smiles at my greeting. "Ready to go? It's just up the street, so I figured we'd walk?"

"Yeah, that sounds good," I reply nervously.

We make small talk on the way to the restaurant. Quirky little tidbits that get us making up faux stories that have us cracking up laughing. He puts himself on the street side of the sidewalk, putting his hand on my lower back as we pass other people. His presence puts me at ease, so I'm pleasantly surprised when we stop at a place called Hippy Dippy. It's a cute pizza place with hipster retro vibes throughout the restaurant. Once we're seated and the waitress takes our order, that's when the real conversation starts.

"So where are you really from Kamryn? I am asking you this now since I was shut down the first time I asked." He says with a smirk that has my face flaming with a blush.

"I am actually from Philadelphia. Born and raised."

"So that explains the accent. You didn't want to stay there for school?"

This part I dread telling people. "You want the real truth? Or some fake truth?"

"Real truth, please."

"Penn U was a solid choice. My family is there. I know the city. Anytime my parents talked about college, they would say that they had the best time of their lives being part of the Greek world. Both of my parents were part of the founding members of their chapters. Penn U is very Greek heavy, so when word got around that they had two legends in their midst the Greek life dedicated a wall shrine to them. All of their achievements and pictures. So many pictures. My parents would take my sister and me to visit there, despite them never going to that school, and it was unconsciously ingrained in us that that was our path." I take a sip of my water before continuing. "I concluded that the only way for me to not be seen a certain way was to go to a completely different school. So here I am. Does that make sense?"

"Of course it does. We all have to have the ability to spread our wings without the crucifixion of others. I think you made the right choice."

"Thank you. Not only was Greek life part of the reason I didn't want to go there, but the school wasn't what I wanted."

"What were you looking for in a school?"

The waitress coming over pauses our conversation as she places our pizza in the center of the table. We both tell her thank you and then get situated.

"I can't really explain it. It's more that I felt it. When I toured here, I got goosebumps. I felt a calmness that I had never felt before. I didn't think I'd feel that anywhere else." I take a bite of pizza once it's cooled. I felt like I was rambling so I take the opportunity to take a breath.

"And your major is psychology?"

Him remembering, even my major, is such a tiny gesture but it means the world. "That's correct."

"What are your end goals for being a psychology major?"

"I would love to have my own practice. General counseling isn't too stuffy. But maybe a psychologist in a hospital. I have a while before I have to figure that out. Then again I keep going back to being a teacher. And oh my goodness I need to stop talking." I cover my face as embarrassment takes hold.

Mason's chuckle is somewhat comforting. "I've been asking you the questions. I'm just surprised you figured that all out in your first year. Most don't."

"Yeah. I took a psychology class as an elective my junior year, and I was hooked. Nothing else really mattered."

"You are probably the most ambitious freshmen that I've ever met."

"Thanks, I guess. Well what about you? Was it always a dream of yours to play at such a high profile college?" I ask ready to have the attention off of me.

He leans back in his chair, now that I've turned the conversation to him. "Football was never even part of my plan. I just did it in high school to have something to do. But colleges took notice and I got offers all over South Carolina. I wanted something that was far from home, but not too far that I couldn't leave if I had a family emergency. My original plan was always art school or even majoring in art therapy."

"Art school?"

He nods his head. "I had really bad ADHD growing up. My parents took me to a bunch of specialists. They tried putting me into music classes, I tried writing, and building; but nothing quite worked. Until one day in middle school, we had to take an art class as a mandatory elective and I guess that's when it clicked for me. Apparently, my teacher called my parents to let them know I finally focused on something for longer than two minutes. They never pushed me into it, which I think that also helped. But I continued with it. Entered into some contests during my junior and senior years of high school. Placed in the top three and even entered nationally for some shows."

"Wow. So how did those shows go?" I ask genuinely curious.

"I actually placed in the top ten," he says so casually.

"That's amazing. Now I can say I know a famous artist."

"I wouldn't take it that far," Mason says modestly.

"Honestly, I never would have pegged you for an art guy.

Don't get me wrong, but you look more like someone who'd be into journalism or sports broadcasting or even engineering. But if you don't mind, and since you said you wanted to go to art school, I'd love to see some of your work."

His eyes widened after I said that. "Really?"

"Absolutely. Anyone who says what they really want to do is respected in my book. But what is your major?"

"I couldn't just let art go. It was a safe place for me when the world was too chaotic. So I'm actually double majoring in Art Therapy and Finance."

"So you didn't stray too far from what you wanted. That suits you."

As we continue talking through dinner, we find we have a lot more in common. Brooks is a much-respected name in Greek life as well. He joined a fraternity his freshman year but doesn't advertise it like others around campus. He tells me all the places he wants to travel to and I tell him mine. And throughout dinner, I find myself warming up to him more than I would have thought possible. He's sweeter than I anticipated. But I guess he gets that from the example that his parents have set for him.

We're still talking about anything and everything under the sun long after dinner is over. After we left the restaurant we decided to take a walk around campus, because neither one of us wanted the night to end. I'm quickly realizing that Mason had a phenomenal example of how to treat a woman when we both notice how late it's getting when he walks me back to my dorm. If neither of us had early classes the next day, I'm sure that we could've kept talking until the sun came up.

"I had a lot of fun tonight Kamryn."

I peek over at him out of the corner of my eye and see his hands shoved deep into his front pockets.

"So did I. More fun than any date that I've ever been on." Backtrack. NOW!

His head pops up at the word date. "So you saw this as a date?"

"Oh god. I didn't want to assume anything. That's only if you saw it that way." I mentally slap myself in the face repeatedly.

He takes my hand in his and leads me to the side of the building out of sight from passersby.

"Mason, I'm sorry if I assumed anything." I just blew it with the most amazing guy that I've ever known.

Mason gently cradles my head in his hand. "I don't do this on first dates. Or when I barely know the person. But it's something about you Kamryn. May I?"

He's asking to kiss me. Ding! Ding! Ding! We have a winner.

I find my voice amidst the blood roaring in my head. "May you what?"

His hand tucks the hair behind my ear and curves around the back of my neck. "May I kiss you?"

I nod my head.

"I need the words Kamryn."

"Yes. You may kiss me."

Mason leans down and is just an inch from my lips, hovering. Is he waiting for me? I stretch to my tiptoes and close the distance as our lips carefully meet. His lips are soft, not overly small or big, but the right size to where we fit together like a puzzle piece. It's an innocent kiss. A get-to-know you kiss. It's like he's waiting for me to make the next move.

His tongue lightly darts out and traces my bottom lip. I open my mouth a little more and that's when it happens. As soon as our tongues meet, Mason puts a hand on my lower back, the other on the back of my neck tightens and pulls me up against him leaving no room for anything between us. Walking us back against the brick wall for support. Fireworks explode behind my eyelids and I feel this kiss everywhere.

I think that's what expertly defines Mason. Sweet and approachable to the outside world. Sexy and dominating the person he's with.

Our tongues dance and battle for control. He wins, but not before placing his thigh between my legs. The friction of his thigh on my center has me rolling my hips desperately seeking more of the friction I desperately want. His hand that's on the back of my neck travels down my body before landing my thigh and giving it a squeeze. The whimper he elicits from me is almost embarrassing.

After a few minutes of over the clothes groping and some innocent ass grabbing, he reluctantly breaks our kiss. Our foreheads rest against each others and my chest heaves from the effort it takes to catch my breath.

"You...wow." He slowly removes his leg from between mine and makes sure I'm balanced before standing up straight.

I'm still a little dazed and breathless from the kiss, my gaze fixated on his lips. "Right back atcha champ." Is all that I can manage to get out.

"I have an away game this weekend. But do you wanna go to breakfast? Maybe Friday morning? I know a place that's good, but we have to get there right as they open."

I'm gonna fall fast for him. I just know it. "Sure. I'd love to. I have my only class at ten."

We walk back to the front of the building as slowly as we can.

"I'll see you Friday. Get some sleep."

"Okay. Thank you for tonight." I kiss him on the cheek and then walk into my dorm. I look over my shoulder once I'm inside and see him watching me walk away. I'm in so much trouble.

The good kind of course.

8

KAMRYN

fter our date, Mason and I have been texting non-stop. Well as much non-stop as possible. With his crazy busy football schedule and my preparing to rush, it's been hectic to say the least. So when Friday rolls around I'm finally able to breathe a sigh of relief.

> Mason: Meet me at Stacks at 8.

> Me: Okay. I'll see you in a bit.

"So I take it things are going good with Mason?" Sarah asks.

The college schedule took some getting used to. Eight AM classes are much different than waking up everyday for high school. But Sarah and I have both managed since we're both natural early risers despite neither of us having early classes on Friday's.

I pull my hair back into a braid and run some mascara through my lashes. Then throw on some leggings and a thin long sleeve shirt with a few spritzes of perfume, before calling it a day.

"It's only been a few days." I start and move to sit on my bed. "But I'm already falling hard for him. He's a perfect gentleman. He's sweet, attentive, and he makes me laugh. He's just so easy to talk to. We never run out of things to say. He gives me butterflies."

Sarah looks over at me with a smile before she asks, "And what about Liam?"

"What do you mean?" I ask and pick at a hangnail.

She pins me with that look. "You know what I mean. Kam, he's your best friend. He deserves to know that you're seeing someone."

"You're the one that said I needed to get over whatever it was that was brewing between the two of us." I tell her pointedly.

"Yeah. I did. Again, Kam, he's one of your best friends. And I know for a fact that after y'all's FWB arrangement, he might be waiting for you to make the next move." Leave it to Sarah to be my voice of reason.

I turn and look at her. "He blew me off. So I took matters into my own hands and moved on."

Sarah gives me a pointed look. "Kamryn, boys run when they're scared. It's just what they do."

"How do I break it to him?" I ask and drop back on my bed, looking up at the ceiling.

"Honestly and truthfully."

I ponder over what to say and then pull out my phone to text him. Not thinking I'd get an instant response from him.

Me: Can we meet up this afternoon? At the fountain? I need to talk to you about something.

Liam: Sure. I have practice til 3. And I wanted to talk to you as well. We can meet up after.

Me: Perfect. See you then.

~

"Done." I tell Sarah and stand up, taking her keys that she's holding out to me. "But if this blows up in my face–"

"–You can say I told you so."

I pause at the door and turn to face her. "Exactly. Thank you for letting me borrow your car."

"You're welcome. Have fun!"

I smile the whole walk from our room to the car. It's strange how everything has felt right since I met Mason. This realization that life can be crystal clear in its direction that life can take you on. In the short time I've been in his life and he in mine, I find myself lighter. I find myself smiling and realizing that happiness is more attainable than I thought. Mason is exactly who I need in this period in my life.

I make the short drive to the small breakfast spot and see him waiting by the door. My body lights up as we make eye contact. As I get out of the car and walk towards him, that lightness I felt before I'm noticing isn't a fluke. It's real.

"Hi," he greets.

"Hi back." I tell him.

He takes my hand in his and opens the door up to the restaurant.

Hand holding is an underrated physical connection. The sparks of light that ignite when mine and Mason's hands touch, sparks the giddiness I've waited for. He transfers my hand to his other as he opens the door for us and places it on my lower back as we walk inside. We get a table for two and settle in for our first of many dates.

This breakfast has been amazing. No matter how many times I've had breakfast in South Carolina, it never fails to amaze me. The company isn't so bad either.

The restaurant is cozy with wood tones throughout. The smell of coffee and maple syrup permeate the area. Tables with character marks and local prints and paintings hang on the wall with huge Bay windows lining the front of the restaurant letting the morning light shine through the space.

The place was just filling up by the time we got there. So we got lucky with the intimate two-seater table that has our legs and feet caging the other. Our conversations isn't forced, we laugh easily, and I've truthfully never felt more giggly. We end up eating off each other's plates as the food is too good to not just restrict ourselves to just our meals.

When our plates are empty, we stack them and settle back into our chairs. Watching the slow hustle and bustle as more people come into the restaurant.

"So I was thinking..." Mason starts by way of conversation.

"Oh no."

"What?" He looks alarmed

"Nothing good ever starts with 'So I was thinking'." I say with a smile and air quotes.

That gets a chuckle out of him. "You're right. I'm sorry. But I was thinking about something. It's a good thing." He looks at me expectantly as he sits forward.

"Go on," I encourage him. I have a hunch of what he's about to tell me.

"I like you Kam. I have fun with you. You're different in a

good way. It sets you apart from the rest of the other girls on campus."

I take that as a good thing. "I like you too, Mason."

"I know that we just started hanging out, and I know that we're both really busy. And I don't want to do the whole talk for a month or longer to see how it goes." He takes my hand in his as if he needs the contact to get him through this. "But, I was wondering if you'd like to make this official? Make us official. It's going to take a lot of work to have alone time. But I think we can do it."

I lean in closer to him, because his energy is just something that I now crave. "Are you asking me to be your girlfriend?"

Now it's his turn to blush. "Yeah. I am."

"My answer is yes." The smile that spreads across my face can't be tamed.

Once our breakfast is paid for, Mason walks me out to the car.

"Thank you for breakfast." I tell him. Breakfast dates are underutilized meals in the date category.

Our hands swing gently between us. The giddiness I feel with officially being his makes me floaty.

"Of course. I wish we didn't have an away game this weekend." He admits as we stop next to the driver's door.

"I'll be able to see you on Sunday, right?"

Mason nods his head. "You and me. Movies all day."

"Sounds perfect."

First kisses as boyfriend and girlfriend are nerve wracking. Yes, we've kissed, but this is different. There are so many questions that run through my mind. Which way do you turn your head? Are we using tongue? Does my breath smell? Are we kissing? Or are we just hugging?

WHAT IS THE RIGHT CALL?!!

Mason pulls me in for a hug and rests his cheek on top of my head. My arms go around his waist. Our bodies mold together and I bask in the warmth of his body heat. I soak in his warmth and his masculine scent with a twinge of sweetness from the syrup. Other than that, it's all Mason. His heartbeat is steady and pumping against my ear. His arms are holding me to him as if he'll never get the chance to do so again.

That lightness I talk about, can he feel it too?

Pulling back to look into his eyes, I see his gaze switching between my eyes and lips. So I make the decision and take the leap. Leaning up on my toes and pressing my lips to his ever so gently and making us 100% official, is better than any kiss that he could give me.

Mason's body crowds mine against the car. His hard body against my soft. Our lips move together. His tongue licks along my bottom lip as one hand goes to the back of my head, holding me in place, while the other slips under my shirt and pushes my lower body into his groin.

"I have to go." Mason says before kissing me senseless. His tongue tangles with mine as we lean against the car.

"Mm hmm." *Kiss.* "Yeah." *Kiss.* "You should really go." *Kiss.*

Neither of us attempt to make a move to stop kissing. This is better than a sugar high if you ask me.

After a few minutes, we slow the kiss down, and finally pull back from each other. Our foreheads resting on each other as we tempt our heart rates to go back to normal.

"I'll see you Sunday." Mason says and pulls open my door.

"Good luck tomorrow." I say and place one last kiss on his lips.

Once the door is closed and I'm buckled in, Mason steps back from the car as I drive away.

I'm literally floating on a cloud for the rest of the day. My Friday class is a breeze and the professor takes pity on us and lets us out of class twenty minutes earlier.

Everything is great. Until I remember that Liam and I are supposed to have a talk this afternoon. And my cloudless day turns into a pending rainstorm. The lightness I felt hours before with Mason, dissipates to what feels like anchors on my ankles. But I'd rather him hear it from me than someone else. That's what friends do, right? Protect each other from getting hurt. Well, not protect, but shield them from the brunt of it? That's what I'm doing for Liam. I don't want to hide anything from him.

~

5 hours later

I'M SITTING by the fountain in the middle of the quad, texting Mason when Liam calls out my name. I look up and see him walking towards me with a smile on his face.

Things haven't been the same between us since that last time we were together. Maybe it's that we're finding who we're supposed to be while in college and it doesn't include each other. For so long it was Liam and Kamryn. Now it's us and other people.

There's been this river between us and I don't know how to cross it. There's no bridge, no boat, and no rocks to jump on to cross over to him.

My phone buzzes with an incoming text from Mason, but I lock it before smiling up at Liam.

"Hey stranger. Long time no see." Liam says by way of greeting me.

I'm nervous to talk to him. *Why am I nervous?* "Hey yourself. I know, I've just gotten pretty busy lately. Sorry about that."

I think I'm about to break his heart.

"No problem. So what did you want to talk about?" He takes a seat next to me and looks at me like I hung the moon. Oh, Liam. I absolutely did not hang the moon.

"I actually wanted to tell you something." Deep breath Kamryn. You can do this! I face him and tuck a leg underneath me. "Do you remember that big back-to-school party a couple weeks ago?" He nods. So I continue. "Well, I met someone there. It wasn't planned. Well for me it wasn't. Sarah kind of introduced us. But we hit it off and hadn't seen each other until about a week later. Then we went on a date that Tuesday and then another one this morning. We made it official right after."

I look at him to gauge his reaction. If he's hurt then he's hiding it damn well.

I see a little twitch in his jaw before he looks at me with a small smile on his face. "What's his name?"

"Mason Brooks."

Liam's eyes jump to his hairline. "You're dating the starting QB for our school?"

I nod. "I know it's completely random. But he's a good guy and he makes me laugh and I'm really happy."

"That's great Kam," Liam responds, surprising me.

"Really?"

"Yeah. As long as you're happy."

"I am. Thank you Liam."

We both look out onto the quad. Not knowing what to say. But knowing something else should be said.

"I just–I know we said we'd let the other know when we met someone. And things have been so weird between us. But I thought I should let you know rather than you finding out from someone else."

He looks at me with a furrowed brow, choosing not to say anything.

"What was it that you wanted to talk to me about?" I ask, referring to our text exchange earlier.

Liam shakes his head and a small, closed smile covers her face, but doesn't reach his eyes. "It's nothing important."

Fuck. The silence between us is no longer the comfortable silence that I once had with him. Instead it's awkward. It was never like this when either of us dated in high school. Then again, we never slept together.

"I'm gonna go." I tell Liam after minutes of us staring at nothing and the silence being too brutal to stand. "You're still my best friend. That doesn't change anything." I kiss Liam on the cheek and head back to my dorm.

That could have gone better. But it could've gone worse.

9

LIAM

Fuck.

I played the role of best friend too well. Listening to Kamryn gush about her new boyfriend and how happy he makes her. How dumb am I to think that she and I would just fall together? I could've made her happy. At least I think I could have. But to think that our hookup could have been the beginning of us and I ruined it because I got scared. I wanna kick my own ass. Regret twines its way through my body and it's the only feeling I can latch on to.

It's a Friday and the football team is on the road leaving the campus quiet. Too quiet.

Me: Any parties tonight?

Brandon: None near campus.

Nash: Might head to one in the next city over.

Me: I'm in.

Chance: Do we need to supervise?

Nash: You mean cockblock?

Chance: No, I mean make sure y'all don't get arrested.

Me: We could use a getaway car.

Me: I mean a designated driver.

Me: Or should I just call you the babysitter?

Chance: Don't be a dick.

Nash: My buddy at Tempest just told me they're having a big party tonight.

Me: It's settled.

Brandon: Why do I feel like this is about to be a long night?

"You're dating the starting QB for our school?" My question plays on a loop over and over again. Losing someone I almost had hurts worse than having them and losing them. No matter how I try to play it, I know my ghosting Kamryn set me up to lose her long before I ever got to have her.

My mind keeps going back to move-in day. How it was so easy for us. Those early nights of our arrangement wrapped around each other. The trust that was already there.

I'm in love with my best friend. And I just lost her to someone that I can never compete with.

I drop my things off in my room before heading to the showers. Male freshman athletes have a whole dorm building to themselves. It's convenient and it's quiet when practices, games, and/or matches are scheduled. But on this particular weekend when a quarter of the dormitory is quiet because they're part of the football team, this place is a ghost town.

I try to black out the hurt that's doing its best to make itself known. I had years to tell Kamryn I had feelings for her. Years! But I squandered it by keeping her in the friend-zone and dating other girls that didn't look like her.

Frustrated, I dry my body off and rough dry my hair with the towel before throwing it in the hamper. I search for a pair of jeans that are decently clean and a long-sleeve black henley. Slipping on some boots, I grab what else I need and head towards the guys off campus apartment.

I had the option to be their roommate. But I wanted to be on campus so I could be closer to Kam. Call it clinging to home, but it was what I needed. *She* was what I needed to feel closer to home.

I make a detour into the liquor store with the new fake ID I got. My plan is to forget that my best friend found someone else. My plan is to forget. Forget that a dare was what set us in motion. That a dare was what gave me a taste of what I could have had. If that involves me passing my time with girls that aren't Kamryn, then so be it.

If she can be happy with him, then why can't I?

Tempest University isn't much different from our university. The athletes stick together and the sorority girls do their best to catch the eyes of the frat bros. Me? I'm just here to get a buzz and maybe hookup. I take a couple shots before moving to the makeshift dance floor. I find myself sliding up behind a curvy brunette and she looks over her shoulder at me with a smirk on her face.

"Is this okay?" I ask as I place my hands on her hips. Because even in my buzzed state, I still know how to ask for permission.

"More than okay," she responds before rolling her hips into mine.

Someone turns down the lights and the dance floor gets more crowded. Our bodies press closer. My hands roam down her body as she leans her head back on my shoulder. She pushes her rolling hips harder into my groin and settles my hand on her hips as I let her feel all of me.

Stopping suddenly, she takes my hand and pulls me through the thick crowd. Leading me to a hall off of the main room, she opens a door and peers into the room. It must be vacant as she pulls us in, slams the door closed, pushing me up against the door, and then kisses me.

My mind takes a second to process before I'm kissing her back. I lean forward and grab her by the back of her thighs and her legs wrap around my waist.

I break the kiss because I should at least know her name despite this planning to be a one-time thing. "What's your name?"

I look around and find the short bed that's about knee height and I walk us forward before I drop her on the mattress and lean over her with my hands pressed on either side of her head. This is no-strings attached sex. Which is what got me in this mess in the first place. I hover over her, waiting for her answer.

"Lyla," she tells me. "And your name?"

"Liam," I tell her, ignoring how cute our names sound together.

"I'm not looking for a boyfriend," she says as her hands tease the hem of my shirt.

I pull my shirt off the rest of the way and then toss it to the bed. "And I'm not looking for a girlfriend. Just sex."

"Perfect. And just one night."

"Deal." I agree and then press my lips to hers again. I

move my lips to her jaw, down her neck, over her breasts covered with her dress. Before continuing down her body and landing with a soft thud on the floor as the hardwood bites into my knees. I look up at her as I run my hands under her dress to the barely-there waistband of her thong. She nods her head and lifts her hips before I'm pulling them down her legs and tossing the scrap of fabric to the floor.

Flipping the skirt of her dress up, I blow cool air on her bare pussy.

She gasps a strangled "Fuck." Before sliding her hands through my hair and pushing my mouth towards her pussy.

You don't have to tell me twice. I latch onto her clit and my tongue flicks the taught bud in quick motions as I slide a finger into her. The sting of my hair being pulled heightens and I add another finger. Pumping them in and out, stroking her inner walls. Lyla's moans and cries of pleasure spur me on. I pull my fingers out of her and replace them with my tongue. Lapping up her arousal as she clamps her legs around my head. I pay attention to her clit as I slide two fingers into her again. Pumping and twisting, urging her to come. My fingers find the spot that has her drenching my hand and her scream is barely audible over the sound of the party in the living room.

When her orgasm fades, I pull my fingers from her and stand back up to my full height. Holding eye contact I suck her release off my fingers and she pulls down the front of her dress down and plays with her rosy nipples. "Are you just gonna stand there?" she asks, her voice is husky, turning my erection to an almost painful feeling.

Grabbing my wallet and pulling out a condom, I toss it on the bed next to her and swat her hands away as I rip her dress off. It goes flying over my shoulder as I suck a hard pointed tip into my mouth. My hand plays with the other nipple, lightly twisting and pulling until she's moaning my name.

I back away and pull my pants down to my thighs. Reaching behind me I pull my shirt off and toss it to the bed. I don't miss the appreciation as she rakes her gaze over my body. Leaning forward, I grab the condom, I tear open the foil and roll the condom down my length.

Her legs spread in invitation, but I quickly flip her over to all fours. I won't do missionary anymore. But this, seeing her perky ass and wet cunt in my face, yeah this works.

I tap her clit with the head of my cock and watch the shudder move over her body as I slide through her slit. I breach her opening as I slide my length inside of her. Pulling out and pushing back in, coating my length in her arousal before her cunt envelopes my cock.

Lyla's moan has my dick twitching before I start thrusting inside of her. Her pussy is warm and tight, just the way my cock likes it. She arches her back causing me to slide deeper.

"Holy fuck," I mutter as I lengthen my strokes.

"Harder," she urges.

Don't have to tell me twice. I perch a leg on the bed and pound into her. Her moans are the encouragement I need. Her ass matches my strokes as she throws it back, thrust for thrust and I'm seconds from blowing my load.

"I need you to get there Lyla." I grit out. Her pussy strangles my cock. "What do you need?" I need to come now. And when she grabs my hand and places a finger on her puckered hole I know that this will send me over.

I lean forward and put my thumb in front of her mouth. "Suck," I tell her. She doesn't hesitate. When I feel my thumb is wet enough, I pull it from her mouth and run my finger around to her asshole before circling and slowly pushing in and lightly pumping.

That movement has her pussy fluttering and my thrusts stuttering before she's screaming my name as she comes.

"That's it Lyla," I call out before my balls draw up and I'm coming harder than ever. I pull out my thumb and grab onto her hips as I work myself through my release with animalistic thrusts. When I'm spent, I pull out of her with a wince and collapse onto the bed beside her attempting to catch my breath. My jeans are still around my thighs so I pull those up and continue to look at the ceiling.

"Fuck," I hear from next to me. "Well that was fun," Lyla breaks the silence after we're done catching our breath.

I look over at her, letting out a chuckle. "Yeah."

That regret sinks back in and I turn my face away before letting her see in too deep.

The bed moves beside me as Lyla gets up and grabs her dress. I don't make a move to look at her.

"I know this was a one-time thing. And I'm okay with that. But if you need someone to have fun with, hit me up." She tells me. Lyla finds a scrap piece of paper and a pencil. Jotting down her number she places it in my jeans pockets. Crawling over my body, she waits until we're eye-to-eye. "I don't know who she is and I don't really care. You're special, Liam. And I hope you know that."

With a lingering kiss to my cheek she crawls off me and slips out of the room. The sound from the party infiltrates before I'm flooded in silence once again.

I don't regret the hookup. I did it all of the time in high school when I never thought I'd get a chance with my best friend. Now that I had my chance with her and she's with someone else, the regret paired with emptiness, claws at me. Threatening to drown me in the hurt. I could blame

Kamryn for this. I could. It would be so easy for me to do so. But I've had years to tell her I have more than a crush on her. So I can't blame her no matter how badly I want to.

My role in her life is simple now. I'm the supportive best friend and if that's the only way to have her in my life without losing her, then that's what I'll do.

10

MASON

"**P**arty tonight?" I hear one of my teammates ask.

    I look at him like he's insane. Yes, we won the game. But it's technically a school night. "Absolutely not. You should be looking at film for our next game. That block you missed took the wind straight out of me."

He looks like I took his favorite toy from him. "Fine."

> Me: Hey sweetheart. We're almost back on campus.

> Kamryn: Can't wait to see you 😊

I pinch myself often since meeting Kamryn. I didn't intend to date anyone in college, let alone in my junior year. But when we met, I felt like I just knew. That she would be my game changer.

My phone buzzes with another message from Kam.

> Kamryn: *when you win a game* playlist

A smile creeps over my face and I pop my headphones

in and cue up the playlist. Britney Spears sounds through my headphones. To Queen, Maroon 5, and Michael Jackson. My girl has some good music taste.

An hour passes and the telltale signs of campus getting closer make itself known as Palmetto trees line the bus's path to our drop-off. Once parked, the guys gather their things and crowd the aisle to get off.

"No practice tomorrow, but there is conditioning tomorrow guys." The coach announces before we're out of earshot.

Catcalls and whistles sound as the guys file off the bus. Confusion swirls, but I mostly ignore them. But that confusion clears when I step off the bus and see Kamryn holding a sign:

Here for the
Hottest QB
in SC

"Hi." She says with a laugh.

I take in her chocolate brown hair pulled up in a haphazard bun with short curly tendrils framing her face. Our school logo on the front of her sweatshirt swallows her body whole and I jog a couple of steps to her before enveloping her in a hug. At 6'5" my body dwarfs her. I feel protective of her in a way I can't begin to explain.

"I could get used to homecomings like this." I tell her.

She stretches up to her tiptoes and places a kiss on my neck that has my heart hammering out of my chest. "I prefer if you stay here, but I'm all for celebrations."

I smush a kiss on her cheek before releasing her. I don't need to go into the athletic training room, despite the hit I took on that missed block. I'm sure I'll regret it and feel the effects the next time we have a full pads practice. Our hands link together as we walk hand in hand toward my car. This feeling of disbelief that she's here is mind boggling.

The ride back to my dorm is in comfortable silence as the radio plays whatever song is trending at the moment.

I've never been around someone where the silence is comfortable. My teammates despise silence. Always needing to fill said silence with conversation. But with Kam, the silence is easy. In the short time we've been together, we've sat in silence and have had meaningful conversations. I cherish both of those moments with her.

Finding a parking spot is easy as it's a late Sunday morning so students are either on their way back to campus from home or a party at another university.

We get out of my car and meet around the back before walking into my dorm.

"Do you wanna order food so we don't have to leave your room for a while?" Kamryn asks.

We take the elevator up to the fourth floor of the dorm. Since this is the upperclassmen dorm, it's fairly quiet. Few guys walk to other rooms for video games. But other than that, not a peep is made.

I give her hand a little squeeze before letting go to unlock my door. "Sounds good and we can go to the cafeteria for dinner."

I got lucky in the dorm room aspect. As upperclassmen, we have the option to share a room or have a single. Being around the team day in and day out made my decision easier–so I chose the single. It's big enough for a full size bed, an oversized loveseat couch, a dresser with enough surface area for my TV, and a desk. Kamryn saunters into my dorm and sets her bag on the desk in the corner. I never thought much about having a girl over. On the rare occasion, it was a quick party hookup at the frat house. But with Kamryn, I've never been so glad I have a single room. And I like that she makes herself at home so quickly.

"Look at us communicating. I mean it is with food, so not much we can mess up on." Kamryn says with a smirk.

A smile attaches itself to my face. I lay out on the couch and hold my hand out for Kamryn. She comes with ease and settles her body next to mine. Her arm wraps around my waist and I feel her body instantly relax.

I play with a curl that's fallen out of her bun. Letting this moment wash over me like waves gently rolling to the shore.

"How was your Saturday?" I ask and press a kiss to the top of her head.

"It was too quiet. I never realized how much life a football team brings to a school."

"Ah...so you missed me?" I ask jokingly.

Her head pops up and she rolls her eyes. "How much bigger will your ego get if I say yes? But I don't feel like I deserve to miss you this soon."

My arms tighten around her when she settles her head back down on my chest. "I think you can miss anyone you want to. Time shouldn't be a factor in that. Because I'll let you in on a secret. I missed you too."

Kamryn burrows her face more into my chest and tightens her arms around me. My mind drifts off to the possibility of her and me in the future. The thought is quick and one of the reasons I never thought to date in college was because some girls never date with pure intentions. As soon as some girls find out you're an athlete with the possibility of going pro, any true connection you think you have with them fly out the window. But I don't get that feeling with Kamryn.

When we met, she seemed to have no clue about the extent of my influence. That's not me being a narcissist, but helping put the football team back on the collegiate map, my face has been plastered all over campus since I was a freshman. I could also say the same about her. Kamryn is magnetic. She might not know it, but I see the way people flock to her. She has a calming yet demanding presence that manages to make smooth sailing even smoother.

I reach over to the coffee table to grab the remote. Knowing neither of us will truly pay attention to the movie, I put it on a Fast & Furious movie. My hands drifting up and down her back while I drift away in thought looking at the TV screen.

Sometime later, I wake up with a new movie on and Kamryn's face turned towards the screen. Her body securely draped over mine.

"Did I fall asleep?" I ask. My voice is scratchy from the sudden use.

I look over at the clock and see it's just past noon. So not a terribly long nap, but enough to feel slightly well-rested but also confused as to what decade it is.

"I did too. You have some magical hands Mr. Brooks." She tells me cheekily.

"Is that so?" I question her as my hands roam down her back and to her ass.

Her breathing changes, so I know it's affected her. "Mm hmm."

I give her a squeeze and move her legs so she's straddling me. The movement wakes her up more so when she sits up she takes my hands in hers.

"I think it's time we had that talk." She pouts.

I'm assuming I know where she's going with this, but I

need to make sure. "Talk? Like the boyfriend and girlfriend talk? Or…"

"The sex talk, silly goose." Her gaze drops and she plays with the strings of my hoodie.

"Well my parents had the birds and the bees talk with me in high school. You might be a little late to that conversation." I attempt a joke.

She gets a stern look on her face that has her brows scrunching. "I'm serious. Sex is whatever to some people. I've done the casual thing. I've done the relationship aspect of sex. But with you…something about sex with you could be different and I don't want it to mess anything up."

A breath leaves me. Part of being in a relationship that can go physical is having those types of conversations. And she's right. "You're right. I know you are. But just so you know, I haven't been with anyone since the summer. Which may seem strange, but early practices and coming to campus earlier than others didn't leave that much time for that." Her eyes dart around my room and then focus on the strings of my hoodie. "Sweetheart, what's wrong?"

"Um, well up until recently I was in a situationship with someone."

"How recently?" I tilt her chin up so I can see her eyes.

"About a week before we met. But he and I made a promise to each other that if and when we met someone we'd stop. He had already pulled away before I met you. And once I met you, I knew I couldn't see him and I going further than we already had. So that Monday I went to the free clinic and got tested. I'm all clean. And protected. I just thought you should know."

I give her a reassuring smile. "I'm glad you told me. To be honest it's good we had this talk now. I'm clean too by the way."

"Oh. Okay. Good. That's good," Kamryn responds jittery.

"Okay." I start and sit up with her still in my lap. "Sweetheart, I don't want you to be nervous. Not around me. I can assure you that when we do get to that stage in our relationship, we'll be perfect together."

"So we stick to first base?" Kam asks as she moves to trail kisses on my jaw to my neck. Her hands snake under my shirt and tease my abs causing them to constrict.

"What's your idea of first base, sweetheart?" I gather her hair that she took out of the bun in one hand. She moves closer and rolls her hips over my now hard cock.

"Lots and lots of kissing."

"What else?" This girl is gonna make me lose my mind. "How fast til we're at second base?"

She takes her hands out from under my shirt. "Over the clothes touching and groping. No skin on skin."

I groan from the loss of her skin on mine.

"As for how fast we get to second base. That's up in the air."

I take her face in mine and smash our mouths together. My tongue seeks entrance right away and hers meets mine stroke for stroke. My breathing stutters to a halt. This is our first kiss not outside or in front of a crowd. It's just us. The realization has my heartbeat kicking up speed.

I flip our positions as smoothly as I can on this tiny couch and rest my weight on her. Kamryn's legs wrap around my waist as she rolls her hips into me. She breaks the kiss and I take the moment to trail a path down her jaw, kissing her neck that has her whimpering, and down to her chest.

We make eye contact as I hover over her chest. Her eyebrow lifts in a challenge.

So I take it. I take a shirt covered nipple in my mouth

and tease the other one with enough pressure that it makes her eyes roll back and a moan slip free. I take my other hand and trail it down to her legging-covered limbs and I feel the heat between her legs. Knowing she's just as affected as I am turns me on even more. Her legs spread further as my thumb brushes her clit.

I pull away from her chest and look into her eyes as I rub her clit through her leggings. The hitch in her breath. How she strangles my forearm as I sense she's getting closer.

When she stops breathing, I plunge my tongue into her mouth just as she falls over the edge. I feel a dampening as I continue to rub her from opening to clit and I rub her through her orgasm before slowing down my movement. Our kiss slows to where I just peck her face with kisses until she's a giggling mess beneath me.

"First base is good." Kamryn says when her laughter subsides.

The look in her eyes has me wanting to pinch myself. How did I get so lucky? I'll have to thank Sarah for introducing us.

"So, a few more dates until a home run...got it." I say with a wink.

"Easy buddy," she starts with a chuckle. "I'm looking for quality dates."

And quality dates are what she gets.

"Blue, forty-five. Blue forty-five." My center snaps the ball to my waiting hands and I drop back in the pocket. Scanning the field for my receiver, I spin out of an almost tackle and pray that my offense holds the defense off so we can gain some yards.

One of my receivers breaks free as I run a couple yards down field before throwing it to him on my run. A lineman manages to tackle someone from the opposing team before one of my guys is brought down at the twenty-yard line.

We're playing against one of our conference rivals on Homecoming weekend. Alumni, boosters, and fans pack the stadium. There's nothing like the rush we get when we have a home game and the fans fill the stands. But with this game, the stakes are higher. This game determines whether or not we have a high enough seed to make it to the playoffs. It's the fourth quarter. We have one timeout left. I know my team is tired. Hell, I've been running on all cylinders since the game started and even I'm gassed.

My line and I look to the sideline for the next play. It's a quarterback sneak where I pray my O-line holds the defense while I tuck the ball and run. This play opens me up to any hit so I'm hoping my guys hold strong.

We get into position and I call out the play. As soon as the ball is snapped a path is cleared for me as I take off running through the path my guys created and off towards the end zone. The sound of the crowds cheering is deafening as I break a weak tackle from a safety. My legs carry me swiftly and safely across the line of the end zone.

What happens next is a blur. My teammates rush me and I look up to see that we're up by double digits. Giving us a big lead. Special teams run onto the field for the field goal. There's ten seconds left on the play clock. The field goal is easily made leaving us with seven seconds of play. When the ball is lined up and the whistle is blown, the ball is kicked and I sit back and take it all in. I watch as the seconds wind down on the clock. As we take the field again and line up for the snap, I take in a fortifying breath. When the ball snaps I spike it to the ground.

We just punched our ticket to the playoffs.

The student body and fans rush the field. Confetti is blasted from the cannons at the rafters. My body is jostled as congrats are shouted all around. But I'm waiting for that one person whose voice washes over me like a wave.

When I see her, my world clicks into place. Having her here, during one of the most incredible moments of my life. I can see it all flash before me. Us in the future. I know it's quick.

And when I see her getting closer to me and fighting her way through the boisterous crowd my body settles.

"You did it, baby!" Kam says as she launches herself into me.

She lathes kisses on my sweaty face. Not caring for the sweat that's transferring to her clothes or how bad I smell. I bask in the only person whose attention and accolades mean to me. Having her here on a celebratory game melds together with us in the future.

One thing is for certain. I need to do everything in my power to keep this girl with me for the rest of time.

11

KAMRYN

January 2011

"I see you and Mason survived Winter break not attached at the hip?" Sarah teases as she blows on her still drying nails. She texted me a couple days before returning to campus for second semester that we're due a roommate pamper session. I missed my best friend, so I agreed instantly.

"Hey, you set us up. I just want you to remember that." The smile on my face is evident and I focus back on painting my toenails.

"Yeah, yeah. Invite me to the wedding and make me a godparent."

A blush covers my entire face. "Winter break was hard. We texted non-stop and called each other on Christmas and New Years. I think my parents were glad when it was time for me to head back here."

"You love sick girl." Sarah teases with laughter that dies down when she sees my face. "Wait. Really?"

"It's getting there. I'm so..." My voice trails off as the

thoughts that come to me when I think about Mason and I's relationship. "I still get butterflies around him. He constantly makes me feel safe and protected. When I'm not with him, I'm always waiting for the next time I *can* be with him. I didn't know relationships could be this easy."

Sarah leans her head on my shoulder. "I'm happy for you, bestie."

"Thank you."

IT'S BEEN a few days since my realization that I more than like Mason. Every time I'm with him the words threaten to come out like word vomit. But I hold them back because I know it's not the right time. Plus I'm scared he won't feel the same.

I'm walking from the library when I see Liam walking out of the athletics building. "Hey, stranger."

"Hey, Rynny. How are you?" Liam's hug warms me from the unexpected chill in the south.

I feel like a bad friend. Liam and I haven't been the friends we were since our arrangement and then when Mason and I started dating, our friendship took a backseat. That was the last thing I wanted. But flaunting my relationship around Liam didn't seem fair either.

"I'm good. Ready for this semester to get busy. Are you ready for baseball?"

"I'm so ready. You're coming to the home opener, right?" The light in his eyes when seeing him talk about baseball warms me to my core.

I was always there at the first home game of every season. "You still want me there?"

His eyes widen almost comically at my question. "Are

you kidding? Of course I do. Whatever gave you the idea that I wouldn't?"

"Well, for one we haven't been the friends we were before everything happened. Two, we haven't really talked in months. And three, I'm dating someone." Those are the three biggest reasons.

"It would mean a lot to have you both in the stands." Liam tells me with no hint of humor, just plain honesty.

"Okay. We'll be there." I start to walk away but turn back. "It was good to see you, Liam."

A soft smile plays on his face. "You too, Kamryn."

February 2011

It's been five months since Mason and I started seeing each other. And it hasn't been as easy as we wanted though.

Starting a relationship in the thick of football season and on top of Rush Week, we had to get creative. Add on the holiday breaks and our relationship was off to a slow start. But with time management skills we made our relationship work. We would wait for each other outside of our classes to get our daily fill of each other. Along with texting each other non-stop as it was the best way to talk to each other when time was short.

But now that I am officially a member of Kappa Beta and football season is done until the fall, Mason and I have more time for each other. With it now being spring semester things are looking up for everyone.

"So what do you have planned for the summer?" Mason and I are walking to dinner and it's still a little cold out so we're not as wrapped up together as I'd like to be.

"Easy cowboy. It's not even spring break yet." I tease and bump into him.

"I'm just trying to make some plans. Seeing into the future and all."

His words stop me in my tracks. "The future? You see me in your future?"

Mason turns to face me. "Of course I do. Kamryn, I know we haven't been together that long, and I know that it's quick, but I love you."

My eyes glaze over at his admission. I knew I had been feeling something more than like for him for quite a while.

"You love me?" I squeak out.

"Yeah, ya goof."

"How do you know?"

"How do I know?" He looks up at the sky before looking back down at me. "When I'm not with you, I wonder when I'm going to be with you next. When I'm with you, I lock away every little thing you do. I've memorized your different little laughs, the way your nose crinkles when you don't like something, the way you stick your tongue out while taking pictures, and the way you look at me like I could bring you the moon and the stars. Kamryn, I have never felt this way about any girl that I've dated. And trust me, there have not been many. So, I want to spend the summer with you and hopefully beyond that. I want to travel and explore new things with you. Kamryn, I love you."

A tear escapes from the corner of my eye. "I love you too. So much."

Mason places his thumb and index finger under my chin and gently tilts my head up. He lowers his lips to mine in a slow kiss. I grip his hips to pull him closer to me and tilt my head to deepen the kiss.

"Let's get out of here." I say between kisses.

"I thought you wanted food?" Mason asks me.

Shaking my head, I hook my fingers into his belt loop to keep him anchored to me. "Later."

Mason looks around to see if anyone saw what we were doing. Once he notices that we're in the clear, he leads us back to his dorm room and luckily for us we don't run into any of his teammates. We've had some very heavy make-out sessions and were both grateful for no interruptions. But tonight is the night that we give each other all of it. All of us.

Finally.

Once we're in his room, Mason locks the door behind him and I turn around to face him while wringing my hands in front of me, a nervous tic that never went away. We both shed our jackets and beanies. For a few seconds we just stare at each other. And before losing all of my confidence, I walk over to Mason and bring his mouth down to mine.

Our tongues meet in a soft dance.

Rhythmic.

In sync.

That's how I would describe this kiss. That's how I would describe Mason and I. We've been in sync since the night we met. Mason brings his hands up to my hips to pull me closer to him and then walks us to his bed. When the back of my legs hit the bed, Mason breaks the kiss.

"Are you sure? I don't want to move too fast for you."

I love that he's so considerate of me. We've taken our relationship slow for a reason. We wanted to get to know each other on a mental and emotional level before we brought sex into our relationship. It's made us as individuals strong, but made us as a couple even stronger.

So I answer him by pulling my shirt off and unclasping my bra. Leaving me completely bare from the waist up. Then slowly and torturously, I unbutton and unzip my jeans, then slowly pull them off. He's still standing with his jaw slack eyes on my nipples that are pointed from his stare. I start pulling up the hem of his shirt to start with and with his height can only pull it up so much. When Mason tosses his shirt to the side, I place kisses on each of his pecks, flicking my tongue over his nipples; then travel up tasting and teasing him. I linger on his collarbones, and then trail kisses and nibbles up his neck. Mason's breathing has sped up and I feel his erection through his jeans.

Before I trail up to his jaw, Mason hooks his hand behind my neck and brings his lips to mine. His mouth assaults mine and I welcome it. Not breaking the kiss, he quickly sheds his jeans and then his hands trail down my body to cup my backside picking me up so I have no choice but to wrap my legs around his waist. Slowly he lowers us to the bed and is careful not to crush me from his weight.

"Are you sure?" He asks again.

Instead of responding, I hook my toes into the waistband of his boxer briefs and push them down. I bring my hand between our bodies, rubbing my thumb over the tip of him, feeling the wetness of pre-cum. Mason moans while I work him up and down, and circling the tip of him. He thrusts into my hand while he lathes my neck in kisses and nips of his teeth.

After I slow down and release him he continues his trail down my body. He pays equal attention to my nipples. With his mouth and tongue sucking my nipple to a hard peak, his other hand pinches and rolls my nipple until I'm panting and squirming beneath him. His mouth's attention goes to the other one until I feel like I could come like this.

"Baby, I'm gonna come." I pant out.

"Do it." He says as he continues the suction of his tongue

and pinching my nipple with his other hand. He adds the right amount of pressure and I fly.

An explosion of color explodes behind my eyelids as I come.

But he doesn't let up.

"Let's go for number two." He says as he slides down my body and off the bed pulling me with him so I'm hanging off. Kisses are peppered down my body and to my lower stomach as he places my legs over his shoulder. With his eyes locked on my own, he swipes his tongue from entrance to clit, before latching on my clit.

"You're so good at this." I moan out.

He looks back up at me and holding my stare he pushes a finger into my entrance. I clench around his finger as his tongue continues lapping at my clit. Mason adds another finger and makes the slow come-hither motion that has me moaning out his name. His fingers continue stroking my walls as he sucks on my clit. "Relax for me baby," Mason instructs as he adds a third finger. The fullness is inde-scribable.

His fingers start pumping in and out of me. Stroking me as if it were his dick instead of his fingers. The obscene sounds my pussy makes as he pumps his fingers in me, has a rush of wetness coming. He holds eye contact as he curls his fingers inside me all while sucking on my clit. The moment has me coming against his face.

Mason extends my orgasm as he continues pumping his fingers and sucking on my clit. "Yes baby. Make a mess all over my face." His mouth and tongue make my orgasm last longer than ever. The sensation is never ending as Mason continues to draw my orgasm out before he slows down his movements and places kisses on my inner thighs. Trailing them up my body. He rests his forehead on my stomach before pulling away from my body. Confidence oozes from him as he opens his nightstand drawer to grab a condom.

When we had the talk all those months ago, we still decided that condoms were staying in our relationship. Neither of us are ready for the step that's bigger than either of us. Do I see that in our future? Yes. My heart feels as if it's about to burst out of my chest. We've played with and teased each other. Learned each other's bodies. Learned what's made us lose control. When he turns around, he holds eye contact as he rolls the condom on. The intimacy with that look speaks volumes. It's no wonder Mason prepped me. He's massive.

Mason climbs back on the bed and kisses me while settling between my thighs. My body tenses at the brush of his cock against my sensitive clit and he breaks the kiss, looking to me for one last confirmation. I tilt my hips up to meet him and that's all the answer he needs. He lines himself up at my entrance and slowly pushes in, inch by inch.

"Oh god," I moan.

"It's just Mason," he says as he gives me time to adjust to his size. Mason's hips flex as he continues to enter me. "You're so tight, baby."

"And you're so big." His responding smirk has me chuckling. The small movement is intense so I stop instantly.

"Can I move?" He asks once he's filled me completely. His breaths are coming in quick spurts.

"Yes. Please."

Mason pulls out slowly and pushes back in. My arousal coating him as he sets a rhythm and after a while I feel it building. Lifting my hips to meet his thrusts makes him feel deeper.

"Harder, Mason."

And he does, because I know he needs to. He hooks my leg over his shoulder causing him to slide deeper as his thrusts continue their punishing rhythm. My breathing has sped up and a light sheen of sweat has formed on both of us. I drag my nails down his back urging him on. I'm so wound up and I know Mason can tell.

Letting my leg go, he pulls himself up to his knees, lifts my hips off the bed and pounds into me. My body feels weightless in his hands as I feel another orgasm on the horizon.

"Your pussy hugs my cock so well," Mason grinds out.

I clench around him. The angle hitting the right spot that takes my breath away.

He brings his hand between us and rubs my clit. And that's all it takes for me to scream out his name.

"That's it, love. Come for me," he encourages.

My orgasm takes my breath away. Mason comes as I pulse around him and then I feel him widening inside of me. His thrusts become erratic and more punishing. Drawing our climaxes out for as long as possible. When he's spent, he collapses on top of me. I rake my nails up and down his back to slow his breathing down.

"I love you." He says when he pops his head out of the crook of my neck.

"I love you too." I say and smack a kiss on his lips.

He starts to get off me but I don't want him to, so I try to lock my arms tighter.

"Sweetheart, I have to throw the condom away."

I groan but let him get up anyway.

Before Mason gets back in bed, he walks over to the sink in the corner of the room and wets a washcloth. Walking back over to the bed in all his naked glory, he swipes the washcloth between my legs and wipes himself off as well. Tossing the washcloth in the hamper, he pulls his boxers back on and hands me his shirt to wear.

And for the rest of the night we lay in his bed. With the TV on for background noise and talking about anything and everything. Making love more times than I can count. And no sooner than not, I finally drift off to sleep.

May 2011

Summer break is officially here. My last final was the hardest out of all my classes and my brain is officially fried.

"Hey, baby. How was your last final?" Mason asks when I plop down in a chair next to him in the cafeteria. My head lands on his shoulder and I finally feel myself relax. "That bad huh?" Mason says with a chuckle and kisses me on the top of my head.

"Why was it a requirement for me to take physics again? That's not the path I'm headed."

Mason places another kiss on my temple. The gesture is so him, that my heart weeps. "The only thing you should be dreaming about is the white sandy beaches that we'll be surrounded by for the next month."

It takes a minute for my brain to register what he just announced. My head pops up. "We got the beach house?!"

"We sure did. We leave next week. That should give us both time to go home and grab beachy clothes and not school-y clothes."

I give him a loud kiss on the lips. "I love you. I love you. I love you."

"I love you, too."

"I need to go pack up my stuff. Bye!" With one last kiss I sprint to my dorm room.

12

KAMRYN

A week later, Mason and I are driving down the final stretch of road to the beach house. A whole month alone with absolutely no interruptions is my favorite kind of summer. Mason slows down the car as he turns his signal light on. When he turns and the trees give way to a beautiful bungalow, my jaw goes completely slack.

"I take it you like it?"

I'm still speechless. "Like it? I love it. You did good babe."

I lean over the center console and kiss him on the cheek. When Mason said he was going to pick out a beach house for us for a month in the summer, I didn't believe him. I jokingly told him to pick something cute with a few bedrooms. And I gotta say that he exceeded my expectations.

"Thanks. Let's go take our stuff inside and explore." He says after we've parked.

We get out of the car and take our stuff into the foyer. It's a beautiful one-story house. The foyer opens right up to the living room, where we can see the white sandy beach just beyond that. To the left of the living room is a full chef's kitchen with light gray granite countertops, white cabinets, stainless steel stove, and light brown/ taupe wood flooring flowing throughout the house.

The rest of the house is spectacular with a movie room and a home gym with a steam room. The primary bedroom has a California King Bed that has French doors leading out to the porch and down to the beach. The other bedroom is simple with a queen size bed and a small dresser. The furniture contrasts perfectly with the cabinets in the kitchen. The white contrasting with the light brown/ taupe flooring looks simple, but timeless.

"What do you think?" Mason asks when he comes up behind me. He wraps his arms around my waist and leans his head on top of mine.

"It's beautiful. You chose what I would have picked."

"What would you like to do first?"

I turn around and pull him with me towards the bedroom. "Christen the bed of course."

Mason chuckles as he follows me. "Kamryn Rawlins. What am I going to do with you?"

"I can think of a few things." I say and start by taking off my shirt. I don't think he noticed I wasn't wearing a bra. I start next on the button of my shorts and then my zipper; and then I slowly shimmy out of them until I'm only in my lace thong.

I can see Mason's Adam's apple bobbing up and down as he swallows and his chest is heaving.

"You have way too many clothes on. Don't you think so?" I ask when I walk towards him. I grasp the bottom of his shirt and he helps me pull it off the rest of the way. My fingers trail down the middle of his torso and enjoy the way he shivers at my touch.

It gives me a thrill that Mason doesn't mind my being

forward sexually around him. I think it makes him a little shy that I'm more blunt with what I want. I've always been that way. But with him it's on a whole other level.

I unsnap the button on his shorts and run my knuckles down the front of his pants while unzipping them. I slide my hands into the back of his shorts and pull them down as best as I can before he takes over that part. *Hey, I may have no problem getting him undressed, but with all this muscle it's hard to finish the job!* Once his shorts are off I pull him closer to me. His erection is starting to peek through his boxer briefs and I can't wait anymore. And apparently neither can he.

Mason brings his mouth to mine and we walk back to the bedroom. Once in the room, he picks me up by the thighs and slowly lowers us to the bed. My panties come off when he lowers himself down my body. I'm so wet for him that any foreplay will just set me off. But Mason tests me out anyway by pushing one finger in and working me up. Then adds a second finger to bring me even closer to the edge. When I'm about to come, he pulls out his fingers but quickly replaces those by pushing himself inside me. Instead of the fast pace that we're used to, Mason takes charge by setting a slower pace. My orgasm comes out of nowhere. I feel it in my toes and then see actual fireworks. Mason comes not too long after me and slows down to ride it out.

"Do you think it's weird we hardly ever fight?" I ask Mason after I finished cooking dinner for the two of us.

We've been here for almost two weeks and it's been so relaxing. The beach has been a regular occurrence. But we've also gone into town and went to an older movie theater that plays black and white movies, zip lining, paragliding, paddle boarding, and we even rode horses on the beach last night.

"Eh...I don't think it's weird. But it's definitely unusual. Why? Do you want to fight with me?"

I narrow my eyes. "No. I was just asking if it was weird. So what are we doing tonight?" I ask to change the subject. I don't like fighting with people. It makes me too sad to even think about it.

I look over at Mason and he's wearing a smile that could rival the Cheshire Cat.

"What's that smile for? You're making me nervous."

"You have two options. And yes, I'm making you choose because this particular thing is for you."

"Okay," I reply nervously.

"Karaoke or a live band?"

"Those are my two options?"

"Mm hmm," he responds without giving anything away.

"I guess I'll go with a live band."

"Perfect! Cause you're their lead singer tonight."

Did I hear what I thought I heard? "Wait...what?"

"You heard me. Go get ready. We're leaving very soon."

"Mason..."

"What? This is supposed to be fun." He says and pulls me into his lap.

"I know. But I've never sung in front of people. Only you and my family. This is big."

He places a kiss on my temple. "You'll be great. I know you will. If you get nervous, just look at me...or close your eyes until you get comfortable."

"Fine." I groan into his neck.

WHEN MASON and I walk into the bar & grille that I'm supposed to be singing at, I see that it's pretty crowded and that takes my nerves to a new height. I do see that band that I'm singing with and they look to be about mine and Mason's age.

"Okay everyone. We have someone new that's going to be singing with us tonight. Her boyfriend actually reached out to us on social media and he sent us some of her work, and I think y'all are gonna like her. Come on up here, sweetheart." The guitarist says pointing at me.

But my feet are planted to the floor. I'm so nervous my knee creases are sweating and I'm standing up. Mason gives a slight nudge in the direction of the stage. The crowd starts with a slow clap when I finally make my way to the makeshift stage. I introduce myself to the band and ask them if they know *A Natural Woman* by Aretha Franklin. They nod their heads and smile.

"Hi everyone. I'm Kamryn. And I guess I'm gonna be singing tonight. This first one is a classic by Aretha Franklin." I turn and nod to the band.

The music starts and I wait for my cue. Before I know it, I look out to the crowd that's still growing to see them singing along and dancing in their seats. I lose myself in the song, swaying to the music, as this song conveys what I feel when I'm with Mason.

When the song ends, I take my bow. Still in disbelief that I finished that song without my voice cracking. I can't believe I sang that song to begin with. Go big or go home, right? I sing about six more songs until we take a little break. Surprisingly I'm not nervous anymore. I walk toward Mason who's got a huge smile on his face.

I wrap my arms around his waist and kiss him. "Thank you."

"You're welcome. I just pushed you in the right direction. That was all you babe." Mason says and moves my hair out of my eyes.

For the next twenty minutes I ask Mason what he thought of the songs I chose and what songs I should sing next. I love that he pushes me to go after what I want even though I don't know if I want it.

The guitarist taps me on the shoulder and nods to the stage. "That's my cue. Don't drink too much." Then I kiss his cheek and I'm off to the stage.

"Well I see we have some new faces in the crowd. If you're just joining us, I'm Kamryn, this is Cody on the guitar, Mitch on the keyboard, and Tony on the drums. For this next song, I may just need Mitch. If any of you are Adele fans, then on her first album she did a cover of *Make You Feel My Love* by Bob Dylan and I had literal goosebumps. So if you don't mind, then that's what I'm gonna start back up with." I nod to Mitch and he starts the piano intro. I feel the thud of the keys in my chest and let the lyrics flow through me and out into the crowd.

Any Adele song can make anyone feel something. Yeah, I may not relate to a ton of her songs now that I'm happy with Mason. But that doesn't mean I can't act.

We decided the second half of this should be ten songs. The songs that we've done have ranged from old to new, country to pop to hip hop to singer-songwriter.

"This last song is by Lady Antebellum. I was hooked when I heard a cover of this song on YouTube. Since I go to school in South Carolina I've gotten back in touch with my love for country music. Nothing says country music like listening to Darius Rucker at a football game. But anyways, the last song of the night is called *American Honey*."

This song is summer in a bottle. I would be crazy not to

sing while here. So that's what I do. It's something about this song that takes me home. Summers in Philly while doing nothing and everything. Yeah, Philadelphia is far from the south but that's what this song reminds me of. It reminds me of home.

The crowd cheers for us when we're done. But I step aside and make sure all the love is showered on the band.

"Thank you guys for letting me sing tonight. I had a lot of fun." I tell them while they start to pack up their equipment. "Well, if you guys are ever in Columbia let me know. I'll come out and watch."

Cody is the first to speak up. "Of course. I think you may have gotten us more exposure, so thanks for that. Take care Kamryn."

"Yeah. You too. Bye guys."

AFTER THE INTENSITY OF PERFORMING, Mason and I decided to keep the rest of the summer in the beach house simple. We only had a week left and relaxing was the main priority for us. Morning walks on the beach, laying out, movie marathons, waking up making love and going to sleep making love, and so much food. I got to know more about Mason on a deeper level in that month than I have in the last 9 months we've been together. After sleeping in the same bed, I'm not sure how I'll be able to sleep alone once we get back to school.

And before we know it, our time in the beach house has come to an end and we're driving back to Mason's parents' house. I will time to slow down or come to a halt. But that's not the way time works. Time is inevitable. Time is constant. Time is always moving.

After spending the weekend with Mason and his family, I make the drive back up to Pennsylvania where I'll be until it's time to head back to school. Mason heads back a little earlier than me for camp and then we're off to the races for another year of school. My second year and his final year.

I didn't think I'd be the girl that found the one to spend her days with so soon. But every relationship that I've admired has been one that started this early. Look at my parents. They found each other at eighteen and have been married almost twenty years. I want that.

But can I have it?

~

TEN HOURS LATER, I'm pulling down my parents' street and blasting out the last of a Lady Gaga song when I pull into the driveway. I see their cars in the carport and my sister's car on the street.

Me: I'm home.

Mason: Okay, great. Come back now.

Me: Don't tempt me. I'll see you in a few weeks.

Mason: Counting down the days. I love you.

Me: I love you too.

Saying those words, whether in person or over text, never gets old. I put my phone in my purse, turn off my car, and open the trunk to get my suitcase out. Getting out I stretch my body before walking to the back and hefting out my bag. I risk a glance across the street at Liam's house, but see no movement.

I haven't talked to him since the baseball home-opener. As much as it hurts that he and I have drifted apart, I have to learn to accept that.

"Mom? Dad? Jax?" I call out when I push through the front door.

Our dog Jersey trots over to me with his tongue flopping out.

"Hello handsome, boy." I greet him as I give his body a rub and kiss the top of his head. When he feels I've greeted him enough, he leads me to the backdoor that leads to the patio and pool. Showing me that's where my family is congregated.

I wander back to the fridge and grab a beer before wandering outside.

"Kamryn!" My mom announces as she rushes at me. My mom is my best friend, but she's still stern when she needs to be.

"Hi, Mommy." I greet when she wraps me in a hug.

"How was your trip?" She asks as she releases me.

I walk over to kiss my dad on the cheek and sit on the lounge chair next to my sister. "It was good. We spent most of our days at the beach, playing tourist, and Mason got me to sing in front of a massive crowd."

My Mom and Dad look at me in shock.

"I know. I wanted to wring his neck when he told me that. But I ended up loving it." I can't stop the smile when I remember how it felt to be up on that stage.

"That's really great, Kammy," my sister says next to me.

My family knows I don't sing in public. They've always encouraged me to just give it a try. But anytime I would even attempt to look at a stage I would lose all ability to form words. So they stopped pushing me.

. . .

LATER THAT NIGHT, I'm sitting in the sunroom reading a book when my mom comes and sits next to me.

"So how are you really?"

My mom is the one I spill a lot of my guts too. Some may think we're too close. But having a parent that will not only be your parent, but your sounding board means everything.

I set my book to the side. "I'm tired. But my body is also wired with happiness. I feel like a firework ready to take off into the night sky."

"How are things with Mason? We'll have to make it down there for a game to finally meet him in person."

The problem with living out of state is that it's not easy to take your friends or your significant other home to meet the parents. They've met over the phone and it's only upped the nerve-factor for when they do finally meet.

"I am so hopelessly in love with him, Mom. I know you always told me not to tie my happiness into another person, but with him I couldn't help it. He's pushed me to be a better person. He's helped me realize the things that I always worried about, weren't such big things to worry about in the end."

She gazes at me with her mother's smile. "Just remember to have your own happiness. I don't want you to lose that glow I've seen in you since you were born."

"I won't, Mom. I promise."

My mom kisses my cheek before heading upstairs to bed and I think back on our talk.

I've always felt I was the bright light in my family. Not that they're Eeyore's or anything. But there was never a day that went by when laughter didn't infect my family and I was the root of that laughter.

Promises are never meant to be broken, and in this instance I hope to finally keep this one.

13

MASON

August 2011

This summer flew by way too fast. As someone whose summers have always been about practicing with minimal days off, this year was a welcome change. I feel more well rested than I ever have before. I owe it all to the girl who completely has my heart.

The month with K solidified my thought that I could seriously see myself marrying her. I know the revelation is fast, but she brings out a side of me I never knew existed.

When our beach house bubble burst, we spent the next few weeks with my parents. Celebrating the fourth of July and taking Kamryn to my old high school, before she went back home for the last couple weeks of summer. My summer isn't as long as hers and I had to get back early for practice and training. It's my senior year and a lot is riding on me now.

Going pro was never the goal. But somehow, someway this game became something more than a game. And as cheesy as it sounds, playing on a bigger stage sounds more intriguing every day.

While on break, I received an email from my coach. Him emailing me is nothing new. It's how he prefers to communicate. As soon as I finish unpacking what I can I head to his office. So that's where I am now.

I knock three times on my coach's office door.

He looked up at the knock. "Ah. Come in Mason. Close the door please."

I do as he says and make my way to a chair in front of his desk.

You know those moments when everything is smooth sailing in your life? You have everything. But you also have this sense of foreboding that you can't shake no matter what. For some reason I feel that now. And it's not a good feeling to have.

"How was your summer?" He asks by way of casual small talk.

Coach and I have always had an easy relationship. When I got scouted to play here, I did all of my research and discovered he won two national championships with his alma mater. So I knew I was in good hands when I came to this school. This football program specifically. When I managed to join a fraternity, he pulled me aside and said it was good having a brother on the team. His statement stopped me, until he showed me his ring with the same crest as the one I now bore.

"It was good. I did a lot of relaxing."

"That's good. I wanted to talk to you about this season. I know that when you were in talks about getting drafted, you wanted to graduate first. And I 100% backed you up on that. But now that it's your senior year, I need your focus 100% on football. No distractions."

Do you remember that sense of foreshadowing? My skin prickles with goosebumps.

"Distractions? What do you mean by distractions? Don't beat around the bush. What are you getting at coach?"

"Your girlfriend." He says with no hesitation.

"What about her? She's been good for me. I haven't gone out like I used to, I've been to all the conditionings that were optional. Again, what about her?"

"I need you to be completely dedicated to the game. And I can't have my number one prospect for the draft distracted because of some girl that he's dating."

"I am 100% dedicated to this game. You know that. When have I been distracted? She's not just some girl." Now he's really pissing me off.

"End it. Or else your dreams of playing in the NFL can disappear."

I look over his shoulder at the practice field. Anger running through my veins. "Coach, for the longest time I used to look up to you. Idolize you as a brother if that's what you want to hear. Not anymore. If you want to start working on a new QB for this season go ahead. I'll walk out on this team right now if that's what you're getting at. But I'd take back everything you just said because I refuse to put a game that's only temporary ahead of something that has a chance to be permanent. If you want me as your QB you will not threaten my future, whether it be my professional or personal future." I don't wait for him to respond. Instead I jump out of the chair I was in and yank open his office door. Slamming it closed in my exit.

Is he serious? When has an NFL draft prospect ever broken things off with their girlfriend because their coach wanted them to?

Dump Kamryn? She's the best thing that's ever

happened to me. Statistically, my game has gotten better since we've been together. Yeah I slacked off and performed like a middle schooler when we first started dating. But I worked through it. The team still won games. I led them to the National Championship for crying out loud. She pushes me to do the optional workouts, she encourages me to hang out with the team when I'd rather spend time with her. Neither of us would survive a break up.

I'm walking around campus and looking at places that have meaning to me like I'm already leaving. Do I want to play in the NFL? What college football player doesn't dream of it? But it was never my plan though. Football was never part of that plan. Coach knew that when he was scouting me back in high school. But do I have to give up the one girl who finally reminded me how to breathe to have that?

I pull out my phone to call my mom. And she answers on the first ring.

"Hey, baby boy."

"Hey, mama."

"How are you? And how's Kamryn? Do you know when she'll be back to school?"

My parents and siblings love Kamryn. Honestly, what's not to love?

"She's good. She's driving down tomorrow. And going to use the few days before school starts to get back in the swing of things."

"That's good. Now you know I love you. But I also know you didn't call me just as a courtesy. Tell me what's up." She's never one to beat around the bush.

Taking a cleansing breath before I explode, I recap the conversation with her. "Coach asked me to his office to talk about the draft. He also said that this season he needs me 100% dedicated, which I already am. Football is everything to me. But he also said for me to do that, I have to end things with Kamryn or he'll make sure I don't get drafted." I leave out the part of me threatening to quit because she doesn't need to know that.

My mom gasps at that last part. "Well I know none of that was ethical. And threatening you in no way is acceptable. He could lose his job for that if it ever gets out. But I have no doubt that the man is completely serious. You and Kamryn love each other. Maybe when the dust settles and you get a few years under your belt you two can find each other again."

"Are you really suggesting that I break up with her? I'll be so distracted that scouts won't even consider me. Has anyone thought about what I want? Y'all are always trying to lead me in the right direction. But when I finally have something that I want forever, I can't have it." I'm having a tough time controlling my emotions. Give up the woman I love for a game that I'll maybe get ten years out of if I'm lucky. And that doesn't even include injuries. What's ten years playing a game versus a lifetime with the one I love?

"I'm not saying do that before or during the season. I love Kamryn like another daughter and so does your dad, brothers, and your sister. She challenges you and pushes you to be a better man. And I have seen that change in you. But if the love that you two have is real, then I have no doubt that Kamryn will be more than understanding."

I choke down my emotions. "But what if she doesn't? What if this breaks her and I so badly that neither of us can recover? What then?"

"Oh, honey. I can't answer that for you. Only you can. Focus on the two of you for now. Love her. Cherish her. And when the time comes, look her in the eye and tell her that it's for your future and possibly both of y'all's future. I wish I could be there with you. Just know that I love you and your father and I aren't going anywhere."

"I know. I love you too. Bye, Mom."

"Bye, sweetheart."

If this isn't a fantastic end to the summer. I can't do it. If I have to make good on my threat to quit the team now, then I will. Football is temporary, I know that. But a love like what Kamryn and I have could be forever. I feel it in my bones.

"Hey baby! I'm about ten minutes out." Her voice sounds far away, but I know it's because she's talking through Bluetooth.

"Want me to help you move your stuff in?"

"Pretty please with me on top?" She begs.

She gets a chuckle out of me. "Of course. I'll see you in a bit. I love you."

"I love you, too."

I told my coach this morning that if he wanted me to break up with Kamryn, then it would have to be after the season ended or I quit. He wasn't pleased at what I said, but when I told him that if I broke up with her before the season started then I'd be uncommitted to the game and unfocused. And that his chance of winning the National Championship would be shot. That sobered him up and he agreed. His reputation also wouldn't survive if word got out that I quit and why.

I still haven't had time to process everything that he wants from me. Break up with my girlfriend to focus on getting drafted. What draftee has ever made it through this process without a significant other by their side? The only other option would be marriage, but neither of us is ready for that. I'll already barely see her once the season starts and her sorority starts with rush week and bids. I can't add that to her already full plate.

The Kappa Beta house isn't too far from campus so that's where I am now waiting for her to pull up. Kamryn was lucky to get a room to herself her first year in the house. I think it also had something to do with her being a Rawlins. Her car honking pulls me out of my own head.

The feeling that I get when I see her is indescribable. It's like I can breathe again. I jog over to her car and she barely puts it in park before jumping out to hug me. I call her my little koala because of how she wraps her arms and legs around me. She pulls her head back to kiss me hard and passionately. How did I ever live without her? We slow down the kiss when we hear the cheering and whooping of other students. Kamryn reluctantly releases her grip on my body and slowly slides down the front of my body. She looks up at me with a devilish grin before placing a kiss in the middle of my chest.

I'M WALKING out of class when I see Kamryn talking to Liam some little ways down. Her back is to me so it's the perfect time to scare her. Liam sees me walking up and I put my finger to my lip to keep him quiet. He continues his conversation with her as if nothing is happening. Liam slightly raises his eyebrows to give me a sign of when to scare her and that's what I do.

"Ohmygod!!" Kamryn shrieks as she jumps out of her skin and then turns around and smacks me in the chest.

Liam and I are both bent over with laughter trying to catch our breaths.

"This isn't funny! I could've hurt myself...or peed my pants."

I sober up some to hug her close to me. "I'm sorry babe. I just couldn't pass up the opportunity. Thanks man." I say and dap Liam up.

"Yeah. No problem. Any chance to scare Rynny. Anyways, I've got to get running or I'm gonna be late for practice." Liam says with a chuckle still lingering.

"I hate you both." Kamryn says with a cute little scowl on her face.

Liam wraps his arm around her shoulder. "You never could. Later peeps."

"Later Liam." I call out as he waves. Kamryn is still pouting when I take her into my arms. "Come on babe. You can't be that upset with us."

She arches an eyebrow at me. "Payback is a dish best served cold."

"Is that what you're planning in that mischievous mind of yours?"

"I guess you'll just have to follow me to find out." Kamryn says and slips out of my embrace.

I'm too shocked to even process what she's staying and also a little turned on that she's planning something to get back at me. My mom's words ring in my head *"Just enjoy your time with her while you can"*. God I love this girl so much. Damn what I said earlier. I'd marry her right now if I could. Kamryn turns around when she notices I'm still firmly planted on the spot.

"You coming superstar?"

I smile at the name she's given me and jog over to where she's waiting for me. "I love you so much."

"I love you too, baby." She says as she wraps both arms around my waist.

November 2011

"This food looks amazing, Mrs. Brooks," Kamryn says with wide eyes.

It's Thanksgiving break. But not quite Thanksgiving. Every year, we play our rival Clifton on Thanksgiving Day. And since my whole family and Kamryn are coming to the game we're celebrating on Tuesday instead.

"Thank you sweetheart." My mom tells her with a smile.

What I love about my relationship with Kamryn is that she's gotten along so well with my family. My brothers and little sister love her, my dad appreciates that she can hold her own when it comes to talking about sports, and my mom loves how she's dealt with everything else that comes with dating the star QB of a Division I college. My extended family even loves how she puts up with me and I've officially gotten the seal of approval. Which is why it makes this Thanksgiving so bittersweet for me. I know it'll be our first and last. And having to put a time stamp on a relationship that's changed you immensely breaks a little piece of my heart each day.

"Baby, are you coming outside?"

I look at her a little clueless.

"Football. Don't worry, I'll be the quarterback. I'd probably out-throw you anyways."

My family tries to hide their laughter by covering it up with coughs. I look around at all of them with narrowed eyes. Kamryn looks up at me with such amusement as she cracks through my tough guy façade.

"Fine. Loser has to clean up with all the dishes."

She holds her hand out to shake. "Deal."

One Hour Later

"Make sure you use soap and extra elbow grease on that pan." Kamryn says from the living room.

Yeah my team lost. And it wasn't on purpose I guarantee you that.

My dad, brothers, and I have set up an assembly line of sorts.

"That one's a keeper." My dad says to me but only loud enough for me to hear.

My chest aches a bit at the reminder that I have to let her go soon. "Yeah. I know she is." I say with a thick throat.

~

January 2012

Well, we made it to the National Championship. But we lost by a field goal. It wasn't that we played terribly or that I was off my game. The other team just played better. This loss puts a nail in the coffin on my collegiate career and also my relationship with Kamryn. With the season over I have my coach and mom in my ear, telling me that it's time. I've been pulling away and dodging Kamryn for the past two weeks. Making up excuses as to why we can't hang out. It's breaking my heart more than she knows. She knows when something is wrong. Kamryn is intuitive like that. But she's also her own worst enemy. I couldn't tell her what was going on. So I know that she has been beating herself over what she did to make me pull away.

The clock is ticking, so I have to do it now. If I want the dream of playing in the NFL and my coach and my mom think the only way I can get there is with no distractions, then I have to. And there's no better time than now.

So I'm waiting outside of Kamryn's last class, and then I see her. Bundled up in a jacket and beanie. The wind blows her hair in front of her face before she pulls it behind her. I quickly whip out my phone and take a picture of her. Knowing that this will be the last time I see her beautiful face unbroken.

My heart is in my throat. My head and heart are warring with the outside world, demanding that I not do this. When she spots me, I see her falter. I see the trepidation, nervousness, and sadness in her beautiful brown eyes as she walks towards me. The glow that she so effortlessly radiates has dimmed because of me. And I hate that I've put that look of doubt in her eyes. I dimmed this vibrant girl and I hate myself for that.

"Hi." She says nervously when she stops in front of me. Almost so quiet that it comes out more as a whisper.

The only time I've heard the nervousness in her voice was when we ran into each other after our first meeting. How I wish I could go back in time to that moment. Where everything was new. Without the voices of my coach and mom telling me I need to end this.

"Hi." I hold my hand out to her and give her a tentative smile. "Come take a walk with me?"

Chewing on her lip, she reluctantly takes my hand and we walk towards a bridge not too far from campus. Kamryn told me that hand-holding was an underrated form of physical connection. And I have to agree. Every time I got to hold her I locked all of those moments away. When we find a spot to stop on the bridge, she lets her hand fall from mine and turns to face me.

"Did I do something?" Her question comes out as a

broken whisper and barely audible over the sound of the river flowing below us. It's right here that I know that I've broken her.

This is going to be harder than I thought. "No, baby. It was nothing you did wrong. But there is something. And it has been tearing me up."

Her eyes are glassy with unshed tears. "What is it?"

Hell, even I'm having trouble keeping my emotions in check. Or even looking her in the eyes. But she deserves my honesty. Honesty and trust is what our relationship was built off of. And I'm throwing it all away because I've been dishonest and less than truthful for the last few months.

"Before we started dating, I had a lot of NFL scouts looking at me. I was one of the top draft prospects. But I made a promise to myself and my parents that I would graduate college with a degree that would support me long after football ended. So I passed on entering the draft last year. Then when training and practice started back up in August, Coach said that the NFL was looking at me again. That I had always been on their radar." I take a deep breath before continuing. This is where I break both of our hearts. But in all honesty, I know they're already beyond broken with no hope of repair. I blow out a deep breath and hold her eye contact.

"Coach said that in order for me to get drafted, I needed to be 100% focused on the game. No distractions. All of my commitment needed to be on football. He said he had the power to make it that I wouldn't even be considered for the draft and that the only way to do that would be if I had no ties left here."

I steel myself as I look at her and witness the moment my words click. Her spine straightens even more and her face drops. "No ties here, meaning me?"

I nod my head because my emotions are way out of whack.

"You've known since August? When in August?" She asks right before the dam of emotions breaks.

"The day before you came back to school."

"Oh my god!" Kamryn exclaims. Her hands covering her mouth as she backs away from me and then paces down the bridge a little then back. "Five months! You've known for five months that you had to end it with me. Why? Why did you string me along when you knew...knew that we had an expiration date?!"

When I get the courage to look back into her eyes, I see the tears forming. Knowing that I put those tears in her eyes is like a dagger to the heart.

"Because I love you and you make me a better man."

"That's bullshit and you know it! A better man would have fought for us." Her voice cracks at the word *us*. "A better man would not have strung me along and then avoided me for weeks! You're a coward."

Those three words hurt harder than any hit a defenseman could make. "I did try Kamryn! You don't think I've dreaded this? You don't think I bartered with everything I have to not do this? Do you think I want to walk away from you? I don't! You are the *best* thing that has ever happened to me. You are the absolute love of my life. It has been killing me knowing that we were on a timeline. And it tears me up because I know that breaking your heart is the worst and last thing I ever thought I would do. But I knew I wanted us for as long as possible. And I didn't want to push you away, baby. But I had to prepare myself somehow by not being around you." I tell her as I desperately plead my case.

When I look at her, tears are streaming down her face

and her hand is over her mouth again, trying to keep her sobs from echoing in the space around us.

They say a picture is worth a thousand words. Only it's not a picture. Because pictures tend to fade over time. Pictures can get ripped, or lost, or water damaged, or even stolen. When they were talking about pictures being worth a thousand words, they meant this moment. Where you can remember every detail: the weather, the time, the day, and the aching scene in front of you right down to the tears trailing a path down her face. It's a picture that wins awards when the emotions of the subject have the ability to smack you in the face.

That's what I did to Kamryn. I broke not only me, but I actually broke her when I promised to myself I never would.

I have no right, but I pull her sob-wracked body to me despite her resistance.

Kamryn's body stays stiff in my arms, but speaks what I've been thinking about since August. "I don't know how I'm supposed to do this Mason. You're my best friend. I don't know how I'm just supposed to walk away from you. I can't just walk away from you." Her body shakes with the silent sobs that are wracking her body.

I run my hands up and down her shaking back trying to soothe her as best as I can, knowing that these words I say will and can never be enough. At least not anymore. A few tears escape from me as I kiss the top of her head. "I don't know either. But I do know that one day, you'll thank me for letting you go." She's shaking her head no, knowing that I'm wrong. Even I know that I'm wrong. Because despite both of our breaking hearts, I continue telling her what she needs to hear in an attempt to move on. "You'll thank me when some guy sweeps you off your feet. I'll still be happy for you even though that guy isn't me. Your happiness is the most important thing in the world to me." The words taste bitter as I confess to her one of my biggest lies to date. I pull away from her to look her in the eyes. "You are one in a million Kamryn Rawlins. And I am so glad that I got to be a part of your life. To be loved by you. To know you. I will love you forever."

"I will love you for always." I know she means that, because one thing Kamryn is, is honest and loyal to a fault.

I know I shouldn't, but I lean down for one last kiss. One last kiss to hopefully tie her to me. But all too quickly Kamryn pulls away, and walks away from me. Her sobs follow her as she walks away from me. It kills me that I just destroyed the one person who didn't deserve it. It kills me to know that I can't be the one to follow her anymore to make sure she's okay.

I HAVEN'T SEEN Kamryn around campus in about a week. My first instinct when I woke up was to text her. It had been my routine since last year. But I lost the right to know what she's up to the night I broke up with her.

As soon as I went to my coach's office and told him what I did, he made a call. The next thing I knew I was scheduled to go to my first combine in February. But at what cost? I had to muster all of the excitement when he told me when I was set to go. Could he tell? That my excitement for this game isn't as strong as it was five months ago? When he told me I was scheduled for February, I slammed the door as I left his office. Still nothing could prepare me for the aftermath.

I heard the whispers all over the campus. The looks of shock from the students in my classes and the look of disdain from my fellow athletes. I called my mom after it happened and she said that it would get better and I *will* heal.

The only problem is that with each passing moment and each passing day, it doesn't feel like it will get better and I don't feel like I'll ever heal.

"You saw her around campus right?" I hear one of my teammates say when I walk over to them at a table in the cafeteria. It's been a few days, and the whispers have barely died down. I don't think they've noticed me yet, but one of them finally does.

"Hey, Mason."

"Hey guys. What are y'all talking about?" I say absent-mindedly as I take a seat.

"Nothing in particular."

They all look at each other conspicuously, thinking that I'm not paying attention. The only problem is that I know who they're talking about.

"How did she look?" I finally ask, already regretting the question.

They all look at each other like this is a trick question. Mike is the first one to speak up.

"Honestly, she looked wrecked. It was as if her light completely went out. I've never seen her like that. It was heartbreaking to see."

I look away and choke down the emotions that are threatening to overspill.

"If it makes you feel any better, you both look the same." He says as an afterthought.

I snap my gaze back to my teammates. "Feel any better? Tell me something. Have you ever had to do something so big that had the potential to ruin everything? I had to break up with the love of my life when I didn't want to. I have had my mom and coach breathing down my neck since August to break up with her." My teammates' eyebrows shoot up to their hairline with that confession. "You didn't see how she reacted that night. The light you talked about being out, you weren't there seeing it dim right in front of your eyes. So no. It doesn't make me feel any better."

I stand up quickly and look around to see that the whole cafeteria has fallen silent and is looking at me. Without making any more of a scene I quickly head towards the exit of the cafeteria, my steps faltering when I see Liam standing just inside the threshold. A thousand words pass between us before he can manage to stop me. In that brief moment, my memory takes me back to when he and I had our first and very brief talk about Kamryn.

"Brooks!" I hear my name yelled out in the athletic building and turn around to face a guy I've seen but haven't been introduced to.

"Yeah?" I respond to him as he's in front of me.

He holds his hand out. "Liam Taylor. I'm Kamryn's best friend."

It all clicks. For some reason, I never would've put it together that he was the arrangement she was talking about. I'm not a jealous guy, but seeing him makes me want to punch him in the face. He had years to tell her how he felt.

"Nice to meet you." My hand meets his and he tries to intimidate me with the strength of his hold. I pull my hand from his. "Did you need something?"

He shakes his head in a nonchalant way. "Just wanted to say thanks for making my best friend happy. She deserves it. As long as you don't hurt her we won't have any problems."

"I have no intention of hurting her. I promise you that."

Not wanting to talk to him because I ended up breaking my promise, I rush out of the cafeteria and back to my dorm continuing to choke down my emotions while fighting tears the whole way there.

I know they say men aren't supposed to cry. That it strips our man card and it makes us more feminine. *Blah, blah, blah.* But what is so bad about men being in touch with their feelings? If anything it helps us be more attune to what is happening around us.

For the rest of my time as a "normal" college student, I put my head down and got to work. I focused on my classes and the one-on-one training sessions with my conditioning coach. I avoided my former teammates as the looks they gave me burned.

I did my best not to seek out Kamryn on campus and beg for her to take me back. That we can keep our relationship a secret. But by the time I got back from the combine and sat through the draft, it turned out the next seven years would be a test of my willpower.

14

KAMRYN

May 2012

Have you ever had a dream where you're the butt of a joke but you have no idea why. Every person you pass stares at you. Silently and not so silently laughing at your utter humiliation. Picture that. But it's not a dream. It's real life. It's my life. And walking through campus those next days after word got around was hard. Trying to ignore the whispers that the star quarterback broke up with the sorority legend was hard to deal with. Because I was the butt of every joke. I was the one they were laughing at.

Mason was my once-in-a-lifetime love. Not a lot of people get that in their adolescent years. And I know I'm young. I know adults believe that when you're young you don't know what love truly is. But in the year that we were truly together, I felt invincible. I felt like with any obstacle that came my way, with him by my side I could conquer anything.

It's been four months since he broke up with me.

Sarah held me the night I came back to our room. I was

inconsolable the rest of the week. She let me wallow without judgment when I needed to. She held my hand when the pain of my heartbreak tore down every last one of my defenses. She made sure I went to class when I was supposed to, I even took different routes to my classes to avoid seeing spots that Mason and I frequented, I did the bare minimum in my sorority (I think they all understood), I avoided the cafeteria at all costs, and I avoided going to any baseball games for fear of him being there.

I avoided life.

It was hard making that life adjustment. I went from being so blissfully happy. I was on cloud nine happy. My life was great.

Until suddenly life wasn't so great. I was no longer on cloud nine. I was no longer in my happy bubble. I withdrew from college life. I became the person I never thought I'd become. The withdrawn and sad person I strived never to become, I became. I thought time would help heal that wound, but I felt it only getting worse.

The light I had promised would never go out, went out. I have no idea how to get it back.

As soon as my last final ended I got in my car and drove straight home. I didn't bother saying goodbye to my sorority sisters, especially Sarah. She deserved more than what I left her with. And I didn't bother waiting to tell Liam good luck in the College World Series. I just couldn't do anything. I had barely put my car in park in the driveway when my mom opened the door and I ran right into her arms. She just held me and let me cry, like she knew that this would be the hardest heartbreak that I'd ever go through.

"I know sweetheart." My mom says fighting against her own tears. "I've got you. Always, sweetpea."

SINCE COMING HOME three weeks ago I powered down my phone and all I've done since is lay in bed. I know I should live some semblance of a life over the summer and prepare for the next school year. But I'm just too emotionally drained. And when I think I've run out of tears to cry, they start right back up.

A knock on my door startles me from my wallowing.

My mom pokes her head around my door to see in. "Honey, Liam's here. He's worried about you. May he come in?"

I can't respond. Just thinking about turning around to look at my mom in response has tears streaming down my face. It's quiet for a few seconds but then my bed shifts and then I'm cradled against a hard chest. Liam turns me around and slowly rocks me, caresses my head, and tells me all the things I need to hear. I sob more and Liam continues to reassure me that everything will be alright. And when I'm all cried out, Liam just lays here with me. He never pushes me to talk or tells me to get on with my life. The occasional tears fall and he just pulls me closer, placing a kiss on the top of my head. And it's all I need.

I wake up the next morning to a warm body behind me. Last night blurs with the previous nights until I remember Liam had come over. And he stayed the night? How did my parents not kick him out? I kind of liked having him here. I know I shouldn't say that. He's my best friend. Forgetting everything that happened between us last year that hasn't changed. My heart is still in pieces on that bridge back in South Carolina.

The waters between us may have gotten murky, but we cleared it up. Liam became the best friend I had growing up.

He got along with he who shall not be named. I didn't expect him to come over yesterday. But that's what friendship is. And despite it being way too soon for my heart to beat for anyone else, this feels good. Laying here with him, spooning, it feels right. So I snuggle up closer to him and hear him grunt.

I freeze, then slowly turn around and face him. My throat is hoarse from misuse and crying. "I'm sorry."

He opens an eye to respond to me. "A beautiful girl like you does that to me and you should be sorry."

His words do something to me. As soon as I remember everything, my nose begins to burn and I feel my eyes water with new tears. I do my best to push them away for a bit. "Liam, thank you for last night. And I'm sorry for using you as my tear towel." I say, my voice raspy from crying and overall lack of use. The tears that threatened to fall over, fall.

"Kamryn, I don't want you to be sorry." He pushes my hair back behind my ear and lets his hand linger on my cheek. His thumb swipes away the lingering tears. "I just don't want you to be hurting anymore."

"I know. It's gonna take me some time. But I'll be the same old Kamryn soon." That's a lie if I've ever heard one.

"I know you will." Liam says. I think he believes me.

And before I know it he's closing in. Eyes zeroed in on my mouth. I shouldn't let him kiss me. I should turn away. Because kissing someone, never mind the fact that it's Liam, it's too soon. But I think I need him to. I need to feel something. I think I need this physical connection with someone to show me that I won't be broken forever.

Is it healthy? Not even a little. This could be the biggest mistake I make.

I've thought about what it would be like to kiss Liam again. There were times when we'd be at the same party and

I'd see him making out with a girl. I'd remember what his lips felt like pressed against mine. It was never envy that made me want that with him in public.

I melt into the kiss and he takes it from there. It's like a light has been relit within me.

Our tongues clash together in this heated moment. We grab at each other trying to get closer. I move the blanket up to move over and straddle Liam. Between my oversized T-shirt and panties along with Liam's gym shorts and T-Shirt, the thin fabric isn't doing a great job in concealing anything. When I feel his erection, my breath hitches. I moan and roll my hips along the length of him. Liam's hands tighten on my hips and he takes control.

Liam flips us over so he's on top, and the feel of his weight on top of me is so much better this way. The feel of his cock trying to push its way through my underwear has the pressure building fast. My hands move on their own accord and roam up and down his back and chest and then under his shirt to feel his rippled abdomen. My hand slips into the waistband of his pants where I start to stroke him.

Liam breaks the kiss and buries his head in my neck. "God Kamryn, that feels so good."

I continue to stroke him when he pulls my hand away and pins it along with my other hand above my head.

"You have no idea how long I've waited for this again."

I look up at him puzzled. When I wanted more Liam was nowhere to be found, he ghosted me. It hurt but I moved on.

He hooks his fingers in the waistband of my panties. "May I?"

I nod. "Yes."

Liam slowly slides my panties off and then throws them over his shoulder somewhere. His hand is still on my thigh, waiting for permission.

I nod again. "Yes."

Liam slips a finger into my opening and goodness! It's like my body comes alive again. He slowly works me up, pumping his finger and then adds another, curling to hit the spot that makes me arch my back for more and cry out. Liam kisses me to silence my cries. His tongue tangling with mine matches that of his fingers stroke for stroke.

I'm so close and he knows it. He rubs the pad of his thumb on my clit and I'm gone. My orgasm explodes through me. I moan into the kiss as my orgasm continues to ripple through me. Liam continues to rub me, only slowing down to bring me back to earth.

I wrap my legs around him to stop him from climbing off me. "I want you inside me. Now."

Liam rolls off me to take his shorts off and I open the drawer to my nightstand to grab a condom and toss it to him. Once it's on, Liam hovers over me.

"Are you sure?"

I dig my heels into his butt and pull him closer to me. *No. Not even close. But I want to feel something. Anything.* Avoiding eye contact, I line his cock up at my entrance. "Yes. I'm sure."

That's all the permission Liam needs as he slowly enters me. Pushing his cock in inch by inch. Stretching me and filling me to the hilt. We both groan out from the feeling. And then he's moving inside of me. Bring his lips to mine all the while kissing me like he has all the time in the world. Moving at a steady pace. I break the kiss because this position is too intimate and not at all what I'm wanting with him.

Our bodies move in perfect rhythm. My hips meet his and I feel the first tingle knowing I'm close to another orgasm. Liam starts to pump faster, his pelvis hitting my clit working to get me off and then finding his release.

I put my hand over his mouth to muffle his groans. Biting my bottom lip as my climax rips through me. Tears sneak out the corners of my eyes, giving way to my continual breaking.

What have I done?

Our eyes clash and I can see the walls he's putting up. Liam rolls off of me after the last of his orgasm fades. Did I really just have sex with my best friend again? It didn't mean anything to me. Now I'm pretty positive it meant something to Liam. Did it actually mean something to him this time?

I turn to face him, because I have to say something. "Liam…"

He puts his finger to my lips effectively silencing me. Giving me a tiny smile. "I know that it didn't mean anything to you. And I know that you're still hurting. So when you're ready I'll be here."

He's rendered me speechless. Which is not an easy thing to do. He kisses my hand and gets dressed. "I'll see you later Kam."

All I can do is watch him silently get dressed and leave.

I screwed up big time.

When I hear the front door close, the tears fall in a steady stream down my face.

THE SUMMER WENT by in a whirlwind of tears and regret. I made it out of the house a few times with Emily and my mom. I think they were both scared for me and took me to some workout classes to take my mind off my heartbreak and my mistake with Liam. We were on a stroll downtown when a high school friend, Megan, ran into us. She told me about the boutique she works at participates in trunk shows. I'm not sure what sparked life back in me. But hearing that led me to checking one of the shows out. Soon after I went to Michael's and picked up a sketchbook to give my mind something else to do. I started sketching the clothes characters on TV were wearing. Once I filled that book up, I went back and got ten more. When I told my parents I wanted to switch majors, they told me to stick with that or I'd be on my own for school.

But all too quickly as my healing journey became routine, it was time to head back to school. Once I said goodbye to my parents and Jax, I started my nine and a half hour drive back to school. It was a good drive to get some thinking in. A little bit too much thinking. As a psychology major instead of analyzing others, I spent the time analyzing myself. I'm too messed up in the head for that and I'm glad I made the decision to change courses.

Traffic has been relatively light so far. Even if it is in the middle of summer. The only part that I do get stuck in is I-95 in Virginia, which is always the norm.

All too soon I'm pulling back up to the Kappa Beta house. I'm still lucky enough to have my own room. I love living in the house, but sometimes I need my own space. And since I'm a third year, my responsibilities have increased so needing my own space will have its advantages.

"Kamryn!"

"Sarah! How are you?" I ask her as we hug. I haven't seen my best friend since I left right after finals. I felt bad for not texting with her. But I needed a break. Unfortunately that included school friends.

"I'm so good! Went on vacation to Bora Bora and then went to Las Vegas for a while. How are you?"

"I'm good. Better," I tell her honestly.

"You look good. For a second, I didn't think you'd come back here."

Neither did I. "I considered it. But I can't let him get in the way of that."

"That's really good to hear."

"Yeah. I'm ready for smooth sailing this year. I decided to change my major. It might mean more school, but I could always double up this year and possibly take summer classes back home. It's not like I have anyone bidding for my time."

"What are you changing your major to?"

"Fashion. I realize that it's not the most lucrative, but it's what I want."

Sarah's eyes get big and a gasp escapes her. "I'm glad to hear that. Let's go unpack and then go get food. I want to hear all about it."

"Sounds good."

ONCE MY COUNSELOR helped me make the major switch, it was smooth sailing afterwards. But when Rush Week and then Bid Day rolled around, I wasn't as into it as I should have been. I have my little 'squish fam' that keeps getting bigger and I should be more open to them. I put on my happy face and welcomed a new member to my little family.

I'm walking from the art building to the house when I spot Liam. Right in the direct path of my way back. I can't turn around now. That'll make me look like I'm avoiding him...but I am avoiding him. UGH!! Might as well face him now. Or try to walk past him without him noticing me, yeah like that'll happen.

I'm halfway past him when he calls my name and stops me in my tracks. I turn around slowly and plaster a fake smile on my face. "Hey, Liam."

"I haven't seen you around lately. How are you?"

"I'm good. Just really busy. I changed my major, so now I'm basically playing catch-up." I say by way of holding up my portfolio case.

His eyebrows raise. "Oh wow."

"Yeah. So how have you been?"

My conversations with Liam have never been this awkward. We've never had to make small talk to talk about things. And I'm realizing that with everything that went down, I don't see how either of us can get back to that.

"I've been good. Baseball is going well so far even though it's fall ball. I haven't seen you around in a while."

Oh crap! This is why I've been avoiding him. I look down before responding. "Yeah. Like I said, I've just been really busy. Speaking of, I should probably go. I have a ton of work to do for class." I turn to leave but his hand on my elbow stops me.

"Kamryn, did I mess this up? Did I ruin us?" he asks in a hushed voice.

"Not at all," I say as my shoulders sag in sadness. The tears I thought had officially run out, make their reappearance.

Stepping close and still keeping his voice low to avoid any listening ears, he asks me. "You could've fooled me. Kamryn, you could've stopped us. Why didn't you stop us?"

He's gonna hate me. "Because I was hurting and you were there. God Liam, you have been my best friend since I was seven. I gave into what I was feeling at that time and...somehow, I think I knew you felt more. And I'm so sorry." One blink and the tears will fall.

"So that's why you've been avoiding me?"

I shake my head vehemently. "That's not–"

He looks away and puts up a wall cutting off my response. "I think maybe we should go back to how we were last year. I won't seek you out and I won't text you. You can keep avoiding me and now I'll start avoiding you."

If I didn't think my heart could break twice in one year, then I was wrong. I can't hold back my tears anymore while looking Liam straight in the eyes. "I think that's for the best too." I turn around and walk away as a sob overtakes me.

I don't know if I can do this anymore. So far everyone that I've loved has left. How much breakage can my heart take? Have I pushed them away? Is it me that makes people not want to stay?

December 2012

Winter break could not have come at a better time. I need my spin classes and Pilates back in my life. And maybe even some family time.

"How's it goin' Jax?" I ask as I plop down on the couch. A rerun of Grey's Anatomy plays out on the TV and the season six finale draws my attention a little.

"It's goin'." Jax responds.

I nod my head in silent approval and acceptance of her answer. I know I've been a terrible sister. Knowing my sister is in her first year of college should be giving us loads to talk about. But I've just felt so numb this last year and nothing has been able to wake my body up.

Jax turns down the volume on the TV before turning her attention to me. "Are you happy Kam? Because I see this girl that I think is my sister. And some days I see the old you fighting to make its return. So are you happy?"

No one has asked me that. "Honestly?"

"Always."

I turn to look at her; but focus on something over her shoulder instead. "No. The person I thought I saw a future with deserted me. And I screwed up my friendship with Liam." Taking a deep breath. "I've never been more unhappy than I am in this moment." My words come out choked.

"Well, what will make you not unhappy?"

I swallow the lump in my throat and attempt to keep the tears away. "I wish I knew. I keep trying to look on the good side of things, but I just can't." The more I spill to my sister, the faster the tears I tried so hard to keep from spilling over, spill over. "I wish I knew what happiness felt like again, Jax. I wish I knew what it was like to dance around the living room at the sorority house. I wish I knew what interacting with friends felt like. But I don't. I just can't move on from this pain. I don't know how."

My sister looks at me with pity and I hate it. I hate that I'm not the girl I was when I went away to school the first year. I hate that I'm not the sister she needs. I hate a lot of things. I hate that my promise to never lose the light that lit me up is broken. But most of all I think I hate love the most.

IT'S OFFICIALLY the opening season for spring sports. That means that baseball games will be everyone's main focus til the end of the school year.

"Kamryn, are you going to the baseball game?"

"Oh, no not today, Maggie." I say and go back to my sketches.

I attempt to get back to what I was working on but I still sense her staring at me.

"Are you sure? It's the first game of the season."

"She said she was sure, Maggie." Sarah snaps coming to my defense.

Maggie turns to walk away and I cast a thankful glance at my best friend.

"I know you said you didn't want to go to the game and I know it's because of Liam," Sarah begins as she sits next to me. "But are you sure you don't just want to show your Striper pride?"

"I can't, Sarah," I say, my throat threatening to close up.

"Are you ever going to tell me what happened between the two of you?"

I take a shuddering breath and turn to look her in the eye. "We slept together."

"What?!" Sarah's eyes practically bug out of her face and looks around to make sure that none of our other sisters heard. "When?"

"Over the summer," I confess.

Sarah urges me to continue.

"Okay, the cliff notes version is that he came to my house when he got home from baseball and comforted me the whole night. When I woke up, it was like another part of me took over. So I used him to make me feel good. But then he said something along the lines of I've waited for this for a long time. And I freaked the fuck out. Liam knew and when it was over, he got dressed and left."

"Wow..."

"That's not all," I start. "I saw him before Thanksgiving break after avoiding him like the plague and he asked if our friendship was ruined. I didn't know how to answer that. So he basically broke up with me. And I don't know if we'll ever be friends again." My eyes water, but the tears don't fall.

"Oh, honey." Sarah says and draws me to her in a side-hug-cuddle.

I have no tears left to cry. I just stay in her embrace completely numb.

After a while I back away from Sarah. "You should go to the game. I know all the other girls are going."

"I don't want to leave you alone."

"Sarah, I'll be okay. I promise." I say, giving her a watery smile. I just want to be alone.

She looks torn for a moment before relenting and getting dressed for the game. Leaving me here with my thoughts and my sketchpad. This isn't my sketchpad for class. Call me whatever you want. A sucker for pain. But since I started sketching, I have this one scene from my life that's been on replay since the day it happened. Us on the bridge. Me trying to hold back my tears. Him appearing to be strong.

I keep redrawing the scene from different angles in hopes that it will have a different outcome. But every single time, it ends. The scene. Us. Him standing alone on the bridge with my back in the distance.

I can't stop the sob that comes out unexpectedly and it's at this moment that I've never felt more alone. Broken.

15

KAMRYN

Late July 2013

My last summer of freedom. I decided to go to New York, but only for part of the summer. It was the greatest learning experience and I'm so grateful to my teachers that pushed me in this direction. I did some interviews with well-known designers to get a feel for what inspires them for their pieces and why. How do they adjust to the changing trends? And I was able to help pick out outfits for models for an upcoming fashion show. The feeling that I got behind the scenes made me realize that I was finally on the right path.

But now I have a month before my senior year begins, I'm already ready for this year to be done. The last two years were not a walk in the park for me. So the fact that I'm able to say I *can* graduate despite the heartache says something.

I've decided not to go crazy with spin or pilates this month. Instead I decided to take up running and have spent most mornings out on ten mile runs. On the last mile of my run, I run right into Liam as we're turning corners.

Liam holds onto my arms to steady me. "Whoa there Usain Bolt!"

"Oh god! Liam, I'm so sorry." Breathless from the run and the run-in, I place my hands on my hips and look up at Liam.

"Don't worry about it. I'll see you later Kamryn."

"Liam, wait!" I wrap my hand around his forearm before he runs off. He turns around and looks at me with a neutral expression. I used to be able to know what he was thinking like he did with me. That was the best part of being friends with someone for as long as we were. Before the intimacy blurred that solid friendship we had, we knew each other. Now we're like strangers to each other.

"I'm so sorry. I'm sorry that I was the cause of our friendship falling apart. I'm sorry that I didn't realize how much of an idiot I was and not seeing it. I'm just sorry for everything." My breath comes faster as I fight the onslaught of tears. I miss Liam more than I thought possible and I hate that I was the reason we fell apart.

He looks down and shakes his head before looking back up at me. "You have nothing to be sorry about. I knew that you were still going through a hard time."

"I was. I kind of still am. But I miss you Liam. I miss just talking to you, seeing you, and just being near you. I miss our friendship more than anything."

"God I miss you too." Liam says as he pulls me in for a hug.

After everything I've been through in the past couple of years, I just let it out. I lose the battle as the tears start streaming down my face with no intention of stopping. My body shakes from the sobs.

"Sshhhh..." Liam coos while placing kisses on the top of

my head every few seconds. He holds me tighter in an effort to hold me together.

Eventually my tears run out and I pull away from Liam. He lightly runs his thumbs underneath my eyes to wipe away the remaining tears.

"Kamryn, I don't want to push you or anything. I'm done doing that. My pride was hurt more than anything after your admission. We should talk one day, okay? And I'll wait for you as long as possible."

That gets a chuckle out of me and I lean up on my tiptoes and kiss Liam on the cheek. "Okay. I'll see you around Liam."

"Yeah, see ya."

I BLINKED and my last summer as a college student is over. I'm back at school a week earlier as a tour guide for prospective students. Better late than never, but I decided to get more involved on campus. I'm already involved with a handful of activities, but what's one more thing?

"And here is the Art Building. You'll find Graphic Design, Fashion, Photography, Fine Art...basically anything that involves thinking outside the box." I tell the group on our Monday tour. When we complete our walk-through of the Arts Building, we make our way across campus. I answer questions as needed. Some questions are serious and some questions are not. So I put more effort into the serious questions.

"Next we have the Athletic Building. While I can't get in there on my badge alone, it's where all of the coaches' main offices are, the athletes have their own auditorium, and they have a communal weight room." Even while I let the group know what's held in this building, I'm still in awe. This university continues to dish out whatever they can for the breadwinners. I can't say I blame them. School spirit is high when all of the teams have winning records.

We continue our walk across the quad. It takes me back to my first time touring here. I did three tours, just to be sure I wasn't making any rash decisions to possibly come to school with my best friend. During the year we weren't talking, I found myself regretting the decision to come here. But I push that regret away when I realize all I've got to experience here.

I take the group through the rest of the building that I can get into. Questions from parents arise and I answer them as politely as possible. We pause in the quad before heading to our last stop. "Any final questions?"

A bunch of hands shoot up. Such eager beavers. I point to a shy looking girl. "What is your major?"

"I was a Psychology major. And then I made the switch to Fashion." She and the others look at me inquisitively, so I expand a little on why I made the switch. Telling them that I had some personal reasons for making this switch. But ultimately I hope to weave psychology and fashion together. This seems to appease them and maybe confuse them. But I choose not to expand any further. "Next question."

A preppy looking freshman boy asks, "Where are the fraternity houses?"

I arch a finely plucked eyebrow at him. "This university is so much more than Greek Life. So if you're only deciding to come to CSU for Greek Life, then you should reevaluate why you want to come to this school. They look for more than just physical looks. You have to have the grades, a good social media background, extracurricular activities, and some recommendations from former teachers."

"What sorority are you in?"

"Uh, I don't remember saying that I was in one. But I am in one."

"Which one?"

"Kappa Delta. I was a legacy."

A well-put-together girl that I have a feeling will rush as soon as she can, speaks up, "Wait your last name isn't Rawlins is it?"

"Yes it is."

"OMG! Your family is a legend in the Greek world."

I give a tight-lipped smile. "Thanks."

I continue on with the final stop on the tour for them. As sports are huge at this school, I take them to the closest outdoor facility which happens to be the baseball field.

"This is our last stop of the day," I tell the group. "Since the football field is a little too far for us, I hope you don't mind us stopping by the baseball field."

I go on about the accomplishments this program has made and in the distance, I see some of the baseball players are walking out of the fieldhouse when we get there, which happens to be Liam and Chance.

Chance pulls me into a bear hug and spins me around before noticing our audience with shocked looks on their faces. "Fresh meat?"

I lightly punch him on the arm. "No. Prospective students. Giving them the tour...all that good stuff. The baseball field was the last stop."

"Interesting..." Chance starts and then turns to the wide-eyed newbies. "Well, I'm Chance. Shortstop. And this ugly guy right here is Liam. Star pitcher."

Liam gives them a shy little wave and his gaze sneaks over to me.

"Any questions children?" Chance asks them.

A bunch of hands shoot up and I shoot Chance a devilish grin. "Answer away Mr. Popular."

I step next to Liam as Chance does all the talking.

"He really does have a knack for this, doesn't he?" Liam asks so only I can hear.

I cover my chuckle behind my hand. "He'd be a great talk-show host if the MLB doesn't draft him."

"That he does. Are you going to the back-to-school party Kappa Mu is throwing on Saturday?"

Hesitation hits me. I may be leading this tour, but my sole focus is on Liam. "I was thinking about it. Why?"

"No reason," Liam looks at me and it appears that Chance is done answering questions. "Looks like he's done. I'll see you around Kam."

"Bye, Liam."

"Hey, Mommy."

"Hi, Kamryn. How was being a tour guide?"

My parents thought it was hilarious that I chose to do this. But really I did it to get out of the house because the sooner I'm here, the sooner I can leave.

"Exhausting. I honestly think that some of them were only interested in Greek Life or being an athlete. But none of them looked like they played sports at all. I don't think any of them let what I told them sink into their pea-sized brains."

"Tsk tsk, my darling. You were like that too, remember?"

I groan at what my mom just pointed out. "Yeah, I remember."

"Are you just doing this one tour today?"

"No. I have several that I'm signed up for throughout the year. So I think about six in total."

"Well, if fashion doesn't work out, you could always be a stewardess."

"Mother! That's it, I'm hanging up on you."

My mom is laughing on the other end. "Fine. I'm done. Have you seen Liam?"

"Yeah." I tell her and clear my throat. "We talked for a bit."

"It'll get easier sweetheart."

Unexpected emotion takes over. I swear this year I'm set to turn my emotions off. It's exhausting feeling everything so deep. "I know it will. Hey, I gotta go. I'm helping some of the girls move their stuff in. I love you. I'll talk to you later."

"Bye sweet girl, I love you too."

Okay, I lied to my mom. I'm not helping any of the girls move in because none of them are coming back until closer to the weekend. Call me a bad daughter, but I can't talk about Liam without getting all choked up. And just seeing him today did something weird to me. Maybe it's the whole saying *absence makes the heart grow fonder* or something like that. But what I do know is that I refuse to be the mopey girl from the last two years. I'm going to enjoy my final year as best as I can.

And I get to work on my senior project, which I'm super excited for.

When I walk into the dimly lit bar, I find that it's pretty much empty sans three other people. So finding a spot to sit at the bar isn't that difficult.

"What can I get you darlin'?" The bartender asks me.

"Tequila on the rocks, please."

"Coming right up."

It's times like this when my mind wanders back to Mason. It's almost football season. And I haven't let my thoughts wander to him or football for over a year. It's the beginning of the school year that's the hardest for me.

"Here you go. Do you want to start a tab or close it out?"

I debate it for a second but then I slide him my debit card. "Start a tab please."

The bartender nods at my response and goes to another customer. Holding the glass up, I tip my head back and the Tequila slides down my throat in a smooth movement.

"A girl that doesn't flinch when she drinks tequila is dangerous to anyone that gets close to her."

I know that voice anywhere. Liam. "You should know." I spit at him.

"Ease up, Kam."

I turn to look at Liam and see that he's got his guitar slung over his shoulder. "How did you know I was here?"

"Come on–it's the only bar close by that has a stage for singing."

I look at him with a raised eyebrow.

He holds his hands up in a defensive manner. "Okay, Sarah told me. Come sing with me."

I haven't sung with Liam in a long time. He always knew the songs that worked for me. It's also one of the ways we became so close and how our friendship has lasted so long. The last time I sang in front of a crowd was when Mason arranged it. So now I guess I associate singing with him. Which opens the barely healed wound.

"Do you know *All I Ask* by Adele?"

He nods his head. But has a pensive look on his face.

"Okay." I unlock my and pull up my phone's camera,

switching it to the video mode. I turn to the only female bartender. "Will you record this for me please?"

She takes my phone. "Sure thing."

A few more people have wandered into the bar and are looking like they don't want their afternoon booze fest interrupted by my singing. Oh well. I don't care. Liam plugs his guitar into the amp and hands me the microphone.

"Hey guys. I'm Kamryn and this is my...uh, friend...Liam. We're going to play a song, or a few for y'all. This first one is for all you brokenhearted and it's *All I Ask* by Adele." Liam looks at me questioningly. But I nod for him to start regardless.

I look out to the crowd as I belt out the lyrics. Some have glassy eyes from either the alcohol or the song, and others are really listening to the lyrics.

A tear escapes and I quickly wipe it away. Is this the closure that I need? Can I move on from this? Can I love again? It still hurts like hell. I still miss Mason like no tomorrow. Because I'm carrying around my broken heart like it's a prize. It's not. I finish the song and the room erupts in applause. I look out at the room and even the employees have stopped what they were doing to applause. I wipe my tears as best as I can.

"Thank you." I go to stand up and requests get thrown out to us.

When I turn to Liam, he shrugs like it's not my fault that they love me.

"Okay. I'm only doing one more song and this one is a duet. Have any of you seen the movie Country Strong?"

Some hoots are all I get.

"This song is *Give into Me*."

Liam starts up the guitar and the familiar tune of the song swims through my veins. But when he opens his mouth to sing, his voice warms my body and it feels like last summer all over again. Why did I choose this song? Him looking right into my eyes like he can see into my soul is unraveling everything that I've tried putting together. Does he like me? If this were us our freshman year, I would've been all over him. But we're not those people anymore and he ran from us before we could even begin.

I can't look away from him. It is hardly an option. We've sung this song before. Just way before anything like what happened last summer happened. He was just my goofball best friend. We did everything together. Until I proposed that stupid arrangement in hopes that he and I could become more than friends.

My body unconsciously drifts towards him as we continue to sing about giving into each other. Whether as friends or more my mind is now conflicted. The words we sing to each other, like a back and forth conversation, wondering if our time is now.

Our stares linger after the song is over and the crowd goes insane. I break the stare first and walk off the short stage to get my phone and quickly pay my tab. I can't go back on my word now. I can't have feelings for Liam again. But whatever it is I'm feeling isn't slowing down my racing heart. I care about Liam as a friend. Did I maybe think that he and I would turn to more than friends? I'd be lying if I said I didn't think about it. He pushed me away. When I started to feel more, he pulled back. So I moved on.

I quickly uploaded the grainy video to Facebook in my haste to get out of the bar. In no time at all my phone is blowing up with text messages about my performance. But I ignore them all. A small part of me was hoping that a certain someone would see it. Would he see how broken I still am? Or would he think that I've moved on? Did he move on? My phone rings with Jax calling.

"Hi, sister."

"Kam! Those songs. Why would you do that to yourself?"

I stop in my tracks. She knows why those songs are special to me. An unexpected sob escapes me before I have a chance to answer her. "I don't know. I wasn't thinking."

"I thought you were doing better?" After a beat of silence, she speaks up again. "Maybe it's time you talk to someone."

Talk to who? A shrink that would just tell me that it's okay to feel the feelings. That it's okay to mourn what almost was? Almost. That's such a heartbreaking word.

"I'll think about it. I'm gonna go. Bye, Jax."

"Bye, Kam."

I continue the walk back to campus with tears streaming down my face. Maybe my sister is right. Maybe I do need to talk to someone. But that means finally opening all the way up. And I've done a fine job of mashing down those feelings this past summer.

THE REST of the week passed by in a blur. Thankfully none of my sorority sisters have talked about my performance. Either that or Sarah got to them first. But that didn't stop the rest of campus from talking about it. Everywhere I walked I heard the whispers *"She sang those songs for him"* or *"Look how broken she still is"* or my favorite yet *"Move on already, he has"*.

That last one really hurt. Since this is such a large campus, you'd think that people would bypass those observations. Or find something else to talk about entirely. But not at this campus. Hearing the part about him moving on threatened to split me open right on the spot. I haven't kept tabs on him. But considering that my mind goes to him more than I'm allowed to say, I probably should. He's allowed to move on. And so am I. But the idea of actually moving on, after planning our future together terrifies me.

16

KAMRYN

August 2013

It's been about two weeks since the bar with Liam and I've replayed that day for fourteen days.

"So planning on kissing anyone tonight Kam?" Sarah asks as we're walking down the solo-cup-littered street towards the party. You know *the* party of the year. She asks me this question every time. Well, she didn't have a chance to ask me our sophomore year because...yeah. And she didn't ask me last year since I never left the sorority house. So I think this is her way of getting back into the swing of things.

I look at her shocked because she's never this bold with her questioning. "No. I think I'm done dating. Besides, no one here is catching my eye." I end on a secret confession.

I also may just be a little tipsy. Another thing that I've hidden from people is how much I've started to drink. But since this frat party is basically booze fest I blend right in.

"Look," Sarah starts. "I'm not saying date anyone, but I don't know why you don't just kiss—" But she's cut off abruptly when we see Liam standing there looking at me differently while his frat buddies cheer on some random partiers. It's been like this since our summer run-in and that unfateful day at the bar I can't get out of my head. "Okay, why aren't you guys together again? Because the way he's looking at you, is so not in the friendship type of way. I noticed it three years ago and I'm noticing it now. Kamryn, he is into you." Sarah points out.

For the past week, when Liam and I did somehow cross paths, he was who he was during our first year here. Only I'm seeing things with a new set of eyes. Lingering glances here. Prolonged touches there. Do I think Liam's attractive? ABSOLUTELY!! Even when I wasn't single, that fact remained. Liam Taylor is hot. Do I want to risk our extremely fragile friendship again for something that might fizzle out...again? NO! We already crossed that bridge once and it completely backfired.

As much as he wants, he can't be the Band-Aid that magically tries to heal me. And I think our not speaking all last year is proof of that. We both deserve better than that. Liam has respected the friendship line that I have so firmly drawn in the sand. So why do I get the feeling that someone's about to cross it?

"I told you." I say as we rush past Liam and his friends. "I don't want to risk a repeat of freshman year. It was complicated enough with us being best friends. But throwing sex into that mix amped the complication factor up. And I'm just getting him back, I don't wanna ruin that." My back burns with the intensity of his gaze as I hurry us past them.

"I get that Kam, I really do. But you know how he feels about you. Everyone knows how he feels about you. Why not just take the plunge for real this time? Maybe it could work out and this would be what you need?" My best friend asked me thoughtfully.

"I just...can't."

It's not that I'm scared of Liam. It's that I'm scared of more. I'm scared of putting myself out there for the next person to emotionally crush me. But that's what crushes do, right? They crush you from the inside out leaving nothing but your former self in its wake when it does pass.

THIRTY-MINUTES later with another almost empty cup, I'm leaning against a pillar watching a game of beer-pong, when the hairs on the back of my neck stand up. Liam. He's one of the few guys my body is acutely aware of.

"I thought I might find you here Rynny." Liam says as he uses my nickname for him. He also uses it when he's been drinking. He's standing so close to me that I can feel the heat of his body and smell his cologne. To distract myself, I tip my head back to finish the last of my drink then turn to face him. I haven't looked this close into his eyes in almost three years.

"You know–" I start to say but I'm cut off by Liam crushing his lips to mine.

Shock overtakes my body because it feels like deja vu. Suddenly that shock turns into recognition, and I'm kissing Liam back. Our tongues move together as I put my hand on the back of his neck to pull him closer to me and at the same time he grips my hips and pulls me into him

I roll my head to the side to get some much-needed air into my lungs. "Liam, I need to talk to you. In private."

He kisses me one more time and then takes my hand to pull me upstairs to his room.

Once in his room, I open my mouth to speak but Liam

puts his finger over my mouth silencing me. "Kamryn, let me go first. Okay?" He starts and I nod my head. "You've been my best friend since second grade. I remember that day like it was yesterday. I walked in so scared because I was the new kid and had no idea where to sit. But this short, curly-haired little girl waved me over to sit next to her. And the rest is history. We played spin the bottle, hormones were starting to change the way us boys saw you girls. Of course we thought we were too cool to play that juvenile game. But we did. And you were my first kiss at twelve years old. I didn't show it, but when that bottle landed on me, I was nervous Kam. Not only were you my first kiss, but you were my first crush." He tells me.

I look at him with a thick throat and unshed tears that he remembers stuff like that. It's been almost ten years since that game and so much has changed. Yet the bond that formed when we were seven has stood the test of time. No, we weren't always the best of friends. But the mutual love we had for one another beat out all of those odds.

He cups my cheek gently. "That first day of college, when you kissed me to prove Allie wrong, I thought that would be the turning point for us. But I was wrong. I thought when we started our just sex arrangement that would be the moment we became an 'us'. Then I got scared of my feelings for you, so I ran. I stood by on the sidelines and watched you and Mason fall harder than ever for each other. To see my best friend happy was all I wanted. But I can't lie and say that I wasn't mad that it wasn't with me you were happy with. Watching from the sidelines was hard. And I don't want to do that again." His eyes roam over my face. Almost as if he's finally seeing me in a new light.

"If I'm being honest...you scare the crap out of me. Knowing that you want a forever kind of love scares me because I've never had that. I never thought I could have that because taking the next step with you, with anyone, scares me. From the time we were little you talked about finding your Prince Charming. I laughed it off because that's what little shits like me did. As I got older and things changed, I thought *maybe*. I thought, 'I want to be that guy for you'. I don't want to be scared anymore. I definitely don't want to lose you again. The summer that everything went to shit, I knew how vulnerable you still were. If I were a stronger man, I should've been the one to stop it. But I saw that moment as my 'finally' and I jumped at it. Kamryn, I've loved you since I was twelve even before I knew what love was. You've seen me go through every awkward phase that no one other than their mom should see. I want to be the guy that you come home to and complain about a bad manufacturer. I want to be your sounding board when you're struggling through your sketches. I want to be the one that makes your dreams come true, if you'll let me."

He's saying all the things that I need to hear. "But is it that simple?"

"It can be."

"We already went down that road once Liam. What makes you think that this can work?" I ask him nervously. Putting myself back out there after just vowing to myself to swear off men for the year...I mean who does that?

"Because I know you like the back of my hand. I know that you hate sushi. You love the color black. Your favorite season is winter, but you'll say it's summer just to please people. You have an amazing voice. You put me in my place and have since we were kids and I want you to keep doing that until we're old and gray. I could go on and on."

My heart and my head are at war. "But is that what you want too? Is marriage and kids what you want? Am *I* what you want? Part of the reason I shied from ever thinking of taking the next step with you was because I saw the girls you'd go after and not once had I heard you talk about settling down and wanting a family."

"The only reason I went after those other girls is because I never thought we'd get to this place. But now that we're here, I can't imagine anywhere else I'd rather be. You're the only one I can imagine having a family with."

I say nothing. What can I possibly say that'll make this a smooth transition?

"I know you're still raw from what happened. With me and with him. I want to do what I can to help you. I want the fictitious future we talked about freshman year to become real. I want the dreams we dream together to become real. I want us by each other's side when we get life changing news. I want to look up in the stands at my games and see you cheering your head off. I want you to look out in the crowd at your fashion shows and see me cheering with your family. Kamryn, we're not who we were three years ago. But we can be better," he says.

What he's saying makes sense. Taking our friendship to the next level is the logical thing. But I'm still fighting myself with whether or not to finally give in.

I clasp my hands behind his neck before I start. "I'm still iffy about relationships. I mean, I just swore them off not even an hour ago. Because being in one again terrifies me. I went in headfirst with the last one and look at how that ended up. I'm not comparing you two, but you're both athletes. But being pushed aside again for a sport would literally take me out of the game. What I don't want is if I say yes to giving us a chance, that'd I'd be pushed to the side because you're being pressured to focus on the game. I need a promise that whatever happens with baseball, that that would never happen. That our relationship can and will be permanent." I say and release a winded breath. "I have plans and dreams that I always pictured someone by my side celebrating those with, and I them. I have this picture in my mind that is so clear of that. And I'd hate for that picture to become distorted."

"What are you saying Kamryn?" Liam asks as he pulls me into him so we're flush together. Not an inch of space can fit between us.

"That sometimes the people in the pictures change. I'm saying that if these aren't just words to get in my pants, then I'm yours."

He smiles. "Promise. Baby girl, I'm all in."

"Good." And I crush my mouth to his.

It takes two seconds for Liam to react. Then he's kissing me back and lifting me in his arms. My legs wrap around his waist as he walks us back to his bed.

It feels like summer all over again, but much different. I'm not as broken and Liam isn't holding me together. We get to have a complete do-over for our first time together and it's not under the pretense of a dare. We're obliterating the whole friend zone category between us.

Carefully, so as not to crush me under his weight, Liam gently lowers us to the bed. His body covers mine as our hands explore one another. Taking the time to rediscover places on each other's bodies that make our breaths quicken and arch into the other's touch.

My hands slip under his shirt, feeling the warmth of his torso. I trace the ridges of his taut stomach and move up to place my hand over his racing heart. Like mine, it feels as if it's going to jump out of his chest.

Liam pulls back on his knees and slowly pulls the hem

of my shirt up my body and once it's off he throws it across the room like it offended him.

"Yours too." I instruct as I pull at the hem of his shirt. "Off."

He gives me that cocky smirk I've seen him give so many opponents as they approach home plate for their at-bat. But this one is different. It turns my insides more molten than anything. It turns my wanting him into needing him.

When he goes to pull his shirt off I move in on his belt and jeans. I make quick work of unbuckling and unbuttoning, but he has to roll off me completely to take his pants off. When his pants are off, I take advantage and move to straddle him. Kissing down his chest, letting my hardened nipples graze his skin.

As I move lower, I look up at Liam and see nothing but pure animalistic need swirling in his blue eyes. I'm sure mine mirrors his, but as I make the first swipe across the head and lick up the first bead of pre-cum, his eyes roll to the back of his head and his hand sinks into my hair.

I tease him more by quickly and lightly fluttering my tongue at the very tip. All the while working the base of him as my fist moves up and down slowly. I continue to torture him the way I know he would torture me.

I want more of him too, so I take all of him to the back of my throat. Contracting as soon as I'm full of him, bobbing up and down, and then slowly coming back up lightly grazing my teeth. I repeat that until he's swearing more than a sailor when I cup and massage his balls.

"Holy fuck, Kamryn! Let me come! Please..." Liam pleads.

"Not yet." I say, right before I go down a little further and suck his balls in my mouth. One at a time. Massaging them with my tongue. I let them slip out of my mouth, but continue to massage them as I go back to sucking on Liam like a lollipop. Swirling my tongue around the head and then the vein that runs up Liam's length.

I hear Liam's intake of breath. "If you don't want a mouth full of my cum, I would move." He warns.

But I keep the suction on Liam's cock and hear him swear as I feel him swell before he shoots his load down my throat with a roar. I continue to work him through his orgasm, moaning at the taste of him and licking up every drop. When he's come back down from his high, I slowly release him from my mouth. but not before dropping a kiss to the tip of him.

I crawl back up the rest of his body and wait for him to come back to his body.

"Hot damn woman." Liam says still out of breath. His arm is thrown over his eyes as his chest heaves for air.

"I'll take that as a compliment." I tell him as I pepper kisses on his neck and his jaw. Kissing everywhere but his lips.

Liam finally opens his eyes and turns his gaze to me. "You should. But for my plan, you are wearing way too many clothes."

"Is that so?" I ask while rolling my hips over his semi-hard erection. My jeans rubbing on his bare skin has him gripping my hips to stop my movement. I lean down to whisper in his ear. "You should probably solve that then."

In a flash, Liam has us flipped and me on my back, arms pinned above my head. He's hard again which gives me a thrill.

"What do you want, Kamryn?" Liam asks huskily.

Easy. I think to myself before telling him what I want. "You. Your tongue, your hands, your cock. All making my toes curl and me crying out your name."

Liam stills his movements before catching himself. "Fuck." He says before kissing me hard.

He moves to kiss my cheek, down the side of my neck, nipping at my collarbone, and suckling kisses at the tops of my breasts. Reaching behind me to unhook my bra, Liam slides the straps off my shoulders and tosses my bra to the side. With my breasts free, Liam moves back up to my face. He plunges his tongue in my mouth as his calloused fingers tease my nipples to a hardened peak and I feel it all the way to my clit. His tongue matches the twisting of his fingers over my nipples, pulling a gasp from me. I feel him smile into the kiss as he flicks his fingers across my nipples again and again until an orgasm just from nipple stimulation takes over my body.

"Fuck, fuck, fuck." My breath comes in gasps as the orgasm flows through me.

When my breathing returns to somewhat normal, Liam trails his lips back down my neck, placing a kiss on my collarbone, and pulling a nipple in his mouth. He circles the taut bud with his tongue, flickering his tongue in fast licks, before sucking and twirling his tongue. All the while his other hand is showing my other nipple the same attention. Twisting lightly and pulling upward until my nipple is elongated, barely touching the sensitive tip while circling his finger over top. One more flick of his tongue and twist of his finger over my nipples and another orgasm takes over.

"Liam!" I cry out with tears from all of the pleasure sneaking out of the corner of my eyes. I don't know if I can handle another orgasm, but Liam is already moving to my pants. Unbuttoning and unzipping my jeans, I should be embarrassed with how wet I am. But I don't care. When my jeans and underwear are off, Liam slides his body down the bed and puts my legs over his shoulders.

Keeping his eyes on mine the whole time, Liam swipes his tongue up my center before circling my clit that has me crying out. He does it again and dives deep. Plunging his tongue in so deep all I feel is warmth. His eyes close in pleasure as he moans and kisses my pussy, sliding and swiping his tongue inside me until I see the stars bursting behind my closed eyes. Liam adds a finger to his movements and then another. His thick fingers move with precision while his tongue focuses on my clit. The feeling as if I'm floating outside of my body has me wanting to move away so Liam places an arm around my hip keeping me in place.

Not satisfied with the way I keep moving, Liam pulls out his fingers and wraps his other arm around my other hip. He pulls me closer and dives into my pussy. Not letting me move, his tongue moves in that expert way that has my toes curling on his back.

"I'm close." I pant out.

Liam takes that as a cue, and uses his fingers to spread me wide open. His tongue dives inside and has me on the precipice of another explosive orgasm. Suddenly, Liam pushes two fingers inside me, curling them in a 'come hither' movement that has me squeezing his head with my thighs.

"I need you to get there, Kam. One more for me," Liam encourages.

My body is wrung out. I don't think I can come again. He continues eating my pussy like it's his last meal. He hardens his tongue on my clit and the new pressure has me coming harder than ever.

"Fuck yes." I hear a slurping noise but can't even bother to care as I continue to come harder than I have in a year.

"I can't go anymore." I cry out to Liam.

He slows down his movements and crawls up my body,

kissing me so I taste myself. A slow kiss that has my breathing accelerating and my hands pushing him into me. He slides off the bed, walking over to his desk and pulling the drawer open to get a condom. I hear the tear of the wrapper and watch as he rolls the condom on before climbing back on the bed and hovering over me. His dick slides through my slit, my release coats his condom-covered cock and my hand slides up around his neck to pull him down for a kiss.

I get lost in him. It still feels new. He still feels new as our tongues dance together. His hand travels down my body, hooks my leg over his hip, and eases inside me.

"Damn you feel good," Liam says when he's balls deep.

I can feel my walls still pulsing from the aftereffects of my last orgasm.

"How do you want it, Kam?"

Pushing his hair back to look in his eyes. "Slow and steady. I want to feel all of you."

Liam pulls out slowly before rolling his hips and pushing back in. It causes us both to groan. "I can do that."

Liam sets a delectable pace that has my body tightening up and on the edge of release. He pumps his hips in slow, short movements before pushing all the way in. His pelvic bone hits my clit that has me moaning out his name. I bring my other leg up and connect it with the other at the base of his spine. The movement shifts our angle and he hits that spot that has me screaming out his name as my orgasm takes over. Liam drives wildly into me before finding his own release.

"Holy shit." I say when I come back down from my high. My pussy is still fluttering with the after effects and Liam is still inside. I squeeze my inner muscles milking the last of him while lightly running my nails up and down his back.

He kisses me fiercely before pulling out and rolling over to his back. "Marry me. Now. I need sex like that every night."

I feel the bass from the music at the party downstairs and turn to look at him. "That's the only reason you'd marry someone? Mind blowing sex?"

"Of course not. But if sex was like that for everyone, then I'm positive divorce rates would be slim to none." He and I both chuckle at that. "I'm keeping my promise to you. I want to be your everything Kamryn."

"I want that too." I tell him sincerely before leaning over and giving him a kiss.

This feels good. Way better than good.

December 2013

My last final of the semester is over. Between sorority events, dating Liam, supporting him with baseball, and being in the Arts Building non-stop; I've barely had a chance to breathe before something else needed my attention. But now, winter break is here and we get a full month to rest before gearing up for our final semester.

It still hasn't hit me that I'm on track to graduate, until I've walked across the stage. But I have five months before that day is set to make its appearance. So for now, I'm focusing on the present.

A knock on my door pulls my attention to it. And the hunk of muscle in the doorway. Throwing my dress on my bed, I hop over to Liam.

"Hi," I wrap my arms around him to greet him with a kiss.

I go to pull away, but his hand on my lower back stops me. His gaze tracks over my face. Sending my heart into my throat. We've been together since the night of the party. Together being a tame word. We've been inseparable. Almost like when we were kids. But this is so much more. I look into his beautiful blue eyes and see the boy I knew turned into the man I love.

Liam and I stayed holed up in his room that first weekend. Getting food and condoms delivered instead of leaving the cocoon of his bed. When I went back to the sorority house that Sunday night, the questions were one after the other until I spilled the beans. Sarah almost burst my eardrums when she found out we were dating. Then proceeded to say "I told you so."

Being with Liam has been so easy. I put in the work to heal my own broken heart. But as the days went on, he helped repair the broken that I couldn't fix. We haven't told each other those three words yet. I'm not sure if it's him respecting the speed in which we've gone in our relationship because of me or if he's just as scared as I am to say those three words. Sure, we've said them in our friendship. But saying 'I love you' to a friend is much different from saying those to the person you're dating. It's that next big step in your relationship.

"Hi, beautiful." Liam places a kiss to the tip of my nose before letting me get back to packing.

We're about to make the long drive back home. Thanksgiving was our first long-distance drive together which is surprising as we used to take trips together all of the time. The amount of times I looked over at him driving almost drove me to having him stopping the car. As hot as he is when he plays baseball, nothing could have prepared me for watching him drive us home.

I pick up my discarded dress as Liam takes a seat at my desk. "Are you all packed?"

"Yep. The car is all gassed up too. Snacks and Red Bulls are in the cooler, as well as a blanket for you."

I can't stop the words from coming out. "I love you." I did it. Looking at Liam, speechless, makes me wonder if I should have waited. "Yo..you don't have to say it back. But this is what I feel for you. I love you, Liam Taylor. So much."

His legs propel him out of the chair and straight for me. Liam takes my face in his hands and kisses me. I rise up on my tiptoes, wrapping my arms around his neck. The lightness that I feel, that I felt before and haven't felt in years, has made its way back.

"You have no idea how long I've waited to hear you say that. I love you too, Kamryn Rawlins."

We stand there in each other's arms. Foreheads pressed together. The love surrounding us is over a decade in the making. My heart feels fuller than it has in a while and I owe it to the boy I met when I was seven making my heart flutter fourteen years later.

We break apart and I put the last of my clothes for break in my suitcase. My toiletries are already packed, so I toss those in my other bag. Taking another look around my room, we make our way to Liam's car. The drive home goes by faster when you're with someone that makes everyday things enjoyable. We stop once at the North Carolina border and then again at the Maryland border. And after nine hours in the car, Liam is pulling into my parents driveway. I could have easily walked with my stuff from his house, but his generosity is one of the things I love about him.

I walk around the back of his car but he shoves me out of the way.

"Jerk," I tease him.

"A jerk you love," he tacks on.

I lean up on my toes to kiss his cheek. "Yeah, I do love you."

A look is shared between us. A look that says more than words can say. Liam breaks our stare and pulls my suitcase out of his car. I go back around to the front to grab my purse and phone. Not bothering to knock, I open the door that puts us in the mudroom.

Animated conversation and laughter greets us when I open the door. "Mom? Dad? Jax?" I call out.

Liam sets my suitcase by the kitchen before taking my hand and leading us to laughter that greeted us when we walked in. When we enter the living room and see both of our parents laughing at something the other apparently said. My bet is on Liam's dad.

My mom must see me out of the corner of her eye and screams. Scaring all of us, especially me, as I've never heard my mom make that loud of a sound.

"You're together?!" She screeches from her spot on the couch.

"Surprise!" I sarcastically cheer.

The delay is comical and then all-hell breaks loose. Both of our moms rush off the couch and crush us in hugs that only moms can.

In the span of time it took for Liam and I to get to this stage in our relationship, we both completely spaced in telling our parents. We didn't think it was necessary to tell our parents then as we were still getting used to being together. But in the few weeks between then and now, it's like our relationship grew tenfold. Questions are thrown at us right and left and while we answer them, this is also a reminder as to why we waited for as long as we did. I hear the word 'wedding' tossed around before the next question is asked.

Liam and I manage to escape our parents to head outside to the patio. He stokes the fire in the pit and motions me to join him on the lounge chair and iIt's not long before Liam breaks the silence and hums the wedding march. I do my best to suppress the laughter that's bubbling but fail miserably.

"Did I tell you my mom was planning our wedding when we were in high school?" Liam asks.

I let out a sigh. "I'm convinced our mom's had a thread going back and forth as to when to announce that. My mom took every chance she could to say how she was planning our wedding. Although she started leaving breadcrumbs sooner than high school."

"They can't rush us yet." Liam says and attacks me with kisses making me giggle.

"I agree. Although being married to you really wouldn't be a bad thing."

"Oh, really?"

"Yeah. I'd be the hot wife at your games. Oh my gosh! I'd be a WAG!" I exclaim and half-turn on the lounge. Liam looks at me strangely.

"What the hell is a WAG?" He asks me.

Now it's my turn to look at him strangely. "Are you serious? It's a wife and girlfriend. Every professional sports team has them. The wives usually alienate the girlfriends, so you better put a ring on it as fast as you can." I say with a teasing lilt to my voice.

"I love you." Liam states right before he tickles me and I'm gasping for breath.

My thoughts run wild. And before I know it, the holiday

break flies by and we're back at school gearing up for our final semester.

KAMRYN

April 2014

"Let's go boys!" Sarah shouts from our spot on the lawn.

Liam and the guys have a game against one of their division rivals and this game determines their seed position and if they're on the right track to making it to the playoffs, then regionals, then super-regionals, and then the championship series. I look around the packed stadium full of garnet, white, and black; with few clusters of blue and gold throughout the crowd. The smell of popcorn and boiled peanuts fill my senses and the heat from the late April sun and humidity warms my skin.

As I watch our guys switch out for defense, I can't help but think back to earlier in the week.

"You're not superstitious?" Why I've never asked Liam this I have no clue. I'm straddling his backside as I massage his back and shoulders. He doesn't need me to do this, but I like touching him.

A moan slips free as I dig into a tight spot. "Shit. Um, not really. At least I never thought I was."

"Any pre-game rituals?"

"Does stretching count?"

I slide my thumbs down his back with enough pressure that he squirms. "Baby. But no, stretching doesn't count. Actually, I would hope you did that before and after every game." I pay a little extra attention to his pitching arm before placing a kiss on his shoulder and sliding off next to him. "Are you nervous for this game?"

Liam, still laying on his stomach, turns his face to me. "Not as nervous as I should be. Granted this is the game that determines our division spot. It'll help with you watching."

"You're such a mush." Pushing his hair back from his eyes, I lean forward and press a kiss to the corner of his mouth.

"Are you happy, Kam?" Liam asks. It's not unusual for him to ask me this.

"The happiest." Is as honest a response as I can give him.

A squeal pops free as Liam pulls my body to his and I lose my breath as he tackles my body with tickles. Only when I'm sputtering and begging for mercy does he stop. And what he does after, makes me forget that we were talking about his nerves and what this game means.

My gaze tracks Liam's every movement as he rounds to the back of the pitcher's circle. He's up in the count with only a runner on second and two outs. The score is up in our favor, so this should be the final inning.

I've asked Liam if he can hear certain people in the crowd. He claims he shuts out everything. Which is why he's been so successful at this game. I do wish the scouts took notice of him though. He's been beating himself up that not one has reached out. As his girlfriend, I do what I can to alleviate his worry.

"Here we go Liam. You got this babe!" I watch his deep inhale and the pull back of his shoulders before he steps up to the rubber. He told me that would be his sign that he heard me. In a sold out crowd, knowing that he heard my voice brings warmth to my body.

Liam gets the sign from Chance, places his fingers on the ball that's hidden in his glove, and does his wind-up sending the ball towards home plate. I hold my breath, along with the rest of the crowd, as I wait for the ball to reach Chance's glove. The smack of the ball to his catcher's glove and the resounding "Strike three" from the umpire has the crowd going wild.

Cheering along with my friends and the crowd, I watch from the outfield as the team rushes Liam. This game was huge for them. While Liam said he wasn't nervous, I noticed him triple check his bag before he left for the field. Which he's never done since I knew him.

Our school fight song plays from the speakers as we watch our boys celebrate on the field. They make their way to the outfield where the majority of the student body is congregated to bask in the cheers. Liam and I magnetize our way to each other, stopping at the outfield fence.

"I'm so proud of you." No other words could explain how I feel for him and the team.

He links our fingers together through the fence. "Thank you baby. Are you going to wait around or head back to the house?"

My eyebrows scrunch in confusion. "You're not going out to celebrate?"

"I'd rather celebrate with you."

"Deal." I lean up on my tiptoes to give him a kiss through the fence.

Liam gives me another look before walking back over to

his team. Seeing his happiness for this game makes my happiness his. Laughing to myself as he jumps on the guys I make my way back to Sarah and our group.

"You two are staying in to celebrate, aren't you?" Sarah surmises as I link my arm through hers.

I give her a *duh* look. As much as I love being out with friends, I love staying in with Liam even more.

May 2014

"Can you guys believe that we're graduating today?" Sarah asks our group before we have to line up.

"I didn't think the day would come," I say in all honesty.

Liam wraps his arm around my shoulder and kisses my temple. "But you are. And I am too. And so is Chance."

"You're right. Thank you, baby." I say and lean up to place a kiss on his lips.

"Alright graduates, time to line up." One of the professors says.

"I'll see you after." Liam says and kisses me quickly.

"Of course."

Walking towards the art and fashion department has me feeling all out of sorts. I still pinch myself that I'm graduating on time. I also didn't think Liam and I would be friends again, let alone dating. But these last nine months with him have been more than I could've ever imagined. He was my best friend before all of it. And now we get to go live our lives together for the time being.

"I'm so happy I met you here." Nina says when we get set up in the processional. She was one of the first fashion majors to befriend me. I was worried that jumping into a group so soon, I'd be ostracized. She was even one of my champions for when I skipped the intro level classes.

"So am I. Let's stay in touch okay? We could definitely help each other out."

"Of course." She says and hugs me.

While the last couple of years may have been the most challenging, it has been memorable beyond words.

"Justina Celeteste Pierce." The speaker calls. I clap for my friend as she gets her "diploma"

"Kamryn Michelle Rawlins." The speaker calls for me. "Thank you." I say as I grab my "diploma" and shake hands with the president of the school. I look up in the stands to see mine and Liam's families cheering for me.

Later after the ceremony I head off in search of our family's since they sat together. While en route to my family, I have several professors stop me to tell me about internships. I promised I'd email them all. With this praise from professor's I now consider friends, I'm confident that I made the right choice with my newer major.

When I make my way through the throng of other families celebrating their graduates, I see my boisterous group. "Congratulations!!" I'm bombarded with hugs and handed flowers and leis and more hugs and enough kisses on my cheek to last a lifetime.

"A picture of you and Liam!" My mom tosses out.

"Where is Liam?" I ask looking around. I didn't think he was too far behind me, but he's garnered a following from being the starting pitcher.

"I'm sure he'll be around soon. Let's just take one of you, Kamryn."

I won't say no to that. I hold up my diploma frame and my flowers.

"Taking pictures without me huh?" Liam says in my ear.

"Of course not. You're just on time." I say and turn around to look up at him.

It's been a wild four years. So many ups and downs. But one thing I am eternally grateful for is finishing college with my best friend.

"I love you," Liam tells me. Since I opened the floodgates in December, he says those three words every chance he can.

"I love you too." I smile up at him and lean up on my toes to press a kiss to his mouth. I intend for it to be a quick kiss, but Liam grabs the back of my head to intensify it. Slipping his tongue inside eliciting a moan from me.

"Okay! Okay! Enough of that!" Jax says, breaking us out of our kiss.

The rest of the afternoon passes by without a hitch. We took as many pictures as we could with our families and friends. When the space began clearing out, we went to the obligatory graduation celebration dinner. Our parents began the embarrassing tale of when they first noticed the crushes we had on each other. The walk down memory lane is great, but it has me itching for the future.

Settling into Liam's side and playing with his hand that's linked in mine, I look around at our families. How meshing them together was seamless and effortless. Liam's chest rumbles under my cheek and a smile pulls at my lips. I didn't know how much I'd come to love the sound of his laugh. He's my breath of fresh air and what I never knew I needed. I can't wait for the rest of our life together.

～

"Are you ready to head back?" I ask him as we put the last box in the back of his truck.

"Yeah. Are you ready to live together?" Liam challenges back.

"Of course. I've put up with you since we were seven. What's the rest of my life?"

Liam chuckles before pulling me towards him. We managed to find an apartment not too far out of the city. It's a nice two-bedroom with a workout facility and pool, gate access and assigned parking. Our parents decided to help us out for the first year with rent as we both work to get on our feet.

"Very funny. I'll see you in about ten hours, Ms. Rawlins."

"That you will, Mr. Taylor." I kiss him hard before pushing away and jumping into my car.

Since we left campus later than usual, we got a late start on making the drive back home. So Liam and I made it to our parents houses just before midnight. With all of the driving, we decided it best to wait to move-in once it's light out and we're well-rested.

"Hi Jersey." I say when our black lab greets me at the door. "Don't wake people up." I let him out back to the bathroom while I fill up a glass of water.

It's in the quiet that the doubt creeps in, making me wonder if I'm doing the right thing with Liam. We've only been together not even a year. Even during our last year we stayed with each other as much as possible. Between baseball and my senior project, it was tough. Liam led his team to another CWS win. So we haven't been able to enjoy the whole summer, but what's left of it I'm hoping we'll treasure together.

I'm pulled out of my thoughts by Jersey scratching at the

back door. Tomorrow starts the madness. "Goodnight boy." I say as I pet him and go to my room.

I FEEL like I just fell asleep when my alarm goes off. I stare up at the ceiling in my childhood bedroom. The feeling hasn't sunk in yet that I'm moving out. It's scary.

My phone chimes with a text from Liam.

Liam: Rise and shine sleepyhead.

Me: I'm awake silly. About to get up and get ready. I'll see you at the apartment.

Liam: See you soon.

I'm making the right decision. I know I am. But I can't stop the nagging feeling in the back of my mind that's telling me something isn't right.

I go through the motions at what feels like 2x speed. And before I know it, we're unloading the final box into the living room. The overwhelming sensation hits hard but knowing we have a couple of months to settle in before our new jobs start, takes some of the pressure off.

Liam and I work like a well-oiled machine. Working efficiently in setting up our bedroom as that's the best way to move-in, or so our parents have told us. We set up the living room and mounted the TV on the wall. Which is the number one tester for any relationship. Ten hours later and our apartment is habitable. We're a little sweaty but not stinky but a lot cranky and a lot hungry. We're not 100% unpacked, but the big things have been done and we can breathe a sigh of relief.

After our parents left and a pizza was delivered, it's just Liam and I snuggled on the couch after our showers.

"Are you happy baby?" I ask him.

"The happiest." He responds with a hard kiss to my lips. His kiss softens as I sink into him. The kiss isn't rushed. The kiss isn't a means to an end. The kiss is the start of our new beginning. Liam slides my leg over his lap and pulls me over to straddle him. Our breathing grows heavier as our kisses become more frantic. I slide my hands under his shirt and pull it up his body and fling it behind me. He moans into my mouth as my hands explore his body.

I'll never tire of exploring him. He's always working out and always practicing. Keeping his body in tip top shape for baseball and it makes me a very happy girl. I break the kiss and trail my lips down his body. Nipping at his jaw. Sucking on his neck. Playing with his nipples because it drives him crazy. As I slide down his body, I pull his pajama bottoms down with me as I go. Freeing his erection that now bobs against his stomach. I wrap my hand around him and lower my mouth to his tip. Kissing the head of his cock like I was kissing him.

Swirling my tongue around the tip and flicking at his opening.

"Fuck you're too good at that." Liam groans.

A few months later and we're finally settled into our apartment. It took us most of the summer and partway into fall, but we finally did it.

I managed to get a job at one of the local middle schools teaching. It wasn't ideal, but I'm also grateful that the community college had an opening for a fashion design teacher. So I do that part-time along with the full-time teaching job.

Liam hasn't had it so easy though. He's still waiting for a call-up to the major's but that chance dwindles daily. He continues to work out and hit the batting cages daily. But as each day goes by, he starts to slip further away from me. It's like his happiness is tied to baseball. I get it, but baseball can only last for so long.

With the lack of a call, his appearances at work have been abysmal at best. More times than I can count, his boss has called me letting me know that he's not shown up for work on time and sometimes not at all. I get that call sometimes twice a week and every time I come home, I dread what I might see inside. Like right now.

"Liam?" I call out when I walk through the door. No answer. "Hello?" I know he's home. His truck was in the same parking spot it was in yesterday.

"Hey." He finally replies from his spot on the couch. Headset on for his video game that he plays all of the time. Our apartment isn't exactly big, so I know he heard me the first time.

"Hey. How was your day?" Setting my bag and the mail on the table, I turn to him in hopes that I have his full attention. The hope I had fizzles out as I see his attention still on the TV.

"It was okay."

"That's good."

We've been doing this routine for the past two weeks. I ask about his day and then all of it stops. After I change into something comfortable I come back out to see him in that same spot. With the same focus on the game instead of me.

"Have you given any thought to what I suggested?" I tread lightly because as the days have gone by, Liam has gotten more and more withdrawn. Not just from me and our relationship, but all of his motivation has seemed to have left him.

"No."

"Liam, it's better than nothing."

"It's a pity thought." He bites out.

Huffing out an unamused laugh. "No it isn't. I'd rather you do that, than me come home and see you burning a hole in the couch. I don't want to be in the eye of the storm if you don't get the call that you're hoping for. But maybe if you'd get off your butt and help someone other than your-self, you might get the call that you want."

He's looking at me like I lost my mind. "Says the woman that's teaching instead of designing."

"You think this is what I want to do for the rest of my life too? No. But I have to do something before getting to the big stuff. You don't get that. Nobody hits it out of the park on their first at bat."

"I do. I was destined for the majors."

"You promised!" I yell. "You promised that we wouldn't push the other away if our dreams didn't come true."

Liam smiles and it's one that he gives opponents when they're at the plate. "I guess I lied."

I grit my teeth together so hard I fear they'll crack from the force. I feel the telltale sign of tears threatening to fall, but I will not give him the satisfaction of knowing he upset me. I look at the man I love and it's like looking at a stranger. And instead of giving him more of my words, I turn on my heel and head to our bedroom–slamming the door as I go and locking him out.

∼

IT'S BEEN six months since I've shut down with Liam. He got a call to join a farm team, but he turned that down. Sarah and I told him it was the stupidest decision that he ever made. It led to the biggest fight that we ever had. And for a month straight he moped around the apartment. He called out of work and didn't help out around the apartment. I remember what I told him because it's still so fresh in my mind. The boy I loved is slipping away from me, and I have no idea how to keep him here.

I came home from work more frazzled than ever. That day the students were more intolerable than before. I had endless meetings and the last thing I wanted to do was come home to my boyfriend who thinks his life is over without baseball.

"Liam...I cannot live like this." Pushing away my still full dinner plate, frustration and exhaustion coats every word. I'm so tired. I'm mad. I feel like I've failed in my professional life and the one person I thought would be present to assure me I haven't failed, is focusing on his own failure.

He barely spares me a glance before going back to his phone. "Like what?"

"Like this..." I point around the apartment and then point a finger at him. "I swear if you don't get your life together in one week, I'm out. I'm done. Because I refuse to support you like this."

I stormed out of the apartment after that. It appeared to work. He called the sister high school for the middle school I worked for and started as a TA. He wasn't exactly thrilled, but when the baseball coach approached him for help he didn't turn it down. I guess you could say things are getting better for him. For me. For us.

18

KAMRYN

TWO YEARS LATER

November 2017

"Liam, where do you see us?" I ask him while we're lying in the bed of his truck.

We have a rare warm night for February and Liam called me asking if I'd like to watch the night sky with him. It's where I can see the stars so clearly out here along with the sound of crickets chirping as the soundtrack to our night.

This spot became a bit of a safe place for us. It was the one spot where we could see the sun rise and the sun set. But tonight this night is buzzing with anticipation. Because despite there being no clouds in the night sky, I can't see the stars. I can't see the moon. Gone is the dreamer that's stayed in a stagnant spot too long.

I guess I thought that once Liam and I solidified things it'd be smooth sailing. I expected there to be bumps in the road, because no relationship is smooth sailing. But once the MLB never called him things went kind of downhill. Sure, he's had offers from Triple A teams and he's even coaching, but it's 'not the same'. Sarah and I have both told

204

him to take the offers they give him. But with no guarantee, it was never enough for him. I think that baseball is baseball. Every major league baseball player has started with a farm team.

"I remember that night so clearly." My voice is thick with emotion as I speak. "You said you see a future with me, but when I bring it up you shrink back? Why?"

Out of my peripheral, I see him run his hands down his face out of frustration and pushes himself up to a seated position. He hangs his head and drapes his arms on his knees. "Why do you do this Kamryn? We've been together what, four years?" I nod and he continues. "So why do you keep pushing a future and marriage with us? I thought things were good for us?"

I think about what he's asking from me and I come up with no reason as to why he's suddenly slowing down. I feel completely duped.

"Are you kidding me right now?!" I sit up from where I was laying down. "One of the reasons we're together is because you promised you'd give me that happily ever after that I dreamed of. *You* promised. I spent a year with someone who pushed me aside for his dream and I never thought I'd relive that again. I can't keep sacrificing my dreams just because yours aren't coming true. That's selfish. *Why* do I keep pushing for marriage? Because *you* promised. Because *you* made me, me again. Because *you* brought me back from heartbreak when for the longest time I didn't think I'd get me back. But with you I did. With you I was beginning to see that happily ever after I had always hoped for." I'm exhausted.

I thought we were getting somewhere. I thought we were both moving towards that path together. When we had that big blowup fight a couple years ago, we went to therapy.

Ultimately, we were advised that having separate living arrangements would be for the best. It worked for us. I found a cute little cottage that became my safe space. We started going on dates again. Liam started wooing me again. The butterflies that had vacated my body returned with vengeance and I fell in love with him all over again. The harder he re-pursued me, the easier it was to ignore the bigger plans we had made. We started focusing on the then and now. Not really giving marriage a second thought. But in the midst of our falling back in love, that picture was beginning to look clearer and clearer. That the future I thought was out of reach was so close. The words I thought were just words, were finally backed up with actions. Liam wooed me. Yet it seemed like he hid even the deepest part of him from our therapist and me.

He looks out to the water crashing on the shore and I know that I hit the nail on the head. "I thought that maybe, I'd be enough for you. That you would change your mind about marriage and kids. That what we had would be enough and that you wouldn't want a piece of paper or the picket fence with the two point five kids to make what we have legit. I just don't think I can be the man you need me to be, when I'm not even the man that I want to be." He says looking into my eyes.

"Your nobility is really trying to disguise your actions as manipulation. Is that what that was at the party? You manipulating me into being with you? Finally having me after he was out of the picture? Was any of it real?" I ask with tears burning my eyes and emotion clogging my throat.

"Of course it was real Kamryn!" Liam asks exasperated. "What do you want me to say? That I'm sorry for stringing you along? That I'm no longer the man you thought I was? My mind and feelings have changed. I don't want to get married, and I don't want to have kids. I just want things to be like they are now."

We sit staring at each other with our chests heaving. And just like that the future that I had perfectly envisioned with him was slipping through my fingers. In fact, it's not even in my grasp anymore.

I think back to every single one of our dates. The time and effort in which he planned them out. The promises. The interest. And then I look back at them with new eyes. The dates that never veered off to talks about the future. They always focused on the past and how good college life was. How could I have been so blind? It's like we're walking down mirroring roads where mine is freshly paved and his is littered with potholes.

"If you think I'm happy with the way things are now, then you don't know me at all, Liam. I grew up wanting a husband, a marriage, and a family. I grew up wanting what each of our parents have. I grew up! Did the last two years not teach you anything?."

Is it so wrong that I want to have it all? I keep giving little tiny pieces of myself to those I'm in relationships with. And by the end they're left with all of me. But what about me? What am I left with?

I run my hands through my hair in frustration at a loss of what to do. Tears of frustration finally spill over. Deciding to do the one thing, I wish I didn't have to do. "Liam, I think we should take a break. From us."

He straightens up in a panic. "What?! NO! Kamryn, I love you."

"I love you too, Liam. So much that it physically pains me. Do you remember our freshman year?" I wipe the tears away that have poured down my face and glance over at him to see him nodding whilst looking at me. "Before that dare, I thought that would be it for us. That what our parents saw when they looked at us, was finally happening. But then you ignored me and every text I sent went without response. Oh my god." I say as the sudden realization that he never planned for full commitment. If he could so easily ghost me when he got scared with his feelings, then what did that say about him now?

Liam reaches over to grab my hand but I snatch it away.

"No. Oh my God. I am so stupid." Scrambling to put my shoes on. I can't believe I was so blind to not see it. "We need...no, I need some time. And you need to figure out if you're letting me go or you're letting me in." At what point do you just throw in the towel? At what point do you decide that you've finally had enough?

"Kamryn, if you walk away I don't think I'll come back from this. I won't survive. Just give me some time. Please." The plea in his voice almost makes me change my mind. Because all I see is a scared little boy.

With clear eyes as if I'm seeing this relationship from an outsider's perspective, I give my full attention to the boy who's been in my life since I was seven years old. My lips tremble with new sobs and fresh tears that threaten to steal all the power over this talk. "I can't be the one to make you change. As much as you want me to, I can't. I deserve someone who is willing to meet me halfway and then some. You're not doing that for me Liam and it is exhausting being the one that's all in."

"Baby, please just give us some time. Give me some time, please." Liam pleads with me and I don't miss the tears welling up in his eyes. It's almost enough to make me call the break off. Almost.

But when is too late, too late? Is it when your safety net

is threatening to tear apart at the seams? Because too late can't be when everything is supposed to go right.

I look up into the night sky trying to gather what little strength I have. "Liam, I've already given you four years. If we're completely honest, I've given you almost twenty years. Just give us some space. Give *me* some space. And when you're ready to admit forever is what you want with me, then I'll be there." I give him a lingering kiss on the cheek. "I love you. I will *always* love you. And nothing can change that. I wish I could stop wanting what I want. But I can't compromise my needs for what you think I should want. Call me when your needs and wants, line up with my needs and wants." I slide out of his truck and walk to my car without a glance back.

I'm not being hard on him. If anything, I've been patient with him. Too patient. Should I have walked away those years ago? Should I have given him another ultimatum? Did we rush into this?

My phone rings and I see Jax's name and picture pop up. "Hey, Jax."

"Hey, sissy. What's wrong?"

"I think Liam and I are done." The admission hurts more than I realize.

"What? Why?"

"He doesn't..." The tears break the dam. "He broke his promise to me."

"Kam, I'm so sorry."

I sniffle as tears threaten to fall. "Yeah, so am I."

I once heard that broken promises are just false hopes and full of emptiness knowing that they won't be kept. Is it irrational to hold on to a promise in hopes that you'll be chosen along with it?

19

LIAM

I feel like I'm losing everything and it's all my fault.

Once again, the girl I love is slipping right through my fingers. And this time I have no one to blame but myself.

Of course Kamryn is upset. I promised her everything that night. But how can I hold onto that promise when I can't even keep myself afloat?

In the three days since Kamryn walked away, I've felt like the world was at a standstill. I also felt forgettable. My dream of playing professional baseball is getting further and further out of my reach. Sarah says she's made calls everywhere. They all say that I should start with a Farm Team. I know how grateful I am to get those suggestions. But none of them could guarantee me a spot in the big leagues.

My dreams are out of reach. And I have no one to blame but myself.

My life is falling apart. Instead of reaching out to the girl I love more than anything I'm letting it all slip away. I can't make her happy if my dreams can't come true. But letting her go seems impossible to do.

I'm losing everything. And I have no one to blame but myself.

I pull the shoebox down from the shelf in the back of my closet. Walking back to my bed I open it up. My life with Kamryn is in this box: our past, present, and future resides in this box. I pull out the ring box that's been stashed in this box. I bought the ring over a year ago. We made strides but it was never the right time. I wasn't where I needed to be in my life and that pushed her away. Now I don't know if we'll ever have a 'right time'.

Closing the box, I head out to the living room and grab some pieces of paper and envelopes I know are stashed here from when Kam lived here. Running a hand through my too long hair, I take the paper and envelopes to the table and get to writing five letters. I pour out all of my feelings and regrets to those I know want the best for me. But I've continued to fail them because no matter how much work I put into myself, I don't think it will matter.

I lost everything. And I have no one to blame but myself.

20

KAMRYN

D o you ever get that feeling in the pit of your stomach like something bad is about to happen? You have absolutely no idea what it is, but when that feeling comes true it all makes sense? It's the timing of the inevitable that's eventually going to move towards warp speed.

It's been three days since me and Liam's argument. Three days and not once have I seen his truck in the parking lot when I drive by to go to work. I haven't talked to him and he also hasn't reached out to me. That hurts more than I'd like to admit. But maybe he's decided that our futures no longer line up and he's given me an out.

When I finally catch up with Emily and tell her all that's happened, she's just as shocked as I am. Emily and I have been friends since she moved to Philadelphia from New York in high school. But we got even closer once she started dating James, Liam's best friend.

"He did not say that!?" Emily exclaims in surprise.

"He did. I know what I want. He wanted it too, but something changed with him. It's like when his dreams failed, he decided mine should too. Am I overreacting? Am I being too hard on him?" It's the questions that have been rolling around in my head for the last few days. But I need to voice them outloud.

"Kam, you know that boy adores you. I've talked to Liam and it looked like the stars were put in his eyes every time someone mentioned you. You also have a right to feel the way that you do." Emily says as my phone rings with Liam calling.

For the first time in three days, my heart drops.

"It's Liam." His smiling face looks back at me as my phone is lit up.

"Answer it!"

"Hello."

"Kamryn, you're right. I feel like I've messed up everything with us!" Liam says and I hear the whooshing of cars and trucks going by. "Kamryn, baby, I'm so sorry."

"What the hell man?!" James says in the background.

"Liam. What are you doing? Where are you? Is that James with you?" I'm now completely curious and a little nervous.

"You wanted space, so I think I'll give it to you permanently."

He's so matter-of-fact about our break that it tears me up inside. "That's not what I meant Liam, you know that. I don't want it permanently."

I hear the acceleration of his truck.

"Well, that's what you're getting Kamryn."

"Liam, what are you doing?! That's not what I want! Liam stop the truck!" I yell into the phone. Emily, sensing my fear, is gripping my hand and looking at me with wide eyes because her fiancé is in the truck as well.

"You don't get to tell me what to do anymore Kamryn.

You're done with me. You made that perfectly clear." Liam cries into the phone.

"I'm not done with you Liam! I will never be done with you. I just wanted space...time to think. Time for you to think." I say trying to plead with him to stop the truck.

"Hey, man." James timidly started. "Why don't you pull over and let me drive?"

Emily starts crying because she is just as scared as I am. I heard the roar of his truck's engine and the honking of horns as I'm assuming he's speeding past cars.

"Liam please!" I pleaded with him. "I want you in my life. I need you in my life, just not like this!" I tell him. Plead with him to just see reason.

"It's always up to you. And what you want Kamryn. Well, I'm done thinking about what you want. Doing what you want." Liam sneered.

"Pull the truck over!" James said at the same time I said, "Liam stop the truck!"

The line was quiet for a minute but then we heard it. The sound of James swearing, the screeching of the tires, the crashing, and the crunching of metal hitting something.

And then nothing.

NOTHING MOVES SLOWER THAN TIME. Take a minute on the treadmill. What's actually thirty seconds feels like one whole hour. A microwave minute feels like an hour-long lecture class. But in this case time stopped. It's like that moment in TV shows when something monumental happens to one of the main characters and the world moves in warp speed around them, but instead it's all moving at a normal pace.

Time, in this exact moment, has stopped.

10 seconds.

My phone dropped from my hand.

10 seconds.

I couldn't move.

10 seconds.

I couldn't speak.

10 seconds.

I barely registered Emily hysterically crying next to me. And I vaguely hear the sound of Liam's ringtone and it takes a few seconds for me to move into action.

10 seconds.

"Liam." I scramble to pick up the phone and answer breathlessly. Hoping with every fiber of my being that it's him on the other end of the line. "Liam, if that's you please say something."

"Uh, no ma'am. This is Officer Lake. I was the first on the scene of the accident. Are you a relative?" he asked me. My mind was a cloud of nothing.

"Uh...um. No. I'm his girlfriend." I finally responded. A cold sweat spreads over my body.

The officer cleared his throat. "I'm not supposed to do this over the phone. But ma'am your boyfriend was doing twice the posted speed limit. I chased him as much as I could. As soon as I radioed for backup that's when it happened. We're transporting both passengers to Covington Memorial Hospital if you want to meet them there. But I will warn you, it doesn't look too good for them."

10 seconds.

It was just 10 seconds.

I say nothing in response as I hang up the phone. "Em, they're being transported to Covington. The officer said it doesn't look good for either of them."

10 seconds.

That was all it took for our lives to change forever.

It's the funny thing about time. It either passes you by in the blink of an eye. Or it draws out to where it's moving so slowly that you feel like you've aged at least five years.

But what about when time ceases to exist? You can't go back. You can't magically find the rewind button in hopes that words that already left their mark could be undone.

In this case, time was my enemy. Whatever deity or cosmic God heard my plea just laughed in my face. In this case in time, I had hoped that whatever deity or cosmic God was listening, I hoped that this was some sick and twisted joke.

10 seconds was all it took for me to stop believing in time and the great timing of life.

21

KAMRYN

-Lola Lawrence

Shock

As the phone falls from my hand, my body goes numb as countless memories of us together fly through my mind like a movie reel. Every memory in chronological order. To our first meeting. To puberty changes. To both of us celebrating each other getting our licenses and then our first cars. To graduating high school and going to college together. To us falling in love. To the last time I walked away.

Is it all gone? Are we no longer able to create new memories? Ones where we loved loud and forgave with quiet whispers and sneaking kisses. Is it really all gone? To the future I thought we'd have. To the love that I had hoped would last our lifetime.

The hope that I carry, thinking everything will be okay, tries to say lit. I try to stay hopeful. But the hope dims out as I pray to whoever is listening that this is all a bad dream. That I'm going to wake up. That Liam is going to be the one to call me. But all of the hoping and praying slips through my fingers as I see Emily barely holding on. Her sobs over-taking her body as the realization that her fiancée is gone.

I don't remember the drive in the car or the walk up to the hospital. As the memories of us refuse to stop playing as a montage.

I don't remember anything as the doctor tells us they didn't make it. My crumbling to the floor as the life I had imagined with the boy I'd known since I was seven is ripped from my grasp. The hope that I carried is snuffed out with the realization that this is the reality I'm living. As the tears that I hoped would stop just fall faster as time ticks on.

I don't remember Jax coming to pick Emily and I up from the hospital and taking her back to her apartment before ending at my house. Silent sobs wrack my body as the soul deep ache of losing the other part to your being starts to sink in.

I don't remember any of it. I don't want to remember any of it.

Five days pass me by. Five long days where I lived but I didn't exist. Because I knew that as this day approached, existing would be the last thing on my mind.

There is a light knock on my door as Jax sticks her head inside my bedroom. My sister and Sarah have been my saving grace through it all.

"Kamrny, it's almost time to go," Jax says from my closed bedroom door.

I'm in a motionless state. I don't remember anything that's happened in the last week. I don't remember waking up or getting dressed for the funeral. And I don't even remember the drive to the church where the funeral is being held.

"I'll be right here the whole time." Jax says as she holds my hand and leads us to sit near Liam's family.

I wish I could hit the rewind button to last week. How has it only been five days? It hits harder the closer and closer we get to our seats. I just want to go back. To when I didn't give him that ultimatum. Where I made him tell me his reasoning for breaking his promise. Where I just gave him more time. Time to prove to me that we weren't just settling into a domestic partnership. Time to realize that we could've had it all. Time is ungraspable at the moment when your whole world is crumbling down around you.

Time and the what if crush me as I realize that at the end of the day, none of it truly mattered.

As I sit in the church with trembling lips and silent tears running down my face; I can't help but hate myself for the way that I handled things with Liam. Maybe he was more fragile than I thought. Maybe he was suffering from depression. How could I have not seen it?

Guilt

I wanted to be a psychologist for crying out loud! The self-hatred for myself that I couldn't see his struggles, slaps me in the face. I should have seen it.

I failed him.

I feel like I have this giant Liam-shaped hole in my heart at what I lost with him. All that Liam's family had lost.

The reverend talks about how precious life is. And how every day on this earth is a gift that should never be wasted.

As we get to the cemetery and settle in our seats, family members of his whom I never met tell stories of a boy who was nowhere close to matching what they described about him. Liam's parents were looking at me expectantly when it was time for me to give the last speech. Jax and Sarah give my hands reassuring squeezes before I stand up and walk to the front.

> *"Only people who are capable of loving strongly can also suffer great sorrow, but this same necessity of loving serves to counteract their grief and heals them."*

–Leo Tolstoy

Denial

I close my eyes to steady my heart and calm my breathing. I muster up every bit of strength that I can to spill the words that only sound right on paper.

"When I thought about funerals, I'll admit I pictured this happening in seventy years. I would tell stories of Liam and the life we lived. The children we had. The love we lived for. Never in my wildest dreams did I think I'd be talking about our stories now." I begin as my eyes begin welling up with tears.

"We first met in the second grade. I made him sit next to me because he was the new kid in class and we soon bonded over anything and everything that seven year olds could bond over: bugs (his favorite), who could be the first to the monkey bars at recess (he was faster), who could throw a baseball the furthest (me until I taught him). To who could get their driver's license first (him because he was older than me by two months). From elementary school to high school, we spent all of our free time together. Our parents couldn't separate us." I look at Liam's parents and his sister Angie with a shaky smile on my face.

"From the time we were seven years old, we were inseparable. Our parents teased us about getting married. And when you're seven years old and a girl, boys have cooties. It was just the rule when you were a kid. Marrying my best friend seemed gross, because then I would have to kiss him." I pause and laugh with the sorrowful crowd. "But as we got older I noticed slight changes and then in college I stopped seeing him as a boy with cooties." I look up to the sky knowing that Liam is looking down. My smile is strained as I do everything I can to keep the tears from falling.

"My, oh my how our parents were right. Even though Liam frustrated me to no end, I knew in the end that he was the one for me. He helped put me back together when I never thought I'd be whole again. But unbeknownst to me, I couldn't do the same for him." My voice cracks as the tears I've tried with all of my might to keep from falling, end up falling in rivers down my cheeks.

"I never thought I'd have to say goodbye to my best friend at twenty-five before we got engaged or before we could grow old together." I cover my mouth to suppress my sobs. "For almost twenty years he was the best part of my days. I never imagined I'd have to say goodbye to him at all. Mr. and Mrs. Taylor, thank you for raising an amazing young man. I'm so thankful that I was part of his and your lives, even if it was for a short time. Liam, a part of me wishes that I could just go back in time. I'd remember every single thing that we did together in detail. The last time we saw each other, I told you I loved you. And that I would always love." I finish with tears falling in thick streams down my face.

With a breath of finality, I sit back down as the reverend says a few more heart-warming words. When it comes time, Liam's casket begins lowering into the ground and my tears continue to fall faster than ever. The finality in this final goodbye hits me like a sledgehammer to the face. Sobs upon sobs escape from me. Crippling me from my upright position to hunched over in my lap. Jax pulls my body into hers as if she could take this pain away from me. But knowing that her efforts are futile. One-by-one, and in little groups, people grabbed handfuls of dirt and threw them onto the casket.

Goodbye my friend, my love. Until we meet again.

Depression

Knock! Knock! Knock!

"Come on Kam, open the door!" Jax shouts from the outside.

After Liam's funeral I continued to shut everyone out. I stopped functioning. I stopped living. My company which was just getting started was put on the back-burner. I'm surprised with myself that I'm still half-way functioning.

"Kam, it's been a month. Open up...please?" Jax pleaded with me.

You may be wondering why my sister doesn't just use her key to come inside. Well, I took it off her key ring when she wasn't around and she finally noticed. The last month has been hard on me. I carry a lot of guilt around. Not just for Liam's parents, but for Emily and James. They didn't deserve any of what happened. I spent the past month crying and wondering if there was something that I could've done.

"I'm unsure which pain is worse - the shock of what happened of the ache for what never will."

-Unknown

A week later I hear a different voice pleading with me to open the door. One that I haven't heard since the funeral. One I didn't think I'd hear again. And for the first time in five weeks, I open my door. To my surprise there are two people I never expected to see again standing at my door.

"Hi Mr. and Mrs. Taylor." I say shakily. Tears that I thought had dried up, pool in my eyes and spill over.

"Oh, sweetie." Mrs. Taylor said and pulled me into a big hug. It was then that I let all of my tears go unabashedly. I just cried. For how long? I don't know. Standing in the threshold of my house with the people that were a second set of parents to me.

After a few minutes we move to sit on the couch, when Mrs. Taylor breaks the silence. "I know what you're going through sweetheart. And trust me, it has not gotten easier for us. But shutting out the world is no way to live, Kamryn."

I look up in surprise as if she knew that's what I was doing.

"Jax called us." Mr. Taylor says with a shrug and wraps his arm over my shoulder pulling me into his side. "And that's not the way that Liam would have wanted you to live your life."

I nod absentmindedly just to agree with him. The truth is, I don't know what Liam would have wanted from me. I don't even know what Liam wanted from himself.

Mrs. Taylor places a box she brought on the coffee table. "I was going through Liam's room at the house and his apartment, and brought some things that you might want." She tells me.

When I look up at her, her eyes have glassed over from unshed tears. Liam's and my relationship was rocky but still somewhat stable. When I moved out, I had hoped with every fiber of my being that we could get back to the good place we were in before. It worked for a while. But then it didn't. I have no clue where our paths diverged.

"You don't have to open it now." Mr. Taylor says as they stand to leave. "Just know that our son loved you with all of his heart. And so do we Kamryn. You will always be a part of our family even though he's not around anymore." With final hugs and kisses on the cheek, I see them to the door.

I walk over to the box that's sitting on my coffee table, afraid of what I might find in it. Elbows perched on my knees and hands clasped under my chin, I stare at the box. "Liam you better not have any secrets," I say out loud to myself.

Blowing out a breath, I open it up to find one of his ratty t-shirts that I always slept in, a couple of pictures in frames of us at our high school and college graduations and one of us at my last birthday before he died, a bottle of cologne that I loved when he wore it, and a black velvet box.

And like the moment when I received that phone call,

time just stops. My body freezes until I have no choice but to let a sudden rush of air into my lungs. A choked sob comes out of me. With shaking hands, I open the lid to find a 1.5-carat engagement ring. I cry an earth-shattering cry. I cry for a man who did want to give me the world. I cry for what I lost and what I could have had with Liam. And I cry for all of the guilt that I still feel.

Grief is a funny thing. I shouldn't say it's funny. But it's an unexpected feeling. Where you don't know whether to cry buckets of tears. Or comfort those who are sobbing uncontrollably. Or yell into the void in hopes that this current situation you find yourself is just a bad dream you'll wake up from.

Grief makes you feel things. It makes you uncover those long-forgotten emotions. Tapping into whatever pain that threatens to unweave your carefully structured life.

Grief seeps deep into your body until that's all you know.

I DON'T KNOW how long I laid on my couch with tears slowly flowing when I heard the doorbell ring. When I didn't answer it after a minute a soft knock followed.

"Kamryn. It's Emily," she says softly from the other side of the door.

I sit up and look at the door like it might explode at any second. When she knocks on the door again, I find myself standing up to open the door. With a final cleansing breath, I open the door and see Emily. And when I see her, the tears start all over again and I crumple in on myself. Emily comes in and closes the door before hugging me and crying for all that we've lost.

"I'm so sorry. It's all my fault. I should've seen it." I say through choked sobs.

Emily shakes her head. "No it's not Kam. You were not his fixer. You didn't make Liam get into his truck. You didn't make James follow Liam into his truck either. They were both their own people. Neither you nor I could have predicted that would have happened. Liam should've made the decision to get help on his own. You were not his caretaker. Again, you were not his fixer. And I will keep telling you that until it sticks."

I nod my head because I know she's right, but that still doesn't stop the guilt from nagging at me. I wipe my eyes with leftover tears before I say something to my friend. "That's why I haven't talked to you since it happened. I carry so much guilt because you two were supposed to get married soon. And because of mine and Liam's problems, that got taken away from you. I'm so sorry." I say through a tight throat.

Emily shakes her head with tears in her eyes. "Stop apologizing. Yes, James was my soulmate and one true love. I'll miss what I was supposed to have with him. And I don't know if I'll ever have that with someone else. But he wouldn't want me wallowing in his loss. I know that he'd want me to move on, to live my life and be happy. And I know Liam would want the same for you. So let's move past this, Kam. We have to move past this. Not just for them, but for us."

Anger

For the last few months, I've been seeing my therapist on a consistent basis. As open as I am, it was hard for me to let out all that I was feeling about losing Liam. In my sessions I was either crying, or silent and watching the clock tick away; or my mind was just empty. My therapist thought that it'd be good for me to go and visit Liam's grave. Tell him all that I had been telling her. That even though I might feel dumb for sitting and talking to a rock, that he's actually listening. So that's where I'm at now.

It wasn't hard for me to find Liam. It's weird, but even in death I'm drawn to him.

When I walk up to the grave I place some fresh flowers down. Nothing too girly because I know he wouldn't like it. I look down at his grave for a few seconds and then take a seat in front of him.

"I know I should've come a long time ago. I just couldn't. It's been too hard on me. But I'm guessing you already knew that." I take a cleansing breath to get my thoughts back in order. "I've been seeing our therapist again. Well, I guess it's my therapist now. It's actually been somewhat good for me. She said that instead of me venting all of my frustrations out on you to her, I should just come to you. But isn't that what therapy is for? They ask the questions, and I answer them?" I huff out a bitter laugh.

I look across the cemetery. The leaves sporadically, falling as if the dearly departed are sending silent messages to their loved ones on earth.

"It wasn't supposed to be like this, Liam. We were supposed to grow old together. Be happy. Have kids and a marriage. A lifelong friendship. But you were just so damn selfish. I hate that you thought this was the only way out.

That you not only took your life, but you took James's life. You took Emily's fiancé away from her. You took another family's son and brother and grandson away from them."

I slap my hand over my mouth as a sob escapes. "I just wanted you to know that I'm so angry at you. Why, Liam? Why did you think it would be so easy for me if you weren't around anymore? Is it because you knew you couldn't give me what I wanted? Because I have the ring you were going to propose to me with. How long were you going to wait? Did you not think I would have said yes? Did you not think you were good enough? I would have said yes. You knew this. You knew I wanted this with you. You put me back together when I thought I would have been broken forever." I take a cleansing breath and swipe away the tears. "I'm sorry. I don't want to yell at you. I do want to say that I will wear the ring. Your ring for as long as I can. It is everything that I hoped it would be. And then I'll be moving on. I need to try to move on by letting you go. One day I'll bring my kids here and tell them about you. I may even introduce you to my future husband. Who knows what the future holds for me now. I'll love you forever Liam. Goodbye."

Acceptance

Emily was right. The next few months were not easy in any way. In fact, the rest of the year was anything but easy. I got through the hardest period of my life. It was a slow start, but I did it. I buried myself in restarting my company. Sarah and Jax made sure to be there for Emily and me whenever we needed them. I haven't talked to Liam's parents since they came to my house that day all those years ago. And I'll admit that things got pretty dark for a while.

I wore the engagement ring that Liam picked out for me for about a year afterward. But when I was talking to my therapist, she suggested that it wasn't healthy but that I shouldn't rush moving on. When I finally took the ring off, I had an emergency session with her. I figured she'd be better to go to than to go to a bar; which I still did.

I still have periods of time when I just lock myself in my house and cry. I'm told that's normal. Depression isn't something you kick out the door when you have a good day.

During that grieving period, I sought an outlet I tucked away for too long. Fashion. Through my grief and working on myself, my therapist told me the best way to find joy is doing what I love to do. And with the endless encouragement from my family and friends, my brand finally took off. I named it Ryn & Co., which is what Liam used to say when my sorority sisters and I would go anywhere together. It's a bit like having him with me.

And I'm still riding the high of now finishing my third New York Fashion Week. I'm hearing great things about the line from critics, but now it's time to start putting the finishing touches on my spring line for its debut.

They say that time heals old wounds. But what about the new wounds? Or what about the old wounds that never truly healed? They just had a layer of tissue paper on them. I always knew that time and love were finicky things. I just never knew how finicky.

PART II

22

MASON

TWO YEARS LATER

September 2019

"You're being traded Brooks." My coach says as soon as I sit in his office.

Not what I expected on a Tuesday morning. This sudden news has me more off guard than it should and I'll need to rip into my agent for not keeping me in the loop.

"When? Why?" I ask, getting a little ticked off. I'm also trying to mask my hurt, but I feel like it's coming off more like a child whining. I've been playing in the league for almost eight years. I just turned thirty last month and am in my prime. I've continued to get stronger and in turn that's helped me become one of the best QB's in years.

These past eight years have been some of the most challenging in my life, it's also been enjoyable but again, far from easy. The training my first year knocked me on my ass. And then the practices were grueling. During the three months of training camp my rookie year, I always went back to my apartment and crashed. On top of my rookie year I was still heartbroken. I rarely went out. I hung out with some of the rookies when interviews would be held at the facility. And some might have even called me a monk because I hadn't even touched a groupie or glanced in the direction of any woman. I'm a one woman type of man, and the only woman I want likely still hates me.

I wasn't completely celibate. But when I needed a release, one night stands were my go-to. Just never in my personal space. I also always made sure that I never led any of my hook-ups on. And trust that many of them tried their hardest to get me to be the one to change for them. But my heart would never be in it though. Those women deserved more than someone who never had more than an inch of their heart to give.

My coach's goodbye speech brings me back. "They're making the announcement tonight. Cincinnati just lost their number one QB to a career ending injury and the backup has lost three games in a row. Badly. And the rookie that they do have is nowhere near ready. We have a good QB roster thanks to you. You've helped lead this team to some impressive wins and two Super Bowls. You should be proud. Carolina is proud of you."

It's on the tip of my tongue to suggest that one of them be traded. But that's not how this game–this business works. And as the words "you're being traded" continue to sit heavy in my mind, I have an out of body experience. My limbs feel like they weigh a ton, my tongue feels glued to the roof of my mouth, and my mind feels as if I'm walking through the world's thickest fog. I can't get my thoughts together as I realize my time here has come to an end.

"Thank you, sir," I reply slowly.

"You're welcome. I know your agent will talk to you as he's already been made aware of what's happening."

And that's exactly why I'll need to have it out with my agent. I pay him a great deal of money to not let news like this happen without my knowing.

My coach continues, "Now the deal is a five-year contract with the option of a two-year extension. You'll be playing for the five-year contract with a worth of $290 million and if they pick you up for the two-year option it'll be a guaranteed $60 million. If you do happen to get injured, they have the option to buy you out, but that's fairly unlikely. They're already putting a lot of money on you. Which is a good thing. Cincinnati has a ton of cap space so you shouldn't have to worry about that. Now you'll be given a lot of hate by fans because you'll be one of the highest paid QBs in the league. But I have faith in you Mason. Now get out of here. Go home and start packing."

In a daze I stand up and shake my coaches–well now former coaches and owners hands. Carolina was the team that drafted me right out of college. Surprisingly, I've been here since then which is rare for anyone who plays this game. My family loved that I was so close to them and so did I.

But I also felt like I was too close to her.

I'll never tell anyone this, but I kept tabs on her. Or I at least tried to. It was hard. While I was getting ready for my rookie year, I was still mourning a very hard heartbreak. I heard through the grapevines that she was struggling and that she avoided a lot of social activities. Which seemed strange to me since she was the social chair for her sorority. And when word got back to me that she had moved on with Liam, it stung. But it had been well over two years since I had ended it with her. And I came to the conclusion that if I would have wanted her to move on with anyone, it would be with him. Because I knew that he could take care of her.

Until the accident happened. And it no longer seemed right to keep an eye on her.

That news shook those of us who went to college with him. My phone lit up with text messages asking if I talked to Kamryn. I hadn't but I had to play aloof because saying that she and I hadn't talked since before I was drafted makes it seem like I cut her out of my life. Which was the furthest thing from the truth. But I was at the funeral, hiding in the back because making my presence known during a time she lost someone she loved would've made it a selfish move. And that was not the time for me to give her a shoulder to cry on. I have no idea what happened in their relationship, but I respected her grief.

But watching her speech to him. The way she continued to break as each word poured out of her beautiful mouth, it tore me apart. Each tear that fell, I wanted to storm up to the podium and hold her. But I couldn't. Because she wasn't mine to hold. So I stood in the back helpless and watched as she broke. And then I watched as she was yelled at by one of Liam's best friends. It took everything in me not to step in and punch the living daylights out of him. But when the funeral was over I walked away. And since that day, I did what I could to push her from my mind.

One thing that has me questioning this move, is that she and I always talked about settling down in Cincy. It appealed to both of us. It had the sports, the nightlife, the culture, the city life and the suburban/ family life. I don't know if she ever moved there. If she stayed in Philly or moved out west. I have no idea.

Like I said, I stopped checking up on her. For my sanity and healing, I needed to.

"Hey, Mom."

My relationship with my Mom was tense when I started

my rookie year. I don't think she understood the heartache that I endured so I kept her at a distance the first year and it shifted the family dynamic for a while. Over the years my resentment towards her faded and in its place is a solid mother-son relationship. I kept my siblings out of the loop with that part of my life as they didn't need to be in the crossfire that was my life at the time. But it didn't stop the texts from my siblings asking if I was coming home when I had breaks during the off-season.

"Hey sweetheart. What's going on? Shouldn't you be at practice?" My family also knows my practice schedule should they need to get in touch with me at the last minute.

"I should. But I just got word that I'm being traded."

"What? Where? Why?"

I snuff out a quiet laugh. "Yeah. Cincinnati. Apparently, the starting QB is out for the rest of the season and the backup QB has lost three straight games. I don't know. It's all a business."

"That it is. I'm sorry Mason." Sadness is laced in her voice. She loved that I played close to home. It's not that I went home frequently. But having the option to pop in for a visit when I needed a break from football was welcome.

"It's alright. Well, hey, I gotta go. I need to call my realtor and see if she can find something for me fast." I tell her when I stroll down the hallway.

"Okay. I'll talk to you soon. I love you."

"I love you too, Mom."

As I finish cleaning out my locker, I'd like to say that a rush of emotions hit me. Like a montage of my time playing here plays behind my eyes. But it never comes. While I'm sad to be leaving the team that's been my home for the last almost decade, I'm excited to try a new team. Like my coach said, I've done all I could for them and it's time for me to try somewhere else and leave my mark there.

~

THE MOVE TURNED out to be relatively smooth. All I needed to do was call a moving company and they packed up what I couldn't do on my own.

My realtor found something outside of Downtown Cincinnati so close to the stadium that I could walk. It's been a few days and I'm now as settled as I can be in my new place when I see a magazine based on local talent. It's a blog type magazine where it focuses on local talent or talent that moved here and is now picking up.

The article is doing a feature on the company called Ryn & Co. The designer began putting it together in her last two years of college, but it fell to the back burner before she could get it funded. Then she had some personal life changes that ended with her scrapping the entire brand as a whole. Until one day she picked right back up where she left off, and her company has only gotten more successful. She's been all over the place for work and even did three shows in New York for fashion week. The article was truly enlightening. Until I flip the page that identifies the designer. *The face of Ryn & Co is none other than Ms. Kamryn Rawlins.* It goes on to highlight her accolades and gives a picture tour of her office. She's even more beautiful than she was in college. When I notice the baseball and football stadiums flanking her in the background, my heart thumps an erratic beat.

In my shock of this being her interview, it hits me that she did move here and she's made a successful name for herself. In the upclose picture, I don't see a ring on her finger, but that doesn't mean she's not dating anyone. That tiny spark of hope tries to ignite itself so that one day we could reconnect. The other part of me fears that if she is dating someone else that our time to ever be an us again, is truly over. But as I look at her face in the picture, it's clear that she looks sad. And worn down. Like she hasn't had any time to absorb the changes that happened to her.

As much as I dread seeing her, I'm also clinging on to the little bit of hope that tries to ignite.

Will she be angry? Of course she will. I expect nothing less.

Will she cry when she sees me? God, I hope not.

That time with us on the bridge still haunts me. I can still see the tears that stream down her face. Hoping that the words I'm spewing are that of a lie.

My phone beeps with a text from some of the guys I played with my rookie season that got traded here around my fourth year at Carolina. They said there's a new dance club and they're going to if I want to join. I'm not usually a club go-er, but it's a way to get my feet wet in this city. The group chat popped off when they got the news that I was being traded here. It makes coming to a new team easier as the chemistry we had those first few years in the league was something out of textbook football.

Me: Time and I'll be there.

Jordan: 10:30

Me: Great

On my short ride from the airport, I noticed how eclectic the city was. Whilst it was still early that people were still at work, what I saw when I was driving through got me excited. I'll have to reach back out to my realtor to see if she has any recommendations for me to venture around to. What I loved most about living in Charlotte was how the city would block off the streets every weekend with vendors and small businesses that would set up shop for the day.

I shake myself out of the one day possibility of roaming the city without anyone causing too much fanfare over seeing me in public. It's the one down-side to being an athlete and having your face advertised all around the city you play for. Although, since my trade hasn't been made public, that shouldn't be too difficult for now. I like being able to roam the streets anonymously. And that is one thing I miss about college. I'm aware that comparing apples to oranges doesn't work. But playing in college and being able to walk around freely, was a breath of fresh air.

My phone buzzing with another incoming text makes me realize I just spent the last thirty minutes daydreaming. I toss the magazine onto the coffee table and make my way to the primary suite. I'm a man that likes living simple and I know that's hard to do when I have the money that I do. But I have to hand it to Arabelle, my realtor, that she set me up in a good spot. Since I needed a place to live and not a lot of time to do that, she found a highrise with some of the sickest views I've seen.

Since the apartment was inspected last month, we were able to waive all the contingencies. With me paying in cash, the apartment was mine in no time. She helped me with my last place and knew I liked living in places that exude warmth. Instead of marble floors throughout, my place has hardwood floors throughout the main living space with new carpet in the bedrooms. The newest technology is fitted throughout and I made a deal with myself to learn the system. I have my iPhone and that alone was a task to get used to from a Blackberry.

I get ready in no time. My clothes are already hung up in my closet and in the dresser, so getting dressed is easy.

Jordan: Headed to the club.

Me: Headed there shortly as well.

I take a deep breath and walk out the door to a city that's set to welcome me with open arms.

23

KAMRYN

"Kamryn, let's go!" My sister shouts at me from downstairs.

"I'll be down in a second Jax." Spitting hair out of my face after responding to my sister. "Alright zipper, all you have to do is zip up without splitting." I cheer for myself as I put my boots on. I mentally add wider calf boots to my to-do list to make. I swear companies have a thing against women with curvier and athletic bodies. My calves are not small as I kept up with my running that I started in college and added boxing back into my fitness routine. I spritz the finishing touches of perfume on before I bound down the stairs.

"It's about time. I've been waiting forever." My sister says exaggeratedly to me.

Ignoring my sister's quip, I make sure Lucy and Poppy, my golden retriever and black cat, don't have to use the bathroom and that they both have food and water for the night. When they're all set I grab my clutch and keys off the table then walk out to my car without waiting to see if my sister is following behind me.

It's been two years since my life was completely

changed. I won't lie and say that I've been able to cruise by without any emotional blips. The first year after Liam's death was hard. My growth these past two years have been a rollercoaster at best. There were times when I doubted every action I made. There were times I was tempted to call it quits on everything and stay in my hometown.

I made it a year post-Liam when living there became too suffocating. Pennsylvania haunted me and everywhere I went I saw him. Every move I made was calculated. With as large a size as the town that I lived in, I couldn't breathe. I felt as if I was back in college and the whispers just wouldn't stop.

My therapist preached to me about the ability to grow. So I put that growth into action and I moved out further west. I'm still close to my parents. They're a short two hour flight or a nine hour drive if I need to really think. But I couldn't stay there. I couldn't force myself to relive that horrific day. Because that's exactly what I did.

For weeks, the sound of that phone call played on a constant loop. I couldn't drive that stretch of the highway without hyperventilating. Anytime I heard the phone ring, my mind would flashback to that day. For weeks, I isolated myself by replaying mine and Liam's last interaction. If I stopped asking him the big questions, would he have surprised me with big answers?

Some days the *what if* narrative haunts me when my thoughts go dark and I wonder if my actions during that time of my life could have been different.

What if. What. If. What...if.

If I had let the *what if's* win, my brand would still be something written on pages. The pages slowly yellowing until they were just dreams on pages. I would have never been able to find an investor to take a chance on me. I would have never had the success that I do now. So I can't focus on the *what if's*, because then I wouldn't have what I do now.

But most days are like today.

I'm indifferent to how I'm feeling most days and unfortunately to those around me. My mind is not a healthy place to be most of the time and I work on it weekly with my therapist. She is confident that one day life will just glow again. I've had it once and I hope that I can have it again.

There are several ways in which my life has changed. I don't visit CSU anymore, even though being a Kappa Beta alumna, it's highly encouraged that alumni visit once a year. But I just can't do it. After losing Mason and then Liam–that place holds too many memories I never wish to revisit. I stopped doing a lot of things that used to bring me joy. I haven't sung in public since after Liam died. A lot of things I did in my daily life were tied to my bond with him. The past me and the me now, are just two completely different people. But isn't that just part of growing up? Isn't that just life? Growing up and moving on? Because I can't think of anyone who has the same hobbies or interests from high school, and even college, as they enter their late twenties.

I tap my mind along to the song floating from the speakers when Jax turns volume down, breaking me from my not so upbeat thoughts. "You know Kam, I really wish you'd reconsider going away with me for a while. I need a break before I start recording again. I think it would really be good for you. Or even just a vacation. You could use it."

"I don't know Jax." I chance a glance at her and then focus back on the road. "It's not that easy for me to go out of the country or take a vacation. And I've got stuff here I need to work on."

A vacation? I'm trying to remember the last time I did that? Maybe college if I'm being honest. Or even a few years after that. The encouragement to sit and relax with my thoughts now sounds more like torture. On top of running my brand, I have other behind the scenes deals and meetings that require me to stay in the states. Meetings and deals that have been lined up for weeks and sometimes months in advance, aren't things I can easily reschedule. If I wish for my brand to be recognized for more than just clothes, but the message that I hope it spreads, then I can't just leave the country for some rest and relaxation.

In the few years that my brand has been up and running, it's been noticed by celebrities and politicians alike. From seeing my clothes on TV shows and movies, to being tagged on social media. It's something I always dreamed of. I know how much a simple clothing item can make someone's day brighter. So when thinking of what to name each item, I went with inspiring words that I repeat daily and use as calming words. And I like to be involved in all aspects of my brand. I mean, I started this as a one-woman show. From the sketching, sewing, cold calling, cold emailing, and social media. Being busy meant I had very little downtime and I liked that. But now I have a team behind me, and while I still keep my hands in every aspect of my company, those in my life would say I'm no longer run haggard.

When my company continued to get the recognition I dreamed of, and not just by the locals here, influencers reached out with praise for what I'm doing with the clothes I was designing. That got us more recognition than I ever dreamed and blew my short and long-term goals I had for my brand out of the water. I ended up having to shift and speed up my plans by reaching out to smaller and bigger influencers that it urged me to make an immediate session with my therapist to not spiral. It was a tough decision on my part, but I added a dedicated team of influencers to my PR team along with a handful of the working class. I didn't want unattainable expectations to be why my clothes don't sell. So my PR team gets a perfect mix of high-end and affordable clothing.

What I love most about what I'm doing is twice a month we hold events that cater to giving sewing lessons at the local women's shelters in the area and donating to clothing drives. I told myself that when my brand got to a certain status, I would give back. It took a few months for the events to gain traction. But with the help of social media and news channels covering the events, we've expanded more than I could have dreamed.

I'm always busy and trying to find the best way to not lose sight of why I love my job. But like I said, while I'm so grateful for what I have, some days I'm just indifferent to the world around me.

Jax scoffs unladylike. "Kamryn, that is the biggest line of bullshit! You just got back from Fall Fashion Week, your Spring line is complete, and you're already months ahead on your next fall line. You're like a robot. Still going through the motions. What is really keeping you here that you can't pause for a couple of weeks?"

I swallow past the lump in my throat and focus on the road. "Don't push me Jax. Other people depend on me. I don't ask you to stop your work, so please don't ask me to stop mine." I tell her, holding on to my quick anger.

I'm not good at just leaving whenever. Moving out here was already a big step as I was settled in my little cottage. My job worked for me, I knew what times to leave my house to avoid traffic, and the same for when I left for my college teaching class. I thrive on a routine and to just pause that for however long someone wants me to, makes it easy for my anxiety to take over.

"I know you don't want to talk to me about what happened Kam, but maybe text one of Liam's friends and see if they'll talk to you." Jax suggested.

What my sister doesn't know is that I already tried that. I reached out to Chance as he and Liam were the closest. That conversation didn't go well. Understandably though. He was upset with the loss of his best friend. I was the easiest target so he verbally took out his anger on me. Not that I blame him as I managed to keep my anger bottled up. But have I really let it out? Or did I just stuff it away in a little box and hope it never resurfaced? The not resurfacing option is the best bet. I haven't opened that can of worms since that day. And I refuse to do that with my sister around. She doesn't deserve anymore of my wrath.

"Can we please talk about something else? Rehashing the past is the last thing I want to do, today of all days. I just want a fun night out with you and my friends and just forget for a while." I frustratedly tell my sister.

"Okay, Kamryn." My sister says and turns the music back up.

I love my sister, don't get me wrong. But there were just so many other things that I never told her about what happened between me and Liam. We had our issues. With me and Liam, commitment was our biggest issue. Well, his biggest issue. Most people think tying yourself to one person isn't the most important thing in the world. But some people are wired for that lifetime commitment. And unfortunately, some people are not wired for a lifetime commitment to one person. I'm that person who's wired to be committed to someone for a lifetime.

Still I can't help but dwell on the past and wonder what

would have happened had Liam and I not shared that kiss in the cafeteria. Would he and I have maintained the brother-sister relationship? Would we have unconsciously drifted towards one another? Or would I always have that *what if* thought lingering in my head? I think unconsciously he and I were always going to be drawn to the other because we became each other's safe spaces.

It was never strange to me that I had a best friend of the opposite sex. I can't say the same for other people. Because Liam and I never had the need to try to date as we already spent most of our time together. Which, to most, is the natural progression anyone in our position would have taken. Somehow any time either of us tried to date in high school, the other person would and could never measure up. And after a while, those relationships would shrivel up leaving it just Liam and I again. But when my hand was forced in college, I knew...something just clicked. I went into our FWB arrangement with the intention to test our physical compatibility. But the hotter we burned the quicker we fizzled.

Some days I try to picture where and what my life would look like if he were still alive. Would he have been called up? Would he have proposed to me? Would we have moved out here? I have so many unanswered questions that float through my mind on a daily basis. The *what if's* that plague me when the silence in my mind gets to be too much. It's those continual questions that leave the rest of our drive strained.

We get to the restaurant with the sound of the radio breaking up the silence. I hate having disagreements with my sister. Especially when we're set to have a celebratory night on the town.

"Jax, I'm sorry." I tell her when we park and turn off the

car. My sister and I used to have a relationship that wasn't overly lovey, but if it came down to it we'd be there for each other in a heartbeat. It took us until a few years ago to finally find common ground with each other. But who would have thought it took heartbreak for that to happen?

"Don't be." She says and unbuckles her seatbelt, then turns to look at me. "I shouldn't push you. And when you refuse, that should be enough of an answer for me."

We share a forgiving smile that only siblings seem to understand before she's leaning over and kissing me on the cheek and then sliding out of the car.

24

KAMRYN

"I'd like to propose a toast to my best friend Kamryn for finishing an amazing fashion week. And for finishing up her work on her upcoming spring and fall lines. Kam, we are so proud of you. You set your mind to something and got what you wanted. Congrats, Kammy." Sarah toasts me to our group. We all clink glasses and I send a wink to her.

One blessed thing that came out of college was my solid friendship and sisterhood with Sarah. She has seen me at my lowest and me at my highest, she's never one to judge me for my decisions, she was there for me when I thought I had no one, and she helped me when no one else bothered to. I owe her more than just my undying friendship. I owe her my life.

We chat through dinner and traipse down memory lane. We plan what bars and clubs to hit, while praying this night doesn't end in disaster.

The night is still young. We started at a restaurant I was recommended to by a few of my employees and make our way up the strip to the other bars. The girls said they wanted to celebrate all my hard work on the line, but I know what they're playing at. They're trying to get me to let loose and completely move on. It's rare that I ever have a night out. I'm took focused on working and researching for my next lines to think about letting loose. The truth is that I'm terrified that one wrong move will send me back to who I was the year after Liam passed. I was a monster and an expert at self-destruction to my life. And I unintentionally hurt those who meant the most to me. But luckily my sister and two best friends stuck it out.

After two more glasses of champagne and some too sweet shots, we make our way down the strip to a few of the bars. We flirt with college guys whose egos don't know when they're fighting above their weight class and Emily challenges Sarah to get two numbers before we get to the dance club. The overachiever in her gets three numbers and causes us to break out in laughter. And after an over dramatic goodbye to the bar, we make our way to one of the best dance clubs in the area.

This dance club specifically opened up about a year ago and it's grown exponentially. Their marketing team has had visitors from all over the state and it's a place where you can be free to be yourself. As rare as it is, celebrities and athletes will make an appearance or two here. But this club is mainly for those that are looking for a place to forget about the long work week. When the bouncer sees us walking up, he waves us on through. The groans of displeasure from those waiting in line are hard to ignore. But it's all about who you know that grants you direct access.

"Thanks Frankie." We all shout as we walk past him.

We walk down the dark hallway that leads to the club. The DJ is playing an awesome set and the beat flows through my body. I scan the area in hopes of finding an empty section when the owner walks up to us.

"Mike, how are you?" I greet the owner with a hug and a kiss on the cheek.

I knew Mike from back in high school. He was a couple years ahead of me, but we still ran in the same circle. Coincidentally he played football too and was an offensive lineman and played at PennU up until his sophomore year but was forced to stop playing after breaking his leg and tearing his ACL. I felt terrible for him. He was always my favorite teddy bear standing at 6'6" and almost 300 pounds. His talent on the field was unmatched and I knew he was destined for the NFL. We kept in touch and always made it a point to get dinner when I was home from college. Except for those unfortunate summers when I locked myself away from the world. When I found out we lived in the same city, I reached out to him. With both of us being business owners, we make it a point to host events together. Networking is key to keeping your business in the mouths of those who can never seem to shut them and I have dinner with him and his wife once a month. They give me a sense of normalcy in a world that's not so normal.

"Staying busy as always. Congrats on the last show." He says as he wraps his arm around my shoulder.

"Thank you." I tell him.

"I've been meaning to ask how you've been. I know we haven't seen each other in a while, but I wanted to make sure you were okay." Mike says as he leads us to our roped off section.

The anniversary of Liam's death is coming up. It's a date I dread and I'm hoping that's not the case this year. My coping mechanisms are much better as therapy has given me a lot of tools that I now use on a daily basis. The inspiring words are one.

"You know–" I start as I lean into him. "It hasn't been easy but I'm trying not to focus on what's coming up even though it's hard." I end on a shrug.

Mike pulls me in for a hug. "Well for what it's worth, I think you're doing great kiddo."

I squeeze him before letting go. "Thank you."

Mike makes a point to tell us this section is ours for the night and that our drinks are on the house. We all loudly protest, but him having the most gracious heart in the world refuses to take our money.

Jax pops the top on the bottle of Dom Periogn that has been icing and hands out the flutes.

"To an amazing night. To all of the dancing our feet can take. To friendship. And to no regrets." Jax toasts.

Our waitress comes over to get our drink orders and supply us with water. My gaze takes in the energy of the club as the DJ plays a mix that has the beat flowing through our bodies as we dance in our roped off section. When our new drinks are dropped off at the table, we down the shots and then chase them with something stronger. I'm officially at the buzzed level of the night.

Sarah is the one that gets us out of our small bubble. She leads us to a somewhat open section on the dance floor. Laughter is drowned out by the music. People are dancing all around us with not a care in the world. And after the busy year I've had I use it to my advantage. Doing my best to forget about work and upcoming meetings. I close my eyes and let the music wash over me.

I startle as hands land on my waist when the DJ switches to a song that has a heavier beat. Tentatively, the stranger molds our bodies to each other. It's not dirty or romantic. It's almost platonic in a sense. Well, as platonic as grinding in a club can be. I've never been one for dancing with a stranger in the club, but nothing some innocent dancing can't solve. My mind goes back to the trashy reality TV shows I would watch when strangers would hookup in clubs. Do people still do that? Why am I entertaining it?

My eyes close as the DJ switches up the mood by playing Chase Rice's *Ride*. A sultry and sexy cover of the original. Our fast grinding goes from frantic to sensual. Chase Rice sings about riding all night. Our bodies roll and gyrate. Our hands crossed across my torso. My head falls back against his shoulder as his head falls into the crook of my neck. Soon he brings one of my hands up to curl around his neck to anchor us from head to toe. It's almost as if we're the only two to exist. I scold myself that it's only dancing. That he's a random guy. But as hard as I try to wrap my mind around that I'll never see this guy again, my mind tricks me into thinking I will.

As soon as the song ends, my mystery dance partner says, "You wanna go get a drink?" I nod my head and grab his hand as he leads us off the dance floor. I turn to my girls and make a drink motion to let them know where I'm going. I get a thumbs up and an inappropriate hand gesture from Sarah that has me barking out a short laugh and shaking my head at her antics.

As we make our way to the bar all I can think is that this man is tall. Like just about 6'5" to my 5' 5". His body looks like that of a professional athlete with his hair shaved in a nice fade and the curls that are just slowly growing out on top. His brown skin complements what I've seen of him so far...if only I could see his face. It seems he doesn't drip money obnoxiously like other guys I've come across, but he most definitely isn't a cheapskate. It's one of my many talents as a designer. Singling the fakes from the real ones. And he most definitely is a real one.

When we get up to the bar he pulls me to stand in front of him so that he's caging me in. The bartender sees us and asks us what to drink. "I'll take a French 75, please."

I note his watch which is a top of the line Rolex and forearms adorned with tattoos. I can't make them out fully in the dim club lighting, but I see the streaks of black that's inked his skin.

"And I'll take a Jameson and ginger ale." Is what I think I hear but the music drowns out his response.

Not a bad choice in a drink either. The bartender nods to our orders and we thank him.

"So..." I start and turn around to look at the mystery guy. My eyes bulge out of my face. I'm almost convinced I'm seeing things. "Mason?!!!" I screech.

Time ceases to stop. And not in a way that a first kiss seems to always do. But in a face-the-reality stop. In the seeing of the person that broke you for the first time in years, time stops. Over the sound of the club music, I distinctly hear the bartender put our drinks down behind me. In a haste I break free from the cage his arms created and I walk away from the bar without grabbing my drink.

How? Why? Mason and I–well we know how that story unfolded. It was, he was, all-consuming in a way that I never knew could be. I don't know if I'll ever get over the betrayal of him stringing me along for months just to break up with me to pursue his dream of becoming a professional athlete. After that, he was like a ghost. Sure I heard the whispers of how he made it. But what they said afterward, I tuned them out. He broke me and then he was gone with no apology. Not even a phone call later on to make sure that I was okay.

But seeing tonight of all nights, him brings that pain right back to the surface.

"Kamryn, wait up!" Mason yells out.

Realization that we're in a crowded club rushes back to me and I slow down to compose myself, when I should just keep walking. I turn around and look at him with annoyance all over my face. He holds my drink out to me and I reluctantly take it.

"May we go somewhere and talk? Please? I'd love–I have some things that I want to say to you," Mason says in a rush.

This is what I've been waiting for. A chance for me to get years worth of hurt off of my chest. A chance to hear what he needs to say. What he should've said years ago.

I raise a perfectly plucked eyebrow and hold my arm out as a gesture for him to lead the way. Mason leads us outside to an isolated area of the rooftop area of the club and motions for me to sit on a bench as he sits next to me. I take a sip of my drink and wait for him to explain.

"First, I want to say how sorry I am about Liam."

Not how I thought he would start this. My armor slips a little before I lock it back down. Because of course he heard about Liam. You couldn't escape the news of his passing. Our university's Facebook page did a memorial post to him and ESPN reported on him for days. Looking at Mason from the corner of my eye, I nod. "Thank you."

He runs a hand roughly down his face and blows out a breath before getting back to explaining himself to me. "Okay. Here it goes. I never should've let my coach dictate my personal life. I never should have walked away from you."

It's like the sudden stopping of a record. The unmistakable and horrendous scratch before nothing but silence is all that greets me. Of everything I thought he would say, I didn't think he would say this.

"Do you remember the night we met?" He asks out of everything.

I nod. How could I forget? We talked for hours.

"That night, you knocked me on my ass. Everything I thought I knew and planned for got tossed out the window because all that mattered was you and football. I fell hard and fast, because I knew that you were my future. But when my final year rolled around and I got told what to do in order to secure my future–Kamryn, you have to know that I would have thrown it all away for you."

My eyebrows fly to my forehead as he tells me all of this. And while it hurts to hear as it takes me back to that time, I'm glad he's telling me.

Mason leans forward and rests his elbows on my knees, giving me no choice to look away from him. "Do you remember that next week? Us running into each other?"

I nod again because he flustered me more than anyone ever had.

"I saw you walk past the athletic academic wing and rushed out to see you. It was fast, but it was always you. I was enamored by you, Kamryn. By your determination, your beauty, your drive. And I knew I wanted to see more of that. But soon, the closer we got, the quicker other things fell to the wayside: school and football being the two that started slipping. But I didn't care because I started falling for you. My coaches, my team, and my parents weren't happy with me. I told myself that once we found a rhythm things would click back into place. That didn't happen and I was in jeopardy of losing everything."

My mouth is slack as he tells me that because of us he almost lost it all. "Mason–"

"Kamryn, it's not your fault. Please don't think that it is or that we can somehow change the past. After my team talked to me, I started getting back on track. It also helped that you encouraged me to bond with my teammates." We sit in weighted silence facing each other. And this clears up a lot for me.

"You have no idea how much I dreaded each day as it moved closer and closer to our end date." Mason starts and I just want the floor to swallow me whole. "When my coach told me I needed to end my relationship with you to get drafted, I was a breath away from leaving the team. Because how–why would I prioritize a game over you?"

"But you did." I tell him. My voice feels like I swallowed sand.

"I know. And I have regretted doing that everyday for the last eight years. When I was forced to walk away from you the year of the draft it wasn't because I didn't love you. I was so in love with you that I couldn't breathe without you around. After my first three years in the league I had everything that I wanted. I was getting to play a sport that I love, the small group of friends I had were incredible. And my family was unbelievably proud of me. Yet the one thing that was missing was you. I didn't have the one person that supported me behind closed doors to share it with. It's been eight years since and nothing has been the same. This game means absolutely nothing to me if I don't get to share it with the one person that makes my world complete. And that person has been you since I was twenty-one years old."

When he finishes, my eyes are filled with tears that are begging to fall as I struggle to catch my breath. So I hit him back with a question. One that I stayed up all night wondering.

"Why didn't you call me?" I hate myself for the way my voice breaks. "Those last few months were hell for me."

It's the one thing I always wondered. How we could go from 24/7 contact to nothing in the span of a night.

He shakes his head before answering. "Because I would have come back to you in an instant. I would have said to hell with the draft and come back to you. You have no idea the effort it took to not barge into the sorority house the night it happened and beg for you back. With the way I ended things that night, I thought and hoped you'd be better off. I thought you'd be the warrior that I always knew that you were, and you'd just move on."

"There was no *just moving on from you*, Mason. I was broken. I wasn't the same after you. And the fact that the whole campus had a front row seat into my heartbreak was the cherry on top of a spectacular year." The tears that I fought to keep from falling lost that battle. Gently streaming down my face and making me feel weaker and weaker as each tear falls.

"I know. I have no other answer to give you. Other than that, I am so terribly sorry. I didn't want that for you." He pleads with me.

Here goes nothing. "Loving you, the way that I did was so easy. You made it so easy for me to love you. So for you to break me the way that you did–for so long I thought I was the problem. I ran through our entire relationship trying to pinpoint when it all shifted. And for the longest time I thought of what I would say to you. But every time I thought of the words to make you feel even an inkling of what I felt, it would send me into another spiral. I did everything to try and fix myself. I did everything."

He nods his head. "I understand."

"No. You don't. Not even a little bit. My junior year of

school, I shut everyone out. I was broken. And I kept making mistake after mistake. School became my crutch, I hid behind alcohol, and I hid behind this fear that I wasn't good enough until I came to some weird moment of clarity that I'd go nowhere in life if I continued on this path." I take a deep breath to continue. Talking about the boy I loved to the boy I'll always love...well the universe never prepares you for that.

"It was the summer of my senior year, where the fight I had put up for the past year was exhausting. And I was so tired. So I stopped fighting. I accepted any change as it came. That's where Liam comes into the picture. We were at that back to school party at the frat house. He came up to me and said everything that I needed to hear. But by the end of those four years together, I realized that it was never what he wanted. At least not as badly as I did. He said those words because it's what I wanted. My words–and the way I treated him." I bite my bottom lip to hold back the sob that threatens my next breath. "For so long I blamed myself for his death." Tears continue to slip down my face as I voice the words I've only said to my therapist.

I'm grateful that Mason doesn't attempt to placate me. Because no matter the gesture or the words, no one can assuage my guilt over what happened. I've been told that it's not my fault. And very deep down I know that. I wasn't the one who made him get into his truck. I wasn't the one who made him crash his truck. Deep down I know this. But convincing my brain and my heart to get on the same page is difficult.

"When he died two years ago, I didn't know how I would or if I could even pick up those pieces. How does someone move on when their guilt and actions are constantly thrown in their face? Because most people aren't at the epicenter of love and loss. Most people don't have to live with the words they said and the words they never said on repeat."

The words I wished I'd said to Liam constantly play on a loop when the silence creeps in. The guilt keeps me up at night when my mind starts to wander. And the breathing and mind exercises I've been taught only work for a little while. So in the end I let the guilt run its course until sleep takes me.

"For so long I thought of what I would do and say to you if we ever saw each other again. Now that you're in front of me saying these things, I don't know what's right anymore. You say none of what you have means anything without me, but I don't even know what that means. Because I've heard that line too many times to believe it. And I refuse to fall for those words when the actions haven't matched up."

My mind flips back to the days I would sketch that moment on the bridge. I drew it so many times I eventually drew it with my eyes closed. I take a deep breath and steady my heart rate. Looking at him absorbing all that I went through...I can't feel pity for the pain that he caused. "It took a long while for me to even be happy again. Most days I'm still so far from that feeling and person I was before everything in my life crumbled. And here you are, after almost eight years, telling me I've been it for you since college and thinking that we should forget the past–I don't know what to do with that." I tell him sounding more defeated than I should.

Mason shakes his head. "I don't want you to forget the past. Doing so would be selfish of me. But unfortunately, with you selfishness is all I know. You have no idea how many times I wanted to call you just to hear your voice and to know that you were doing okay or to know if you moved on. I am glad that you moved on. That's all I wanted for you. That was my selfishness thinking."

He was always an eloquent speaker. On days we would lay around in his room, he would just read to me and I would float away with nothing but the baritone notes of his voice lulling me to sleep. I could never forget the way he made me feel when we were together. The love difference between him and Liam, were worlds apart. Where Liam's love was like putting us on cruise control, Mason's love was like climbing thirty thousand feet and being put on auto pilot. Still, I felt utterly safe while I was in either of their arms. I would have given the world to be with Mason, but I wouldn't have gotten the world from Liam. Is that what it's like to love and be loved?

Loved? Or love?

"Thank you. I would be lying if I said I didn't want to try again. Because I do. All I pictured that year after was you coming back and us starting again. But I'm finally in a good place and I'm terrified of opening my heart again. I'm terrified of being let down by someone again. Ugh! Second chances–I'm not saying one night is going to make up for years of absence. Because it can't. But I'd like to start over as friends and see how that plays out. But if and when things progress, I need you to know that I'm not dating to date. I'm dating for marriage. They're not a pit stop to something better. Because that person would be my something better." I take a deep breath and look at Mason. I catalog every shape and curve of his face that's only gotten more distinguished as he's gotten older. "Tell me this, in five years from now where do you see yourself?"

"Married. With a kid or two. Maybe three depending on how lucky my wife and I get." He answers without hesitation. A smile threatening to break free as he tells me his answer like he's been waiting for someone to ask him that for years.

And the chills that slide over my body when hearing the words *my wife* come from his lips has me envisioning it as me.

Mason continues on like I'm not picturing it as me, "Maybe I'd take a gig on a sports talk show once I retire that'd allow me to work while the kids are at school and my wife is at work building her empire. I'd make sure that our family understood that celebrating little accomplishments were just as important as celebrating the big accomplishments."

It wasn't a fluke. Chills spread through my body again when he says *my wife*. Also a tinge of jealousy as I imagine him with someone else. But still, that ember threatens to ignite as I still can't help but feel he's placing me in the picture. When it comes to Mason I'm also selfish and that's all I want even though I just told him we'd start back as friends.

"I see a life outside of football that's not all-consuming. I won't lie and say that it's not you I'm picturing, because it is. It's been you since I told you I loved you, all those years ago Kamryn. And it'll always be you. If you do, I don't plan to take this second chance for granted. That's if I get a second chance with you. Because the ball is in your court. I want us to fall in love again, Kamryn. I want the endgame with you."

Fresh tears form at his words. My breath hitches and my head feels as if it's floating in the clouds. His confession on a silver platter just for me. And all I have to do is take it. Yet I hesitate. Remembering the last time he told me he loved me that ended in destruction.

I recross my legs. "I'm willing to give this another chance, as friends. I want to cheer you on at your games, because that's what I did in college. And I want nothing more than to see you in the audience at my shows. I want the life you just painted to be a life with you. But I won't make this easy for you. Like I said–we start as friends. And if that includes friends who push the boundary, then so be it."

Removing a brick from that wall around my heart, while not easy, I do feel it's necessary. Not just because of Mason. But because of me and my family and friends. My heart has been hardened for so long that I don't know how fast it'll thaw.

"What do you want from me Kam?" Mason asks me.

I get a flashback to our first true weekend together. "Dates. Quality dates. And then hopefully we go from there."

A smirk that hasn't changed in the years past, graces his face. "I'm up for the challenge."

I stand up and hide my growing smile behind my drink and take a sip. "Okay, then. I'll see you around."

I'm about to step back into the club when I hear my name called behind me.

"Same number?"

"Yeah. Same number."

I find the girls when I'm back inside. The DJ continues to pop out hit after hit and the patrons dance to their heart's content. But my whole world was just shaken. The love of my life came back into my life. Well, I shouldn't say back into my life. He has to work for it.

Making my way back to our roped off section, I see the girls dancing the night away. I'm hoping they stay on the dance floor as I try and sort through the last thirty minutes. The last thirty minutes in which my world has shifted.

Am I happy to have seen Mason? I hesitate to say yes so

fast. Does the hurt feeling resurface? Yes. Without a doubt, yes.

In all of the romance books I've read, there has always been a good 'on his knees, forgive me' moment. The moment when the guy, or the girl, realizes they messed up and have to do everything in their power to win the forgiveness and love back for their person. Sometimes it's a monstrous gesture and sometimes it's small things that mean more to the couple than even the reader realizes.

25

KAMRYN

The ticking of the clock on the wall, a door closing in the hallway, and a semi-truck's brakes squeaking are the only sounds to be heard in this room. I've yet to say more than a handful of words since my session started. Some days I can't stop talking. Other days, like today, are like this. God bless my therapist. It's why she gets paid as much as she does.

"So Mason's back?" She asks after an undisclosed amount of time.

I cross my arms and heave another sigh. "Yeah."

"This is going to be cliche. But how is that making you feel Kamryn?"

My thoughts have been scrambled since seeing Mason and I knew I needed to see my therapist. She helped me through moving here since my routine was thrown off and with getting to the root of my feelings and thoughts. While she's not the same therapist I had when I was living in Philly, Theresa came highly recommended by my former therapist, Maggie.

I drop my arms and pick at a hangnail, as I try to gather

my thoughts. "I feel ike this should have happened seven years ago. Like..."

"Do you think your hesitance has something to do with Liam?"

"Maybe. I don't know."

Theresa puts her notepad and pen down. It's when I know she's about to get serious. Well, more serious than her job already is. "When was the last time you went and visited with Liam?"

"A few weeks after he died." My response stumps me. Subconsciously I think I knew visiting Liam would never be high on my to-do list. I got everything out that I needed to when I visited Liam. At least I thought I had. Now with my past knocking at my door, I'm not so sure if I ever moved on from the past.

Like most sessions we engage in a silent stare-down. Her, willing me to talk unprovoked. Me, wishing she would prompt something for me to say. My mind is an empty vessel and I break our stare-down to focus back on the hangnail that gets stuck on my shirt sleeve. Our session is slowly running out of time. And that's a good thing. Some days I love my therapy sessions and other days, I dread my therapy sessions. Today is one of those days that I dread my therapy session. While I feel like I have so much to talk about, my brain won't connect to my mouth.

"Thirty days," Theresa says by way of breaking the silence. My head snaps up to her.

"Thirty days for what?"

"Unfortunately, Mason coming back has erased a lot of the progress we've made. So in order for these sessions to continue to be effective, they'll only work if you talk to me. For this assignment I want you to go buy a journal and write in it for thirty days. It can be about anything that happens to you throughout the day. Write it down. Because Kamryn, I know you have so much to talk about. Now it's getting you to talk about it consistently that's a bit of an issue. And not just with me, but your friends and family too."

I always thought I was good with my words. My parents never had to pull teeth to get me to speak. But this feels like a setback.

"I know this is hard for you Kamryn. Just give it thirty days. Then we'll talk again."

The rest of the day is a blur. I heed Theresa's advice and pick up a journal after my session. Being around people is too much effort so I let Olivia, my assistant, know that I'll be working from home for the rest of the day as being a business owner allows me that luxury. I stare out at my backyard and the pond that's the centerfold of my neighborhood with Poppy in my lap and the laughing of *FRIENDS* provides me much needed background noise. Idly petting Poppy proves to be the perfect heart rate soother as her purrs calm me. Taking a deep breath, I pick up my pen and I sketch out mine and Mason's new meeting in the journal I picked up. It doesn't take me long to get carried away with the scene as my mind had been replaying this new meeting since I left him on the rooftop. In the gaps, I write out my thoughts until Lucy nuzzling my leg brings me to a stopping point.

"Yes?" I ask her.

Of course she can't respond since she's a dog, but I assume her nuzzling me means she wants to go outside. I unfold myself from my chair and grab my smaller sketch pad along with my journal, meandering downstairs and out the backdoor to let Lucy run around and hopefully get more inspiration for the rest of my Winter line.

I found myself at a bit of a standstill last week. The truth is that I'm scared I'll run out of ideas and everyone will know that I'm a fraud. It's why I snapped at my sister. I'm not wanting to get too over eager with my designs as I know how fast trends change. But it's hard to stop trying to top my last line.

Picking my journal back up, I flip to a blank sheet. I never imagined reliving traumatic events would lead to cathartic moments. Before I know it, I'm drawing out that night in Liam's truck. The night before life imploded. I draw and rewrite that night because it seems that's when life was on track. Our relationship was in a fragile state, but we were still us. At least we were trying to hold on to what made us an us.

The sun is setting by the time I lift my head up. The string lights in my patio have turned on and the fireflies make their presence known and I look back down at the filled up pages and I feel somewhat lighter. The words I wrote next to the memory I drew can't change the past. And as I look over every detail, I feel almost lighter and I will myself to hold onto this feeling for as long as possible. But something I've learned about myself is that the lightness I strive to have is harder to ignite.

It's been thirty days where I've put my head down and worked. Before my self-imposed focus period, I sent a text to Mason and let him know when I'd be in touch. His resistance was expected because I can't imagine having my life constantly dictated by others. And I'm sure me holding back from him was just another facet of his life being controlled.

As I'm leaning over my design desk trying to smooth out some new sketches I get a knock at my door. "Come in!" I yell without looking up. The bodice on this corset is giving me the most trouble. It's intricate and delicate. Yet my pencil strokes on this sketch are anything but delicate.

Most designers have moved onto technology to do their work for them. Choosing iPads over sketchbooks to make every detail precise. I won't lie and say I don't use technology for my sketches and I do, but for the less complex pieces. But my bread and butter comes from a sketchpad and a pencil before I find a way to transfer my completed designs to technology. Well, usually. Today not so much. So this delivery is a welcome interruption to my not so successful drawings.

"I have a delivery for Ms. Rawlins," A young man announces.

I huff at my work and I look up with confusion coating my tone. "That's me."

He walks over to my desk and places an arrangement of orange lilies down.

"Do I need to sign?" I ask him.

"No ma'am, they're already taken care of. Have a nice day." And with that he leaves.

I walk over to the flowers and take in their beauty. "Who are those from?" My assistant Olivia asks me as she pokes her head into my office.

I pluck the card from the flowers. "I was just about to check who they were from nosey lady."

Kamryn, I can't get you out of my mind.
Come to a home game soon.
Let me know which one and I'll leave tickets.
XOXO, Mason.

I read over the card three times with a smile on my face. The first real smile in thirty days.

"Oooo! Those are pretty. Who are those from?" Jax asks when she walks in my office. I show her the card and she gives me her best I-don't-know face.

"What is that face for?" I ask my sister.

She looks at me like I'm insane. "You haven't shown a man any inkling of interest since Liam. And now all of a sudden you're all doe-eye for Mason again?"

"I'm not doe-eyed for anyone." The beginnings of a panic attack make my fingers tingle. I knew no matter who I started talking to I'd get this type of reaction.

Jax cocks her brow at me. "Okay. Well what happened with Brett? I thought for sure something would brew between you two."

"Brett was a chauvinistic pig who said it was "cute" that I designed clothes. I told him it was "cute" that he was thirty-five and still working part-time at a job meant for high schoolers. Needless to say the guy you thought I would hit it off with was a total bust. Jax, please let me have this little slice of happiness. And if it's with Mason, you have to respect that. If it's not with Mason, then you also have to respect that."

"Okay," she concedes. But I know it's not that easy with her. "I'm just confused why all of a sudden."

"It's not sudden. At least not on my end." A strange feel of exhaustion takes over as I have the need to defend myself. "Jax, I have been working on myself for years. You know this. Letting Mason back into my life, it's not an easy decision. When I saw him that night at Mike's club I was caught off guard. And even he knows that one night isn't enough to take away the pain of the way he left me. So if Mason and I ever make it to an 'us' again, I won't take your negativity."

Jax holds her hands up in surrender. "Okay. You and Mason were good together. I know that. But I just don't want you to get your heart broken again."

I look at my sister and some days it's like we're back to being strangers. When I was in college, and dating Mason, Jax and I were as far from sisters as one could get. So I've missed a massive chunk of her life and I'm wondering if she's projecting some of her hurt onto me.

"I know you don't. Thank you for looking out for me. I'm sure we'll hit the bumps like every relationship does, but I'll be fine. One big mess up and I'm done. I won't put myself through anything like that again." I tell my sister and pull her in for a hug.

I don't want to get my hopes up. Or even jump past the obstacles I know will be in our way. We're both older with so much time lost between us. But time we can gladly make up for. I want to get to know Mason now. I want to get to know the thirty-year old version of him. I want to get to know the thirty-year old that has succeeded beyond all expectations in a sport he only picked up as a hobby. I want to get to know Mason again. Eventually, when the time comes, I hope to fall in love with Mason again.

Because once upon a time, he made loving him as easy as breathing. We were effortless. Nothing with our relationship was forced and he had the uncanny ability to read my mind. He also read my moods like they were a playbook depicting every one of them with accuracy. Can loving Mason again be as easy as breathing?

I'M SITTING at home later that day with a glass of wine, when my phone pings with a text from Mason. I slide to open the message.

> Mason: Hey beautiful. Did you get my flowers?

I snap a picture of them sitting on my dining room table and post it in our message chat.

> Me: Hey yourself. They're beautiful. Thank you.

> Mason: You're welcome. How's your day been?

> Me: It's looking up. How's your day?

> Mason: It's been long. Practice. Watching film. Interviews. It can get tiring and repetitive.

> Me: Oh, I know all about that. I can only say so many things about my new line when I debut it at fashion week. The clothes speak for themselves, but reporters and magazines expect me to say a paragraph about what I designed.

> Mason: That's exactly how I feel in my interviews. My game speaks for itself.

> Me: So it looks like we're one in the same, then. We'd rather let our work do the talking than actually do the talking

> Mason: I like the way you put that Ms. Rawlins. So I was thinking...

> Me: Oh goodness. What now?

I smile in remembrance of when he first said that to me eons ago.

Mason: Smartypants. We have a home game next weekend. I know that it's last minute and you were supposed to choose the game, but I'm just too impatient to wait for your answer. I'm hoping that you live in the city so it won't be too much of a problem for you. You can bring Jax and a couple of friends. I'll have passes for you all to get field access and to sit in a booth. What do you say?

Me: I say that you're an incredibly eager man. When do you need an answer from me?

Mason: Thursday if it's not too much trouble.

Me: Okay. I'll have an answer for you in two days.

Mason: I look forward to hearing from you. Goodnight, Kamryn.

Me: Goodnight, Mason.

26

KAMRYN

I'm out to dinner with Jax, Sarah, and Emily a week later when I tell them about Mason being back in my life.

"But is it moving too fast? Am I moving too fast?" I sit back in my chair with my drink in my hand. I've kept Sarah and Emily in the loop because our schedules clash even when we're all not on deadlines. So we make it a mission to schedule monthly dinners and this dinner is packed with all the goings of our personal lives.

My sister looks at me like I'm an idiot. "Kamryn, when have you ever gone slow with guys? You and Mason were great together. I know I questioned it, but it's obvious that he adores you and he's doing everything that he can to make things right with you. Plus, it really is time that you move on. I'll admit that Brett was not the right choice for you."

I look at Sarah and Emily and they're both nodding their heads in agreement at what Jax said.

"What if I'm scared?" I begin. "He chose football over me before and that crushed me. And after losing Liam, I don't think I could ever put my heart through that again. I have a reason for burying myself in my work these past couple years. Because what if he does it again?" I explain to them.

"It wouldn't be love if it didn't scare you." Emily said with a knowing look.

"You're right, Em. I'm sorry." Sometimes I forget that I'm not the only person who experienced a life changing moment. It's moments when your past comes back into your life that you realize you were being selfish.

Losing James and Liam the same day and the same way, made our shared grief bearable. We may have initially leaned on each other in our shared grief, but I eventually pulled away from her and she pulled away from me. Seeing the picture's of the crash made it harder to be around her because I couldn't help but feel responsible for the accident. No matter the reassurances from my parents, Liam's parents, and Emily–it didn't stop the guilt from overtaking my life.

But with therapy I've still been coming to terms with knowing the accident wasn't my fault and Emily and I have slowly built our friendship back up. What we have now is more of a sister bond than a friendship.

"Don't be sorry Kam. You and I both know what it's like to have the worst of the worst happen. It's time you finally started living again." Emily explains to me.

To say I'm in awe of Emily is an understatement. The pause in our friendship was beneficial for her as well. Emily was able to open her heart up earlier and is slowly toying with the idea of getting back into dating. It hasn't been easy, because no one can replicate what she had with James. They complimented each other better than Liam and I did. So while her happiness isn't overflowing like it was a few years ago, she is slowly getting to that place again.

"So, to love and friendship and to new beginnings." Jax

said as she lifts her drink to the center of the table for a toast. We all giggle and clink our glasses together.

I take a deep breath and say, "I think I'm gonna do it. I think I'm gonna go to the game, and you three are coming with me."

The rest of the dinner passes us by way too quickly. We all talk about anything and nothing. Sarah tells us about the trip her and her boyfriend are planning. Emily says that she's in talks to get bumped up to teaching third grade which is a huge step up from kindergarten. And Jax and I talk about the expectations for my new line. Jax helps me with the marketing along with her thriving Podcast and YouTube channel.

My attention is pulled as I read a couple of pages and then look at my phone. I repeat the cycle while reading the same page over and over and over. Not retaining anything that's happening in the story with the main couple. When I annoy myself to the point of frustration, I pick up my phone to text Mason.

Me: So you said it's a home game Sunday?

Mason: Yes, ma'am.

Me: And how would you react if I told you my answer was yes?

Mason: What?! You're really coming?

Me: I sure am. And the girls are more than excited to see you play as well

Mason: Kam, you have no idea how happy you just made me.

Me: I think I have an idea. And when do you get back in town?

Mason: Thursday evening. We have practice late Saturday morning, then team dinner at 5.

Me: So…no chance for us to see each other before your game?

Mason: I think we can squeeze in a Friday date.

Me: Okay. Well just let me know when .

Mason: Oh I intend to.

Me: Bye, Mason.

Mason: Bye, Kamryn.

27

KAMRYN

I walk into work the next morning almost as if I'm floating. I look around the space that I've created with a fresh pair of eyes. The exposed brick that's barely visible with the amount of clothing racks and mannequins lining the walls. Desks with half completed drawings, swatches of fabric, and pencils spread out creating an array of color in the mess. It's messy, but it's a second home.

Finding this space for the home of Ryn & Co., my high-end line and Kamryn, my affordable line, was a stroke of luck. But what sold me on this space was the view from my, before I knew it at the time would be, office. The baseball and football stadium's flanking my view with the river just barely seen beyond. I've never had to worry about a lull in creativity when the stadiums were bursting with activity. Some days I'd come down to the office on a Sunday during football season for some inspiration. Other times, I'd sneak up to the roof and let the cheers from the stadium light me up. But having my office space here, it felt like a dream come true and a nightmare rolled into one that my office was in view of the two sports where the two great loves of my life could be with me without being with me.

A few hours rolls by when I'm brainstorming in my office, and thinking about reaching out to Nina for a collaborative project, when a courier with a delivery pops into the office. "Delivery for Ms. Rawlins?" he asks.

"That's me," I announce from where I'm standing at my vision board for my next few lines. Once I sign for the package, the courier leaves. And when I see that the return address is posted from the stadium, I automatically know it's from Mason. But why would he send me a box when all I thought I was getting was tickets?

"Olivia, will you bring me a box cutter, please?" I yell to my assistant as I move to put the box on top of my workstation.

She comes back with the cutter and returns to her desk. I always brace myself before opening boxes like these since the last one I got identical to this broke me down.

When all of a sudden a wave of why I felt numb when I saw Mason again, hits me. The box cutter falls from my grasp as I fumble for my phone to FaceTime Theresa. She said to call her anytime and I desperately need to talk to her. As the phone continues to ring I close my door because I don't need my employees in my personal business.

"Hello, Kamryn." Always the professional even with FaceTime.

I cut straight to the chase. "It's a box. The reason why I am the way that I am. The reason I can't let anything out."

"Boxes can mean a ton of different things. Why do you specifically think it means you can't let anything out?"

I stop pacing and make my way over to my chair. Once seated, I swivel and look out of the floor to ceiling window and the two stadiums that host the sports that I've loved and hated. "I remember weeks after losing Liam, his parents stopped by with a box of his things that they thought I'd like to have. Usually I'd be overjoyed with getting a delivery, but–"

Theresa regards me carefully over the video call. Even not in the same space I feel two inches tall. "But what? What brought this on Kamryn?"

"Mason had a box delivered to my office. I was about to open it up when my mind was thrust back in time. Those emotions I felt the first time was all I could feel. And it doesn't matter that this box represents something good. My mind clearly doesn't know how to separate the good and the bad."

For the last two years I continued to expect the bad. Apart from my brand becoming successful faster than I could have imagined, I was always waiting for the shoe to drop.

"It's good you're letting him back in."

"Yeah but what if I let him all the way in and he doesn't like what he sees?" I ask, voicing my biggest fear.

A pitying look from Theresa is the last thing I expected from her as my therapist. In a blink that look is gone and in its place is one of professionalism. "If he doesn't like what he sees, then he is not the one for you. Everybody is broken. Whether it's a little crack or some pieces are completely gone. If Mason is who you hopefully think he is, then he will accept you for all of your broken pieces."

I linger over her words. Barely catching what she tells me as we set a tentative appointment for two weeks from now.

"Open the box, Kamryn. And I'm not just talking about the metaphorical box. Not everything represents the bad.

But you have to let him see what's inside you before you can decide if you want to run."

Our goodbye is quick and I continue to stare out of my office window. I turn over our talk in my head as I do after every session. I do my best to read between the lines, when what's between the lines is nothing. Everything Theresa said is to the point and she validated my hidden fears. With a resounding breath I get up and walk back over to the box. And when I move the flaps of the box I see that the contents are nothing like what I've been given before.

My fears, while not unfounded, are unwarranted.

In this I see: an envelope with four tickets and four box & field passes, three Cincinnati Bengals jerseys with no numbers on the back, a Bengals jersey with Mason's number on it, and a note at the bottom.

> Kamryn,
> I can't wait for you to come to the game Sunday.
> I have Monday off from all things related to football.
> Come to the tunnel with the girls when the game ends.
> Afterward, I plan to take you on an official, unrushed date.
> XOXO,
> Mason

My mood rose after looking over the contents of the box and I couldn't focus on work, so I sent my employees home early. I may have also been nervous about seeing Mason these next three days, so I managed to get last minute pamper appointments. After my toes and nails are done and freshly painted, I swing-by my favorite salon to get a fresh trim and a blowout. As if I wasn't already nervous, the girls in the salon kept asking me about my love life and if they could get the inside scoop on my next line. I just gave them a tight-lipped smile and told them it's all a work in progress.

"Hi, Lucy," I greet with equal enthusiasm when I get home. Poppy views our interaction with as much enthusiasm as she can from her spot on the couch. "Wanna go for a walk?" I ask her. If her wagging tail is any indication, then that'd be a yes. Setting my purse on the table and swapping out my flats for slip on sneakers. "Go get your leash for me sweet girl." I had just planned to take Lucy on a walk around the neighborhood, but I was still full of restless energy so we found ourselves at the dog park. Smiling to myself as I watch Lucy play with other dogs, I can't help but think about this coming weekend. I don't want to move at lightning speed, but I'm at the point where it's all or nothing with anyone I date.

After thirty minutes of Lucy running around playing with other dogs and chasing after squirrels, I whistled for her to come over to me. "Let's go home sweet girl," I say to her while petting her. Clipping her leash back on we make our way out of the park and back home.

28

KAMRYN

I walk to the corner of my bedroom that has my full length mirror and survey what I'm wearing.

My outfit is all black and while on video chat with my girls, I got made fun of for wearing all black. As if they don't know it's my go-to color for any sort of event, date, or regular night out, so attempting to sway me out of my outfit choice to wear color was a lost cause. As a millennial, phasing out the goth phase was a big mistake with my generation. Now look at us. Black jeans for nights out or black jackets to throw over top when running out the door. The goth phase is still truly alive.

My jeans sit high on my hips, with a black lace halter bodysuit that has a deep V in the front. I paired the bodysuit with a black blazer, black clutch with gold detailing that holds the essentials, and black Christian Louboutin heels. For how doom and gloom the color black is, it truly is timeless and goes with everything. Maybe it's my job, but as the years went on, I slowly incorporated this color back into my wardrobe before it took over my entire wardrobe. I hated wearing anything dark in college but I've essentially made it an extension of myself. I'll add bright colors to my style every now and then, but black will always be my signature color.

Thinking of black being my signature color has me wanting to dedicate an entire Ryn & Co. and Kamryn line to the all-black wardrobe. Why I've never done it, I'm not sure but I whip out my phone and make a quick note in it before I forget.

Once I've added that to my list, I check over my makeup before deeming I can't add anything more to my face. My makeup is done simple yet sexy with a simple eye look and deep red lip that helps accentuate the browns from my eyes. The curls from the blowout earlier today have loosened leaving my hair to fall in soft waves down my back. I gave up the fight in trying to get my natural curls to come back. The only time my natural curls make an appearance is if I jump in the ocean and apparently that would require me to actually take a vacation, so they don't make an appearance as often as one would hope.

I ordered an Uber before spritzing perfume onto my pulse points, almost going overboard and drowning myself in the expensive bottle. My nerves are driving me crazy and I'm grateful when the car pulls up so I can leave the perfume bottle on my dresser. Locking up my house I walk to the waiting car and get in and once settled, I give the driver the address. When we pull onto the main road, I'm finally given the chance to look out at the city as she drives me to Mason's condo. After the Uber drops me off I give myself a pep-talk in the lobby of his building before walking up towards the concierge.

I can do this. I can do this. I can do this. I repeat to myself over and over again.

With one last deep breath I step up to the desk and clear my throat.

"Hi. I'm here for Mason Brooks," I announce to the concierge when I finally find my words. I could have easily texted him but my nerves have taken over and any inkling of thought I possessed is gone.

"Name?" The woman typing on her computer asks without looking up at me.

"Kamryn Rawlins," I reply back to her.

She finally glances up with her mouth slightly open and shocked at hearing my name. I don't get that reaction a lot so it brings a small smile to my face.

The concierge clears her throat a few times before calling up to Mason's room. "He'll be down in a minute. But may I just say that I'm a *huge* fan of your line. I buy a couple pieces from each collection and I'm super eager for this next line." She rambles off to me.

I get a little flustered and blush at her compliment. "Thank you so much. That means a lot. I promise you're going to love this new line." I hear the elevator ping and turn to see Mason walk out and my heart does that pitter-patter skip a beat thing it always does when I see him. "Well it was nice meeting you." I tell her as I wave and walk away.

He strolls out of the elevator bay and I have to close my mouth as he prowls towards me. The rust orange, button-down long sleeve he's wearing has the top buttons undone revealing a very tattooed chest and the black jeans he's wearing encase his muscular, quarterback thighs. In the light of his apartment's lobby, he's more handsome than he was in college.

My smile gets even bigger as I walk toward Mason, as if that's even possible, and I let out a squeal when he picks me up and spins me around the lobby.

"Ugh I've missed you Kam," Mason says.

He puts me down and I get lost in his light brown eyes before sputtering out, "Yeah I- I've missed you too."

Pull it together Kamryn!

He puts his arm around my shoulder to pull me out of the hotel and kisses the top of my head. "Let's go eat some food, beautiful."

"So how have you really been? I see football is treating you well," I say the last statement offhandedly.

"You've been checking me out I see." His cheeks lift as he tries to hold back his laughter.

My own cheeks heat after having been caught. "Look, yes! Okay. You're hot. And your body is insane. Football and time has been fantastic to you."

"Not to sound like a dog, time has been wonderful to you as well."

No more hiding the blush that spreads over my body as his gaze roams over my face. Lingering on my exposed chest as my body continues to heat up all over the place.

I take a sip of water because it's only gotten hotter in here.

"Enough body talk. I wanna know how you've been."

The waitress bringing over our wine halts Mason from responding. She also takes our appetizer and entree orders, before heading back to her station.

"Exhausted. I'm pretty much on the go from July to February only slightly lightening my training during the off-season. I've been an obsessive routine follower that hasn't made much time for a life outside of the game. When I was in Carolina, it was easier to see my family. And it made disconnecting from the game easier. But now being here... I'm still trying to figure out those logistics."

"You were..."

Mason nods. "Yeah."

How crazy is it that he was right across the state line for the rest of my time in college. Back to what he said about having no life outside of football. Which is a very interesting take from Mason. "So no life outside of football. What about painting? Did you ever finish your degree? I know how important that was to you."

"I know what you're getting at Kam. I wasn't a total monk so no need to beat around the bush." He's always been one to call me out.

My cheeks burn at having evaded what I really wanted to ask. Truthfully, I have no reason to question his dating life, or even *be* jealous, when I was with Liam.

"Okay. No serious relationship then?" I beat the bullet and just ask him.

"No. It didn't seem fair of me to get in a relationship when my time was so focused on football. I decided that whoever I was with deserved a full-time guy. That couldn't be me when I'm occupied for half of the year."

I let him by with that. Not wanting to get my hopes up that the reason he hadn't been with anyone long term had been because of me. I moved on and he had that right to do so as well. But professional football players date all of the time. I've even made bridesmaids dresses for some of them that got married. So, I refuse to take his answer about not having time. But this dinner is not the place to ask that.

"Well what about painting?" I repeat one of the questions. His talents were unmatched, whether with a paintbrush or his fingers. Maybe I'm biased but his awards weren't pity awards.

"I paint about once a year. The urge to paint was never strong after I got drafted and I can't remember the last time I actually enjoyed it." I sense sadness in his admission.

Maybe I was wrong that our heartbreak was one-sided. He loved painting more than football. To hear he's barely picked up a paintbrush or gotten his hands messy with paints and oils in the years we've been apart hurts my heart.

"I see the wheels turning in that pretty head of yours. Kamryn, I don't want you to think the reason I haven't painted has been because of us. Painting will always be there to welcome me back with open arms. But football became my main priority. It had to. One day, when I settle down, I do hope to get back to that creative place. Because the calm that rushed over me was more intense than anytime I stepped out on that field."

Our waitress brings our food out, halting my response. We thank her and then she's out of sight again.

"That makes me sad to hear. I'm hopeful that you'll get back to it. You were too talented to stop."

Mason busies himself with unrolling his silverware. It's a stalling tactic I've learned to pick up from other people. Never did I think he'd need that kind of avoidance.

"Thank you. That means a lot. To answer your other question, I did end up finishing my degree. It took a couple of years but I managed to graduate. But enough about me. How did you wanting to be a psychologist now become you selling out fashion shows?"

"A loaded question for an extremely loaded answer." I tell him as I push the food around my plate.

"Eat your food Kam. And we have time. I'm not going anywhere."

His demand sends chills coursing through my body.

I take a bite of my food and then wash what's left of my

food down with a swig of wine. "It was the summer going into my junior year. Our breakup was hard and I'd spent the first month of my break wallowing in my room. Nothing helped. And it was also the downfall of my friendship with Liam." I ignore the furrow in his brow, not wanting to tell him how I used my best friend. Maybe one day I'll tell him. But not now when we're attempting to get back on equal footing.

"A friend of mine had dragged me out of my house and took me to a trunk show she was helping out at. Apparently it was the thing I needed. So after that, I went to the arts & crafts store on a whim and scoured the sketchpad aisle. After getting some advice I bought a couple of them and some pencils. As for how I got to designing clothes is kind of simple. Jax was watching something on TV and I got this idea seeing the outfits. I tried making them better as if they already weren't. But even you can admit that sometimes the outfits TV show characters wear aren't always the best." Letting out a breath. "But somehow, my drawings went from sketches of clothes to us that night on the bridge. Drawing that moment became cathartic and torturous. And I drew it so many times that I could've drawn that moment with my eyes closed."

"Kam..." Mason starts.

I shake my head stopping him. "No. It's okay. That pain of losing you was so present. It was this living thing that I used for inspiration and that pain was the only thing that I could grasp onto. When summer ended, I went to my advisor and told her I wanted to make a switch. Of course she wasn't pleased with me. But I was able to double up on my classes. The next summer I joined that same friend at some more small trunk shows and I just got that rush of calmness fall over me. It was at that moment I felt I was in the right space for the first time in a while."

He nods at my food. A not so silent order to keep eating. He does the same and when our plates are almost cleared is when Mason asks the bigger question.

"So how did you get from college to now?" he asks, "I saw in a magazine on local talents and your story was in it."

I blow out a breath that ruffles my lips and take a swallow of wine. "Oi. No one ever wants to take a chance on inexperienced designers especially right after college when I had no investor to help get my line off the ground. So I took a couple of teaching jobs. One at the local middle school and one teaching fashion design at the local community college part-time. It was good. Not ideal. But it kept my skills sharp. The students I taught were–we all had a collaborative relationship. I actually still keep in touch with some of them and few work for me."

He raises an eyebrow knowing I'm leaving out a huge chunk of why my brand faltered for a couple of years.

Our server comes to clear our plates and top off our glasses of wine.

"Before Liam passed, one of the professors at CSU told me an investor was looking to invest in up and coming designers. I remember dancing around my living room because this was what I needed. Once I gave her the okay, she sent the investor my number and email. Up until Liam had passed, we had been in contact every day. At that point, once he passed, nothing mattered to me anymore. I did what I could to survive but I wasn't living. The investor eventually moved on after no word from me. I mean I was grieving and clearly not in the headspace to communicate efficiently with anyone. So I don't blame her."

Most people learn to work through the pain. But I was not one of those people.

"It took me a long while to get back to me. I stumbled a lot. People don't lie about the learning curves as the amount thrown at me threw me off course a handful of times. It was by pure luck that I was able to get my line started again. I had to do a complete re-brand and vision a completely new idea for my line."

"So you got an investor?" Mason asks.

"Actually, no. Not at first. I did everything the organic way. Living in this city created completely new opportunities for me. I started out with tops, dresses, and skirts that I wore around the city. It wasn't until I was out and about when a woman stopped me. Said she'd seen me around town and asked who the designer of my clothes were. When I told her they were all my designs, she asked if I wouldn't mind setting up a meeting. The way my line came to be was like when models get discovered in a mall only it was for my clothes. In the first year, we doubled our profit and I was close to buying her out. It wasn't until last year that I was able to buy her out completely. Making me the sole owner of my brand."

"That's incredible Kamryn." Mason beams.

"It's been a whirlwind for sure. I still keep in touch with Martha, the investor, as my brand really wouldn't be where it is without her." Martha was my guardian angel at a time when I needed something good. She mentored me the best way she could. She pushed me to be a better designer. She saw my potential when I was drowning in my despair. I owe her for more than anyone thinks I do.

"I'm really proud of you, Kamryn."

"Thank you."

That night at the club was full of hurt and, besides the

lobby earlier, this is the first chance we get to stare at each other without the loud music or bustling crowds. To take the other in without the nerves of this date taking over. I catalog the way he's lost his boyish features and in its place are sharp lines. The tattoos that adorned his beautiful skin have me wanting to trace them to see where they begin and where they end. But I don't think we're at that place yet. Or maybe we are and I'm just fooling myself that he and I could take this slow.

The candle light and hush quiet of the restaurant has made talking with Mason easy. Never once has the conversation faltered. We haven't been interrupted by football fans and the wait staff is known for their discretion. Sitting here with my hand in his and his thumb rubbing soft circles into my skin has amped up the kindling sexual tension between us.

"Let's get out of here," Mason says.

He pulls three 100 dollar bills out that covers way more than our bill with enough for a generous tip then wraps my hand in his to pull me out of the restaurant.

"How far away is your place from here?" Mason asks as he pulls me into his side. My body melts into him.

I wrap my arms around his waist and stare up at the man I met when I was eighteen years old. The hurt memories will probably always be a painful wedge between us. But not right here. No, right here is where our lives will change.

29

KAMRYN

It's like we bypassed every nervous gesture to skip to this part. From the drive to my house to the walking into my house. Every second has felt like we're in fast forward mode. Like we're racing against the clock to get to the finale. But I want to remember this.

As soon as we make it inside my house, I go to let Lucy out to the backyard to do her business. And when I turn around I'm met with lust-filled eyes. My heart is racing a mile a minute as Mason slowly saunters over to me. We're standing toe-to-toe. Even with heels on, he still towers over me. It's almost like we're afraid to ruin this perusal of each other. His hand reaches out for mine as he tangles our fingers together before he lifts our arms and places my hand on his neck.

"This can't be real life." Mason murmurs as I watch him categorize me into his mind. What do I say to that? Because I've been saying the same thing since the night after the club. Of all the cities in the states and we're in the same one.

"It's better than a dream that's for sure," I whisper, afraid to break the spell. As much as I want to make Mason work for this, my heart can't take the longing.

The sound of our breathing, or maybe it's just mine, is the only sound in the room. His forehead rests on mine and my arms and hands drop, looping around Mason's lower back as his hand slides up to cradle the back of my head and our lips meet for the first time in almost a decade. My lips tremble and I do my best to disguise the shakiness by pressing my lips harder to his. His tongue licks at the seam of my lips begging for entrance and I part my lips just as his tongue tries again. As soon as we touch, nothing goes slow.

I start to walk us backward, pulling Mason with me, stumbling into the doorjamb of the spare bedroom. The small laugh that escapes us breaks our kiss before we're pulled to each other again like magnets. Our steps are like a forgotten dance as we reach the foot of the bed. He pulls my jacket down my body and lets my arms slip out one by one, tossing the item to the side. Mason breaks the kiss as his hands reach up and unbutton the neck clasp on my body-suit, peeling it down my torso. When he steps back to look at me his eyes go wide with lust and he covers his mouth letting loose a groan when he sees I had nothing on top.

"You're even more beautiful than I remember." Mason surveys as his eyes are slow to undress me while my body heats with the intensity of his gaze. It's as if all sense has left me and I'm frozen–waiting for his next move.

He steps forward and his body crowds mine as he ghosts his hands down my back to my thighs before hoisting me up. My legs instinctively wrap around his waist and a moan escapes as he licks at a nipple that's now in his face. I look down and watch as he blows a puff of cool air on the pointed tip. He pulls my nipple into his mouth with a suction that sends the signal straight to my pussy. My legs tighten around his waist as he pays attention to the other one, twisting and pulling until the pain turns to pleasure. I'm a panting and moaning mess when he lowers us to the bed and my hands guide him up to my mouth. Our lips melt together as his tongue twirls with mine. Mason's hands find the button on my jeans and flicks them open, unzips them, and pulls them down my legs. My bodysuit follows leaving me bare beneath him.

"You are way too overdressed." I say in between kisses.

He sits back on his knees and holds up his arms like a little kid. I slide out from under him and slowly, teasingly start lifting his shirt up. Lightly touching his skin as I go, his stomach clenches as I run light feather touches upward. When I get to the top with his shirt, he helps me remove the rest of it. I bring his mouth to mine as I unzip his jeans and slide my hands to his backside to pull them down his muscular behind and give it a little squeeze. When his jeans are removed, my hands make the journey back to his butt and give it a little squeeze again.

"I love this." I tell him with one final squeeze. He rolls his hips into me causing me to lose my breath and he looks down at me with so much love that my heart skips a beat.

Mason nuzzles his nose against mine and slides off his boxer briefs, showing me what I've missed causing me to lose my breath. I look back up at him and he's got that same smirk on his face that I fell in love with nine years ago. He bends down to pull a condom out of the back pocket of his jeans and rolls it onto his length. Mason bends down to kiss me deeply and we fall back onto the bed. My thighs fall open to accommodate him more. His hand travels down my body and I tense with nerves before his fingers tease my clit before dipping into my pussy.

"Fuck. Your pussy is sucking my fingers in."

Our mouths stay fused together as Mason finger fucks me into oblivion. His tongue and fingers matching in movement has my orgasm slamming into me. As my pussy flutters from my orgasm, Mason enters me in one thrust.

"Oh god," I moan.

"It's just Mason," he says cockily as he waits for my body to relax around the intrusion. I don't have time to make a retort as he cants his hips back and thrusts back into me, taking my breath away.

Our lips meet and Mason starts to move in and out of me at an agonizingly slow pace. Every stroke of his tongue matches the stroke of his cock tunneling inside of me. My hips meet his and the rhythm we set is indescribable. I wrap my legs high around his waist and feel him go deeper and with my hips at another angle, his cock hits my clit every time he enters me. I feel the familiar tingling of another orgasm coming and I pull Mason down to kiss him deeply and clench my muscles around him. My orgasm overtakes me on a slow wave and I moan out his name. Mason drives in harder and faster, prolonging my orgasm. When I feel him swell inside me his thrusts get more erratic and he lets go on a roar.

We stay connected like this, sweaty and satiated, for minutes after our orgasms fade and I feel him soften inside of me. I jolt when I hear Lucy scratching at the back door, begging to come back inside.

"I should go let her back in."

I make to untangle myself from Mason and whimper at the loss of him inside of me.

He stands to grab his boxer shorts. "I'll do it."

I stifle a giggle as he ducks his head to leave the room and hearing the muffled sound of him talking to my dog warms my heart.

The sound of my kitchen sink turning on intrigues me and the blush that covers my face when he comes back with a washcloth solidifies that.

I hold out my hand and shriek when he grabs my leg, pulling me to him at the edge of the bed.

"What are you doing?"

"I got you dirty. It's only right I clean you up." Mason replies with a cheeky grin. Once he's satisfied, he tosses the washcloth to the bathroom and climbs into bed with me.

"Did you think that we would be here?" I ask.

We've been talking non-stop for the past few hours. It's well past two in the morning and I have no clue what time Mason needs to go home.

He kisses the side of my head before breathing out deeply. "Honestly, no. Only because I knew I hurt you pretty bad. Plus, I didn't think I'd ever see you again, let alone get a second chance. But now that we're here, I'm never letting you go."

I look up at him and smile before leaning up to kiss him. The kiss turns deeper as Mason's tongue begs for entry into my mouth. Without breaking the kiss, I slide my leg over his hips to straddle him and feel him harden beneath me. I kiss my way down his neck, sucking on his collarbone, and then fluttering my tongue over his nipple. I look up at him and bring my other hand to his other nipple. With my mouth still covering one, I use my other hand to mimic each other. His cock gets even harder beneath my core.

"Fuck Kamryn." Mason releases on a groan.

I smile against his skin before making my way down his body and sliding his boxers off. When Mason and I dated in college, I never went down on him. It was always him going down on me and I loved it. But now it's my turn to completely blow his mind.

I settle in between his legs and fist his dick. Working him up and down before darting my tongue out and licking up the drop of pre-cum. His answering groan is all the encouragement that I need. Running my tongue up the underside of his cock before sucking on the head. I look up at Mason and meet his gaze as I lower my mouth little by little until I have to relax my throat to fit all of him. I hum my approval around him and that has him fisting the sheets. I repeat the noise before hollowing my cheeks and release him with a pop and flicker my tongue over the tip of him. I bring my other hand between his thighs and massage his balls and I feel his thighs start to tense as I pick up my pace. Bobbing my head up and down on him while my other hand keeps massaging his balls.

"Kamryn," Mason warns. He starts to pull out but I suction my mouth even more. I swirl my tongue around and suction the tip while my fist quickly gets him off. Mason swears as he comes. Thick spurts shoot to the back of my throat. I suck, lick, and clean up every drop before releasing him with a pop and I trail kisses back up his body before our lips meet. Letting him taste what he can on my tongue. Breaking the kiss, I sit back up and look down at him with a smile.

He's still looking up at the ceiling. His chest moving in deep inhales and exhales.

"Earth to Mason. Did I break you?" I ask almost jokingly.

"Woman, I can't feel my legs."

"Then it seems like I did everything right."

Mason tips his chin down and looks at me. A smile graces his face. Scratch that, an evil smile graces his face.

At the speed of light, Mason pulls my body up to straddle his hips. Kissing me senseless while twisting my nipples between his fingers. Grinding my wetness over his cock, he continues to play with my nipples before pulling one into his mouth. Releasing one with a pop he looks at me with a salacious gleam.

"Let's see if I can't get you off just like this." It's a challenge I know that I'll lose.

~

I WAKE up well past noon. We stayed up until the sun started to rise. Only then did we fall asleep. But when I reach my hand out, Mason isn't in bed with me. Panic ensues before I roll over to find a note left on the pillow.

I didn't want to wake you up, but I had to get to practice.
I'll see you Sunday.
XOXO, Mason.

30

KAMRYN

We're walking up to the stadium for the game since it's so close. Choosing to avoid all of the tailgating, because we'd rather eat and drink in the stadium, plus, with Mason getting us passes to get on the field during warmups that swayed our decision to skip the tailgating experience.

"Are you ready?" I ask the girls.

We're being escorted by security and seeing the field from ground level is a whole other experience.

"Oh my God," Jax says in awe. "It's so much bigger from down here."

"Agreed." Emily and I say at the same time Sarah says, "That's what she said."

Once we're on the sidelines, the security guy walks off to let us watch the warmups. I can't believe Mason does this for a living. I thought my stage was massive. His stage makes mine look like a high school stadium.

"These guys look so much bigger on ground level." Sarah says. "I wonder if any of them are single."

"Don't be one of those girls Sarah. It's not attractive. Besides, don't you have a boyfriend?" I scold her and her responding shrug is enough of an answer. "Although, this guy's pretty cute," I say as I see Mason walking over to us.

"Hi ladies," Mason says in greeting.

"Hi Mason," they all greet dreamy.

Mason stops right in front of me so I'm forced to tip my head back to look at him. "Nice jersey."

Since it's veering into late fall, I paired his jersey with high-rise, dark-washed jeans and Nike Air Force Ones. I left my hair in its long natural waves and very minimal makeup.

"Oh this old thing...?"

I'm rewarded with his signature smirk. *Yep*. It's still panty-dropping worthy.

"Get together you two," Sarah instructs us.

Mason wraps his arm around my shoulders as I wrap my arms around his waist and lean my head on his chest.

"Oh that's being framed." All the girls announce.

When the girls swipe through the picture, Mason leans down to kiss my cheek. "I'll see you after the game, yeah?"

I nod, because I don't trust my voice at the moment.

"Bye, ladies."

"Bye, Mason."

I'm still looking at him running back to the field because his butt in those shorts is something else.

"Earth to Kamryn."

I blink a couple times and look over at the girls that have matching grins. My face burns hot at having been caught looking at Mason's butt.

"Let's go and get some food."

"Touchdown baby!" Sarah hoots from our seats. My best friend knows how to garner attention.

Mason hooked us up with the swanky seats in the stadium. He tried convincing me to sit in a box, but I wanted the feel of the crowd. It's the third quarter with five minutes left on the play clock. Mason has done really well for his first season with a new team. He meshes with his offensive line like a well-oiled machine, he's calm under pressure, and he looks healthy. He and I both know that being a professional athlete, and in a high-contact sport like football, an athlete's shelf-life is only so long. That's if they can stay healthy for the entirety of their career. But the fact that he has means his O-line is solid.

The game flies by with very only a few timeouts pausing the speed of the game. Before I know it, the game is over and Mason and the boys won. If that's not a great sign for how the rest of the season should go, I'm not sure what other sign anyone would need. I heard some veteran fans complaining about Mason's ability to last the five years his contract is good for. It took everything in me to defend him. But his game defended himself.

While following the crowd out of the stands and veering off to the side entrance to the locker rooms, I get a text from Mason that he and some of the guys are headed out to a bar. I slow my steps as I respond to him.

"Hey do you guys wanna meet Mason and some of the guys at a bar? He said we could go home, shower to get ready, and then meet them." I watch as the bubbles pop up signaling him typing.

"Hang out with pro football players? Is the sky blue? YES, I will come!" Sarah says. "Hopefully." She's the most boy-crazy and painfully single one of all of us.

Emily and Jax shrug their shoulders, and Jax answers for the both of them. "Why not?!"

Me: Yeah, we're in. We're gonna head back to my place to get ready and then we'll meet y'all.

Mason: Okay. We're going to Goalpost Pub. So whenever you're ready, we'll be there.

Me: Okay. See you soon.

I FORGOT how bad football traffic is even on foot. Which is why I'm glad my house is within walking distance of the stadium. It's a tiring walk, but at least we'll work off some of this food and beer. Once we get to my house, I'm in drill sergeant mode.

"Chop chop ladies! One of you takes the shower upstairs and one of you takes the shower downstairs."

"Ma'am yes ma'am!" They all stand at attention.

"Get out of my face," I say this with their sarcastic remarks.

Those girls are something else. Lucy pushes my hand for some attention. "I know my sweet girl. Let's go potty."

I let Lucy into the backyard and head up to my room to figure out what to wear. My default is a black outfit. But I'm in the mood to shake it up. Walking into my closet I find a dress from one of my first launches. It's a mini dress with cap sleeves and a cinched bodice. I'm still cheating a bit with the black, white, and pink flower design of the dress. But it's casual enough for a bar, but not too casual that it makes me look younger than I should. I heft out my Doc Martens and place them by my bed along with my dress. I'll figure out my hair and makeup after I shower.

"Next!" I hear Jax call from the downstairs bathroom.

"Okay, Kamryn. The bathroom is all yours." The calm and soft tone of Emily sounds from the threshold of the bathroom.

"Thanks, Em."

Once in the shower, I do a quick soaking of my body, then I run the razor over everywhere, even though I just shaved the other day. I make sure to exfoliate and deep condition my hair, which is a challenge in itself when trying to get ready on a time limit. I thoroughly rinse out my hair then wash my body to get rid of the deep conditioner residue. When I step out of the bathroom wrapped in my towel with a towel around my hair Emily is looking at me comically.

"What?"

"I haven't seen you this eager before. It's refreshing."

"Thanks...I think."

I forget that Emily and I weren't around each other when Mason and I first started dating as she's a year younger than me, and stayed home for college, it's easy to forget. One of the downsides to not going home as much in college was that I wasn't around to see James and Emily fall in love. We texted weekly, but being around when they fell in love makes me regret not going home more often.

Once my body is moisturized, I tackle my hair. I did try to continue to bring my natural curls back after college, but once those Pennsylvania winters hit my outfits just went better with straight hair. One of my interns told me about a blowout brush and after giving it a week's test I ditched my flatiron for the brush.

While doing my hair, I run through a list of vendors and influencers that I could work with in an attempt to keep my nerves at bay. I shouldn't be nervous. But this is mine and Mason's first outing since reconnecting and as adults.

Turning off the blowout brush I open my makeup cabinet and debate on what to do. Looking at the time, I decide to keep my face makeup light but pack on the mascara to make my eyes pop. After the final coat I walk into my bedroom and put on my dress. Sliding on some thicker socks and pulling my Docs on, I head down the stairs to let Lucy back inside.

"All set! Anyone else done?" I yell throughout the house as I feed Lucy and Poppy. I hear a collective "Yep", "Yeah", "One second" so I go and put what I need in my clutch.

"Whoa, Kam, you look hot!"

"Well, thank you. You ladies don't look half bad yourself."

We all burst out in giggles.

My phone dings with an alert notifying me that the Uber's out front. "Uber's here."

I give Lucy and Poppy one last pet. Then I lock up my house and we head to the car.

"MASON SAID they're at the back two pool tables." I tell the girls when we walk in.

The Goalpost Pub is a local dive bar that has pool tables and dart boards. I've yet to venture in here, as it's not usually my scene. But if this is the place Mason and the guys choose, who am I to say no?

We're all scanning the bar when Jax says. "I see them. And damn his teammates are hot!"

With that, we head over to the guys. Mason hasn't noticed us yet, but one of his teammates says, "Hot girls coming this way."

Mason turns and his smile is back on. He props his pool

stick on the side of the table, comes over, and wraps me up in a hug. "Hi."

"Hi. Good game."

"Thank you. I'm glad you enjoyed it."

I cock my eyebrow in a playful manner. "I wouldn't say I enjoyed it."

"No?" Mason asks.

"Well, I mean your butt looked *great* in those pants. That part I did enjoy." I was always a sucker for him in his football pants.

"You were always a butt girl. Just as long as you were only looking at mine."

"Eh. I can't make any promises."

Mason laughs and is about to say something else when one of his teammates stops him. "Yo Brooks! Introduce us to your girl."

"Yeah. Introduce me to them."

Mason places a kiss on my forehead before leading us back to the others. "Guys, this is Kamryn."

For all my bravado, I shy a wave at them. "Hi."

"Kamryn, this is Jason, Mac, and Tommy." They all acknowledge Mason when he says their names.

"You look really familiar," Tommy says. "Do I know you from somewhere?"

"I don't know." I reply, giving Mason an odd look.

"Tommy, what are you talking about?" Mason asks.

"Are you a local?" Tommy ignores Mason and goes straight back to me.

"What are with the questions for her?" Mac asks him.

"I'm sorry. It's just...you–your name sounds really familiar."

Oh so this is what he's getting at. "Have you been to New York during Fashion Week?"

Tommy claps his hands together in recognition. "That's it! You're Kamryn Rawlins. Of Ryn & Co."

"Guilty."

"Oh man, my wife is gonna freak. She loves your line."

"Why couldn't you have just asked her, instead of giving her the third degree?"

"I had to make sure I wasn't going crazy." Tommy defends.

"Newsflash Tommy...you're already crazy." Mac says in a loud whisper.

"So how did you two meet?" Jason pipes up and asks.

"College." Mason responds quickly without getting into all the nitty gritty of our relationship. "Let's play some pool. Y'all can get to know her that way."

"You know how to play Kamryn?" Mac asks.

"I may have played a time or two." I respond coyly as I hand my clutch to Jax and walk over to grab a pool stick and wink at Mason.

He's holding in a silent chuckle. On some of our last minute dates, we would go to the student center and play pool. I beat him every time.

"Do you wanna break or rack?" Mac asks. Looks like I'm playing against him.

I mull it over just for fun. "I think I'll break. And no calling the pocket. That just makes you seem like a tool."

"As you wish." Mac says as he racks up the pool balls.

"I might be bad at this." I feign innocence and say as I get in my pool ready position. I really might be as it's been so long since I've last played a game.

"I won't judge you," Mac says with the overconfidence of an athlete that he might have this game in the bag.

Looking up at Mason and the girls who are all holding in their laughter. I focus back on the pool balls in front of me. I set up my hand and place the cue stick in the crease, I take three fake pumps, and then on the fourth time forward I put all my mite into breaking up the balls. I crack it perfectly, sinking two stripes. When I look at Mac he's utterly confused.

"You played me." He says when he finally finds his voice.

I walk around the table to find my best shot. When I see one that I can bounce off the edge I set up there.

"I guess you will never know." I sink two more and then miss on my third. I take a sip of Mason's drink and then settle between his legs.

"It's not nice to fool people." Mac says as he pouts and tries to find a spot.

"It's not nice to assume that because I design clothes, that I can't play pool either."

Mac sinks two shots and misses on his third. "Fine. I'm giving you the benefit of the doubt."

"Thank you." I say and go up to the table to spot my next shot. I find one and sink one, and then the last stripe. "8 ball corner pocket." All I have to do is lightly hit the cue ball for it to hit the 8 ball. And I do just that. I stand upright and look at Mac who is still in a bit of shock. "Good game Mac. It was fun beating you."

I rack my cue and go settle back between Mason's legs. The warmth of his body calms me. It's weird how these years apart didn't dull the feelings I had for him.

Mason places a kiss to my cheek and I soak it in. Wrapping my arms further around his. Securing my body to his.

The rest of the night passes with easy fun. I get to know the guys a little better. They tell me about their time in the league, how many teams they've played for, if they ever had an injury that they thought they wouldn't come back from; are they married or do they have any kids? Are they close with their families? They ask me how I came to be a fashion designer, when my original plan was psychology. And why I decided to launch my brand in Cincinnati rather than Philadelphia. I regal them of how I was heartbroken in college and used that as a way to heal.

When Mason and I were in school, we talked about the possibility of moving to Cincinnati. I mean, Nashville could have always been the plan for us, but we figured a place far enough away from our families was a good plan. Ohio has an equal balance of city-life and home-life. It also isn't far from Pennsylvania or South Carolina so that was a win. When Mason got traded to Cincinnati he said he thought it was a cruel twist of fate...or even karma. I told him the same thing about my line. That I unconsciously made the decision to move here.

31

KAMRYN

Can I sleep standing up? It's the thought that runs through my mind after every Fashion Week. I've just completed another round at Paris Fashion Week and I'm beyond ready to sleep for the rest of the week. The months leading up to the show are non-stop around the office. We eat, sleep, and breathe all things Paris before we're off to the show. While I still have some people in the office working on the Kamryn side of my company, I always give those of us that come back from Paris the rest of the week off.

I'm waiting at the baggage claim when my phone dings with a text.

> Mason: Hey, baby. I have a car waiting for you so cancel the Uber I know you already ordered.

> Mason: Jax has Lucy and Poppy with her at her loft. The girls and I helped set up your staycation so all you have to do is start your bath when you get to your house.

> Mason: Let me know if you need anything else.

I could cry. At the airport baggage claim. I could actually cry. Would I come off as crazy if I just bursted into tears? The flight was long and I could barely relax my body enough to get some sleep. I kept running through the show wondering if I could have done something different. If I could have added more pieces to my line or if I should have taken out certain pieces.

> Me: You have no idea how much this means to me. Thank you. I do need one more thing.

> Mason: Anything, sweetheart.

> Me: You. At my house.

> Mason: I'll be there soon.

I smile down at my phone until I hear the sound of the luggage being dropped to the baggage claim. Moving towards an area that's less crowded, I patiently wait for my bags to make their way to me.

It takes about ten minutes. But once I have my suitcases, I make my way to the waiting cars and see a driver holding up a sign with my name.

"Hi, I'm Kamryn."

My driver is a middle-aged Black man sporting a goatee. He's wearing the standard driver outfit: black suit with a black tie and white button down shirt. He acknowledges me with a smile and tells me his name is Aaron. Grabbing the handle of the backdoor, he ushers me in before tending to my suitcases and putting those in the trunk.

> Me: I didn't need a car to take me home.

> Mason: Let me spoil you, please?

> Me: I guess I have no reason to object?

Mason: None. I'll see you soon.

The ride from the airport is quiet, which I'm grateful for. I'm thankful that Aaron doesn't attempt to make idle chitchat. Once we hit the highway back to my house does my body relax and my eyes start to droop.

I must've drifted off as I jolt forward when the car finally stopped. Looking around I see my house to the right of me and I give Aaron a sheepish look.

"Sorry," I say with a grimace.

"No worries Ms. Rawlins." Aaron volleys back before he's out of the car and hefting my suitcases out of the trunk. My suitcases are set on the ground before I realize that he said more than two words to me.

Gathering my bag and phone I amble out of the car. Giving around a 'thank you', I lift the handles of my suitcases and head up my front sidewalk. I'm almost to the door when the sound of another car pulls into my driveway. Hesitantly turning, I see Mason clamber out of the driver seat.

"You just couldn't wait, could you?" I yell bursting at the seams as Mason does a little jog to where I'm standing.

He picks me up by the back of my thighs. His arms wrap around my body leaving no space between us. "Not a chance, baby."

We stay like this. Wrapped around each other in full view of my neighbors that prefer to sit out front of their houses. The calm I felt that existed before, makes itself known to me now.

"I missed you." I mumble into Mason's neck.

"I missed you too, baby."

I do my best not to compare our relationship from

before to what we're building it to be now. But already, the missing him that I felt is greater than what it was back then. Mason loosens his hold on me and sets me down on solid ground.

"I'll get your bags." Mason turns me around and lightly pushes me to my front door.

Taking that as my cue, I pull my house key out of the side pocket of my bag and unlock and open my front door. Holding the door open for Mason, I breathe out a sigh of relief that my reset period starts now.

Before I can take a step towards my kitchen to sort out any mail that was brought in, Mason redirects me to the stairs. "Go light your candles and start your bath. I'll be up there in a minute."

I've never had anyone here for me when I get home from a show. Stopping, I turn and launch myself at him and kiss him. In the privacy of my home and not on the front steps of my house for anyone to see. I kiss Mason like I haven't done so in years when it's only been a few weeks. And the care in which he's making sure I'm okay after my trip and cared for emotionally threatens to burst me apart.

"Thank you." I tell him.

Three other words are begging to be freed from my lips. But it's too soon. We've barely had more than a week of uninterrupted time. And I know it's quality over quantity, yet it makes it hard to wonder if I'm falling for the man I've built up in my mind or past Mason.

"You're welcome, baby. Now go upstairs." With a kiss to the tip of my nose, Mason turns and walks down the hallway to my kitchen.

Dragging my weary body up the stairs, I hop on one foot to get my shoe off and drop it with a clunk in my bedroom, followed by the other shoe. My socks soon follow, along with my hoodie that kept me cozy the entire flight. Walking into my bathroom I head for the vanity and look for the essential oils, bath salts, and Dr. Teal's of choice for my bubbles. I toss my hair up into a bun and walk back over to the bath, turning the water on high and pulling the stopper. I shuffle back to my bedroom to get the lighter for my candle and light the ones I know will soothe me.When the water is about halfway I fill the tub with my bath essentials then strip off the rest of my clothes and get in the tub. Instantly my body relaxes as the heat from the water and the scent of my bath concoction overtakes my senses.

Sleep is close to overtaking until Mason walks into the bathroom. "Here's your wine, baby."

Peeling my eyes open, I sit up and take a healthy gulp. "Thank you. You wanna join me?"

"Are you sure?"

"Positive." I tell him and scoot forward so he has room.

I watch with rapt attention as he peels his clothes off. The ripple of his abs and the flex of his forearms. He really has gotten more handsome with age. My mouth goes dry when his pants hit the floor. Trailing my eyes up his toned body I meet his smirk as he walks over to the bath.

The water rises as he settles in behind me and pulls me into him. Now my body fully relaxes.

"Did I tell you I missed you?"

His hands knead into the knots in my shoulders. "You did. I missed you too. But I spent seven years missing you." Mason's hands drift down my back to wrap around my stomach as my head falls back to his shoulder. "Us being apart from each other was hard. I don't think we'll ever be done talking about the past. All of the what could've been and what should've been. But I'm hoping with more time we'll be able to talk about our pasts without it hurting so much."

"You really want to do that?" When we met again all those months ago, I knew I'd have to tell him more about how me and Liam came to be.

"I do. There's so much about your life that I know nothing about."

"Baby, that part of my life is so hard." Confessing that life hasn't been all sunshine and rainbows is hard to admit. "Do we have to talk about it now?"

Mason places a kiss to the side of my head. "No. Not now. Why don't you tell me about the show?"

"It was incredible. Paris had rare warm weather so having the show outside was bearable."

"And what collection was this for?" Our fingers twist and twine together and I watch with a giddiness that can barely be contained.

"This was for Spring. It still drives me wild that pieces for new seasons are shown way in advance. But I love seeing what other designers come up with. The buzz from consumers is what makes designing clothes exciting."

"I'm so proud of you. I know I'm coming in on the middle of your success, but it means the world to see you succeed."

My throat feels tight with the sudden urge to cry. I didn't have this type of support with Liam and here Mason is giving it freely. Turning to face him I search his face and look into the eyes that captured my heart when I was eighteen years old. "Thank you. That means the world to me."

Leaning up to touch my lips to his, I only intend for it to be a quick kiss. But Mason's hand wraps around the back of my neck. His thumb softly rubbing along my jawline as he deepens the kiss. Our tongues tangle and dance. Reacquainting ourselves after our time apart. The water feels hotter. Or that could just be my body temperature rising.

As much as I told myself I would make Mason work to get back in my life, I didn't make him work too hard. In my heart I knew that I couldn't. We've both succeeded in our careers, we're living where we dreamed about, and we're with each other for the long haul.

Taking control of the kiss, Mason slows it down. Peppering my lips and cheek with kisses then nuzzling in my neck, he lets out a contented sigh. "I know our talk is coming. But I'm just glad we're moving forward. You're what I've wanted since I was twenty years old."

If you'd have asked me if Mason and I would have found each other when I was twenty, I would have said no. I was so angry at him. Angry that he could just walk away from what we had. Angry that he made no attempt to reach out to me. I was angry that he made me feel unloveable.

"Is it okay if we just move forward day by day? I'm not knocking your wanting us to talk, but emotionally I can only handle so much." Therapy has taught me to accept what I can handle and how much I can handle. That in order for any of my relationships, friendship or romantic, to succeed, the boundaries that I set in place are keys for them succeeding.

His kiss to the side of my head is acknowledgement enough. "Of course, baby. I don't want to rush you."

"Thank you." Leaning back into his body, I let my body relax. And when the water gets cold we take turns rinsing off in the shower before Mason orders me to lay in bed as he makes us dinner.

Thirty minutes later, Mason has brought up a big bowl of carbonara, along with the rest of the wine. When I heard him tittering around in my kitchen, I about exploded. Once we're settled, I press play on my rewatch of *The Vampire Diaries* and we settle into our meal. We eat until the bowl is empty and my thoughts are all over the place. I'm barely paying attention as I think about our bath conversation. Do I want to burst this happy bubble we're living in by dredging up the past? No. But I need to do it in order for us to find our happy ground.

I place my glass of wine on the nightstand beside me and turn down the volume on the TV.

"What's up?" Mason asks me now, giving me his full attention.

"I want to tell you about Liam. If I wait for when I'll be ready to do so, I'll never tell you." I turn and face Mason and pull a throw pillow into my lap. Taking a deep breath, "I slept with Liam a few months after we broke up."

"Huh?"

"Technically it was that summer. I used him. And for some reason it didn't click that he felt more than *just friends* for me. I avoided him and he called me out on it. Our friendship took a hit my junior year. On top of everything, you leaving and him pausing our friendship, I was a wreck."

Mason takes my hand in his. Rubbing comforting circles in a reassuring gesture.

"Things took a turn my final year of school. I apologized for using him and not seeing the depth of his feelings for me."

His eyebrows raise at that and he looks taken back.

"What?" I ask, scared that he's going to say something I might not like.

"Liam ran into me a few weeks after we started dating. He was a bit too possessive over you and it didn't take long to figure out he's who you were sleeping with before you met me. It also didn't take too long for me to piece together that he had more than friendship feelings for you."

I do my best to mentally rewind back to that time. It's hazy but I still don't see it. "How did I miss that?"

"He was your best friend Kam. Did you ever have feelings for him before we first dated?"

The look on my face has Mason nodding his head. "But I never thought he would feel the same for me. So that's when I proposed to the whole friends with benefits arrangement with him."

"Liam should have spoken up. But continue. What happened after you graduated college?"

Looking up to the ceiling in an effort to get my thoughts in order and my words straight. "When he and I got together senior year, he made a promise that if neither of our dreams came true we wouldn't shut the other out. We wouldn't break the promise of supporting each other no matter what." The memory of betrayal washes over me. "When he wasn't getting the call for baseball that he wanted, he shut me out. He told me promises were meant to be broken. It wasn't long after that I moved out. But he still never got the call that he wanted. I pleaded with him, along with Sarah, to take whatever deal comes to him. He never did."

The look of pity on Mason's face for Liam to never get his dream of playing professionally. If Liam could see it he would probably smack it off his face.

"We bounced back for a little bit and had been dating for about four years at this point. I asked Liam if I was just wasting my time with him. If he was ever going to take the next step with us and he said no."

I've spent so many nights lying awake wondering if I could have said something differently. Would he still be alive?

"What happened next–I blame myself for what happened. No matter how many therapy sessions I went to or how many people told me his death wasn't my fault. It can't take the guilt away. I have to live with the sound of his truck being crushed into the back of an eighteen wheeler." Talking about this again sends me back to that day.

Mason throws the pillow to the side and pulls me to him. Wrapping me in his arms. Tears silently pour down my face.

"It was a few weeks after the funeral when his parents came to my house. They did everything to assure me that his death was not my fault. But again, guilt is a bitch. They brought over a box of Liam things that they thought I'd like to have."

Mason continues to rub circles along my back.

"I was broken. Or I thought I was broken. Opening the box of Liam's things made me unfixable."

"What was in the box, baby?" He asks softly and rubs circles on my back.

"I thought Liam didn't want a forever. But that damn box had a ring in it."

I can't get any more words out. I don't need to.

Mason lays us down on the bed. He comforts me.

Part of growing up is realizing that words don't need to be said in a grand way. It's the actions that are meant to do more than the words can say. Mason comforting me in his quiet way says way more than his words ever could.

32

MASON

I push myself harder on the treadmill after practice. Leaving Kamryn this morning was tough. And while I'm grateful for how early practice was, I was also grateful to put some space between us. Hearing that Liam had a ring for her makes me realize that I could have lost her for good. I'm not sure how many times I'll be able to express how badly I felt when I broke her heart–when I broke both of our hearts. The amount of rookies that came into the league with the support of a significant other made their game that much better. While I didn't struggle my first couple of years, I didn't enjoy it the way I hoped I would. And it made me hate my college coach for making me break up with Kamryn for the game.

I'm not a vengeful person. But seeing my teammates having that support spurred something in me. When I had a break from football I jumped on the phone with the athletic director at CSU. I let him know of the conversation Coach had with me and how unethical it was that I should not have any type of romantic relationships while attempting to go pro. I may have been two years too late, but someone else needed to know. The repercussion of that life shaking moment has affected my game more than it's helped. And since the athletic director is a former pro-bowler, who proposed to his then college girlfriend and now wife of twenty years, he made it a point to listen to my frustration. I didn't want what happened to me to happen to anyone else that declared for the draft.

"Brooks!" Someone shouts from behind me and breaks me from my thoughts from that time in my life. I stumble to a stop and grab the towel next to me to wipe off my sweat.

Rolling off the treadmill I see my offensive coordinator standing in the doorway.

Panting out a "Sir" while I drop to the floor for some body weight exercises. This goes beyond what I'm set to do for the season.

I feel him burning a hole through my head. Knowing I won't get away with pushing my body further.

"What's on your mind Mason?" His voice is closer as he takes a seat on the bench beside me.

"Personal things, sir."

"Alright. Stop working yourself to the bone and tell me what's going on. That's an order."

Stopping myself from more bodily torture, I sit up and place my arms overtop of my knees. "I found out my girl-friend could have been engaged had her previous boyfriend not died. And I kicked myself for breaking up with her to be able to get drafted."

The silence is louder than the loudest football stadium as I look at my coach and wait for him to say something.

"I question your college coach's morals for having you do that. Is your girlfriend going to affect how you play this season?"

"No sir. I played better when I was with her in college.

She pushed me to become a friend, a teammate, and a better captain. My stats improved. She was the best part of playing in college."

"For that I hope your coach gets reprimanded. But why are you beating yourself up? Running yourself ragged is not a healthy way to let out your frustration that life could have gone in a different way. You can't change the past anymore than you can predict the future." He tells me.

"I don't know," I huff out. "I guess it just got me thinking that I could've lost her forever, you know?"

When I didn't think other people were in the cards for us, her getting engaged to someone was not something I mentally prepared myself for. Had Liam lived would they have gotten engaged? Would Kamryn even live in Cincinnati?

"Don't dwell on the *what ifs* because it's not healthy. All you'll do is drive yourself crazy. My advice is to talk to your girlfriend. You're both adults and communication is the key to a successful relationship."

Coach gets up to leave and I thank him before he's out the door. I really have no reason to feel any type of way about Liam and Kamryn. But it doesn't sting any less to know about the ring.

> Kamryn: Hey, are you coming back to my place?

I left her asleep in her bed with a short text of 'Practice. Be by later.' I had no clue what else to say.

> Me: Yeah, baby. Let me clean up here and then I'll be over.

～

WHEN I GET to the front door, I give it a test and swear under my breath when it's unlocked. Kamryn told me she never locks her front door when she's home. And I, along with her sister and friends, have scolded her for testing her safety.

"Kamryn?" I call out after I lock the door and stroll down the short hallway that leads into the living room and kitchen.

"In the backyard," I hear from the open patio doors. I empty my pockets, give Poppy some head scratches, and make my way to her backyard. I lean against the doorframe and watch her work. Seeing this new side of her: the focused and wholly talented side of her, brings me more joy than I could possibly explain. It's weird trying to compare the college version of someone to the adult version of them. That's what I've been doing with Kamryn and I need to learn that they're two different people.

Pushing off from where I'm leaning, I make my way to the chair next to her. Lucy brings the stick over to where I sit and I toss it back out into the yard. How do I bring up my feelings? Do I just say what I'm actually feeling or just get straight to the point?

Kamryn notices my thoughts. "Are you okay?"

"I don't know, Kam. To hear that Liam had bought you a ring. Knowing that if he were still alive you'd probably be married to him. You and I would have been a moment in history."

She places her sketchpad on the seat next to her and comes over to where I'm sitting, straddling my lap. Her hands rest on the sides of my neck as her thumbs caress my jaw.

"I don't think Liam and I would've lasted. Subconsciously I was trying to morph what I had with you to something that I could have with him." Kam starts and traces my face with feather-like patterns. "When I found the ring, I was angry and so hurt. I was led on this seesaw by Liam into thinking that we had a future and then no future. It went back and forth for about a year. Him keeping it in the box–do you want to know what I did with it?"

Do I? If she tells me she kept it I might just turn her house upside down to find it. But instead I give a little nod, letting her know that I'd like to know.

"I wore it for about a year. I think it was a way of me holding onto him since I couldn't physically do that anymore. But in one of my therapy sessions, I was advised that by wearing that ring I was holding on to a past that was no longer written in the stars for me. The ring was keeping me from reaching my fullest potential. It was a day in February that I came back and visited Liam. As I was talking to him, I slowly dug a hole in the ground in front of his grave. When it got deep enough, I took the ring off, and I buried it. As much as I loved Liam, that ring was not mine in the real sense. Could it have been mine? Maybe. But since he's dead I have no way of knowing. You two were the greatest loves of my life. I'm not sorry for saying it. But your ring is the only one I can see wearing for the rest of my life when that time does come."

I let out a woosh of breath that I had been holding in. How Kamryn has a way with words that alleviate my own fears, I will never know. Leaning forward to press a quick kiss to her lips.

"I'm sorry I left this morning. I needed my thoughts in order. And comparing myself to a dead guy and wanting to kick his ass isn't fair to either of you."

"You came back," she points out. "That's what matters."

With a subtle nod, I tell her the words I said once before.

Words that held more weight when I broke her heart. "Kamryn, I love you. I always will."

"I love you too. Always have." She buries her face in my neck and wraps her arms around me just as tightly.

We sit like this for what feels like hours although it's probably only minutes. Kamryn in my lap with her face buried in my neck. My arms anchoring her to me as our hearts sync together.

THE PAST MONTH with Kamryn has been as easy as breathing. We've managed to work at our relationship with our schedules as busy as they have been. While the road trips for games have made having a relationship tricky, FaceTime has made it so we can be with each other without being with each other.

But now our schedule is lightening up for the next two weeks. We have our Thursday night game at home and then a Bye Week and I have last minute plans that I'm hoping I won't have to cancel.

I walk down the hallway to my offensive coordinators office the Wednesday before our game.

"Hey, coach. Do you have a minute?"

He looks up from his tablet. "Yeah. Come in Brooks."

Taking a seat in front of his desk, I don't beat around the bush. "I was thinking about taking a trip after the game."

His eyebrows scrunch together. It's very uncommon for any athlete, let alone one that's a starter and in a good seed spot.

"Mason, you know that's not how things are run around here."

"I know. But hear me out." I plead. If I need to get on my

knees and beg I will. He sits back in his chair and gives me a short nod. "When we win on Thursday night, we'll be put at a higher seed in the division. This bye week couldn't come at a better time."

He regards me like I've gone insane. And maybe I have. Going out of the country while the season is still happening is ludicrous.

"Come talk to me after the game."

It's not a no. But it's not a yes. I feel like I just asked my parents to go to the mall.

"Yes sir. Alright, well I'll let you get back to what you were doing." Heaving myself out of the chair, I tap the top of his desk and walk out towards the team locker room.

"ALRIGHT BOYS, I know we're all tired. Jamison, they've been double teaming you all night. Let's use that to our advantage." The noise of the sold out crowd hopefully drowns out what I'm telling my guys. We're up by a touchdown in the fourth quarter. The other team came to play, but so did we. We just need another touchdown to coast into a win.

"Break."

I stay back from the huddle as my O-line heads to their positions. When they're settled, I take my spot behind the center. Looking around at the defense, I lock back in, taking a breath before I call out the play. The ball is snapped into my hands and I drop back a couple of steps, looking for my open guy.

I don't see it. I don't see the hit coming before it's too late. It feels like a semi has crashed into my body. The sharp sting of pain that happens when the force of our bodies landing on the side of my body. And I know that I just cracked a rib.

I try to move my body once the weight of the defenseman is up, but I can't feel the left side of my body. The roar of the crowd fades to nothing as I try to get my brain to send waves to unresponsive body parts.

"Mason. Can you move?" One of the athletic trainers asks me.

I move my right arm and leg.

"Good. How about the other side?"

I manage to twitch my left foot. "I can't move my arm Jeff."

"What about your neck?"

I turn my head left and right. The team doctors continue their on field assessment. Jeff comes back mournfully with a, "We're going to have to cart you off the field."

My nod is all that I can give. I went my whole career without a major injury. Hamstring, quad, and shoulder injuries were easy to come back from. But can I come back from this? The sound of the gator getting closer gets my heart rate pumping. If I could walk off this field to alleviate myself, my teammates, the fans, my family, and Kamryn I would.

I drown out the noise around me. As if that hasn't already happened with the crowd falling to a hush. The only time it's been silent in this stadium is when I come here for solo drills. But now, the silence is because of me.

I'm jostled around and let out a curse as my body is flipped onto a backboard. I keep my stare on the night sky. Not wanting to look at my teammates or my opponents. I distantly hear the crowd of applause as I'm loaded onto the gator. When the cart moves I give a thumbs up to those in the stadium. Not truly knowing if everything is okay. But knowing that this injury may be the one to finally take me out of the game.

"Please let me back to see him," a soft feminine voice says.

"It's against protocol, ma'am. I can't let you back there." A burly voice says.

I look over at Jeff. "If that's Kamryn will you let her back here?"

They have me laid up on a table. The team doctor did a quick evaluation and said there was no explanation for the numbness that I experienced, but an MRI would answer all of the questions.

A flurry of dark chocolate hair and worried eyes enter my line of sight. My girl is trying her best to hold off her tears. I told her I never wanted to make her cry again. This is why.

"Baby, come here." I beckon with my right arm. My left arm is in a sling and I have an icepack on my ribs. It hurts to breathe but I can't stand not holding her.

Kam slides onto the bed next to me. Too carefully for my liking but I know she's doing it because of my injury. When she's settled next to me I feel her body relax.

Her touch is delicate as it slings low over my waist.

I voice the fear and realization, "I think this might be it for me."

"What do you mean?"

"When I got hit, I couldn't feel the left side of my body." I run my free hand up and down her back soothing her. "The team doctor doesn't know why it happened but that an MRI would hopefully explain it more."

"But you can rehab right?" Her voice is so hopeful.

My dad put me into football because he and I needed more stuff to do with our free time. And I'll thank him forever because this game led me to Kamryn. It took me away from her, but it also led me back to her. I can survive without the game, but I can't survive without her.

"I think it all depends on what the doctor says. I'd want to avoid surgery at all costs, so PT would be the best route. But I don't want to think about that."

"Watching you from the box, not knowing what was happening, I was terrified Mason."

One of the biggest risks of playing professionally is getting hurt. College was slightly easier. But I'm playing against guys with way more experience under their belt. So when my O-line fails the other team will take advantage of that.

"I'm sorry, baby."

Kamryn leans up to kiss me. I can't move too much towards her so one kiss is all we can do. We lay here until the game ends and I'm set to go to the hospital. By the boisterous sounds of the team, we at least won the game. I send Kam home because she has a big meeting regarding her holiday line. But the fact that she was here tonight meant the world to me. Now I wait for news to whether or not I can keep playing a game that took me away from the one person I ever loved.

33

KAMRYN

Before designing, I loved the holidays. The rush of last minute shopping, the decorations, and holiday joy. But as an adult the malls are jam-packed, traffic is a mess, and last minute online shoppers threaten to drive me insane.

When I had the crazy idea to drop an affordable version of *Ryn & Co.* and name it *Kamryn*, but also launch it during the beginning of the holiday season; well I'm sure those who worked for me wanted to strangle me. But it's become such a success that we're planning to do quarterly launches. The *Kamryn* line has none of the pieces priced over fifty dollars. It has a mix of patterns that are bold or subtle, neutrals, dark colors, bold colors, casual, business casual, and nights out on the town. My plan is to add shoes to the brand, but our main focus is affordable clothing.

I'm envious of my customers as I wish I had a line like this when I was teaching.

It's been over a year in the making and we finally launched online in November along with a holiday line. Which was perfect timing since most people started their holiday shopping around then. Some look for deals on clothes to refresh their work wardrobe. Our plan is to keep *Kamryn* online for the first year before moving it and *Ryn & Co.* into a storefront here in the city. Now that the holidays are just about over, I have to keep the creative juices flowing and start thinking up designs for spring and summer, on top of my more high-end brand.

My phone rings with a FaceTime from Mason. "Hey, handsome."

"Hey, baby. How are you?"

"Exhausted." I place my glasses on top of my head.

"I'm sure. But I think I have a way to take your mind off of it."

"How so?"

"You. Me. London. Five days."

"What? Baby I don't think I can just drop what I'm doing last minute. And what about football? It's the middle of the season."

His injury scared me. But he assured me he was fine after his MRI. I have no reason to doubt him. Yet standing in the crowd as I watched him go limp terrified me more than I care to admit.

"Yes you can. I already talked to Jax and Olivia. They said they would oversee business while you're gone. And plus, you need a break too. You've been working non-stop and you and your body need a refresh. I have some news about football but I'd rather do that in person."

I chew on my bottom lip and mull it over. I do need a break. I'm starting to stress out and that usually means I don't eat or sleep very well and everything else gets put on the back-burner. "Okay, I'm in. When do we leave?"

"In two days. Can you be ready by then?"

Wow that's soon. "It's short notice, but challenge accepted Mr. Brooks."

"Okay. I'll see you soon sweet girl. I love you."

"I love you too."

London for five days with Mason. This holiday season can't get any better.

I THINK I have everything I need. I keep running through my mental and written list. I've gone over it ten times because I'm that crazy about forgetting something. I've been to London once but it was strictly for work. So the sightseeing I'm hoping to do this time around excites me.

"Jax, will you come help me?" I plead from my room.

I hear Jax running up the stairs with Lucy right behind her. "Let's run through your list again. Yadi yadi ya. Seriously Kam, I think you have everything."

"It's paranoia Jax. Please."

"Okay, okay."

We run through my list again and I'm once again reminded that I'm crazy.

"I told you, you had everything."

"I know you did. Thank you. Are you sure you're fine staying here?"

"Are you kidding? Your house has everything and more. Plus, I have Lucy and Poppy to keep me company. Isn't that right girl?"

Lucy barks and nuzzles Jax's hand for some petting. Poppy, my black cat, side-eyes Lucy for her loud interruption.

"Well I'm glad that she'll be taken care of."

"Of course she will. Make sure your carry-on is packed

and everything is charged up. That's going to be a long flight. And don't forget your airplane pillow. We all know you get cranky when you don't get your sleep."

I roll my eyes at my sister. "You don't know me."

She arches a brow at my statement.

"Okay fine," I concede.

"Glad you agree. Listen, I'm gonna head out. I'll be by in the morning so I'm taking Lucy into the office while you're out so she's not here by herself. I know you don't like that, but the change of scenery will be good for her. Plus, her being cooped up in the house while you're off in London just seems like a fair trade for me. And I think Poppy will appreciate the silence."

I have a black cat and a golden retriever. Still never would've guessed that pairing for me. "Okay. Fine. Go. I'll see you in the morning before I leave."

ONCE JAX IS GONE and I'm sure that I'm not missing anything from my suitcases, I'm cuddled up on the couch with Lucy, reading with the TV on as background noise. I'm just to the good part when someone knocks on my door. Lucy gets up and starts barking, sending Poppy upstairs to hide.

"Who is it girl?" I look through the peephole and see Mason standing there with a suitcase next to him. I open the door, surprised that he's here.

"Surprised to see me?"

"Yes. What are you doing here? I thought you were picking me up in the morning?" I step aside to let him in. When I lock the door and turn around, he captures me in a bear hug.

"I just missed you. And I couldn't wait until the morning."

"You're too sweet. I missed you too."

Mason leads us back over to the couch. He pulls off the blanket from the back and wraps it around us. I look at him curiously, but he just picks back up my e-reader and places it in my hand. As he waits for me to power it back up, he pulls me to him and wraps his arm around my shoulders.

"Read your book." Mason says and kisses me on the temple.

Nights like this are what I dream about. Mason and I settled in complete comfort. He's exactly what I ever wanted in a man. He's selfless, kind, warm, passionate, dedicated, adventurous, loving.

Mine.

"Baby wake up," Mason lightly sings in my ear and presses a kiss to the side of my head. I feel the plane making its descent into the London City Airport.

Traveling first class has its advantages but it also makes me sleepier than I should be. I blame the time zone changes. Or that I'm blindly handing over my trust to two men to make sure that we make it to our destination and I naturally freak myself out til I have to go to sleep.

I open my eyes to Mason looking down at me. I'm always shy after I wake up. And no matter how many times Mason and I have woken up together, that hasn't faded. He still turns me into that bashful eighteen year old girl.

"You're so cute when you blush. What were you thinking about?" Mason notices everything about me. It's one of the things I love about him.

"How you still manage to make me feel like a love-struck teenager. And how I hope with everything in me that that feeling never fades."

Mason leans forward and presses a soft and too chaste kiss to my lips, yet I still feel it all the way to my toes. "Me too, baby."

When we safely land, the captain makes an announcement and everyone aboard claps and cheers. Once the plane is stopped safely, the first class passengers make way to gather their things from the overhead compartment and off the plane.

Mason gets up first and dutifully grabs both of our carry-on bags, leaving me to follow him. Not that I mind. My man has an incredible behind. I will never let him forget it.

"Kamryn? Are you coming?" Mason asks with an all-knowing smirk gracing his face. Oh, he knows all right.

"Eventually," I respond cheekily. Okay, so I'm always horny for him. It's like my lady bits are electronically wired to him. And it makes it a little uncomfortable at times. Okay, a lot uncomfortable at times. Like right now. *Get a move on Kamryn!*

Someone clears their throat behind me, snapping me out of my daze. Heat creeps up my cheeks in embarrassment when I turn around to apologize.

"I'm sorry. I got distracted," I say to the older woman behind me.

She must be in her late sixties to mid seventies. She looks as if she's about to reprimand me when she looks past me at Mason. "It's no problem sweetheart. I would've gotten distracted too." She ends with a wink.

And with that I walk towards my amused boyfriend who thankfully lets me pass him to leave the plane.

"It's not funny!" I say to Mason as he tries to control his amusement.

"It's very funny. You can't keep your eyes off of me."

"Okay, Mr. Ego. Let's reign that in just a bit."

"Only for you angel face."

I let that name pass. He knows that's my least favorite pet name. "So what's the plan now?"

"Well, we'll get our luggage. Find our car. And then eat and sleep for the rest of the night. And then tomorrow we start our exploration. How's that sound?"

"Perfect," I say. Because it really is perfect that he's planned all of this out.

We walk with the rest of the passengers to baggage claim and wait off to the side immersed in each other.

"I want these five days to be all about us. I want new memories. I want new firsts with you," Mason says.

As if I need more convincing. I wrap my arms around his waist and slide them under his sweatshirt and caress his back. "Yes. I want all that too."

Mason gently tips my chin up so we're eye to eye. "I love you, Kamryn Rawlins. You've been the only girl for me. You've been the only girl to see me for me. And not just as an athlete. As a human being. Thank you."

"You don't have to thank me for loving you."

Mason presses another soft kiss to my lips. It's still not enough so I push forward on my toes to make it last longer. But whimper when he pulls away.

"I know, baby. But if we get started I'm not going to be able to stop." Mason explains pulling me closer to his front. And if what's poking me in the stomach is of any indication that he's as turned-on as I am, then I know I'm in for a fun night.

I place a kiss on his sweatshirt-covered chest and breathe out a frustrated breath.

"You two are so adorable." The older lady from the plane says to us. "Honeymoon?"

"No, ma'am. Not yet. One day though," Mason answers.

My heart rate triples in speed. Being with someone that's so sure of what they want never fails to surprise me.

"Well you two are lucky to have one another. Enjoy your trip," the older woman says.

"Thank you." Mason responds before looking back down at me.

"I love you a lot," I tell him.

"Ditto baby girl."

Once we get our bags and wait for the car to pull around, I'm utterly exhausted. That is until I see our hotel.

I hear Mason chuckle next to me, but I'm too enthralled by the beauty of the front of the hotel.

"You like it baby?"

"I—have no words."

"Come on. Let's get our bags, check in, and order some food."

I'm even more impressed when we walk inside. "Wow," I whisper under my breath. I'm almost too afraid to speak at a normal level.

"You've got a little drool." Mason teases.

"Shut up!" I whisper-yell.

"Why are you whispering?"

I lightly shove him towards the front desk. "Go check in." I urge him, embarrassment heating my cheeks.

I watch until Mason gets to the receptionist desk and I look around the hotel in awe. I've never stayed somewhere as extravagant as this. Yeah, my family and I went on some memorable family vacations, and traveling for fashion shows meant staying in whatever hotels were closest to the show. But none of them were like this. Most likely because the focus of those trips wasn't to stay holed up in the hotel for the majority of the time.

"Rendering you speechless is one of my favorite things to do. Let's go," Mason says when he walks back over with the key in his hand.

"Is that because it's the only time that I'm quiet?"

"I am shocked that you would even think that I don't like hearing your voice all of the time." He says with a dramatic hand to his chest.

We step into the elevator and Mason presses the button for our floor.

"How about we play a game?"

"What did you have in mind Ms. Rawlins?"

Hmm. I can play this game. I sidle up in front of Mason and walk my finger up his chest and then back down. Teasing the hem of his sweatshirt and the waistband of his sweats. I hear the choked groan in his throat.

"I don't think I have to spell it out any further. Loser pays for room service. Winner gets to do whatever they want to the loser. As long as the loser okays it. Consent and all of that. Are you up for it?"

Mason clears his throat before answering. "I'm all in."

The elevator dings before I can continue my torture. I feel like a boiling kettle of water that's about to explode with steam. I can't be the only one that's feeling like this. If Mason's kiss and his growing erection were any indication of what he's feeling, then I have no idea who's going to win this little game.

When the door opens and we walk over the threshold, I'm rendered speechless again. Mason has really outdone himself. I've only read about the Garden House Suite in

Vogue, but seeing it in person is jaw dropping. I turn to read Mason since he's reading me. But the only thing I see in his eyes is heat.

And that heat in the pit of my stomach evolves into a full on inferno. My breathing matches that of Mason's. Deep. Heavy. Full of longing in not just our breathing, but in our heated stares.

Slowly, I trail my hands to my cardigan and start unbuttoning it. Taking his cue from me, Mason begins to pull his sweatshirt over his head.

It's a draw. We both lost.

34

KAMRYN

After a day full of catching up on sleep, eating, and sex we've now started our tourist vacation. We're walking towards Big Ben when something Mason said pops in my head.

"What was it that you had to tell me?"

"Huh?"

"You said that you had something to tell me something about football."

"Oh. That. After this season I'm retiring." He says it so nonchalantly, like he's talking about the weather changing and not just changing his whole life.

I think I heard him incorrectly. "Come again."

"Wouldn't you want that."

"I'm serious, Mason."

"I know you are. You remember that hit I took in that last game?"

"Yeah. You just said it was nothing. That it was just a bruise. You lied to me?"

Mason pulls us off to the side. "I didn't at the time. That's what I was told. And that's what it was. Until I tried light

341

practicing. Between throwing through that pain and the hits, I've been told that if I take any other sort of hit, I may lose total mobility. And I don't want that, baby."

"So what does that mean for football?" I'm trying my hardest not to let this news of him stepping away from football affect me.

"I finish out this season as an official player. But I won't be playing. And they can't buy me out with all that money they put up to get me. So I would stay and help out with the quarterbacks. It's unorthodox, but it's what makes sense."

"Are you okay with it?" Because that is the only thing that worries me.

"Honestly, before I even got traded I told myself that ten years in the league is plenty enough. And after the hits over the years and the one at the last game, I'm realizing that my body isn't recovering as easily as it once did. After this season ends, I'm done."

I'm trying my hardest to hold back my tears. But failing miserably.

"Baby don't cry." Mason says as he gently wipes the tears from under my eyes.

"But this is everything that you worked for." I say through a sob.

"It's also what took me away from you. I'm tired of living my life always on the road. I want to settle down in one place."

He makes a lot of sense.

"I don't want you to wake up one morning and regret not playing your last years out."

Mason squats a little so we're eye level. "Hey. I'd rather stop now when I have full use of my body. I don't want to live a life half-functioning. I want a full mobile life with you and one day our kids."

I nod my head through the tears that are still falling.

"Okay. Deep breath." Mason instructs.

I do as he says. Taking multiple deep breaths to bring me back to normal.

"Good girl. I love you. And I don't want that kind of life for me. For us."

"I love you too." I say as he gently wipes the tears from under my eyes.

"Now come on, pretty girl. Let's go be tourists." Mason declares as he wraps an arm around my shoulder and directs us towards Big Ben. I melt into him and press a kiss to the side of his chest.

I love this man more than anything. But I'm terrified that he's gonna wake up missing it more than he loves me. Football tore us apart once. Yes, we found our way back to one another but who's to say that something better won't come around for him? Am I being too negative? Things between Mason and I are better now that we're older. We're both established in our careers. The love we have is stronger and more solid now.

"Have you ever thought about moving?"

"Where did that come from?"

"I dunno. I guess I like the anonymity that both of us have over here. You know?"

Mason nods his head thoughtfully. "I do. But you and I both know that we could never be too far from our family."

"You're right. Oh my god!" I wish I knew other words but those are failing me at the moment.

We've finally come into view of Big Ben. I knew the clock tower was iconic, but wow!

"It's huge." I say in astonishment and hear Mason snicker beside me. "The clock. Not you."

"Uh huh. Well, we can't go in for a tour, but we can take pictures."

"Are you going to retire to become my social media boyfriend?" I joke.

"Absolutely. Although that title will have to change to social media husband."

Giggling and blushing like a schoolgirl, I pull Mason towards an area that's a little less crowded, but still has Big Ben in its view.

Mason instructs me where to stand, how to pose, how to have my facial expressions; I come to find out that he's really good at this and I need to thank his sister.

"Excuse me?" I ask someone that's walking past. Would you mind taking some pictures of us?"

"Of course not. Are you Kamryn Rawlins?"

I'm surprised she recognizes me. "I am."

"I love your clothes. I'm anxiously awaiting your new line to drop."

"Thank you. That means a lot. What's your name?"

"Kate."

"How about as thanks for taking some pictures, I'll send you some stuff from my new line?"

She looks taken aback and shakes her head. "I couldn't. It's just a few pictures. And I really don't mind."

"Nonsense. I really insist. Message me your sizes and address to me and I will send those over to you personally when I get back to the states." I tell her.

"Thank you so much. Okay. Not getting emotional. Let me get your pictures."

I like this girl. Mason hands the camera to her and comes strolling over to me.

"That was sweet of you."

I shrug like it's no big deal. "It's not a big deal."

"Okay, lovebirds. Pose however you want and then we'll do some candid shots."

"Thanks Kate."

"No problem."

"Come here."

I eye Mason with trepidation. He turns me around so my front is to his back. I look up at him with so much love, it actually kind of hurts.

"Okay. Now Mason, I want you to pick Kamryn up. And Kamryn, I want you to wrap your legs around his waist."

"We got this." Mason champions.

I'm giggling like a love-struck teenager as Mason lifts me up effortlessly. I seem to do that even more.

"That's good. Now Kamryn, place your hand that's furthest away from the camera on his shoulder, and rest the other one on his chest."

I do as she says.

"Perfect! Hold that pose!"

Looking into Mason's eyes, I see it all.

Love.

Warmth.

Home.

Future.

Family.

Without thinking and caring that we're in public, I lean down to kiss Mason. It's not anything too hot or heavy. It's the pressure of my lips resting on his.

I pull away before either of us decide to take it any further.

"I think I got some really good ones." Kate announces.

Mason gently puts me back on the ground, and I walk over to her to get back the camera.

"Thank you. You're a lifesaver."

"No problem. I'm just glad I could capture some moments of you two."

I give her a kind smile. "Don't forget to DM me your address and sizes."

"I won't. You two enjoy the rest of your trip."

We watch Kate walk off to wherever it is she's going.

I'm eager to go to the room so I can upload these to my laptop and edit them. But I'm not sure what else Mason has planned for us for the day.

"Come on, let's go back to the room." He says.

"Are you sure? You don't have anything else planned for us?"

He shakes his head and grabs my hand taking us in the direction of our hotel.

"So since we're going to be those cheesy tourists..." Mason begins as we're walking and I look at him to continue. "Let's continue on with the cheesiness."

"What do you have in mind?" I'm insanely curious.

"Another photoshoot at the hotel. But completely undone. No makeup on. No hair done. All natural." He says with twinkling eyes.

"How natural?"

"You'll see. This is my Instagram boyfriend audition."

I laugh at his new title as we walk the rest of the way in comfort.

"Thank you." I tell Mason honestly when we're back in our hotel room.

"For what beautiful girl?"

"For...making me happier than I ever thought possible. For helping me accept that it's okay to relax. For spoiling me with you and not just your money. Although I know none of this is cheap. Thank you for loving me, and for seeing a future beyond next week."

Some days I wonder what would have happened had Liam not passed. Would I already be married? Would I still be a teacher? Would we have ended up splitting not long after marrying?

"You know that I would do anything for you Kam. You don't have to thank me for loving you. That's easy."

"I had a revelation. An epiphany, if that's what you'd call it." I say. Deciding that I should just tell Mason.

"What was that?"

"That I would marry you in a heartbeat if possible."

The words aren't even out for a minute when Mason's lips come crashing down on mine. Stealing my breath as he picks me up by my thighs forcing me to wrap my legs around his waist. Walking to our room, he climbs onto the middle of the bed and carefully lowers us without breaking the kiss. I still can't wrap my head around the strength that he possesses.

My hands travel down his torso and I pull at the hem, raising it until he has to break our kiss to remove his sweater and undershirt. Once his shirt is off, he moves to take my sweater off. Teasing me with soft touches until I'm a writhing mess on the bed. My sweater flies off my body and joins his on the floor.

Mason brings his mouth to mine in a slow kiss while trailing his hands down my torso. When his hands get to my jeans, I'm just about crawling out of my skin.

"Mason, please." I pant and not even care that I sound desperate.

He continues his slow and torturous trail of making me squirm by slowly unbuttoning and unzipping my jeans. He pulls my jeans down just enough as his hand snakes between the fabric. Rubbing my clit through my underwear has me losing my mind. The pressure increases as my orgasm rocks through me.

"Oh my god!" I gasp out.

Mason's mouth covers mine, absorbing my gasps as my orgasm continues to swim through me. His warmth leaves me as he slides his body down the bed and takes my pants with him.

I've barely recovered from the first orgasm before his mouth covers my pussy. My hands grip the sheets and a strangled curse flies out of my mouth.

"Eyes on me baby." Mason tells me. When I pick my head up, he holds eye contact with me as the tip of his tongue flicks my clit before sliding into my opening. The salaciousness of it all has my orgasm sneaking up on me. "That's it. Come for me Kamryn."

My body is weak to his command. Mason places a pillow under my hips and enters me in one slow stroke.

"Christ, baby. I feel your pussy fluttering around my cock." Mason breathes out.

"You're so deep." All I feel is him and the way his cock hits every nerve. "I'm close, Mase."

"Rub your clit for me baby." My legs are placed on his shoulders as he continues his slow, languorous thrusts.

My breath catches in my throat. "Right there. I need to come Mason."

"Me too, baby. Let go."

And I do. My body shakes uncontrollably with my orgasm pulling Mason over the edge as well. His strokes become slower as the high comes down.

Mason falls to the side and takes me with him.

"How'd I do?" Mason asks with all the humor.

"World series win. Super Bowl champ. World cup winner."

"That is quite a prize."

I lean up and rest my chin on his chest. "You are my ultimate prize. I don't mean it to sound cheesy or anything."

I'm rewarded with a cute little smile from him.

I wish for days like this. Where we're tangled in sheets and away from life's responsibilities. Where it's just us two existing in each other's orbit.

35

KAMRYN

FOUR MONTHS LATER

We're walking through Downtown Cincinnati and I can't help but steal glances at my handsome man. He's still got a nice tan from our days spent wandering around the beautiful island that was Santorini and lounging at the beach and pool. And apparently all of the other females can't stop staring at him either.

"What are you looking at missy?" Mason asks when I peek at him for the tenth time.

My cheeks pink in embarrassment like I've been caught with my hand in the cookie jar. "You."

He smiles shyly at me. "And what are you thinking about?"

"Skipping lunch and going back to my place," I say without hesitation.

His eyes darken before he blinks a little and realizes that we're in a public place. "Ms. Rawlins. You are insatiable." He wraps his arm around my shoulder to bring me in closer to him. "Besides...it's good for us to be seen out and about."

Since Mason announced his retirement it freed up a lot of

time for us. Our relationship went fully public. And while there was some criticism and people dug into our past, we haven't let those opinions penetrate us. With my design schedule being way ahead, I've given my employees a full week off. Will I come to regret this? Maybe. But I also have a collaboration with Nina in the works so it's best to come back with fresh minds.

We're meeting the girls and some of Mason's former teammates for food. Since we've been living here we haven't explored the way Downtown should be explored. And the best way to immerse yourself where you live is by eating. Our whole day is planned around food and bar hopping. With mine and Mason's first stop to get a coffee and to split a giant cinnamon roll.

Once our food is purchased and coffee in hand, we find a bench to share our food.

"Ladies first," Mason declares and holds the first bite out to me.

"I'm not just going to bite into it."

He looks at me like I'm insane like I didn't just hold up a whole cinnamon roll.

"You are one weird woman." He proclaims.

I lean in to kiss him on the cheek. "Yeah, but you love me anyway."

"I do."

We eat in relative silence. Watching the mid-morning crowd venture into the still waking up city.

"What are you thinking about?" Mason asks, pulling me from my stare into the distance.

Turning to look at him, I blurt out what I've wanted to ask him since London, "Move in with me. I mean you're there most of the time anyways. And while I love your apartment, Lucy can't run around whenever." I wouldn't be a proper millennial if I didn't think about my dog having the necessary space to run around.

"Are you sure?"

Nodding. "I'm one hundred percent sure."

His answering smile is reward enough. "Yes. I'll move in with you."

It's hard not to compare the future living situation to the past. But like I always war with myself, I'm older. Mason and I already spend most nights together. And as much as I love the view from his apartment, it's not a home. At least not one where a family can be born or pets can roam free.

"So what's next for you two?" Sarah asks when we're at our final stop for the day, Queen City Exchange, and it's just our group with a few other people that decided to stop in for the day.

We've all gorged ourselves on food and drinks that we'll have to UBER to our respective homes.

"Like after here? Or in general?" I think I know what Sarah is getting at. But I want her to spell it out.

She gives me a *are you dumb* look. "In general, smartass."

Blowing her a kiss, I announce to our group, "Mason and I are moving in together."

"It's about time" and "Congratulations" and "When's the wedding?" are tossed out. I wasn't joking when we were in London. I would marry Mason as soon as possible. Now that he's retired and is waiting to hear back from some sportscaster jobs, we have time.

"Enough about us. Emily, where's your beau?"

A blush covers her face. She's been going strong with her new beau for a little bit. I'm still in awe of her resilience to let love back in. While it wasn't as easy for me, she was more open to the possibility of finding the person that fills the missing pieces of her life.

"He's at home, while his son is with his parents."

I look at her quizzically. "He didn't want to come out with us?"

"Kamryn, he owns a bar. The last place he wants to be on his day off is at a bar."

I give her a *you're right* nod.

I look around at the people that have become my people. But the happiness I feel with this group falters when I see Sarah watching the TV with a sad look on her face. I follow her line of sight and see a baseball game on. The truth is that I've been a terrible friend to Sarah. When Liam passed, she dropped everything to be with me. I guess in my grief and in my healing I refused to acknowledge anyone else's grief.

"Sarah. Come with me." I place my drink on the table in front of us and kiss Mason on the cheek before heading over to Sarah.

Our hands clasp as I lead her to the back patio of the bar. When we're seated, I wait for her jaw to unclench. In all the times we've been friends I've never seen her so upset.

"Sarah, I'm sorry."

She looks up at me and a tear falls down her cheek. I feel like absolute shit.

"I've been a terrible friend. Because when Liam passed I could only think about myself. I never considered your part in all of it."

Sarah was interning for the family friend that ran a sports business with agents. She was tasked with getting teams to get Liam on their radar. And as the days dwindled and no teams were calling for him, the defeat on both of their faces crushed me.

"I thought I was fine. It's been years since he passed. But sometimes I'll look around and feel like he should be here."

The day Liam passed, Sarah got news that a team did want him. I never took the time to see how the other people in my life were affected. At the time my grief took precedence.

"Have you seen a therapist? Or at least talked to anyone?" Seeing a therapist helped me. I still see mine regularly.

She shakes her head. Defeat coats her body. Who was once the strongest and confident out of our group is slowly drowning in guilt. I don't want what happened to him to happen to her.

I scoot next to her and wrap my arm around her shoulder, pulling her into me. "I think talking to someone would really help. You've alway been Team Kamryn, well now it's time for me to be Team Sarah. Anytime you need me, I want you to call me." Her body trembles with the sobs I know she's trying her hardest to lock down. "If you need to get away from the city, name the place and I will personally go with you. You don't have to be tough every single day, Sarah. If you want a slumber party, say the word and I'll have Mason do our bidding. You're my best friend and I can't lose you."

We stay like this for however long Sarah needs it. What became a roommate assignee when we were eighteen, has become a lifelong sisterhood that transcends any sorority connection that we made. I catch Mason watching us from the backdoor and give him a small smile.

I almost feel even worse for abandoning the friendships

I had for a relationship with him. While I know he would never make me choose, I do need to find that balance.

36

KAMRYN

Nina: Landed at the airport. Be at your office shortly.

Me: Be waiting with open arms

When we graduated, I didn't take Nina's word to heart about us helping each other out. Tack on my issues with Liam and my spiral through grief and I wasn't in a good headspace to reach out to anyone. Let alone think about fashion design. But when I was thinking of my next line, I was stuck. Call it writer's block for fashion. I did everything, but nothing helped. Not strolling around the city, not watching TV, or listening to music. Nothing sparked for my next line. So I reached out to Nina on Instagram.

It was tricky with a lot of back and forth to get our schedules to match up. She does fashion consulting for the businesswomen and men in the DC metropolitan area. The fear of her rejection to collaborate was always at the back of my mind. But when she stated she wanted to do something other than suits and evening gowns, we both jumped at the chance for her to fly out here.

I'm pouring my first cup of coffee, when a knock sounds at my office door.

"Hey!" I greet as I rush over to Nina. "You're stunning." It's true that Nina was gorgeous in college but the years away from collegiate life have done her well. "Do you want some coffee? Or tea?"

"Coffee would be great."

She sets her bag and sweater on the couch in front of my desk while I get to work on her coffee. "This place is great, Kamryn."

"Thank you."

When I have Nina's coffee prepared, she follows me over to the oversized couch that's in my office. I have a few small mood boards laid out with hopes that it would spark something. But apparently my inspiration and talent have disappeared.

"So what were you thinking?" Nina notes as she shuffles around the mood boards.

Placing my coffee on the floor and kneeling closer in front of the coffee table, I find a picture of a couple of dresses. "Maybe do a dress line?"

Nina looks at me like I just said she was debt free. "Genius."

For the next few hours we pour over every type of dress to make: casual, cocktail, black tie, work casual, little black dress, club dresses, and every type of print, cut, style, and length.

"What about wedding guest dresses?"

We add that to the design board. We sketch until we've filled up multiple pages of our sketch books and Procreate pages. We mix patterns and fabrics. We pull out our phones and look at the dresses we may have worn in the past and alter the designs to have more function that what we had. In the end, we scratch the idea of wedding guest dresses for the time being. And focus on the everyday type of dress.

My stomach rumbles, breaking us out of the zone. "I guess that's a sign for us to take a break. Do you want to go out for lunch, or order in?"

"Order in. I'm not picky," Nina replies.

I order from my favorite deli and then grab us some water.

"So how's life been?"

A soft smile graces her face. "Really good. Work is insane, but it keeps that part of my life full. As for love, my best friend and I started dating about a year ago."

"Is this the guy you were telling me about while we were in school?"

"Yeah. It was...I don't know. I guess it took being apart from him to realize that he's the one for me. College was not an easy time for our friendship. We continually did and said things that hurt the other. But when I moved back home, the next day he was at my parents front door and it was like this fog finally lifted." Nina takes a sip of water before continuing. "As hard as it was going from friends to more than friends, it's also been so easy being with him. He challenges me in a way I never knew I could be challenged."

"You are so in love it's not even funny."

"I am. We have our issues and working them out is never the issue. Because at the end of the day, we both have each other's heart. I know that sounds cheesy, but it's true." The far away look she gets on her face is envious, even for someone in a relationship. "Kamryn, I wanted to say how sorry I am about Liam."

I give her a soft smile. "Thank you. But really it should be telling you how sorry I am?"

"For what?" Her brows scrunch in confusement.

"When you reached out to me, I tossed you to the side."

"That was on me."

"No. In this phase of my life I've been taking accountability of the damage I did to the relationships that were important to me. Your friendship was one of those and I had no idea if you'd wave me off when I reached out. But I'm glad you took a chance."

She squeezes my hand. "I'm glad you reached out. Truly. What we've created has the potential to be huge. Two black, female fashion designers. This is huge, Kamryn!"

Her excitement is contagious in a way I haven't felt in a while. I've gotten stagnant in my work. The creativity I felt when I first started my company has dimmed. But with this line I just know my inspiration and creativity will be flowing.

"But enough about work. We still have time before our food arrives. I saw you and Mason are back together."

"Yeah. We've been back together for almost a year, although it feels like more."

"And you're happy?" Nina asks me.

"So happy. I mean, I have days when I'm not. As I'm sure everyone does."

"Good. I'm really happy for you Kam. This brand you've built is extraordinary." She looks around my office and out into the main floor again.

"Thank you. Any plans for your own brand?"

We get lost in Nina's hopeful plans. Her work plans and her romantic plans. We walk down memory lane and tear up with how far we've come along. Our lunch arrives during our memory lane stroll. And before I know it, it's the end of the day. Meaning Nina has to hop back on a flight to get home.

"Should we tease our collaboration on social media?" I ask.

"I was hoping you would ask."

I pop my head out of my office, "Olivia? Will you come take our picture?"

"Sure thing boss." She says with a sly grin.

I pass her my digital camera and we pose in front of the door to the main floor of the office.

"On three. One, two, three." The flash from the camera is the sign that she took the picture. "Beautiful."

She passes me the camera on her way back to her desk. "Thanks, Olivia."

"Welcome."

Nina and I face each other. My cheeks hurt from how much smiling I've done today and my stomach feels toned from all of the laughter.

"Are you sure you don't want to grab a hotel room?" I question again as we're walking downstairs.

"Positive. It's a short flight anyway."

We lean in at the same time to hug each other. "I'm so glad we're doing this."

"Me too. And anytime you want a tour of DC, you have my number."

A soft laugh slips out. "I'm gonna take you up on that."

The Uber Nina ordered pulls up to the curb next to us.

"This is me."

"I hope you get home safe."

She pulls open the back passenger door. "Thanks, Kamryn. I'll see you later."

I watch the car drive off and head back up to the office.

～

"Mason?" I call out when I get home. Home. It's so weird that we live together.

I hear his steps coming down the stairs. "Hey, baby. How was work with Nina?"

Wrapping my arms around his waist, I absorb his warmth. "Really good. What we have planned is going to be so beneficial for women, and men, that they'll be kissing the ground we walk on."

My head vibrates as his chest shakes with a laugh. "Are you done working for the night?"

"Yeah. Why?" I ask, leaning back to look up at him.

"I wanna take you somewhere."

"I don't need to grab anything?"

"Nope. Well, your phone if you want it."

I do as he says and then we're locking up my house before jumping in his truck. Looking over at him driving takes me back to when he drove us to the beach house our first summer together.

He sees me looking over at him. "What are you thinking about ya goof?"

"Our trip to the beach during our first summer together." It comes out more melancholy than I had hoped. That's when our downfall happened. But even I can't deny that our summer at the beach was epic.

"That was a fun summer," he agrees with me.

I face forward and take in the scenery as he drives.

37

MASON

I'd been pacing and nervous all day. When Kamryn told me Nina was coming in for the day to brainstorm a collaboration, I knew it was the right moment.

When Kamryn asked me to move in with her, that next day I contacted my realtor that I was looking for a house. It was quick work, but she found one that I knew Kamryn would love. As much as I love her house, it's cramped. And I plan to have a family with her. Lots of kids hopefully. The process of purchasing the house was quick. Since I was paying all-cash, it was easy to bypass all of the contingencies.

I got the call early this morning that the house was all mine. So while Kamryn was at work, I went down to my realtors office to sign all of the required papers. Once the keys were in my hand, I enlisted the help of Kam's girls to set up an epic surprise.

While the house is a done deal, I have no clue where her head's at. She gets lost in that beautiful mind of hers some-times, and while it's scary she always comes back to me.

Peaking over at her as I slow down and turn into a gated

neighborhood, I bite the inside of my cheek to stop from smiling.

"Mason, where are we?" My curious koala asks.

Leaning out of the truck to insert the code and then sliding back in, I tell her. "You'll see."

She eyes me nervously, but remains quiet. I know it's taking everything in her not to ask questions. The drive to the back of the neighborhood takes about five minutes. And in that time Kamryn opens her mouth to say something but closes it at the last second. It brings me some joy to know she's at a loss for words.

I pull up to our house, just saying that to myself brings a lightness I haven't felt in quite some time, and the gasp Kamryn lets out is the sweetest sound.

"What is this?" Her voice is so quiet, almost a whisper.

Parking the truck in the driveway and shutting it off, I turn to her. "We're building a life together, Kamryn. And as much as I love how cozy your house is, we need a bigger home. So this is ours."

"You bought us a house?"

I bring her hand up to my mouth and kiss it. "I did. Do you want to see inside?"

"Yes." She leans forward before getting out and fusses our lips together. "I love you."

"Ditto." Grabbing the keys I open the door and hop out. I meet her at the hood of my truck and her excitement is barely contained.

We walk up the front walkway and I unlock the door. Pushing it open I lean down and scoop Kamryn in my arms.

"Oh my god!" She shrieks with laughter as her arm loops over my neck and I carry her over the threshold bridal style. "It's beautiful."

I place her on her feet and close and lock the front door. "Come on. Let me give you a tour."

I take her through the downstairs which boasts a huge kitchen, a dining room fit for twenty people, a guest room, and an expansive living room. We make our way upstairs and my heart hammers a little more. On one side of the second floor is the primary suite with a spacious walk-in closet and bathroom with a soak-in tub and standing shower. The other side of this floor has three bedrooms with plenty of closet space and bathrooms in each room.

I stop in front of a door to the attic space.

"What's this?"

"A surprise I really think you're going to love." Opening the door, I usher her in first and follow her up the second set of stairs. I know she's seen the surprise when she stops at the top of the stairs.

Standing next to her, I look at what she sees. Rose petals are scattered throughout the room, with a row of them leading to the center. Battery-operated candles give the room a romantic glow. Placing my hand on the small of her back I lead her to the center of the room.

Tears have already formed in her eyes and when I drop down to one knee those tears have spilled over and onto her beautiful face.

"Do you remember the night we met? I remember it clear as day. I tried a terrible line on you, which you called me out on. From that night on I was hooked. I didn't know it at the time, but you changed my life for the better. I'll never be able to take away the hurt that I caused you the first time. And I promise to never hurt you like that again. The night we met was the night my life changed. Never did I think I could love someone as much as I love you. Kamryn, would you do me the honor of becoming my wife. Sharing and expanding this life that we've created is all I want to do with you. Kids, traveling, support, and more love than either of us know what to do with. Will you marry me?" I hold out the ring I had hiding at my condo. It's an 18k solitaire engagement ring from Tiffany's.

Picking out a ring for Kamryn was easy. My girl is extravagant but she's also a simple girl. She loves her high end clothes but isn't afraid to get her hands dirty with some gardening or gorging on some food.

Words fail her as she nods her head emphatically. Then she says the one word that changes everything, "Yes."

EPILOGUE

Kamryn

10 Years Later

"Carsyn Grace, take your brother and sister inside please." I watch my seven year old grab her siblings hands. The twins are almost four and it's never a dull day around the house. We're in Philadelphia for the week as my parents are celebrating their fortieth wedding anniversary. Which is insane.

Jax is flying in tomorrow with her husband, Emily is already with her parents and fiancé, and Sarah is flying in with her family. It's hard to imagine that we're all settled.

"Are those my favorite grandbabies?" My dad boasts from the garage.

The sound of joyful children squealing and laughing brings tears to my eyes. But a sense of dread slides over my body. I've visited back home occasionally, but not nearly enough and never for this long. My other motive was to visit with the Taylors. They were my family for nearly twenty years. But when Liam passed, that relationship frayed until it fizzled away to nothing.

"Go on, baby. I've got our babies." Mason encourages from behind me.

He's been so helpful when it comes to my anxiety of seeing them. He'd hold me at night while I cried over my warring decision to visit them. And to visit Liam.

Turning, I hug him and make my way across the street. I feel like I've gone back in time. I made this walk so many times when I was a kid, I could have done it blindfolded. But I'm not that little girl who rang the doorbell and asked for Liam to come play outside. So much time has passed that I have no idea what to expect.

Looking over my shoulder, I see Mason and my dad standing in the driveway watching me with encouraging smiles. With a deep breath, I ring the doorbell and wait.

I wait for the past to smack me in the face.

I wait for the possible judgment.

The door opens and I hold my breath.

"Kamryn?" A girl a little younger than me asks.

"Angie? Is that you?" She surprises me with a crushing hug. I wrap my arms around her and her body relaxes, as does mine. I didn't realize I was holding tension until my mind caught up with my body.

"Angie? Who's at the door?" The question is distantly asked before it's trailed off and an inhale is all I hear.

It's like looking in a mirror when I see Liam's dad standing in front of me. Had Liam lived, he would've looked just like his dad.

"Mr. Taylor," I breathe out at a severe loss for words. The last time I saw them was almost fifteen years ago. While I spiraled, they had to keep moving for their other kids. I was young. I had no clue how to manage grief the right way. But what was the right way to grieve?

"Kamryn. Come in, please." Angie steps back and allows for me to cross into the house.

The back of my eyes burn with emotion. "Thank you."

Walking into the house is surreal. Seeing it after all this time and I expect Liam to come barreling down the stairs. But the house is quiet and Liam is not going to come barreling down the stairs.

"Greg, who was at..the door? Kamryn?"

"Hi, Mrs. Taylor."

The words are barely out before I'm crushed in her embrace. It's such a difference from the last time I saw these broken parents. After greetings are exchanged in the foyer, I'm pulled to the living room. And it's as if nothing has drastically changed in this space. I could just pretend that I didn't lose my best friend.

We talk for what feels like days, when it's only hours. I update the people who were a second family to me, on my life after I moved to Cincinnati: my brand, Mason, and my kids. While they tell me they've been healing every day since, it's good to know that they've come to accept that Liam isn't struggling anymore. I know the struggles of healing from loss.

"So what brings you home?" Greg asks.

"My parents. They're celebrating their fortieth wedding anniversary. I thought what better time than to bring the kids and spend a week down here."

A smile hits Susan's face at the mention of my kids. "Tell us about your kids."

My smile must mirror Susan's because just the thought of talking about my kids makes me feel lighter. "Carsyn, she's seven going on twenty. She's full of sass and the energy in her never drains. Then the twins, Hayden and William, were a complete surprise." Twins don't run in our family, so naturally it sent Mason into overprotective mode. But it made me love him even more. I don't tell them middle names, or what we call William, as I'm not sure how they would react to it. Before and after Liam died, I knew I wanted my kids to honor someone important to me. Liam was that someone.

My time at the Taylor's comes to an end. They'll be at my parents' anniversary party this weekend, so Susan promises we'll have more time to catch up. With a few more hugs I'm out of their house and walking back across the street to my parents house. The sound of laughter greets my ears as Hayden runs to me when I walk into the living room.

"Hi, baby girl. Are you having fun?" I tickle her neck with kisses and inhale her toddler smell. While Carsyn took after me for a while, she's now all Mason. William keeps up with both of them, but Hayden is all me.

Walking over to the loveseat where Mason is sitting, I drop down next to him and swing Hayden around, placing her in the cradle of my legs. I catch my moms eye and a look of understanding passes us. Mason swings his arm over my shoulder and blows raspberry kisses on Hayden's cheek.

Seeing Mason as a dad was a whole other experience. He was with me every step of the way. He took the load off of me before I even had the chance to carry it. I fell in love with him all over again.

"Are you okay?" Mason asks, keeping his voice low.

"Yeah. It was good seeing them." And it was good seeing them. But they're not the only ones I want to see, Mason knows that.

We flew in early for this particular reason. I wanted my visit with Liam to be early enough so that it wouldn't put a damper on my time here. The kids don't know about him. We're not sure when or what to tell them.

I turn and our gazes clash. A look of understanding passes and he knows it's time.

"Mom? Dad? We're gonna head out."

"The kids will be fine here sweetie. Take your time." My dad tells me.

Mason walks to the foot of the stairs and calls the kids down. The herd of elephants that are my babies barrel down the steps.

"Mommy and Daddy have to go do something. And we can't take you."

"Where are you going?" Carsyn asks.

She's been questioning things since the time she could form sentences. "I'll tell you when you're older."

"You always say that Mommy," Carsyn says with a tease in her voice.

I kiss her on the cheek. "Then I'm doing my job right. Behave for your grandparents. We won't be long." I kiss William on his forehead and transfer Hayden to my mom who leans in to kiss me on the cheek.

Mason and I duck out fast because if we don't, we'll never leave.

WE STOP at a grocery store to pick up some flowers and the sun is just starting to drop from its highest peak of the day. Getting out of the car, I lean against the car looking at his headstone. It still feels like another world that his passing happened. And in a way I guess it is.

Mason, my supportive husband, stands next to me. He

doesn't say a word. He doesn't pressure me to speak. He just lets me be.

Pushing off from the car, I turn to Mason. "I'll be right back."

He pulls me into him and rests his lips against my forehead, "Take your time, baby. I'm not going anywhere."

I turn and walk towards Liam's headstone. Squatting down, I place the flowers in front of his resting spot and take a seat. "Twelve years is insane. I have so much to catch you up on." And I do. I tell him about moving away, finding Mason and letting him back into my life, my work, the world I've created, and my kids. I shed some tears as I tell him William's middle name. Two first names for a kid is unheard of, but I wanted a way for Liam to be present. So William "Liam" Grey Brooks, while it's a mouthful, my little boy wears the name proud.

"I just want you to know that you changed my life. I wish you were still here. I wish I could change so many things about our time together." I get up from the ground and brush off the leaves and dirt that have gathered on my clothes. "I hope you know I'll always love you. Bye, Liam."

Placing a kiss to the top of his headstone, I turn and walk back to my husband.

Mason

I watch my wife walk back towards me with a smile on her face. I said what I needed to as I watched her walk down memory lane with her best friend. I'll never compete with the friendship they had. While I'm upset that he's no longer here to hear her laugh or see her smile, I can guarantee that he's watching over her from above.

Holding my hand out when she's within reach. "You ready to go?"

"Yeah." She leans up and presses a kiss to my lips. "Let's go home to our babies."

Babies. Yep, that's right. The girl I met when she was eighteen has three of my kids. She's just as gorgeous now as she was back then.

We make the drive back to her parents house just in time for dinner. It's chaos from the beginning to end, but I wouldn't have it any other way. But I'll never tell Kamryn that I want more kids as our three keep us occupied all hours of the day and night. When dinner is done and the kids are bathed and tucked in bed, I retreat to Kamryn's childhood bedroom, which has thankfully been redone.

I slide in next to her as we get ready for bed. She's been a little quieter from the events that took place today. And I don't blame her for it. But I also won't push her to speak about how she's feeling. She usually comes to me when she's ready.

We shut off the lights, save for the light on the night-stand, slide into bed and turn the TV on low. Kamryn slings her leg between mine and wraps her arm around my waist, letting her head lay on my shoulder.

Alone time is never alone, but when we're at Kamryn's parents house they tire our children out better than we ever could.

"Thank you," Kamryn breaks the relative quiet. She slides her leg fully over my waist and sits to straddle me. Her hands fall to the hem of my shirt to keep the talk light. "I don't know how you always know what I need. Whether it's a loud night with the kids or a quiet night just the two of us."

My hands fall to her hips. "Ten years together is enough to know what you need."

"What about you?" She questions. "What do you need?"

"You and our kids' happiness are all that I need. I know I can never fully protect you all from things that bring you happiness, but I can do my best to try."

Her lids lower and I get the niggling suspicion she's about to take this heart to heart and throw it out the window. "You know what I need?" She asks as she rubs her pussy over my boxers.

"Kamryn, don't you dare." I chastise. While we do have three kids, I'm still not comfortable having sex at her parents house. Because let's face it, my girl is not quiet.

Her hands slide under my shirt, pushing it up until I'm forced to lift my arms. My shirt flies across the room and her hands land on my chest. "I want my husband to make love to me."

When she puts it like that, it's hard to say no. So I make love to my wife. I love on her body and pay attention to the marks on her stomach that brought our children into the world. I take her fast and hard the first round. But by the second round, when the sun is starting to rise above the horizon, I take it slow. I tease her body, bringing her to the edge multiple times, before she finally falls over and taking me with her.

I was twenty years old the night we met. And at that time I had no idea I'd met my perfect match.

ACKNOWLEDGMENT

I started this book in 2018 when my relationship was failing. The heartbreak I experienced helped these words form. But I sat on them because this was a different version of my diary. So, thank you to the broken heart that pushed these words along.

Next, I have so many people to thank. First, Kalie Gerwig for befriending me in 2020 and then being the most excited best friend to read my words, along with being an amazing PA I would've been lost.

My alpha readers, Kaylee and Hallie, you two are blessings in the book world. I'm so glad for the help along the way.

My beta readers, Danielle, Kendra, and Cassie you three were the best hype girls during this journey. I lived for your comments and DMs for this book.

To my sister, Robyn, and my bestie, Jess, you two were the best encouragers for getting this book out in the world.

To the dark cubicle at work where a lot of these words were formed, thank you. I truly could not have written this surrounded by co-workers. To the bookstagram community that got hype when I first teased this book in 2021, thank you.

To you, the reader, for taking a chance on my debut book and allowing me to take up space in your Kindle. I hope you enjoyed these characters and this world as much as I did.

Until next time,
Elleese Black

ABOUT THE AUTHOR

Elleese Black is a thirty-something millennial. With a degree in Psychology, she took her love of the subject to dive into fictional characters. She grew up reading romance books with swoon and tears, fortunately, they all end with a happily ever after. When she's not writing or working, she's a cat mom to two zany cats, taking spin classes or doom-scrolling until the wee hours of the night. Elleese loves to hear from her readers. So send her a DM on Instagram (@elleeseblack.author), she'll love it!

Sign up for my newsletter:

ALSO BY ELLEESE BLACK

The Night We Met

Make It Without You

Let It Be Me

Somewhere Only We Know - Late Summer 2025

www.ingramcontent.com/pod-product-compliance
Lightning Source LLC
Chambersburg PA
CBHW031203010826
48971CB00013B/1273